NORTH SEA
Calais
Flanders
Artois
Crécy
Somme R.
Amiens
Coucy
Paris
Champagne
Seine R.
Reims
Meuse R.
Orléans
Loire R.
Dijon
Berry
FRANCE
Burgundy
Bourbon
Limoges
Lyon
Dauphiny
Avignon
Toulouse
Languedoc
Foix
MEDITERRANEAN SEA

THE SHE WOLF

BY MAURICE DRUON

The Accursed Kings

The Iron King

The Strangled Queen

The Poisoned Crown

The Royal Succession

The She-Wolf

The Lily and the Lion

The King Without a Kingdom

THE SHE WOLF

Book Five of The Accursed Kings

MAURICE DRUON

Translated from French by
Humphrey Hare

HarperCollins*Publishers*

HarperCollins*Publishers*
77–85 Fulham Palace Road,
Hammersmith, London W6 8JB

www.harpercollins.co.uk

First published in Great Britain by Rupert Hart-Davis 1960
Arrow edition 1988

Published by HarperCollins*Publishers* 2014

1

A catalogue record for this book
is available from the British Library

ISBN: 978-0-00-749133-9

Printed and bound in Great Britain by
Clays Ltd, St Ives plc

MIX
Paper from
responsible sources
FSC C007454

FSC is a non-profit international organization established to promote the responsible management of the world's forests. Products carrying the FSC label are independently certified to assure consumers that they come from forests that are managed to meet the social, economic and ecological needs of present and future generations, and other controlled sources.

Find out more about HarperCollins and the environment at

www.harpercollins.co.uk/green

'History is a novel that has been lived'
E. & J. de Goncourt

'It is terrifying to think how much research is needed to determine the truth of even the most unimportant fact'
Stendhal

'She-wolf of France, with unrelenting fangs,
That tear'st the bowels of thy mangled mate . . .'
Thomas Gray

Foreword

GEORGE R.R. MARTIN

Over the years, more than one reviewer has described my fantasy series, *A Song of Ice and Fire*, as historical fiction about history that never happened, flavoured with a dash of sorcery and spiced with dragons. I take that as a compliment. I have always regarded historical fiction and fantasy as sisters under the skin, two genres separated at birth. My own series draws on both traditions . . . and while I undoubtedly drew much of my inspiration from Tolkien, Vance, Howard, and the other fantasists who came before me, *A Game of Thrones* and its sequels were also influenced by the works of great historical novelists like Thomas B. Costain, Mika Waltari, Howard Pyle . . . and Maurice Druon, the amazing French writer who gave us the *The Accursed Kings*, seven splendid novels that chronicle the downfall of the Capetian kings and the beginnings of the Hundred Years War.

Druon's novels have not been easy to find, especially in English translation (and the seventh and final volume was never translated into English at all). The series has *twice* been made into a television series in France, and both versions are available on DVD . . . but only in French, undubbed, and without English subtitles. Very frustrating for English-speaking Druon fans like me.

The Accursed Kings has it all. Iron kings and strangled queens, battles and betrayals, lies and lust, deception, family rivalries, the curse of the Templars, babies switched at birth, she-wolves, sin, and swords, the doom of a great dynasty . . . and all of it (well, most of it) straight from the pages of history. And believe me, the Starks and the Lannisters have nothing on the Capets and Plantagenets.

Whether you're a history buff or a fantasy fan, Druon's epic will keep you turning pages. This was the original game of thrones. If you like *A Song of Ice and Fire*, you will love *The Accursed Kings*.

George R.R. Martin

Author's Acknowledgements

I AM most grateful to Georges Kessel, Pierre de Lacretelle and Madeleine Marignac for the invaluable assistance they have given me with this book; to Brigadier L. F. E. Wieler, CB, CBE, Major and Resident Governor of the Tower of London, and Mr J. A. F. Thompson of Balliol College, Oxford, for their generous help; and to the Bibliothèque Nationale and the staff of the Archives Nationales in Paris for indispensable aid in research.

Contents

Part Two: Isabella in Love

Part Three: The Disinherited King

Part Four: The Cruel Invasion

The Characters in this Book

THE KING OF FRANCE:

CHARLES IV, called the Fair, fourteenth successor to Hugues Capet, great-grandson of Saint Louis, third and last son of Philip IV, the Fair, and Jeanne of Navarre, formerly husband of Blanche of Burgundy and Count de la Marche, aged 29.

THE QUEENS OF FRANCE:

MARIE OF LUXEMBURG, eldest daughter of Henry VII, Emperor of Germany, and of Marguerite of Brabant, aged 19.

JEANNE OF ÉVREUX, daughter of Louis of France, Count of Évreux, brother of Philip the Fair, and of Marguerite of Artois, aged about 18.

THE QUEEN DOWAGERS OF FRANCE:

CLÉMENCE OF HUNGARY, Princess of Anjou-Sicily, niece of King Robert of Naples, second wife and widow of King Louis X Hutin, aged 30.

JEANNE OF BURGUNDY, widow of King Philippe V, the Long, daughter of Count Othon of Burgundy and of Countess Mahaut of Artois, aged 30.

THE KING OF ENGLAND:

EDWARD II Plantagenet, ninth successor to William the Conqueror, son of Edward I and of Eleanor of Castille, aged 39.

THE QUEEN OF ENGLAND:

ISABELLA OF FRANCE, wife of the above, daughter of Philip the Fair and sister of the King of France, aged 31.

THE HEIR TO THE THRONE OF ENGLAND:

EDWARD, eldest son of the above and future King Edward III, aged 11.

THE HOUSE OF VALOIS:

MONSEIGNEUR CHARLES, grandson of Saint Louis and brother of Philip the Fair, uncle of the King of France, Count of the Appanage of Valois, of Maine, of Anjou, of Alençon, of Chartres and of Perche, Peer of the Kingdom, ex-Titular Emperor of Constantinople, Count of Romagna, aged 53.

MONSEIGNEUR PHILIPPE, Count of VALOIS and of Maine, eldest son of Charles of Valois and of his first wife Marguerite of Anjou-Sicily, future King Philippe VI, aged 30.

JEANNE OF VALOIS, Countess of HAINAUT, daughter of Charles of Valois and of Marguerite of Anjou, sister of the above, wife of Count Guillaume of Hainaut, aged 27.

JEANNE OF VALOIS, Countess of BEAUMONT, daughter of Charles of Valois and his second wife Catherine de Courtenay, half-sister of the above, wife of Robert III of Artois, Count of Beaumont, aged about 19.

MAHAUT DE CHÂTILLON-SAINT-POL, Countess of Valois, third wife of Monseigneur Charles.

JEANNE, called THE LAME, Countess of VALOIS, daughter of the Duke of Burgundy and Agnes of France, sister of Marguerite of Burgundy, granddaughter of Saint Louis, wife of Monseigneur Philippe, aged 28.

THE HOUSE OF NAVARRE:

JEANNE OF NAVARRE, daughter of Louis X Hutin and of Marguerite of Burgundy, heir to the Kingdom of Navarre, aged 12.

PHILIPPE OF FRANCE, Count of ÉVREUX, husband of the above, son of Louis of France, Count of Évreux, and cousin-german of Charles the Fair, future King of Navarre, aged about 15.

THE HOUSE OF ARTOIS:

THE COUNTESS MAHAUT OF ARTOIS, Peer of the Kingdom, widow of the Count Palatine Othon IV of Burgundy, mother of Jeanne and Blanche of Burgundy, aged about 54.

ROBERT III OF ARTOIS, nephew and adversary of the above, Count of Beaumont-le-Roger, Lord of Conches, son-in-law of Charles of Valois, aged 36.

THIERRY LARCHER D'HIRSON, Canon, Chancellor to the Countess Mahaut, aged 53.

BÉATRICE D'HIRSON, niece of the above, lady-in-waiting to the Countess Mahaut, aged about 29.

THE HOUSE OF HAINAUT:

JEAN OF HAINAUT, brother of Guillaume the Good, Count of Hainaut, Holland and Zeeland.

PHILIPPA OF HAINAUT, his niece, second daughter of Guillaume the Good and of Jeanne of Valois, affianced to Prince Edward of England, aged 9.

THE GREAT OFFICERS OF THE CROWN OF FRANCE:

LOUIS OF CLERMONT, Lord, then first Duke, of BOURBON, grandson of Saint Louis, Great Chamberlain of France.

GAUCHER DE CHÂTILLON, Lord of Crèvecoeur, Count of Porcien, Constable of France since 1302.

JEAN DE CHERCHEMONT, Chancellor.

HUGUES DE BOUVILLE, one-time Great Chamberlain to Philip IV, the Fair, Ambassador.

THE RELATIONS OF THE KING OF ENGLAND:

THOMAS DE BROTHERTON, Earl of Norfolk, Marshal of England, son of Edward I of England and of his second wife Margaret of France, half-brother to King Edward II and cousin to the King of France, aged 23.

EDMUND, Earl of KENT, younger brother of the above, Governor of Dover, Warden of the Cinque Ports, aged 22.

HENRY, Earl of LEICESTER and LANCASTER, called Crouchback, grandson of Henry III of England, cousin-german to King Edward II, aged 42.

THE COUNCILLORS:

HUGH DESPENSER, the elder, Earl of Winchester, aged 61.

HUGH DESPENSER, the younger, son of the above, Earl of Gloucester, the favourite of King Edward II, aged 33.

BALDOCK, Archdeacon, Chancellor to Edward II.

WALTER STAPLEDON, Bishop of Exeter, Lord Treasurer.

The Earls of ARUNDEL and WARENNE.

THE LADIES-IN-WAITING TO QUEEN ISABELLA:

LADY JEANNE MORTIMER, *née* Joinville, great-niece of the Seneschal de Joinville, the wife of Roger Mortimer, Baron of Wigmore, aged 37.

LADY ALIENOR DESPENSER, *née* Clare, the wife of Hugh Despenser, the younger.

THE BARONS OF THE OPPOSITION:

ROGER MORTIMER, the elder, Lord of CHIRK, one-time Justiciar of Wales, aged 67.

ROGER MORTIMER, the younger, eighth Baron of WIGMORE, the King's former Lord-Lieutenant and Justiciar of Ireland, nephew of the above, aged 36.

John Maltravers, Thomas de Berkeley, Thomas Gournay, John de Cromwell, etc., English lords.

THE ENGLISH BISHOPS:

Adam Orleton, Bishop of Hereford.

Walter Reynolds, Archbishop of Canterbury.

John de Stratford, Bishop of Winchester.

THE GUARDIANS OF THE TOWER OF LONDON:

Stephen Seagrave, Constable.

Gerard de Alspaye, Lieutenant.

Ogle, Barber.

THE COURT OF AVIGNON:

Pope John XXII, ex-Cardinal Jacques Duèze, elected at the Conclave of 1316, aged 79.

Bertrand du Pouget, Gaucelin Duèze, Gaillard de la Mothe, Arnaud de Via, Raymond Le Roux, Cardinals and relations of the Pope.

Jacques Fournier, Counsellor to John XXII, future Pope Benedict XII.

THE LOMBARDS:

Spinello Tolomei, a Sienese banker in business in Paris, aged about 69.

Guccio Baglioni, his nephew, a Sienese banker of the Tolomei Company.

Boccaccio, a traveller for the Bardi Company, father of the poet.

THE CRESSAY FAMILY:

PIERRE and JEAN DE CRESSAY, sons of the late Lord of Cressay, aged about 31 and 29.

MARIE, their sister, secret wife to Guccio Baglioni, aged 25.

JEAN, called Jeannot or Giannino, supposed son of Guccio Baglioni and of Marie de Cressay, in fact JEAN THE POSTHUMOUS, son of Louis X Hutin and of Clémence of Hungary, aged 7.

All the above names have their place in history; their ages are given as in the year 1323.

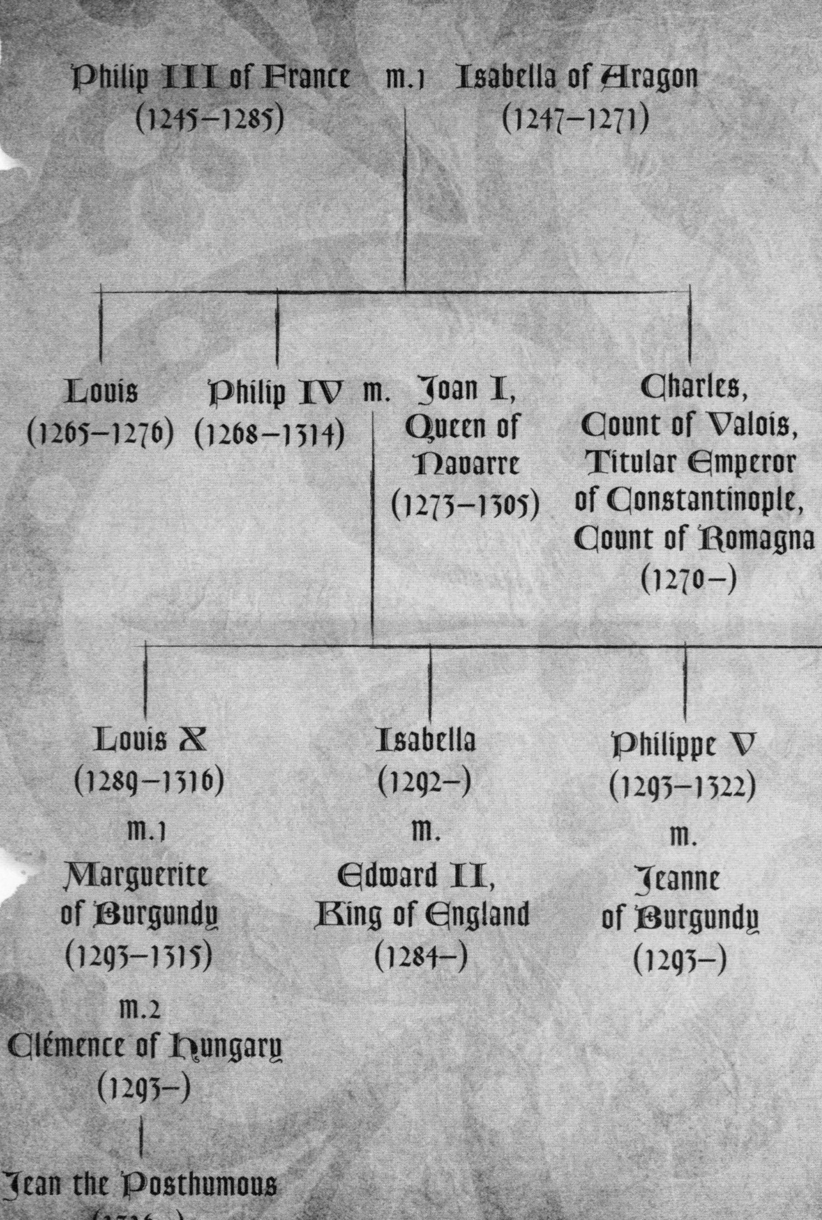

Philip III of France m.1 Isabella of Aragon
(1245–1285) (1247–1271)
Louis
(1265–1276)
Philip IV m. Joan I,
(1268–1314)
Queen of
Navarre
(1273–1305)
Charles,
Count of Valois,
Titular Emperor
of Constantinople,
Count of Romagna
(1270–)
Louis X
(1289–1316)
m.1
Marguerite
of Burgundy
(1293–1315)
m.2
Clémence of Hungary
(1293–)
Jean the Posthumous
(1316–)
Isabella
(1292–)
m.
Edward II,
King of England
(1284–)
Philippe V
(1293–1322)
m.
Jeanne
of Burgundy
(1293–)

m.2 Marie of Brabant
(1254–1321)

Louis Capet,
Count of Évreux
(1276–1319)

Blanche
(1278–1305)

Margaret
of France
(1282–1318)

Charles IV
(1294–)
m.1
Blanche
of Burgundy
(1296–1326)
m.2
Marie of
Luxemburg
(1304–)

The House of Capet 1323

The She-Wolf of France

'I SEE,' SAID ISABELLA, 'that you wish me to be left utterly alone.'

'What do you mean by alone, Madame?' cried Hugh the Younger in his fine, well-modulated voice. 'Are we not all your loyal friends, being the King's? And is not Madame Alienor, my devoted wife, a faithful companion to you? 'That's a pretty book you have there,' he added, pointing to the volume, 'and beautifully illuminated; would you be kind enough to lend it to me?'

'Of course, of course the Queen will lend it to you,' the King said. 'I am sure, Madame, that you will do us the pleasure of lending the book to our friend Gloucester?'

'Most willingly, Sire my husband, most willingly. And I know what lending means when it's to your friend, Lord Despenser. I lent him my pearls ten years ago and, as you can see, he's still wearing them about his neck.'

She would not surrender, but her heart was beating wildly

in her breast. From now on she would have to bear the daily insults all alone. If, one day, she found means of revenging herself, nothing would be forgotten.

Prologue

THE CHASTISEMENTS PROPHESIED by the Grand Master of the Templars and the curses he had hurled from amid the faggots of his pyre continued to fall on France. Fate had destroyed her kings like pieces on a chess-board.

Philip the Fair having died as if struck down by lightning, and his eldest son, Louis X, having been murdered after eighteen months on the throne, Philippe V, his second son, seemed destined for a long reign. But now six years had gone by, and Philippe V had died in his turn before attaining the age of thirty.

Let us look for a moment at his reign which, compared with the tragedies and disasters that were to follow, seems something of a respite from calamity. If you glance casually through a history of the period, it may seem a colourless reign, possibly because your hand comes away from the page unstained with blood. And yet, if we look deeper, we shall see of what a great king's days consist if Fate is against him.

For Philippe V, the Long, had been a great king. By a mixture of force and cunning, of legality and crime, he had seized the crown, when it was at auction to the ambitious, while still a young man. An imprisoned conclave, a royal palace taken by assault, an invented law of succession, a provincial revolt put down in a ten days' campaign, a great lord cast into prison and a royal child murdered in its cradle – or so at least it was supposed – had all been stages on his rapid path to the throne.

On that January morning in 1317, when, as the bells rang out in the heavens, the second son of the Iron King had come out of Rheims Cathedral, he had reason to believe that he had triumphed, and was now free to pursue his father's grand policies, which he had so much admired. His family had all had to bow to his will. The barons were checkmated; Parliament had submitted to his ascendancy, and the middle classes had acclaimed him, delighted to have a strong Prince again; his wife had been washed clean of the stain of the Tour de Nesle; his succession seemed assured by the son who had recently been born to him; and, finally, coronation had endued him with intangible majesty. There seemed to be nothing lacking to Philippe V's enjoyment of the relative happiness of kings, not least the wisdom to desire peace and recognize its worth.

Three weeks later his son died. It was his only male child, and Queen Jeanne, barren from henceforth, would give him no more.

At the beginning of summer the country was ravaged by famine and the towns were strewn with corpses.

And then, soon afterwards, a wave of madness broke over the whole of France.

Driven by blind and vaguely mystical impulses, primitive dreams of sanctity and adventure, by their condition of poverty and by a sudden frenzy for destruction, country boys and girls, sheep-, cow- and swineherds, young artisans, young spinners and weavers, nearly all of them between fifteen and twenty, abruptly left their families and villages, and formed barefoot, errant bands, provided with neither food nor money. Some wild idea of a crusade was the pretext for the exodus.

Indeed, madness had been born amid the wreckage of the Temple. Many of the ex-Templars had gone half-crazy through imprisonment, persecution, torture, disavowals torn from them by hot irons, and by the spectacle of their brothers delivered to the flames. A longing for vengeance, nostalgia for lost power, and the possession and knowledge of certain magic practices learnt in the East had turned them into fanatics, who were all the more dangerous because they disguised themselves in a cleric's humble robe or in a workman's smock. They had re-formed themselves into a secret society; and they obeyed the mysteriously transmitted orders of a clandestine Grand Master, who had replaced the Grand Master burnt at the stake.

It was these men who had suddenly transformed themselves one winter into village preachers and, like the Pied Piper of the Rhine legends, had led away the youth of France: to the Holy Land, they said. But their real goal was to wreck the kingdom and ruin the papacy.

And Pope and King were equally powerless in the face of these visionary hordes travelling the roads, these human rivers swelling at every cross-roads as if the lands of Flanders, Normandy, Brittany and Poitou were bewitched.

In their thousands, their twenty thousands, their hundred thousands, the *pastoureaux* were marching towards mysterious goals. Unfrocked priests, apostate monks, brigands, thieves, beggars and whores, all joined their bands. At the head of these columns a cross was carried, while the girls and boys indulged in the utmost licence, committed the worst excesses. A hundred thousand ragged marchers, entering a town to beg, soon pillaged it. And felony, which was at first merely an accessory to theft, soon became the satisfaction of a vice.

The *pastoureaux* ravaged France for a whole year and, indeed, with a certain method in their madness. They spared neither churches nor monasteries. Paris, aghast, saw an army of plunderers invade its streets, and King Philippe V spoke pacifically to them from a window of his palace. They urged the King to place himself at their head. They took the Châtelet by assault, attacked the Provost, and pillaged the Abbey of Saint-Germain-des-Prés. Then new orders, mysterious as those assembling them, directed them on to the roads to the south. The people of Paris were still trembling with fear when the *pastoureaux* were already flooding into Orléans. The Holy Land was far away; Bourges, Limoges, Saintes, the Périgord and the Bordelais, Gascony and Agenais had to suffer their fury.

Pope John XXII grew alarmed as the flood approached Avignon and he threatened these false crusaders with excommunication. But they had need of victims, and they found the Jews. From then on, the urban populations applauded the massacres and fraternized with the *pastoureaux*. Amid the ghettoes of Lectoure, Auvillar, Castelsarrasin, Albi, Auch and

Toulouse were to be seen here a hundred and fifteen corpses, and there a hundred and fifty-two. There was not a city in Languedoc that did not suffer this expiatory butchery. The Jews of Verdun-sur-Garonne used their children as missiles, and then cut each others' throats so as not to fall into the hands of the lunatics.

Then the Pope ordered his bishops and the King his seneschals to protect the Jews, whose commerce was important to them. The Count of Foix, going to the help of the Seneschal of Carcassonne, had to fight a pitched battle with the *pastoureaux* and drove them back into the marches of Aigues-Mortes, where they died in their thousands, stabbed, bludgeoned, engulfed or drowned. The land of France was quaffing its own blood, devouring its own youth. In the end, the clergy and the officers of the crown joined in hunting down the survivors. The gates of the towns were closed to them; they were denied food and lodging; they were pursued into the passes of the Cévennes. Those captured were hanged in groups of twenty or thirty to the branches of trees. For most of the next two years there were still some bands wandering about; and they ranged as far as Italy before they finally disappeared.

France, the body corporate of France, was sick. Hardly had the *pastoureaux* fever abated, than lepers appeared.

Who could tell whether these tragic people, their flesh corroded, their faces death-masks, their hands stumps, who could tell whether these pariahs, restricted to lazar-houses or infected, pestilential villages, where they procreated among themselves, and whence they were forbidden to emerge without a clapper in their hands, were in truth responsible for polluting the waters of France? For in the summer of 1321 the springs, brooks, wells and fountains were in many places poisoned. And during that year the people of France panted thirstily beside their generous rivers, or drank only with fear in their hearts, expecting death at every sip. And had the Temple anything to do with that strange poison – compounded of human blood, urine, magic herbs, adders' heads, powdered toads' legs, desecrated hosts and the pubic hair of whores – which it was asserted had been introduced into the water supply? Had the Temple incited this accursed race to rebellion, inspiring it, as some lepers admitted under torture, to will the death of all Christians or infect them with leprosy?

It began in Poitou, where King Philippe V was staying; and soon spread over the whole kingdom. The inhabitants of town and countryside attacked the leper colonies and exterminated the members of the diseased race who had suddenly become public enemies. Pregnant women were alone spared, but only till their child was born. Then they were burnt. The royal judges endued these hecatombs with legality, and the nobility supplied men-at-arms. Then the public turned against the Jews once again, accusing them of being involved in a huge, if vague, conspiracy, inspired, so it was said, by the Moorish Kings of Granada and Tunis. It seemed as if France were trying to allay her agony and fear with gigantic human sacrifices.

The wind of Aquitaine was impregnated with the appalling stench of the pyres. At Chinon all the Jews in the bailiwick were thrown into one huge fiery pit; in Paris they were burnt on that island opposite the Château Royal, which so tragically bore their name, and where Jacques de Molay had uttered his fatal prophecy.

Then the King died of the fever and the appalling stomach pains he had contracted in his appanage of Poitou; he died of having drunk the water of his kingdom, poisoned by some of his subjects.

He wasted away till he became a skeleton; and it took him five months to die, suffering the most appalling agonies.

Every morning, in the Abbey of Longchamp, to which he had been carried, he had the doors of his room thrown wide, allowing the passers-by to approach his bed, so that he might say to them: 'Look on the King of France, your Sovereign Lord, the most miserable man in all his kingdom, for there is not one among you with whom I would not change my lot. My children, look on your temporal Prince, and give your hearts to God at the sight of how it pleases Him to sport with His creatures of this world.'

He went to join the bones of his ancestors, at Saint-Denis, the day after Epiphany 1322; and no one, save his wife, wept for him.

And yet he had been a wise King, careful of the public good. He had declared every part of the royal domains, that is to say, France proper, inalienable; he had unified the currency and weights and measures, reorganized the law so that it might be applied with greater equity, forbidden pluralism in public offices, refused to allow prelates to sit in parliament, and systematized the administration of the country's finances. It was due to him also that the emancipation of the serfs was developed. He desired that serfdom should disappear altogether from his realms; he wanted to reign over a people who enjoyed the 'true liberty' with which nature had endowed them.

He had avoided the temptations of war, had suppressed many of the garrisons in the interior of the country to reinforce those on the frontiers, and had invariably preferred negotiation to foolish military escapades. It was no doubt too soon as yet for the people to grasp the fact that justice and peace were necessarily expensive or, indeed, to understand why the King so ardently required their co-operation. 'What has happened,' they asked, 'to the revenues, to the tithes and annates, to the subventions of the Lombards and the Jews, since less charity has been distributed, no wars have been made, and no buildings constructed? Where has all the money gone?'

The great barons, who were only temporarily submissive, and who had only on occasion, and when faced with the threat of war, rallied round the King from fear, had been patiently awaiting the hour of revenge, and now contemplated the death agonies of the young King they had never loved with a certain satisfaction.

Philippe V, the Long, a lonely man who was too much in advance of his time, died misunderstood by his subjects.

He left only daughters; the law of succession he had promulgated for his own advantage now excluded them from the throne. The crown went to his younger brother, Charles de la Marche, who was as dull of mind as he was handsome of face. The powerful Count of Valois, Count Robert of Artois and all the Capet cousins and the reactionary barons were once again triumphant. At last you could talk of a crusade again, become involved in the intrigues of the Empire, traffic in the price of gold, and watch, not without mockery, the difficulties of the kingdom of England.

For in England an unstable, dishonest and incompetent king, a prey to an amorous passion for his favourite, was fighting his barons and bishops. He, too, was soaking the soil of his kingdom with his subjects' blood.

And there a Princess of France was living a life of humiliation and ignominy both as wife and queen. She was afraid for her life, was conspiring for her own safety, and dreaming of vengeance.

It was as if Isabella, the daughter of the Iron King and the sister of Charles IV of France, had carried the curse of the Templars across the Channel.

PART ONE

FROM THE THAMES TO THE GARONNE

I

'No One ever Escapes from the Tower of London'

A MONSTROUS RAVEN, HUGE, gleaming and black, nearly as big as a goose, was hopping about in front of the dungeon window. Sometimes it halted, lowered a wing and hypocritically closed its little round eye as if in sleep. Then, suddenly darting out its beak, it pecked at the man's eye shining behind the bars. His grey, flint-coloured eyes seemed to have a special attraction for the bird. But the prisoner was too quick for it and had already drawn his face back out of danger. The raven continued its constitutional, taking short, heavy hops.

Then the man reached his hand out of the window. It was a long, shapely, sinewy hand. He moved it forward slowly, then let it lie still, like a twig on the dusty ground, hoping to seize the raven by the neck.

But the bird, in spite of its size, could move quickly too; it hopped aside, emitting a hoarse croak.

'Take care, Edward, take care,' said the man behind the bars. 'I'll strangle you one day.'

For the prisoner had given the treacherous bird the name of his enemy, the King of England.

This game had been going on for eighteen months, eighteen months during which the raven had pecked at the prisoner's eyes, eighteen months during which the prisoner had tried to strangle the bird, eighteen months during which Roger Mortimer, eighth Baron of Wigmore, Lord of the Welsh Marches, and the King's ex-Lieutenant of Ireland, had been imprisoned, together with his uncle, Roger Mortimer of Chirk, one-time Justiciar of Wales, in a dungeon in the Tower of London. For prisoners of their rank, and they belonged to the most ancient aristocracy in the kingdom, it was the normal custom to provide a decent lodging. But King Edward II, when he had taken the two Mortimers prisoner at the Battle of Shrewsbury, where he had defeated his rebellious barons, had assigned them to this low and narrow prison, whose only daylight came from ground-level, in the new buildings he had had constructed to the right of the Clock Tower. Compelled, under pressure from the Court, the bishops and even the common people, to commute the death sentence he had first decreed against the Mortimers to life imprisonment, the King had good hopes that this unhealthy prison cell, this dungeon in which their heads touched the ceiling, would in the long run perform the executioner's office for him.

And, indeed, though Roger Mortimer of Wigmore, who was now thirty-six years of age, had been able to endure the miserable prison, the eighteen months of fog pouring in through the low window and rain trickling down the walls, or, in the summer season, the oppressive, stagnant, stifling heat at the bottom of their hole seemed to have got the better of the Lord of Chirk. The elder Mortimer was losing his hair and his teeth, his legs had swollen and his hands were crippled with rheumatism. He scarcely ever left the oak plank that served him for bed, while his nephew stood by the window, staring out into the light.

It was the second summer they had spent in the dungeon.

Dawn had broken two hours ago over this most famous of English fortresses, which was the heart of the kingdom and the symbol of its princes' power, on the White Tower, the huge square keep, which gave an impression of architectural lightness in spite of its gigantic proportions, and which William the Conqueror had built on the foundations of the remains of the ancient Roman castrum, on the surrounding towers, on the crenellated walls built by Richard Cœur de Lion, on the King's House, on the Chapel of St Peter ad Vincula, and on the Traitor's Gate. The day was going to be hot, sultry even, as yesterday had been. The sun glowed pink on the stonework and there was a slightly nauseating stench of mud coming from the banks of the Thames, which lay close at hand, flowing past the embankments of the moat.[1*]

Edward, the raven, had joined the other giant ravens on that famous and melancholy lawn, the Green, where the block was set up on days of execution; the birds pecked at the grass that had been nourished by the blood of Scottish patriots, state criminals, and fallen favourites.

---

* The numbers in the text refer to the historical notes at the end of the book.

The Green was being raked and the paved paths surrounding it swept, but the ravens were unconcerned. No one would have dared harm the birds, for ravens had lived here since time immemorial, and were the objects of a sort of superstition. The soldiers of the guard began emerging from their barracks. They were hurriedly buckling their belts and leggings and donning their steel helmets to assemble for the daily parade which had, this morning, a particular importance for it was August 1, the Feast of St Peter ad Vincula – to whom the chapel was dedicated – and also the annual Feast Day in the Tower.

There was a grinding of locks and bolts on the low door of the Mortimers' dungeon. The turnkey opened it, glanced inside, and let the barber in. The barber, a man with beady eyes, a long nose and a round mouth, came once a week to shave Roger Mortimer, the younger. The operation was torture to the prisoner during the winter months. For the Constable, Stephen Seagrave, Governor of the Tower,[2] had said: 'If Lord Mortimer wishes to be shaved, I will send him the barber, but I have no obligation to provide him with hot water.'

But Lord Mortimer had held to it, in the first place to defy the Constable, secondly because his detested enemy, King Edward, wore a handsome blond beard, and finally, and above all, for his own morale, knowing well that if he yielded on this point, he would give way progressively to the physical deterioration that lies in wait for the prisoner. He had before his eyes the example of his uncle, who no longer took any care of his person; his chin a matted thicket, his hair thinning on his skull, the Lord of Chirk had begun to look like an old anchorite and continually complained of the multiple ills assailing him.

'It is only my poor body's pain,' he sometimes said, 'that reminds me I am still alive.'

Young Roger Mortimer had therefore welcomed barber Ogle week after week, even when they had to break the ice in the bowl and the razor left his cheeks bleeding. But he had had his reward, for he had realized after a few months that Ogle could be used as a link with the outside world. The man's character was a strange one; he was rapacious and yet capable of devotion; he suffered from the lowly position he occupied in life, for he considered it inferior to his true worth; conspiracy offered him an opportunity for secret revenge, and also enabled him to acquire, by sharing the secrets of the great, importance in his own eyes. The Baron of Wigmore was undoubtedly the most noble man, both by birth and nature, he had ever met. Besides, a prisoner who insisted on being shaved, even in frosty weather, was certainly to be admired.

Thanks to the barber, Mortimer had established tenuous yet regular communication with his partisans, and particularly with Adam Orleton, Bishop of Hereford; again through the barber, he had learned that the Lieutenant of the Tower, Gerard de Alspaye, might be won over to his cause; and, through the barber once more, he had set on foot the dilatory negotiations for his escape. The Bishop had promised him he would be rescued by summer. And summer had now come.

The turnkey looked through the spy-hole in the door from time to time, not because he was particularly suspicious, but merely out of professional habit.

Roger Mortimer, a wooden bowl under his chin – would he ever again have a fine basin of beaten silver as in the past? – listened to the polite conversation the barber made in a loud voice for appearances' sake: the summer, the heat, the weather continued fine, very lucky on the feast of St Peter.

Bending low over his razor, Ogle whispered in the prisoner's ear: 'Be ready tonight, my lord.'

Roger Mortimer gave no sign. His flinty eyes, under his thick eyebrows, merely looked into the barber's beady eyes and acknowledged the information with a wink.

'Alspaye?' Mortimer whispered.

'He'll go with us,' the barber replied, attending to the other side of Mortimer's face.

'The Bishop?' the prisoner asked again.

'He'll be waiting for you outside, after dark,' said the barber, who began at once to talk again at the top of his voice of the heat, the parade that was to take place that morning, and the games that would fill the afternoon.

The shaving done, Roger Mortimer rinsed his face and dried it with a towel. He did not even feel its rough contact.

When barber Ogle had gone with the turnkey, the prisoner put both hands to his chest and took a deep breath. With difficulty, he prevented himself shouting aloud: 'Be ready tonight!' The words were ringing through his head. Could it really be true that it was for tonight, at last?

He went to the pallet bed on which his companion in prison was sleeping.

'Uncle,' he said, 'it's tonight.'

The old Lord of Chirk turned over with a groan, looked at his nephew with his pale eyes that shone with a green glow in the shadowy dungeon and replied wearily: 'No one ever escapes from the Tower of London, my boy, no one. Neither tonight, nor ever.'

Young Mortimer showed his irritation. Why should a man who, at worst, had so comparatively little of life to lose, be so obstinately discouraging and refuse to take any risks whatever? He did not reply so as not to lose his temper. Though they spoke French together, as did the Court and the nobility of Norman origin, while servants, soldiers and the common people spoke English, they were still afraid of being overheard.

He went back to the narrow window and looked out at the parade, which he could see only from ground-level, with the happy feeling that he was perhaps watching it for the last time.

The soldiers' leggings passed to and fro at eye-level; their thick leather boots stamped the paving. Roger Mortimer could not but admire the precision of the archers' drill, those wonderful English archers who were the best in Europe and could shoot as many as twelve arrows a minute.

In the centre of the Green, Alspaye, the Lieutenant, standing rigid as a post, was shouting orders at the top of his voice. He then reported the guard to the Constable. At first sight, it was difficult to understand why this tall, pink and white young man, who was so attentive to his duty and so clearly concerned to do the right thing, should have agreed to betray his charge. There could be no doubt that he had been persuaded to it for other reasons than mere money. Gerard de Alspaye, the Lieutenant of the Tower of London, wished, as did many officers, sheriffs, bishops and lords, to see England freed from the bad ministers surrounding the King; in his youthful way he was dreaming of a great career; and, what was more, he loathed and despised his immediate superior, the Constable, Seagrave.

The Constable, a one-eyed, flabby-cheeked and incompetent drunkard, owed his high position in fact to the protection of those bad ministers. Overtly indulging in the very practices King Edward displayed before his Court, the Constable was inclined to use the garrison of the Tower as a harem. He liked tall, fair young men; and Lieutenant Alspaye's life had become a hell, for he was religious and had no vicious tendencies. Alspaye had indeed repelled the Constable's advances and, as a result, had become the object of his relentless persecution. From sheer vengeance Seagrave seized every opportunity to plague and vex him. Slothful though he was, this one-eyed man found the leisure to be cruel. And now, as he inspected the men, he mocked and insulted his second-in-command over the merest trifles: a fault in the men's dressing, a spot of rust on the blade of a dagger, a minute tear in the leather of a quiver. His single eye searched only for faults.

Though it was a Feast Day, on which punishments were generally remitted, the Constable, faulting their equipment, ordered three soldiers to be whipped on the spot. They happened to be three of the best archers. A sergeant was sent to fetch the rods. The men who were to be punished had to take their breeches down in front of the ranks of their comrades. The Constable seemed much amused at the sight.

'If the guard's no better turned out next time, Alspaye, it'll be you,' he said.

Then the whole garrison, with the exception of the sentries

on the gates and ramparts, gathered in the Chapel to hear Mass and sing canticles.

Listening at his window, the prisoner could hear their rough, untuneful voices. 'Be ready tonight, my lord . . .' The ex-Lieutenant of the King in Ireland could think of nothing except that he might perhaps be free this very night. But there was a whole day in which to wait, hope, and indeed fear: fear that Ogle would make some silly mistake in executing the agreed plan, fear that Alspaye would succumb to a sense of duty at the last moment. There was a whole day in which to dwell on all the obstacles, all the hazards that might prejudice his escape.

'It's better not even to think of it,' he thought, 'and take it for granted that all will go well. It's always something you've never even considered that goes wrong. Nevertheless, it's also the stronger will that triumphs.' And yet his mind, inevitably, returned again and again to the same anxieties. 'In any event, there'll still be the sentries on the walls . . .'

He jumped quickly back from the window. The raven had approached stealthily along the wall, and this time it was a near thing that it did not get the prisoner's eye.

'Oh, Edward, Edward, that's going too far,' Mortimer said between clenched teeth. 'If ever I'm going to succeed in strangling you, it must be today.'

The garrison was coming out of the Chapel and going into the refectory for the traditional feast.

The turnkey reappeared at the dungeon door, accompanied by a warder with the prisoners' food. For once, the bean soup was accompanied by a slice of mutton.

'Try to stand up, Uncle,' Mortimer said.

'They even deprive us of Mass, as if we were excommunicated,' said the old Lord.

He insisted on eating on his pallet, and indeed scarcely touched his portion.

'Have my share, you need it more than I,' he said to his nephew.

The turnkey had gone. The prisoners would not be visited again till evening.

'Have you really made up your mind not to go with me, Uncle?' Mortimer asked.

'Go with you where, my boy? No one ever escapes from the Tower. It has never been done. Nor does one rebel against one's king. Edward's not the best sovereign England's had, indeed he's not, and those two Despensers deserve to be here instead of us. But you don't choose your king, you serve him. I should never have listened to you and Thomas of Lancaster, when you took up arms. Thomas has been beheaded, and look where we are.'

It was the hour at which his uncle, having swallowed a few mouthfuls of food, would sometimes talk in a monotonous, whining voice, recapitulating over and over again the same complaints his nephew had heard for the last eighteen months. At sixty-seven, the elder Mortimer was no longer recognizable as the handsome man and great lord he had been, famous for the fabulous tournament he had given at his castle of Kenilworth, which had been the talk of three generations. The nephew did his best to rekindle a few embers in the old man's exhausted heart. He could see his white locks hanging lank in the shadows.

'In any case my legs would fail me,' the old man added.

'Why not get out of bed and try them out a little? In any case, I'll carry you. I've told you so.'

'Oh, yes, I know! You'll carry me over the walls and into the water though I can't swim. You'll carry my head to the block, that's what you'll do, and yours too. God may well be working for our deliverance, and you'll spoil it all by this stubborn folly of yours. It's always the same; there's rebellion in the Mortimer blood. Remember the first Roger, the son of the bishop and the daughter of King Herfast of Denmark. He defeated the whole army of the King of France under the walls of his castle of Mortemer-en-Bray.[3] And yet he so greatly offended the Conqueror, our kinsman, that all his lands and possessions were taken from him.'

The younger Roger sat on a stool, crossed his arms, closed his eyes, and leaned backwards a little to support his shoulders against the wall. Every day he had to listen to an account of their ancestors, hear for the hundredth time how Ralph the Bearded, son of the first Roger, had landed in England in the train of Duke William, how he had received Wigmore in fief, and why the Mortimers had been powerful in four counties ever since.

In the refectory the soldiers had finished eating and were bawling drinking songs.

'Please, Uncle,' Mortimer said, 'do leave our ancestors alone for a while. I'm in no such hurry to go to join them as you are. I know we're descended from royal blood. But royal blood is of small account in prison. Will Herfast's sword set us free? Where are our lands, and are we paid our revenues in this dungeon? And when you've repeated once again the names of all our female ancestors – Hadewige, Mélisinde,

Mathilde the Mean, Walcheline de Ferrers, Gladousa de Braouse – am I to dream of no women but them till I draw my last breath?'

For a moment the old man was nonplussed and stared absent-mindedly at his swollen hands and their long, broken nails, then he said: 'Everyone fills his prison life as best he can, old men with the lost past, young men with tomorrows they'll never see. You believe the whole of England loves you and is working on your behalf, that Bishop Orleton is your faithful friend, that the Queen herself is doing her best to save you, and that in a few hours you'll be setting out for France, Aquitaine, Provence or somewhere of the sort. And that the bells will ring out in welcome all along your road. But, you'll see, no one will come tonight.'

With a weary gesture, he passed his hands across his eyes, then turned his face to the wall.

Young Mortimer went back to the window, put a hand out through the bars and let it lie as if dead in the dust.

'Uncle will now doze till evening,' he thought. 'He'll make up his mind to come at the last moment. But he won't make it any easier; indeed, it may well fail because of him. Ah, there's Edward!'

The raven stopped a little way from the motionless hand and wiped its big black beak against its foot.

'If I strangle it, I shall succeed in escaping. If I miss it, I shall fail.'

It was no longer a game, but a wager with destiny. The prisoner needed to invent omens to pass the time of waiting and quiet his anxiety. He watched the raven with the eye of a hunter. But as if it realized the danger, the raven moved away.

The soldiers were coming out of the refectory, their faces all lit up. They dispersed over the courtyard in little groups for the games, races and wrestling that were a tradition of the Feast. For two hours, naked to the waist, they sweated under the sun, competing in throwing each other or in their skill in casting maces at a wooden picket.

Then he heard the Constable cry: 'The King's prize! Who wants to win a shilling?'[4]

Then, as it drew towards evening, the soldiers went to wash in the cisterns and, noisier than in the morning, talking of their exploits or their defeats, they went back to the refectory to eat and drink once more. Anyone who was not drunk on the night of St Peter ad Vincula earned the contempt of his comrades. The prisoner could hear them getting down to the wine. Dusk fell over the courtyard, the blue dusk of a summer's evening, and the stench of mud from the river-bank became perceptible once again.

Suddenly a long, fierce, hoarse croaking, the sort of animal cry that makes men uneasy, rent the air from beyond the window.

'What's that?' the old Lord of Chirk asked from the far end of the dungeon.

'I missed him,' his nephew said; 'I got him by the wing instead of the neck.'

In the uncertain evening light he gazed sadly at the few black feathers in his hand. The raven had disappeared and would not now come back again.

'It's mere childish folly to attach any importance to it,' the younger Mortimer thought. 'And it's nearly time now.' But he had an unhappy sense of foreboding.

But his mind was diverted from the omen by the extraordinary silence that had fallen over the Tower during the last few minutes. There was no more noise from the refectory; the voices of the drinkers had been stilled in their throats; the clatter of plates and pitchers had ceased. There was nothing but the sound of a dog barking somewhere in the garden, and the distant cry of a waterman on the Thames. Had Alspaye's plot been discovered? Was the silence lying over the fortress due to a shock of amazement at the discovery of a great betrayal? His forehead to the window bars, the prisoner held his breath and stared out into the shadows, listening for the slightest sound. An archer reeled across the courtyard, vomited against a wall, collapsed on to the ground and lay still. Mortimer could see him lying motionless on the grass. The first stars were already appearing in the sky. It would be a clear night.

Two more soldiers came out of the refectory holding their stomachs, and collapsed at the foot of a tree. This could be no ordinary drunkenness that bowled men over like a blow from a club.

Roger Mortimer went to the other end of the dungeon; he knew exactly where his boots stood in a corner and put them on; they slipped on easily enough for his legs had grown thin.

'What are you doing, Roger?' the elder Mortimer asked.

'I'm getting ready, Uncle; it's almost time. Our friend Alspaye seems to have played his part well; the Tower might be dead.'

'And they haven't brought us our second meal,' the old Lord complained anxiously.

Roger Mortimer tucked his shirt into his breeches and

buckled his belt about his military tunic. His clothes were worn and ragged, for they had refused his requests for new ones for the past eighteen months. He was still wearing those in which he had fought and they had taken him, removing his dented armour. His lower lip had been wounded by a blow on the chin-piece.

'If you succeed, I shall be left all alone, and they'll revenge themselves on me,' his uncle said.

There was a good deal of selfishness in the old man's vain obstinacy in trying to dissuade his nephew from escaping.

'Listen, Uncle, they're coming,' the younger Mortimer said, his voice curt and authoritative. 'You must get up now.'

There were footsteps approaching the door, sounding on the flagstones. A voice called: 'My lord!'

'Is that you, Alspaye?' Mortimer asked.

'Yes, my lord, but I haven't got the key. Your turnkey's so drunk, he's lost the bunch. In his present condition, it's impossible to get any sense out of him. I've searched everywhere.'

There was a sniggering laugh from the uncle's pallet.

The younger Mortimer swore in his disappointment. Was Alspaye lying? Had he taken fright at the last moment? But why had he come at all, in that case? Or was it merely one of those absurd mischances such as the prisoner had been trying to foresee all day, and which was now presenting itself in this guise?

'I assure you everything's ready, my lord,' went on Alspaye. 'The Bishop's powder we put in the wine has worked wonders. They were very drunk already and noticed nothing. And now they're sleeping the sleep of the dead. The ropes are ready, the boat's waiting for you. But I can't find the key.'

'How long have we got?'

'The sentries are unlikely to grow anxious for half an hour or so. They feasted too before going on guard.'

'Who's with you?'

'Ogle.'

'Send him for a sledgehammer, a chisel and a crowbar, and take the stone out.'

'I'll go with him, and come back at once.'

The two men went off. Roger Mortimer measured the time by the beating of his heart. Was he to fail because of a lost key? It needed only a sentry to abandon his post on some pretext or other and the chance would be gone. Even the old Lord was silent. Mortimer could hear his irregular breathing from the other side of the dungeon.

Soon a ray of light filtered under the door. Alspaye was back with the barber, who was carrying a candle and the tools. They set to work on the stone in the wall into which the bolt of the lock was sunk some two inches. They did their best to muffle their hammering; but, even so, it seemed to them that the noise echoed through the whole Tower. Slivers of stone fell to the ground. At last, the lock gave way and the door opened.

'Be quick, my lord,' Alspaye said.

His face glowed pink in the light of the candle and was dripping with sweat; his hands were trembling.

Roger Mortimer went to his uncle and bent over him.

'No, go alone, my boy,' said the old man. 'You must escape. May God protect you. And don't hold it against me that I'm old.'

The elder Mortimer drew his nephew to him by the sleeve, and traced the sign of the Cross on his forehead with his thumb.

'Avenge us, Roger,' he murmured.

Roger Mortimer bowed his head and left the dungeon.

'Which way do we go?' he asked.

'By the kitchens,' Alspaye replied.

The Lieutenant, the barber and the prisoner went up a few stairs, along a passage and through several dark rooms.

'Are you armed, Alspaye?' Roger Mortimer whispered suddenly.

'I've got my dagger.'

'There's a man there!'

There was a shadow against the wall; Mortimer had seen it first. The barber concealed the weak flame of the candle behind the palm of his hand. The Lieutenant drew his dagger. They moved slowly forward.

The man was standing quite still in the shadows. His shoulders and arms were flat against the wall and his legs wide apart. He seemed to be having some difficulty in remaining upright.

'It's Seagrave,' the Lieutenant said.

The one-eyed Constable had become aware that both he and his men had been drugged and had succeeded in making his way as far as this. He was wrestling with an overwhelming longing to sleep. He could see his prisoner escaping and his Lieutenant betraying him, but he could neither utter a sound nor move a limb. In his single eye, beneath its heavy lid, was the fear of death. The Lieutenant struck him in the face with his fist. The Constable's head went back against the stone and he fell to the ground.

The three men passed the door of the great refectory in which the torches were smoking; the whole garrison was there, fast asleep. Collapsed over the tables, fallen across the benches, lying on the floor, snoring with their mouths open in the most grotesque attitudes, the archers looked as if some magician had put them to sleep for a hundred years. A similar sight met them in the kitchens, which were lit only by glowing embers under the huge cauldrons, from which rose a heavy, stagnant smell of fat. The cooks had also drunk of the wine of Aquitaine in which the barber Ogle had mixed the drug; and there they lay, under the meat-safe, alongside the bread-bin, among the pitchers, stomachs up, arms wide-spread. The only moving thing was a cat, gorged on raw meat and stalking over the tables.

'This way, my lord,' said the Lieutenant, leading the prisoner towards an alcove which served both as a latrine and for the disposal of kitchen waste.

The opening built into this alcove was the only one on this side of the walls wide enough to give passage to a man.[5]

Ogle produced a rope ladder he had hidden in a chest and brought up a stool to which to attach it. They wedged the stool across the opening. The Lieutenant went first, then Roger Mortimer and then the barber. They were soon all three clinging to the ladder and making their way down the wall, hanging thirty feet above the gleaming waters of the moat. The moon had not yet risen.

'My uncle would certainly never have been able to escape this way,' Mortimer thought.

A black shape stirred beside him with a rustling of feathers. It was a big raven wakened from sleep in a loop-hole. Mortimer instinctively put out a hand and felt amid the warm feathers till he found the bird's neck. It uttered a long, desolate, almost human cry. He clenched his fist with all his might, twisting his wrist till he felt the bones crack beneath his fingers.

The body fell into the water below with a loud splash.

'Who goes there?' a sentry cried.

And a helmet leaned out of a crenel on the summit of the Clock Tower.

The three fugitives clinging to the rope ladder pressed close to the wall.

'Why did I do that?' Mortimer wondered. 'What an absurd temptation to yield to! There are surely enough risks already without inventing more. And I don't even know if it was Edward . . .'

But the sentry was reassured by the silence and continued his beat; they heard his footsteps fading into the night.

They went on climbing down. At this time of year the water in the moat was not very deep. The three men dropped into it up to the shoulders, and began moving along the foundations of the fortress, feeling their way along the stones of the Roman wall. They circled the Clock Tower and then crossed the moat, moving as quietly as possible. The bank was slippery with mud. They hoisted themselves out on to their stomachs, helping each other as best they could, then ran crouching to the river-bank. Hidden in the reeds, a boat was waiting for them. There were two men at the oars and another sitting in the stern, wrapped in a long dark cloak, his head covered by a hood with earlaps; he whistled softly three times. The fugitives jumped into the boat.

'My lord Mortimer,' said the man in the cloak, holding out his hand.

'My lord Bishop,' replied the fugitive, extending his own.

His fingers encountered the cabochon of a ring and he bent his lips to it.

'Go ahead, quickly,' the Bishop ordered the rowers.

And the oars dipped into the water.

Adam Orleton, Bishop of Hereford, who had been provided to his see by the Pope and against the King's wish, was leader of the clerical opposition and had organized the escape of the most important baron in the kingdom. It was Orleton who had planned and prepared everything, had persuaded Alspaye to play his part by assuring him he would not only make his fortune but attain to Paradise, and had provided the narcotic which had put the Tower of London to sleep.

'Did everything go well, Alspaye?' he asked.

'As well as it could, my lord,' the Lieutenant replied. 'How long will they sleep?'

'Two days or so, no doubt. I have the money promised each of you here,' the Bishop said, showing them the heavy purse he was holding under his cloak. 'And I have also sufficient for your expenses, my lord, for a few weeks at least.'

At that moment they heard the sentry shout: 'Sound the alarm!'

But the boat was well out into the river, and no sentry's cries would succeed in awakening the Tower.

'I owe everything to you, including my life,' Mortimer said to the Bishop.

'Wait till you're in France,' Orleton replied; 'don't thank me till then. Horses are awaiting us at Bermondsey on the farther bank. A ship has been chartered and is lying off Dover, ready to sail.'

'Are you coming with me?'

'No, my lord, I have no reason to fly. When I have seen you on board, I shall go back to my diocese.'

'Are you not afraid for your life, after what you have just done?'

'I belong to the Church,' the Bishop replied with some irony. 'The King hates me but will not dare touch me.'

This calm-voiced prelate, who could carry on a conversation in these circumstances and in the middle of the Thames as tranquilly as if he were in his episcopal palace, possessed a singular courage, and Mortimer admired him sincerely.

The oarsmen were in the centre of the boat; Alspaye and the barber in the bows.

'And the Queen?' Mortimer asked. 'Have you seen her recently? Is she being plagued as much as ever?'

'At the moment, the Queen is in Yorkshire, travelling with the King; his absence has made our undertaking all the easier. Your wife' – the Bishop slightly emphasized the last word – 'sent me news of her the other day.'

Mortimer felt himself blush and was thankful for the darkness that concealed his embarrassment. He had shown concern for the Queen before even inquiring about his family and his wife. And why had he lowered his voice to ask the question? Had he thought of no one but Queen Isabella during his whole eighteen months in prison?

'The Queen wishes you well,' the Bishop went on. 'It is she

who has furnished from her privy purse, from that meagre privy purse which is all our good friends the Despensers consent to allow her, the money I am going to give you so that you may live in France. As for the rest, Alspaye, the barber, the horses and the ship that awaits you, my diocese will pay the expenses.'

He put his hand on the fugitive's arm.

'But you're soaked through!' he said.

'No matter!' replied Mortimer. 'A free air will dry me quick enough.'

He got to his feet, took off his tunic and shirt, and stood naked to the waist in the middle of the boat. He had a shapely, well-built body, powerful shoulders and a long, muscular back; imprisonment had made him thinner, but had not impaired the impression he gave of physical strength. The moon, which had just risen, bathed him in a golden light and threw the contours of his chest into relief.

'Propitious, dangerous to fugitives,' said the Bishop, pointing to the moon. 'We timed it exactly right.'

The night air was laden with the scent of reeds and water, and Roger Mortimer felt it playing over his skin and through his wet hair. The smooth black Thames slid along the sides of the boat and the oars made golden sparks. The opposite bank was drawing near. The great Baron of the Marches turned to look for the last time at the Tower, standing tall and proud above its fortifications, ramparts and embankments. 'No one ever escapes from the Tower . . .' And, indeed, he was the first prisoner who ever had escaped from it. He began to consider the importance of his deed, and the defiance it hurled at the power of kings.

Behind it, the sleeping city stood out against the night. Along both banks, as far as the great bridge with its shops and guarded by its high towers, could be seen the innumerable, crowded, slowly waving masts of the ships of the London Hanse, the Teutonic Hanse, the Paris Hanse of the Marchands d'Eau, indeed of the whole of Europe, bringing cloth from Bruges, copper, pitch, wax, knives, the wines of the Saintonge and of Aquitaine, and dried fish, and loading for Flanders, Rouen, Bordeaux and Lisbon, corn, leather, tin, cheeses, and above all wool, which was the best in the world, from English sheep. The great Venetian galleys could be distinguished by their shape and their gilding.

But Roger Mortimer of Wigmore was already thinking of France. He would go first to Artois to ask asylum of his cousin, Jean de Fiennes, the son of his mother's brother. He stretched his arms wide in the gesture of a free man.

And Bishop Orleton, who regretted that he had been born neither so handsome nor so great a lord, gazed with a sort of envy at this strong, confident body that seemed so apt for leaping into the saddle, at the tall, sculptured torso, the proud chin and the rough, curly hair, which were to carry England's destiny into exile.

2

The Harassed Queen

THE RED-VELVET FOOTSTOOL on which Queen Isabella was resting her slender feet was threadbare; the gold tassels at its four corners were tarnished; the embroidered lilies of France and leopards of England were worn. But what was the use of replacing the footstool by ordering another, if the new one were immediately to disappear beneath the pearl-embroidered shoes of Hugh Despenser, the King's lover? The Queen looked down at the old footstool that had lain on the flagstones of every castle in the kingdom, one season in Dorset, another in Norfolk, a winter in Warwick, and this last summer in Yorkshire, for they never stayed more than three days in the same place. On August 1, less than a week ago, the Court had been at Cowick; yesterday they had stopped at Eserick; today they were camping, rather than lodging, at Kirkham Priory; the day after tomorrow they would set out for Lockton and Pickering. The few dusty tapestries, the dented dishes, and the worn dresses which constituted Queen

Isabella's travelling wardrobe, would be packed into the travelling-chests once again; the curtained bed, which was so weakened by its travels that it was now in danger of collapsing altogether, would be taken down and put up again somewhere else, that bed in which the Queen took sometimes her lady-in-waiting, Lady Jeanne Mortimer, and sometimes her eldest son, Prince Edward, to sleep with her for fear of being murdered if she slept alone. At least the Despensers would not dare stab her under the eye of the heir-apparent. And it was thus they journeyed across the kingdom, through its green countryside and by its melancholy castles.

Edward II wanted to be known personally to the least of his vassals; he thought he did them honour by staying with them, and that a few friendly words would assure their loyalty against the Scots or the Welsh party. In fact, he would have done better to show himself less. He created latent discord wherever he went; the careless way he talked of government matters, which he believed to be a sovereign attitude of detachment, offended the lords, abbots and notables who came to explain local problems to him; the intimacy he paraded with his all-powerful chamberlain whose hand he caressed in open council or at Mass, his high-pitched laughter, his sudden generosity to some little clerk or astonished young groom, all confirmed the scandalous stories that were current even in the remotest districts, where husbands no doubt deceived their wives, as everywhere else, but did so with women; and what was only whispered before his coming was said out loud after he had passed by. This handsome, fair-bearded man, who was so weak of will, had but to appear with his crown on his head, and the whole prestige of the royal majesty collapsed. And the avaricious courtiers by whom he was surrounded helped considerably to make him hated.

Useless and powerless, the Queen had to take part in this ill-considered progress. She was torn by two conflicting emotions; on the one hand, her truly royal nature, inherited from her Capet ancestors, was irritated and angered by the continuous process of degradation suffered by the sovereign power; but, on the other hand, the wronged, harassed and endangered wife secretly rejoiced at every new enemy the King made. She could not understand how she had once loved, or persuaded herself to love, so contemptible a creature, who treated her so odiously. Why was she made to take part in these journeys, why was she shown off, a wronged Queen, to the whole kingdom? Did the King and his favourite really think they deceived anyone or made their relations look innocent by the mere fact of her presence? Or was it that they wanted to keep her under their eye? She would have so much preferred to live in London or at Windsor, or even in one of the castles she had theoretically been given, while awaiting some change in circumstance or simply the onset of old age. And how she regretted above all that Thomas of Lancaster and Roger Mortimer, those great barons who were really men, had not succeeded in their rebellion the year before last.

Raising her beautiful blue eyes, she glanced up at the Count de Bouville, who had been sent over from the Court of France, and said in a low voice: 'For a month past you have been able to see what my life is like, Messire Hugues. I do not even ask you to recount its miseries to my brother, nor to my uncle of Valois. Four kings have succeeded each other on the throne of France, my father King Philip, who married me off in the interests of the crown . . .'

'God keep his soul, Madame, may God keep it!' said fat Bouville with conviction, but without raising his voice. 'There's no one in the world I loved more, nor served with greater joy.'

'Then my brother Louis, who was but a few months on the throne, then my brother Philippe with whom I had little in common, though he was not lacking in intelligence . . .'

Bouville frowned a little as he did whenever King Philippe the Long was mentioned in his presence.

'And then my brother Charles, who is reigning now,' went on the Queen. 'They have all been told of my unhappy circumstances, and they have been able to do nothing, or have wished to do nothing. The Kings of France are not interested in England except in the matter of Aquitaine and the homage due to them for that fief. A Princess of France on the English throne, because she thereby becomes Duchess of Aquitaine, is a pledge of peace. And provided Guyenne is quiet, little do they care whether their daughter or sister dies of shame and neglect beyond the sea. Report it or not, it will make no difference. But the days you have spent with me have been pleasant ones, for I have been able to talk to a friend. And you have seen how few I have. Without my dear Lady Jeanne, who shows great constancy in sharing my fortunes, I would not even have one.'

As she said these words, the Queen turned to her lady-in-waiting who was sitting beside her. Jeanne Mortimer, great-niece of the famous Seneschal de Joinville, was a tall woman of thirty-seven, with regular features, an honest face and quiet hands.

'Madame,' replied Lady Jeanne, 'you do more to sustain my courage than I do to maintain yours. And you've taken a great risk in keeping me with you when my husband is in prison.'

They all three went on talking in low voices, for the whisper and the aside had become necessary habits in that Court where you were never alone and the Queen lived amid enmity.

In a corner of the room three maidservants were embroidering a counterpane for Lady Alienor Despenser, the favourite's wife, who was playing chess by an open window with the heir-apparent. A little farther off, the Queen's second son, who had had his seventh birthday three weeks earlier, was making a bow from hazel switch; while the two little girls, Jane and Alienor, respectively five and two, were sitting on the floor, playing with rag dolls.

Even as she moved the pieces over the ivory chess-board, Lady Despenser never for a moment stopped watching the Queen and trying to hear what she was saying. Her forehead was smooth but curiously narrow, her eyes were bright but too close together, her mouth was sarcastic; without being altogether hideous, there was nevertheless apparent that quality of ugliness which is imprinted by a wicked nature. A descendant of the Clare family, she had had a strange career, for she had been sister-in-law to the King's previous lover, Piers Gaveston, whom the barons under Thomas of Lancaster had executed eleven years before, and she was now the wife of the King's current lover. She derived a morbid pleasure from assisting male amours, partly to satisfy her love of money and partly to gratify her lust of power. But she was a fool. She was prepared to lose her game of chess for the mere pleasure of saying provocatively: 'Check to the Queen! Check to the Queen!'

Edward, the heir-apparent, was a boy of eleven; he had a rather long, thin face, and was by nature reserved rather than timid, though he nearly always kept his eyes on the ground; at the moment he was taking advantage of his opponent's mistake to do his best to win.

The August breeze was blowing gusts of warm dust through the narrow, arched window; but, when the sun sank, it would turn cool and damp again within the thick, dark walls of ancient Kirkham Priory.

There was a sound of many voices from the Chapter House where the King was holding his itinerant Council.

'Madame,' said the Count de Bouville, 'I would willingly dedicate all the remainder of my days to your service, could they be useful to you. It would be a pleasure to me, I assure you. What is there for me to do here below, since I am a widower and my sons are out in the world, except to use the last of my strength to serve the descendants of the King who was my benefactor? And it is with you, Madame, that I feel myself nearest to him. You have all his strength of character, the way of talking he had, when he felt so disposed, and all his beauty which was so impervious to time. When he died, at the age of forty-six, he looked barely more than thirty. It will be the same with you. No one would ever guess you have had four children.'

The Queen's face brightened into a smile. Surrounded, as she was, by so much hatred, she was grateful to be offered this devotion; and, her feelings as a woman continually humiliated, it was sweet to hear her beauty praised, even if the compliment was from a fat old man with white hair and spaniel's eyes.

'I am already thirty-one,' she said, 'of which fifteen years have been spent as you see. It may not mark my face; but my spirit bears the wrinkles. Indeed, Bouville, I would willingly keep you with me, were it possible.'

'Alas, Madame, I foresee the end of my mission, and it has not had much success. King Edward has already twice indicated his surprise, since he has already delivered the Lombard up to the High Court of the King of France, that I should still be here.'

For the official pretext for Bouville's embassy was a demand for the extradition of a certain Thomas Henry, a member of the important Scali company of Florence; the banker had leased certain lands from the Crown of France, had pocketed the considerable revenues, failed to pay what he owed to the French Treasury, and had ultimately taken refuge in England. The affair was serious enough, of course, but it could easily have been dealt with by letter, or by sending a magistrate, and most certainly had not required the presence of an ex-Great Chamberlain, who sat in the Privy Council. In fact, Bouville had been charged with another and more difficult diplomatic negotiation.

Monseigneur Charles of Valois, the uncle both of the King of France and Queen Isabella, had taken it into his head the previous year to marry off his fifth daughter, Marie, to Prince Edward, the heir-apparent to the throne of England. Monseigneur of Valois – who was unaware of it in Europe? –

had seven daughters whose marriages had been a continual source of anxiety to this turbulent, ambitious and prodigal prince, who inevitably used his children for the promotion of his vast intrigues. The seven daughters were by three different marriages for Monseigneur Charles, during the course of his restless life, had suffered the misfortune of twice becoming a widower.

You needed a clear mind not to lose your way amid this complicated family tree, to know, for instance, when Madame Jeanne of Valois was mentioned, whether the Countess of Hainaut was meant or the Countess of Beaumont, the wife of Robert of Artois. Just to help matters, the two girls had the same name. As for Catherine, heiress to the phantom throne of Constantinople, who was by the second marriage, she had wedded in the person of Philip of Tarantum, Prince of Achaia, an elder brother of her father's first wife. It was, indeed, something of a puzzle!

And now Monseigneur Charles was proposing that the elder daughter of his third marriage should wed his great-nephew of England.

At the beginning of the year, Monseigneur of Valois had sent a mission consisting of Count Henry de Sully, Raoul Sevain de Jouy and Robert Bertrand, known as the 'Knight of the Green Lion'. To curry favour with Edward II, these ambassadors had accompanied him on an expedition against the Scots; but, at the Battle of Blackmore, the English had fled and allowed the French ambassadors to fall into the hands of the enemy. Their freedom had had to be negotiated and their ransoms paid. When, at last after a number of unpleasant adventures, they had been released, Edward had replied, evasively and dilatorily, that his son's marriage could not be decided on so quickly, that the matter was of such great importance that he could make no contract without the advice of his Parliament, and that Parliament would be summoned to discuss the matter in June. He wished to link this affair with the homage he was due to pay the King of France for the Duchy of Aquitaine. And then, when Parliament had at last been convoked, the question had not even been discussed.[6]

In his impatience, Monseigneur of Valois had taken the first opportunity of sending over the Count de Bouville, whose devotion to the Capet family was undoubted and who, though lacking in genius, had considerable experience of similar missions. In the past, Bouville had negotiated in Naples, on the instructions of Valois himself, the second marriage of Louis X with Clémence of Hungary; he had been Curator of the Queen's stomach after the Hutin's death, but that was not a period he cared to recall. He had also carried out a number of negotiations in Avignon with the Holy See; and in matters concerning family relationships his memory was faultless, he knew all the infinitely complex inter-weavings that formed the web of the royal houses' alliances. Honest Bouville was much vexed at having to go back this time with empty hands.

'Monseigneur of Valois will be very angry indeed,' he said, 'since he has already asked the Holy Father for a licence for this marriage.'

'I've done all I can, Bouville,' the Queen said, 'and you can judge from that what weight I carry here. But I do not regret it as much as you do; I do not want another princess of my family to suffer what I have suffered here.'

'Madame,' Bouville replied, lowering his voice still further, 'do you doubt your son? He seems to take after you rather than after his father, thank God. I remember you at his age, in the garden of the Palace of the Cité, or at Fontainebleau . . .'

He was interrupted. The door opened to give entrance to the King of England. He hurried in; his head was thrown back and he was stroking his blond beard with a nervous gesture which, in him, was a sign of irritation. He was followed by his usual councillors, the two Despensers, father and son, Chancellor Baldock, the Earl of Arundel and the Bishop of Exeter. The King's two half-brothers, the Earls of Kent and Norfolk, who had French blood since their mother was the sister of Philip the Fair, formed part of his entourage, but rather against their will so it seemed; and this was also true of Henry of Leicester. The last was a square-looking man, with bright, rather protruding eyes, who was nicknamed Crouch-back owing to a malformation of the neck and shoulders which compelled him to hold his neck completely askew, and gave the armourers who had to forge his cuirasses a good deal of difficulty. A number of ecclesiastics and local dignitaries also pressed into the doorway.

'Have you heard the news, Madame?' cried King Edward, addressing the Queen. 'It will doubtless please you. *Your* Mortimer has escaped from the Tower.'

Lady Despenser, at the chess-board, gave a start and uttered an exclamation of indignation as if the Baron of Wigmore's escape were a personal insult.

Queen Isabella gave no sign, either by altering her attitude or expression; only her eyelids blinked a little more rapidly over her beautiful blue eyes, and her hand, beneath the folds of her dress, furtively sought that of Lady Jeanne Mortimer, as if encouraging her to be strong and calm. Fat Bouville had got to his feet and moved a little apart, feeling himself unwanted in this matter which purely concerned the English Crown.

'He is not *my* Mortimer, Sire,' replied the Queen. 'Lord Mortimer is your subject, I should have thought, rather than mine; and I am not accountable for the actions of your barons. You kept him in prison; he has escaped; it's the common form.'

'And that shows you approve him! Don't restrain your joy, Madame. In the days when Mortimer deigned to appear at my Court, you had no eyes except for him; you were continually extolling his merits, and you have always put down the crimes he has committed against me to his greatness of soul.'

'But was it not you, yourself, Sire my Husband, who taught me to love him at the time he was conquering, on your behalf and at the peril of his life, the Kingdom of Ireland, which indeed you had great difficulty in holding without him? Was that a crime?'[7]

Put out of countenance by this attack, Edward looked spitefully at his wife and found some difficulty in replying.

'Well, your friend's on the run now, running hard towards your country no doubt!'

As he talked, the King was walking up and down the room, working off his useless agitation. The jewels hanging from his clothes quivered at every step he took. The rest of the company followed him with their eyes, turning their heads from side to side, as if they were watching a game of tennis. There was no doubt that King Edward was a fine-looking man, muscular, lithe and alert. He kept himself fit with games and exercises and had so far resisted any tendency to stoutness though his fortieth birthday was close at hand; he had an athlete's constitution. But if you looked closer, you were struck by the fact that his forehead was utterly unlined, as if the anxieties of power had failed to mark him, by the pouches beginning to form beneath his eyes, by the uncertain line of the curve of the nostril, and by the long chin beneath the thin, curled beard. It was not an energetic or authoritative chin, nor even a really sensual one, but merely too big and too elongated a chin. There was twenty times more determination in the Queen's little chin than there was in this ovoid jaw whose weakness the silky beard could not conceal. And the hand he passed from time to time across his face was flaccid; it fluttered aimlessly and then tugged at a pearl sewn to the embroidery of his tunic. His voice, which he hoped and believed was imperious, merely suggested lack of control. His back, which was wide enough, curved unpleasantly from the neck to the waist, as if the spine lacked substance. Edward had never forgiven his wife for having one day advised him to avoid showing his back if he wished to gain the respect of his barons. His knee was shapely and his leg well-turned; indeed, these were the best points of this man who was so little suited to his responsibilities, and to whom a crown had fallen by some curious inadvertence on the part of Fate.

'Haven't I enough worries and difficulties already?' he went on. 'The Scots are always threatening and invading my frontiers and, when I give battle, my armies run away. And how can I defeat them when my bishops treat with them without my permission, when there are so many traitors among my vassals, and when my barons of the Marches raise troops against me on the principle that they hold their lands by their swords, when some twenty-five years ago – have they forgotten? – it was determined and ordered otherwise by King Edward, my father. But they learned at Shrewsbury and Boroughbridge what it costs to rebel against me, didn't they, Leicester?'

Henry of Leicester shook his great, crippled head; it was hardly a courteous way of reminding him of the death of his brother, Thomas of Lancaster, who had been beheaded sixteen months before, when twenty great lords had been hanged and as many more imprisoned.

'Indeed, Sire my Husband, we have all noticed that the only battles you can win are against your own barons,' Isabella said.

Once again Edward looked at her with hatred in his eyes. 'What courage,' Bouville thought, 'what courage this noble Queen has!'

'Nor is it altogether fair,' she went on, 'to say that they rebelled against you because they hold their rights by their swords. Was it not rather over the rights of the county of Gloucester which you wanted to give to Sir Hugh?'

The two Despensers drew closer together as if to make common front. Lady Despenser, the younger, sat up stiffly at the chess-board. She was the daughter of the late Earl of Gloucester. Edward II stamped his foot on the flagstones. Really, the Queen was impossible. She never opened her mouth except to tease him with his errors and mistakes of government.[8]

'I give the great fiefs to whom I will, Madame. I give them to those who love me and serve me,' Edward cried, putting his hand on the younger Hugh's shoulder. 'On whom else can I rely? Where are my allies? What help, Madame, does your brother of France, who should behave to me as if he were mine, since after all it was in that hope I was persuaded to take you for wife, bring me? He demands that I go and pay him homage for Aquitaine, and that is all the help I get from him. And where does he send me his summons, to Guyenne? Not at all. He has it brought to me here in my Kingdom, as if he were contemptuous of feudal custom, or wished to offend me. One might almost think he believed himself also suzerain of England. Besides, I have paid this homage, indeed I have paid it too often, once to your father, when I was nearly burnt alive in the fire at Maubuisson, and then again to your brother Philippe, three years ago, when I went to Amiens. Considering the frequency with which the kings of your family die, Madame, I shall soon have to go to live on the Continent.'

The lords, bishops, and Yorkshire notables, who were standing at the back of the room, looked at each other, by no means afraid, but shocked rather at this impotent anger which strayed so far from its object, and revealed to them not only the difficulties of the kingdom, but also the character of the King. Was this the sovereign who asked them for subsidies for his Treasury, to whom they owed obedience in everything, and for whom they were to risk their lives when he summoned them to take part in his wars? Lord Mortimer must have had good reasons for rebellion.

Even the intimate councillors seemed ill at ease, though they well knew the King's habit of recapitulating, even in his correspondence, all the troubles of his reign whenever a new difficulty arose.

Chancellor Baldock was mechanically rubbing his Adam's apple above his archidiaconal robe. The Bishop of Exeter, the Lord Treasurer, was nervously biting his thumbnail and watching his neighbours out of the corner of his eye. Only Hugh Despenser the Younger, too curled, scented and overdressed for a man of thirty-three, showed satisfaction. The King's hand resting on his shoulder made it clear to everyone how important and powerful he was.

He had a short, snub nose and a well-shaped mouth and was now raising and lowering his chin like a horse pawing the ground, as he approved every word Edward said with a little throaty murmur. His expression seemed to imply: 'This time things have really gone too far; we shall have to take stern measures!' He was thin, tall, rather narrow-chested and had a bad, spotty skin.

'Messire de Bouville,' King Edward said suddenly, turning to the ambassador, 'you will reply to Monseigneur of Valois that the marriage he proposes, and of which we appreciate the honour, will most certainly not take place. We have other views for our eldest son. And we shall thus put a term to the deplorable custom by which the Kings of England take their wives from France, without ever deriving any benefit from it.'

Fat Bouville paled at the affront and bowed. He looked sadly at the Queen and went out.

The first and most unexpected consequence of Roger Mortimer's escape was that the King of England was breaking his traditional alliance. By this outburst he had wanted to wound his wife; but he had also succeeded in wounding his half-brothers of Norfolk and Kent, whose mother was French.

The two young men turned to their cousin Crouchback, who shrugged his heavy shoulder in resigned indifference. Without reflection, the King had casually alienated for ever the powerful Count of Valois who, as everyone knew, governed France in the name of his nephew Charles the Fair. Caprices such as this have sometimes lost kings both their thrones and their lives.

Young Prince Edward, still motionless by the window, was silently watching his mother and judging his father. After all, it was his marriage that was being discussed and he was allowed to have no say in it. But if he had been asked to choose between his English and French blood, he would have shown a preference for the latter.

The three younger children had stopped playing: the Queen signed to the maidservants to take them away.

And then, with the greatest calm, looking the King straight in the eye, she said: 'When a husband hates his wife it is natural he should hold her responsible for everything.'

Edward was not the man to make a direct answer to that.

'My whole Tower guard dead-drunk,' he cried, 'the Lieutenant in flight with that felon, and my Constable sick to death with the drug they gave him. Unless the traitor's malingering to avoid the punishment he deserves. It was up to him to see my prisoner did not escape. Do you hear, Winchester?'

Hugh Despenser the Elder, who had been responsible for the appointment of Constable Seagrave, bowed to the storm. He was thin and narrow-shouldered, with a stoop that was in part natural and in part acquired during a long career as a courtier. His enemies had nicknamed him 'the weasel'.

Cupidity, envy, meanness, self-seeking, deceit, and all the gratifications these vices can procure for their possessor were manifest in the lines of his face and beneath his red eyelids. And yet he was not lacking in courage; but he had human feelings only for his son and a few rare friends, of which Seagrave indeed was one. You could better understand the son's character when you had observed the father for a moment.

'My lord,' he said in a calm voice, 'I feel sure that Seagrave is in no way to blame.'

'He's to blame for negligence and laziness; he's to blame for allowing himself to be made a fool of; he's to blame for not suspecting that a plot was being hatched under his nose; he's to blame perhaps for his bad luck. And I never forgive bad luck. Though Seagrave is one of your protégés, Winchester, he shall be punished; and people will no longer be able to say that I'm unfair and that my favours are lavished only on your creatures. Seagrave will take Mortimer's place in prison; and perhaps his successor will take care to keep a better watch. That, my son, is how you rule,' the King added, coming to a halt in front of the heir to the throne.

The boy raised his eyes to him and immediately lowered them again.

Hugh the Younger, who knew how to turn Edward's anger aside, threw back his head and, gazing up at the beams of the ceiling, said: 'It's the other criminal, dear Sire, who's defying you most contemptuously. Bishop Orleton organized the whole thing himself and seems to fear you so little that he has not even taken the trouble to fly or go into hiding.'

Edward looked at Hugh the Younger with gratitude and

admiration. How could one not be moved by that profile, by the fine attitudes he struck when speaking, by that high, well-modulated voice, and that way, at once so tender and respectful, of saying 'dear Sire', in the French manner, as sweet Gaveston, whom the barons and bishops had killed, used to do? But Edward had learned from experience, he knew how wicked men were and that you never won by coming to terms. He was determined never to be separated from Hugh, and all who opposed him would be pitilessly struck down, one after the other.

'I announce to you, my lords, that Bishop Orleton will be brought before my Parliament to be tried and sentenced.'

Edward crossed his arms and looked round to see the effect of his words. The Archdeacon-Chancellor and the Bishop-Treasurer, though they were Orleton's worst enemies, looked disapproving for they could not help standing by members of the cloth.

Henry Crouchback, who was by nature a wise and moderate man, could not help making an effort to bring the King back to the path of reason. He observed calmly that a bishop could be brought only before an ecclesiastical court consisting of his peers.

'Everything has to have a beginning, Leicester. Conspiracy against Kings is not, so far as I know, taught by the Holy Gospels. Since Orleton has forgotten what should be rendered to Caesar, Caesar will remind him of it. Another favour I owe your family, Madame,' the King went on, addressing Isabella, 'since it was your brother Philippe V who, against my will, had Adam Orleton provided to the see of Hereford by his French Pope. Very well. He shall be the first prelate to be sentenced by the royal judiciary and his punishment shall be exemplary.'

'Orleton was not originally hostile to you, Cousin,' argued Crouchback, 'nor would he have had any reason to become so if you had not opposed, or if your Council had not opposed, the Holy Father's giving him the mitre. He is a man of great learning and strength of character. And you might even now perhaps, precisely because he is guilty, rally him to your support more easily by an act of clemency than by a trial at law which, among all your other difficulties, will draw upon you the anger of the clergy.'

'Clemency, forbearance! Every time I'm scorned, provoked or betrayed, that's all you have to say, Leicester. I was implored to spare the Baron of Wigmore, and how wrong I was to listen to that advice. You must admit that had I dealt with him as I did with your brother, the rebel would not be fleeing down the roads today.'

Crouchback shrugged his heavy shoulder and closed his eyes with an expression of weariness. How very irritating was Edward's habit, which he considered royal, of calling the members of his family and his principal councillors by the names of their counties, addressing his cousin-german by shouting 'Leicester' instead of simply saying 'my cousin', as did everyone else including the Queen herself. And his bad taste in mentioning the execution of Thomas on every possible occasion, as if he gloried in it. Oh, what a strange man he was and what a bad king. To imagine you could behead your nearest relations and that no one resented it, to believe that mourning could be effaced by an embrace, to demand devotion from those you had wronged, and expect loyalty from everyone while you yourself were so cruelly inconstant.

'No doubt you're right, my lord,' said Crouchback, 'and since you've now reigned for sixteen years you must know the consequences of your actions. Hail your bishop before Parliament. I won't stand in your way.'

And, muttering between his teeth so that no one should hear but the young Earl of Norfolk, he added: 'My head may be set askew on my shoulders, but I'd rather keep it where it is.'

'You must admit,' Edward went on, his hand fluttering, 'that it's simply snapping his fingers at me to escape by piercing the walls of a tower I built myself especially so that no one should escape from it.'

'Perhaps, Sire my Husband,' the Queen said, 'when it was building you were more preoccupied with the charms of the masons than with the solidity of the stonework.'

A sudden silence fell over the company. The insult was flagrant, and most unexpected. They all held their breath and stared, some with deference, some with hatred, at the rather fragile-looking woman who sat so upright and lonely in her chair, and held her own like this. Her lips drawn back a little and her mouth half-open, she was showing her fine little teeth; they were clenched, sharp, carnivorous. Isabella was clearly delighted with the blow she had dealt, whatever the consequences might be.

Hugh the Younger was blushing scarlet; Hugh the Elder made a pretence of not having heard.

Edward would certainly have his revenge. But what means would he adopt? The retort lagged. The Queen watched the drops of sweat pearling her husband's brow. And nothing disgusts a woman more than the sweat of the man she has ceased to love.

'Kent,' cried the King, 'I've made you Warden of the Cinque Ports and Governor of Dover. What are you doing here? Why aren't you on the coast you're supposed to be guarding and from which our felon must inevitably take ship?'

'Sire my Brother,' said the young Earl of Kent, somewhat taken aback, 'it was you yourself who ordered me to accompany you on your journey . . .'

'Well, now I'm giving you another. Go back to your county, have the towns and countryside searched for the fugitive, and see to it personally that every ship in port is visited.'

'Send agents on board the ships and apprehend Mortimer, dead or alive, if he embarks,' said Hugh the Younger.

'Sound advice, Gloucester,' Edward approved. 'As for you, Stapledon . . .'

The Bishop of Exeter stopped gnawing at his thumbnail and murmured: 'My lord . . .'

'You will make haste to London and go immediately to the Tower on the pretext of checking the Treasure, which is in your charge. Then, furnished with an order under my seal, you will take command of the Tower and supervise it till a new constable is appointed. Baldock will make out the commissions at once, so that you will have the necessary powers.'

Henry Crouchback, his eyes turned towards the window and his ear propped on his shoulder, seemed to be dreaming. He was calculating that six days had elapsed since Mortimer's escape,[9] that it would take at least eight days more before these orders could be executed, and that unless he was a fool, which Mortimer most certainly was not, he must already have left the kingdom. He congratulated himself on having joined with the greater part of the bishops and lords who, after Boroughbridge, had succeeded in obtaining a reprieve for the Baron of Wigmore. For now that Mortimer had escaped, the opposition to the Despensers might well find the leader it had lacked since the death of Thomas of Lancaster, and a stronger, cleverer, and more effective leader than Thomas had been.

The King's back bent sinuously; Edward pirouetted on his heels and came face to face with his wife.

'What's more, Madame, I hold you entirely responsible. And, in the first place, let go that hand you've been holding ever since I came into the room. Let go Lady Jeanne's hand!' cried Edward, stamping his foot. 'It's going surety for a traitor to keep his wife so ostentatiously at your side. The people who helped Mortimer to escape well knew they had the Queen's support. Besides, you can't escape without money. Treason has to be paid for. Walls aren't pierced without gold. But the conduit's evident: the Queen to her lady-in-waiting, the lady-in-waiting to the bishop, the bishop to the rebel. I shall have to look more closely into your privy purse.'

'Sire my Husband, I think my privy purse is already sufficiently controlled,' said Isabella, indicating Lady Despenser.

Hugh the Younger seemed suddenly to have lost interest in the discussion. The King's anger was turning at last, as indeed it usually did, against the Queen. Edward had found an object for his vengeance, and Hugh felt all the more triumphant. He picked up a book that was lying near by and which Lady Mortimer had been reading to the Queen before the Count de Bouville had come in. It was a collection of the lays of Marie of France; the silk marker signalled this passage:

En Lorraine ni en Bourgogne,
Ni en Anjou ni en Gascogne,
En ce temps ne pouvait trouver
Si bon ni si grand chevalier.
Sous ciel n'était dame ou pucelle,
Qui tant fût noble et tant fût belle
Qui n'en voulût amour avoir . . .[10]

'France, it's always France. She never reads anything that doesn't relate to that country,' Hugh thought. 'And who's the knight they're dreaming of in their thoughts? Mortimer, no doubt . . .'

'My lord, I do not superintend the charities,' said Alienor Despenser.

The favourite looked up and smiled. He would congratulate his wife on that remark.

'I foresee I shall have to give up my charities too,' said Isabella. 'I shall soon have no queenly prerogative left, not even that of charity.'

'And also, Madame, for the love you bear me, of which everyone is aware,' Edward went on, 'you must part with Lady Mortimer, for not a soul in the kingdom will understand her being near you now.'

And now the Queen turned pale and sank back a little in her chair. Lady Jeanne's long pale hands were trembling.

'A wife, Edward, cannot be held responsible for all her husband's actions. I am an example of it myself. You must believe that Lady Mortimer has as little to do with her husband's errors as I have with your sins, supposing you commit any.'

But this time the attack was unsuccessful.

'Lady Jeanne will leave for Wigmore Castle, which from now on will be under the supervision of my brother of Kent, and will remain there until I have decided what to do with the property of a man whose name will never again be mentioned in my presence except to sentence him to death. I believe, Lady Jeanne, that you would prefer to go to your house of your own free will rather than be taken there by force.'

'I see,' said Isabella, 'that you wish me to be left utterly alone.'

'What do you mean by alone, Madame?' cried Hugh the Younger in his fine, well-modulated voice. 'Are we not all your loyal friends, being the King's? And is not Madame Alienor, my devoted wife, a faithful companion to you? That's a pretty book you have there,' he added, pointing to the volume, 'and beautifully illuminated; would you be kind enough to lend it to me?'

'Of course, of course the Queen will lend it to you,' the King said. 'I am sure, Madame, that you will do us the pleasure of lending the book to our friend Gloucester?'

'Most willingly, Sire my Husband, most willingly. And I know what lending means when it's to your friend, Lord Despenser. I lent him my pearls ten years ago and, as you can see, he's still wearing them about his neck.'

She would not surrender, but her heart was beating wildly in her breast. From now on she would have to bear the daily insults all alone. If, one day, she found means of revenging herself, nothing would be forgotten.

Hugh the Younger put the book down on a chest and made a privy sign to his wife. The lays of Marie of France would go to join the gold buckle with lions in precious stones, the three gold crowns, the four crowns inset with rubies and emeralds, the hundred and twenty silver spoons, the thirty great platters, the ten gold goblets, the hangings of embroidered cloth of gold, the six-horsed coach, the linen, the silver bowls, the harness, the chapel ornaments, all those splendid possessions, the gifts of her father and relations, which had been her wedding presents and whose inventory had been drawn up by the good Bouville himself, before her departure for England. And now they had all passed into the hands of Edward's favourites, first to Gaveston and now to Despenser. Even the great cloak of embroidered Turkish cloth she had worn on her wedding day had been taken from her.

'Well, my lords,' said the King, clapping his hands, 'hasten to the tasks I have allotted you and may each of you do his duty.'

It was his usual phrase, another of those formulae he believed to be royal, and with which he closed the meetings of his Council. He went out and the others followed him. The room emptied.

Evening was beginning to fall over the cloister of Kirkham Priory and, with its coming, a little freshness entered by the windows. Queen Isabella and Lady Mortimer dared not say a word to each other for fear of weeping. This was the last time they would be together before being separated. Would they ever meet again, and what had fate in store for them?

Young Prince Edward, his eyes as usual on the ground, came and stood silently behind his mother, as if he wished to take the place of the friend who was being taken from her.

Lady Despenser came over to take the book that had attracted her husband's eye. It was a beautiful book, and its velvet binding was inlaid with precious stones. She had long coveted the volume, particularly since she knew how much it had cost. As she was about to pick it up, young Prince Edward put his hand on it.

'Oh, no, you wicked woman,' he said, 'you shan't have everything!'

The Queen pushed the Prince's hand aside, picked up the book and handed it to her enemy. Then she turned to her son with a smile of understanding that showed, once again, her little carnivore's teeth. A boy of eleven could not be much help to her as yet; but his attitude was important, all the same, since he was the heir to the throne.

3

Messer Tolomei has a New Customer

OLD SPINELLO TOLOMEI was in his study on the first floor. He moved the arras aside with his foot and pushed open a little wooden shutter to reveal a secret opening which enabled him to keep an eye on his clerks in the great room on the ground floor. By this judas of Florentine invention, concealed among the beams, Messer Tolomei could see everything that went on below, and hear everything that was said.

At the moment his bank and trading-house appeared to be in considerable confusion. The flames of the three-branched candelabra were flickering on the counters, and his employees had ceased moving the brass balls on the abaci by which they kept the accounts. An ell cloth-measure fell with a clatter to the flagstones; the scales dipped on the money-changers' tables, though no one was touching them. The customers had all turned towards the door, and the senior clerks were standing with their hands to their chests, making ready to bow.

Messer Tolomei smiled; from the general disturbance he guessed that the Count of Artois had entered his establishment. An instant later, he saw through the spy-hole a huge chaperon with a red-velvet crest, red gloves, red boots with ringing spurs, and a scarlet cloak that hung from the shoulders of a giant. Only Monseigneur Robert of Artois had this peculiarly shattering way of making an entrance. He set the staff trembling with terror; he tweaked the women's breasts in passing, while their husbands dared make no move; and it seemed as if he could set even the walls quaking merely by drawing breath.

However, the old banker was not particularly impressed. He had known the Count of Artois much too long and had watched him too often. And now, as he looked down on him from above, he was aware of how exaggerated, forced and ostentatious this great lord's manner was. Monseigneur of Artois behaved like an ogre because nature had endowed him with exceptional physical proportions. In fact he was a cunning and crafty man. And Tolomei held Robert's accounts.

The banker was more interested in the personage accompanying Artois. This was a lord dressed entirely in black; there was an air of assurance about him, though his manner seemed distant, reserved and somewhat haughty. At first sight Tolomei judged him to be a man of considerable force of character.

The two visitors stopped at the counter displaying arms and harness. Monseigneur of Artois's huge red glove moved among the daggers, stilettos and the patterns of sword-hilts, turned over the saddle-cloths, the stirrups, the curved bits, the scalloped, pinked and embroidered reins. The shopman would have a good hour's work to put his counter in order again. Robert selected a pair of Toledo spurs with long rowels; the shanks were high and curved outwards to protect the Achilles tendon when the foot exerted a violent pressure against the horse's flank; a sound invention and certainly of great use in tournaments. The side-pieces were decorated with flowers and ribbons with the device 'Conquer' graven in round letters in the gilded steel.

'I make you a present of them, my lord,' said the giant to the gentleman in black. 'The only thing that's missing is a lady to buckle them to your feet. But she won't be missing for long; the ladies of France are soon aroused by people from abroad. You can get anything you want here,' he went on, with a wave at the shop. 'My friend Tolomei, a master usurer and a fox in business, will supply you with everything you need. I've never yet known him fail to produce anything one asks of him. Do you want to present your chaplain with a chasuble? He has thirty to choose from. A ring for your mistress? He has chests full of stones. Scenting the girls before pleasuring them? He'll provide you with a musk straight from the markets of the Orient. Are you in search of a relic? He has three cupboards full. And what's more, he sells gold to buy it all. He has currency minted in every corner of Europe, and you can see the exchanges marked up on those slates there. He sells figures, that's what he really sells: farming profits, interest on loans, revenues from fiefs. There are clerks adding and checking behind all those little doors. What would we do without this man who grows rich on our inability to count? Let's go up to his room.'

The steps of the wooden corkscrew staircase were soon

creaking under the weight of the Count of Artois. Messer Tolomei closed the spy-hole and let the arras fall back into place.

The room the two lords entered was sombrely, heavily and sumptuously furnished; there were massive pieces of silver plate, while figured tapestries muffled every sound. It smelt of candles, incense, spices and medicinal herbs. All the scents of a lifetime seemed to have accumulated among the rich furnishings.

The banker came forward. Robert of Artois, who had not seen him for many weeks – indeed, for almost three months during which he had had to accompany his cousin, the King of France, first into Normandy at the end of August, and then into Anjou for the whole autumn – thought the Sienese was looking older. His white hair was thinner and fell more sparsely over the collar of his robe; time had set its crow's-feet on his face and, indeed, his cheekbones looked as if they had been marked by a bird's feet; his jowls had fallen and swung beneath his chin; his chest seemed narrower and his stomach more protuberant; his nails, which were cut short, were splitting. Only his left eye, Messer Tolomei's famous left eye, which was always three-quarters shut, still lent his face an expression of cunning and vivacity. But the other eye, the open eye, seemed a little absent, a little weary and inattentive, as if he were worn out and less concerned now with the exterior world than with the disorders of his old and exhausted body which was nearing its end.

'Friend Tolomei,' cried Robert of Artois, taking off his gloves and throwing them, a pool of blood, on to a table. 'Friend Tolomei, I'm bringing you another fortune!'

The banker waved his visitors into chairs.

'How much is it going to cost me, Monseigneur?' he replied.

'Come on, come on, banker,' said Robert of Artois, 'have I ever made you make a bad investment?'

'Never, Monseigneur, never I admit it. Payment has sometimes been a little overdue, but in the end, since God has vouchsafed me a fairly long life, I have been able to gather in the fruits of the confidence with which you have honoured me. But just think, Monseigneur, what would have happened had I died, as so many people do, at fifty? Thanks to you, I should have died ruined.'

This sally amused Robert of Artois whose smile, spreading widely across his face, revealed strong but very dirty teeth.

'Have you ever incurred a loss through me?' he said. 'Do you remember how I once made you wager on Monseigneur of Valois against Enguerrand de Marigny? And look where Charles of Valois is today, and how Marigny ended his wicked life. And haven't I paid you back every penny you advanced me for my war in Artois? I'm grateful to you, banker, yes, I'm grateful to you for having always supported me even when I was in my greatest difficulties. For I was overwhelmed with debts at one time,' he went on, turning to the gentleman in black. 'I had no lands but the county of Beaumont-le-Roger, and the Treasury refused to pay me its revenues. My amiable cousin, Philippe the Long – may God keep his soul in some hell or other! – had imprisoned me in the Châtelet. Well, this banker here, my lord, this usurer, this greatest rogue of all the rogues Lombardy has ever produced, this man who would take a child in its mother's womb in pawn, never abandoned me. And that's why as long as he lives, and he'll live a long time yet . . .'

Messer Tolomei put out the first and little fingers of his right hand and touched the wood of the table.

'Oh, yes, you will, Master Usurer, you'll live a long time yet, I'm telling you . . . Well, that's why this man will always be a friend of mine, and that's on the faith of Robert of Artois. And he made no mistake, for today I'm the son-in-law of Monseigneur of Valois; I sit in the King's Council; and I'm in full possession of the revenues of my county. Messer Tolomei, the great lord I've brought to see you is Lord Mortimer, Baron of Wigmore.'

'Who escaped from the Tower of London on August the first,' said the banker, making an inclination of the head. 'A great honour, my lord, a great honour.'

'What do you mean?' Artois cried. 'Do you know about it?'

'Monseigneur,' said Tolomei, 'the Baron of Wigmore is too important a personage for us not to have been informed. I even know, my lord, that when King Edward issued the order to his coastal sheriffs to find you and arrest you, you were already embarked and out of reach of English justice. I know that when he had all the ships sailing for Ireland searched, and seized every courier landing from France, your friends not only in London but in all England already knew of your safe arrival at the house of your cousin-german, Messire Jean de Fiennes, in Picardy. And I know, too, that when King Edward ordered Messire de Fiennes to deliver you up, threatening to confiscate all his lands beyond the Channel, that lord, who is a great supporter and partisan of Monseigneur Robert, immediately sent you on to him. I cannot say that I was expecting you, my lord, but I was hoping you would come; for Monseigneur of Artois is, as he has told you, faithful to me and always thinks of me when a friend of his is in difficulties.'

Roger Mortimer had listened to the banker with great attention. 'I see, Messer,' he replied, 'that the Lombards have good spies at the Court of England.'

'They are at your service, my lord. You must know that King Edward is very heavily in debt to our companies. When you have money outstanding, you watch it. And for a long time past your King has ceased to honour his seal, at least as far as we're concerned. He wrote to us through Monseigneur, the Bishop of Exeter, his Treasurer, that the poor receipts from taxes, the heavy expenses of his wars and the intrigues of his barons did not allow of his doing better by us. And yet the duty he places on our merchandise, in the Port of London alone, should suffice to discharge his debt.'

A servant brought hippocras and sugared almonds, which were always offered to visitors of importance. Tolomei poured the aromatic wine into goblets, helping himself to no more than one finger of the liquor to which he barely put his lips.

'At the moment, the French Treasury seems to be in a better state than that of England,' he added. 'Is it known yet, Monseigneur Robert, what the figures for the year are likely to be?'

'Provided there's no sudden calamity during the month to run – plague, famine, or, indeed, the marriage or funeral of one of our royal relations – there'll be a surplus of twelve thousand livres, according to the figures Messire Mille de Noyers, Master of the Exchequer, placed before us at the

Council this morning. Twelve thousand livres to the good! The Treasury was certainly never in so healthy a state during the reigns of Philippe IV and V – may God put a term to the list of them!'

'How do you manage to have surplus at the Treasury, Monseigneur?' Mortimer asked. 'Is it due to the absence of war?'

'On the one hand to the absence of war and, on the other, to the fact that war is continually being prepared, but is never in fact being waged. Not to put too fine a point on it – the crusade. I must say, Charles of Valois uses the crusade to fabulous advantage. But don't go thinking I look on him as a bad Christian. He is extremely concerned to deliver Armenia from the Turks, indeed just as much as he is to re-establish the Empire of Constantinople, whose crown he once wore though he was never able actually to occupy the throne. But a crusade cannot be organized in a day. You have to arm ships and forge weapons; above all, you have to find the crusaders, to negotiate with Spain and Germany. And the first step must be always to obtain a tithe on the clergy from the Pope. My dear father-in-law has obtained that tithe and, at the moment, the Treasury is being subsidized by the Pope.'

'That interests me very much, Monseigneur,' said Tolomei. 'You see, I'm the Pope's banker – to the extent, at least, of a quarter share with the Bardi, but even a quarter share is a very large sum – and if the Pope should become impoverished . . .'

Artois, who was taking a big gulp of hippocras, exploded into the silver goblet and made signs that he was choking.

'Impoverished, the Holy Father!' he cried as soon as he had

swallowed the wine. 'He's worth hundreds of thousands of florins. There's a man who could teach you your business, Spinello! What a banker he'd have made, had he not entered the priesthood. For he found the papal treasury emptier than was my pocket six years ago . . .'

'I know, I know,' Tolomei murmured.

'The fact is, you see, the priests are the best tax-collectors God ever put on earth, and Monseigneur of Valois has grasped that fact. Instead of being ruthless about the taxes, whose collectors are hated anyway, he makes the priests collect the tithe. Oh, we shall set out on a crusade, one of these days. But, meantime, the Pope pays by shearing his sheep.'

Tolomei was gently rubbing his right leg; for some time past he had felt a sensation of cold in it, and some pain in walking.

'You were saying, Monseigneur, that a Council was held this morning. Was anything of particular interest decided on?' he asked.

'Oh, just the usual stuff. We discussed the price of candles and forbade the mixing of tallow with wax, and the mingling of old jam with new. For all merchandise sold in wrappers, the weight of the wrappers is to be deducted and not included in the price. But this is all to please the common people and show them we have their interests at heart.'

Tolomei listened and watched his two visitors. They both seemed to him very young. How old was Robert of Artois? Thirty-five, thirty-six? And the Englishman seemed much the same age. Everyone under sixty seemed to him astonishingly young. How much they still had to do, how many emotions still to suffer, battles to fight and ambitions to realize. How many mornings they would see that he would never know. How often these two men would awaken and breathe the air of a new day, when he himself was under the ground.

And what kind of man was Lord Mortimer? The clear-cut face, the thick eyebrows, the straight line of the eyelids across the flint-coloured eyes, the sombre clothes, the way he crossed his arms, the silent, haughty assurance of a man who had sat on the pinnacle of power and intended to preserve all his dignity in exile, even the automatic gesture with which Mortimer ran his finger across the short white scar on his lip, all pleased the old Sienese. And Tolomei felt he would like this lord to recover his happiness. For some time past, Tolomei had acquired almost a taste for thinking of others.

'Are the regulations concerning the export of currency to be promulgated in the near future, Monseigneur?' he asked.

Robert of Artois hesitated before replying.

'Oh, of course, I don't suppose you've been told yet . . .' Tolomei added.

'Of course, naturally I've been told. You very well know that nothing is done without my advice being asked by the King, and by Monseigneur of Valois above all. The order will be sealed in two days' time. No one will be permitted to export gold or silver currency stamped with the die of France from the kingdom. Only pilgrims will be allowed to provide themselves with a few small coins.'

The banker pretended to attach no greater importance to this piece of news than he had to the price of candles or the adulteration of jam. But he was already thinking: 'That means foreign currency will alone be permitted to be taken out of the kingdom; as a result, it will increase in value . . . What a help these blabbers are to us in our profession. How the boasters give us for so little the information they could sell so dear.'

'So, my lord,' he went on, turning to Mortimer, 'you intend to establish yourself in France? What can I provide?'

It was Robert who replied.

'What a great Lord needs to maintain his rank. You're accustomed enough to that, Tolomei.'

The banker rang a handbell. He told the servant to bring his great book, and added: 'If Messer Boccaccio has not left, ask him to wait till I'm free.'

The book was brought, a thick volume covered in black leather, smooth from much handling, and its vellum leaves held together by adjustable fastenings so that more leaves could be added as desired. This device enabled Messer Tolomei to keep the accounts of his important clients in alphabetical order and not to have to search for scattered pages. The banker placed the volume on his knees, and opened it with some ceremony.

'You'll find yourself in good company, my lord,' he said. 'Look, honour where honour is due, my book begins with the Count of Artois. You've a great many pages, Monseigneur,' he added with a little laugh, looking at Robert. 'Here's the Count de Bouville for his missions to the Pope and to Naples. And here's Madame the Queen Clémence . . .'

The banker inclined his head in deference.

'Oh, she gave us a lot of anxiety after the death of Louis X: it was as if mourning put her in a frenzy of spending. The Holy Father himself exhorted her to moderation in a special letter, and she had to pawn her jewels with me to pay off her debts. Now she's living in the Palace of the Templars which she exchanged against the Castle of Vincennes; she gets her dowry and seems to have found peace.'

He went on turning over the pages which rustled under his hand.

'And now I'm boasting,' he thought. 'But one must do something to emphasize the importance of the services one renders, and to show that one's not dazzled by a new borrower.'

He had a clever way of letting them see the names while concealing the figures with his arm. He was only being half-indiscreet. And, after all, he had to admit that his whole life was contained in this book, and that he enjoyed every opportunity of looking through it. Each name, each figure evoked so many memories, so many intrigues, so many secrets of which he had been the recipient, and so many entreaties by which he had been able to measure his power. Each figure commemorated a visit, a letter, a clever deal, a feeling of sympathy or one of harshness towards a negligent debtor. It was nearly fifty years since Spinello Tolomei, on his arrival from Siena, had begun by doing the rounds of the fairs of Champagne, and then come to live here, in the Rue des Lombards, to keep a bank.[11]

Another page, and another, which caught in his broken nails. A black line was drawn through a name.

'Here's Messer Dante Alighieri, the poet, but only for a small sum, when he came to Paris to visit Queen Clémence after she had become a widow. He was a great friend of hers, as he had been of King Charles of Hungary, Madame

Clémence's father. I remember him sitting in your chair, my lord. A man without a spark of kindness. He was the son of a money-changer; and he talked to me for a whole hour with great contempt of the financier's trade. But he could afford to be ill-natured and go off and get drunk with women in houses of ill-fame, while talking of his pure love for the Lady Beatrice. He made our language sing as no one before him has ever done. And how he described the Inferno, my lord! You have not read it? Oh, you must have it translated. One trembles to think that it may perhaps be like that. Do you know that in Ravenna, where Messer Dante spent his last years, the people used to scatter from his path in fear because they thought he really had gone down into Hell? And, even now, many people refuse to believe that he died two years ago, for they say he was a magician and could not die. He certainly didn't like banking, nor indeed Monseigneur of Valois who exiled him from Florence.'

The whole time he was talking of Dante, Tolomei was putting out his two fingers again and touching the wood of his chair.

'There, that's where you'll be, my lord,' he went on, making a mark in his big book; 'immediately after Monseigneur de Marigny; but be reassured, not the one who was hanged and whom Monseigneur of Artois mentioned a little while ago. No, his brother, the Bishop of Beauvais. From today you have a credit with me of ten thousand livres. You can draw on it at your convenience, and look on my modest house as your own. Cloth, arms, jewels, you will find every kind of goods you may require at my counters and can charge them against this credit.'

He was carrying on his trade by habit; lending people the wherewithal to buy what he sold.

'And what about your lawsuit against your aunt, Monseigneur? Are you thinking of taking it up again, now that you're so powerful?' he asked Robert of Artois.

'I most certainly shall, but at the right time,' the giant replied, getting to his feet. 'There's no hurry, and I've learnt that too much haste is a bad thing. I'm letting my dear aunt grow older; I'm leaving her to exhaust herself in small lawsuits against her vassals, make new enemies every day by her chicanery, and put her castles, which I treated a bit roughly on my last visit to her lands – which are really mine – into order again. She's beginning to realize what it costs her to hold on to my property. She had to lend Monseigneur of Valois fifty thousand livres which she'll never see again, for they went to make up my wife's dowry, and incidentally enabled me to pay you off. So, you see, she's not quite so noxious a woman as people say, the bitch! I merely take care not to see too much of her, she's so fond of me she might spoil me with one of those sweet dishes from which so many people in her entourage have died. But I shall have my county, banker, I shall have it, you can be sure of that. And on that day, as I've promised you, you shall become my treasurer.'

Messer Tolomei showed his visitors out, walking down the stairs behind them with some prudence, and accompanied them to the door that gave on to the Rue des Lombards. When Roger Mortimer asked him what interest he was charging on the money he was lending him, the banker waved the question aside.

'Merely do me the pleasure,' he said, 'of coming up to see me when you have business with the bank. I am sure there is much in which you can instruct me, my lord.'

A smile accompanied the words, and the left eyelid rose a little to reveal a brief glance that implied: 'We'll talk alone, not in front of blabbers.'

The cold November wind blowing in from the street made the old man shiver a little. Then, as soon as the door was closed, Tolomei went behind his counters into a little waiting-room where he found Boccaccio, the travelling representative of the Bardi Company.

'Friend Boccaccio,' he said, 'today and tomorrow buy all the English, Dutch and Spanish currency you can, all the Italian florins, doubloons, ducats, and foreign money you can find; offer a denier, even two deniers, above the present rate of exchange. Within three days they'll have increased in value by a quarter. Every traveller will have to come to us for foreign currency, since they'll be forbidden to export French gold. I'll go halves with you on the profits.'[12]

Having a pretty good idea of how much foreign gold was available and adding it to what he already had in his coffers, Tolomei calculated that the operation would make him a profit of from fifteen to twenty thousand livres. He had just lent ten thousand and would therefore make about double his loan. With the profits he could make further loans. Mere routine.

When Boccaccio congratulated him on his ability and, turning the compliment in his thin-lipped, bourgeois, Florentine way, said that it was not in vain that the Lombard companies in Paris had chosen Messer Spinello Tolomei for their Captain-General, the old man replied: 'Oh, after fifty years in the business, I no longer deserve any credit for it; it's simply second nature. If I were really clever, do you know what I would have done? I'd have bought up your reserves of florins and kept all the profit for myself. But when you come to think of it, what use would it be to me? You'll learn, Boccaccio, you're still very young . . .'

Boccaccio had sons who were already grey at the temples.

'You reach an age when you have a feeling of working to no purpose if you're merely working for yourself. I miss my nephew. And yet his difficulties are more or less resolved; I'm sure that he'd be running no risk if he came back now. But that young devil of a Guccio refuses to come; he's being stubborn, from pride I think. And, in the evening, when the clerks have left and the servants gone to bed, this big house seems very empty. I sometimes regret Siena.'

'Your nephew ought to have done what I did, Spinello,' said Boccaccio, 'when I found myself in a similar difficulty with a woman of Paris. I removed my son and took him to Italy.'

Messer Tolomei shook his head and thought how melancholy a house was without children. Guccio's son must be seven by now; and Tolomei had never seen him. The mother refused to allow it.

The banker rubbed his right leg which felt heavy and cold; he had pins and needles in it. Over the years, death began to catch up with you, little by little, taking you by the feet. Presently, before going to bed, he would send for a basin of hot water and put his leg in it.

4
The False Crusade

'Monseigneur of Mortimer, I shall have great need of brave and gallant knights such as you for my crusade,' declared Charles of Valois. 'You will think me very vain to say *my* crusade when in truth it is Our Lord's, but I must confess, and everyone will recognize the fact, that if this vast enterprise, the greatest and most glorious to which the Christian nations can be summoned, takes place, it will be because I shall have organized it with my own hands. And so, Monseigneur of Mortimer, I ask you straight out, and with that frankness you will learn to recognize as natural to me: will you join me?'

Roger Mortimer sat up straight in his chair; he frowned a little and lowered his lids over his flint-coloured eyes. Was he being merely offered the command of a banner of twenty knights, like some little country noble or some soldier of fortune stranded here by the mischances of fate? The proposal was mere charity.

It was the first time Mortimer had been received by the Count of Valois, who till now had always been busy with his duties in Council, or receiving foreign ambassadors, or travelling about the kingdom. But now, at last, Mortimer was face to face with the man who ruled France, who had that very day appointed one of his protégés, Jean de Cherchemont, as the new Chancellor,[13] and on whom his own fate depended. For Mortimer's situation, undoubtedly enviable for a man who had been condemned to prison for life, though painful for a great lord, was that of an exile who had nothing to offer and was reduced to begging and hoping.

The interview was taking place in what had once been the King of Sicily's palace, which Charles of Valois had received from his first father-in-law, Charles the Lame of Naples, as a wedding present. There were some dozen people in the great audience chamber, equerries, courtiers, secretaries, all talking quietly in little groups, frequently turning their eyes towards their master, who was giving audience, like a real sovereign, seated on a sort of throne surmounted by a canopy. Monseigneur of Valois was dressed in a long indoor robe of blue velvet, embroidered with lilies and capital V's, which parted in front to show a fur lining. His hands were laden with rings; he wore his private seal, which was carved from a precious stone, hanging from his belt by a gold chain; and on his head was a velvet cap of maintenance held in place by a chased circlet of gold, a sort of undress crown. Among his entourage were his eldest son, Philippe of Valois, a strapping fellow with a long nose, who was leaning on the back of the throne, and his son-in-law, Robert of Artois, who was sitting on a stool, his huge red-leather boots stretched out in front of him. A tree-trunk was burning on the hearth near by.

'Monseigneur,' Mortimer said slowly, 'if the help of a man who is first among the barons of the Welsh Marches, who has governed the Kingdom of Ireland and has commanded in a number of battles, can be of help to you, I willingly give you my aid in defence of Christianity, and my blood is at your service from this moment.'

Valois realized that here was a proud man, who spoke of his fiefs in the Marches as if he still held them, and that he must treat him tactfully if he wished to make use of him.

'I have the honour, my lord,' he replied, 'to see arrayed under the banner of the King of France, or rather mine, since it has been arranged that my nephew shall continue to govern the kingdom while I command the crusade, to see arrayed, I say, the leading sovereign princes of Europe: my cousin Jean of Luxemburg, King of Bohemia, my brother-in-law Robert of Naples and Sicily, my cousin Alfonso of Spain, as well as the Republics of Genoa and Venice who, at the Holy Father's request, will give us the support of their galleys. You will be in no bad company, my lord, and I shall see to it that everyone gives you the respect and honour due to the great lord you are. France, from which your ancestors sprung and which gave birth to your mother, will make sure that your deserts are better recognized than they appear to be in England.'

Mortimer bowed in silence. Whatever this assurance might be worth, he would see that it came to more than mere words.

'For it is fifty years and more,' went on Monseigneur of Valois, 'since anything of importance was done by Europe in the service of God; to be precise, since my grandfather Saint Louis who, if he won his way to Heaven by it, lost his life in the process. Encouraged by our absence, the Infidels have raised their heads and believe themselves masters everywhere; they ravage the coasts, pillage ships, hinder trade and, by their mere presence, profane the Holy Places. And what have we done? Year after year we have retreated from all our possessions and establishments; we have abandoned the castles we built and have neglected to defend the sacred rights we had acquired. And this has all happened as a result of the suppression of the Templars, of which my elder brother – peace to his soul, though in this I never approved him – was the instrument. But those times are past. At the beginning of this year, delegates from Lesser Armenia came to ask our help against the Turks. I give grateful thanks to my nephew, King Charles IV, for his understanding of the importance of this appeal and for giving his support to the steps I then took. Indeed, he now believes the idea to have been originally his. Anyway, it is most satisfactory that he should now have faith in it. And so, as soon as our own forces have been assembled, we shall go to attack the Saracens in their distant lands.'

Robert of Artois, who was listening to this speech for the hundredth time, nodded his head as if much impressed, while secretly amused at the enthusiasm his father-in-law displayed in explaining the greatness of his cause. Robert was well aware of what lay behind all this. He knew that, though it was indeed the intention to attack the Turks, the Christians were to be jostled a little on the way; for the Emperor Andronicos Paleologos, who reigned in Byzantium, was not so far as one knew the champion of Mahomet. No doubt his

Church was not altogether the true one, and it made the sign of the Cross a bit askew; nevertheless, it did make the sign of the Cross. But Monseigneur of Valois was still pursuing his idea of reconstructing to his own advantage the fabulous Empire of Constantinople, which extended not only over the Byzantine territories, but over Cyprus, Rhodes, Armenia, and all the old kingdoms of the Courtenays and the Lusignans. And when Count Charles arrived there with all his banners, Andronicos Paleologos, from what one heard, would not be able to put up much of a defence. Monseigneur of Valois's head was full of the dreams of a Caesar.

It was remarkable, also, that he always indulged in a system which consisted of asking for the maximum so as to obtain a little. In this way he had tried to exchange his command of the crusade and his pretensions to the throne of Constantinople against the little kingdom of Arles by the Rhône on condition that Viennois was added to it. He had negotiated with Jean of Luxemburg about this at the beginning of the year; but the transaction had come to nothing owing to the opposition of the Count of Savoy, and that of the King of Naples who, since he owned lands in Provence, had no wish to see his turbulent relative create an independent kingdom for himself on the borders of his states. So Monseigneur of Valois had resumed plans for the holy expedition with more enthusiasm than ever. It was clear that he would have to go in search of the sovereign crown, which had eluded his grasp in Spain, in Germany, and even in Arles, at the farther ends of the earth. But though Robert knew all these things it would have been unwise to mention them.

'Of course, all the difficulties have not yet been overcome,' went on Monseigneur of Valois. 'We are still in negotiation with the Holy Father over the number of knights and how much they shall be paid. We want eight thousand knights and thirty thousand footmen, and each baron to receive twenty sols a day and each knight ten; seven sols and six deniers for the squires and two sols for the footmen. Pope John wants me to limit my army to four thousand knights and fifteen thousand footmen; he has, nevertheless, promised me twelve armed galleys. He has given us the tithe, but is looking askance at twelve hundred thousand livres a year, during the five years the crusade will last, which is the sum we are asking, and above all at the four hundred thousand livres the King of France requires for ancillary expenses.'

'Of which three hundred thousand are to be paid to the good Charles of Valois himself,' thought Robert of Artois. 'At that price it's worth while commanding a crusade. But to cavil at it would be unbecoming, since I shall get my share of it.'[14]

'Oh, if I had only been at Lyons in the place of my late nephew Philippe during the last conclave,' cried Valois, 'I should have chosen a cardinal – though I wish to say nothing against the Holy Father – who understood more clearly the true interests of Christianity and did not require so much persuading.'

'Particularly since we hanged his nephew at Montfaucon last May,' observed Robert of Artois.

Mortimer turned in his chair and looked at Robert of Artois in surprise. 'A nephew of the Pope? What nephew?'

'Do you mean to say you don't know about it, Cousin?' said Robert of Artois, taking the opportunity to get to his feet, for he found it difficult to remain still for long. He went over to the hearth and kicked the logs.

Mortimer had already ceased to be 'my lord' to him and had become 'my Cousin', on account of a distant relationship they had discovered through the Fiennes family; soon he would become simply 'Roger'.

'Do you mean to say,' he went on, 'that you have not heard of the splendid adventures of the noble lord, Jourdain de l'Isle, so noble and so powerful that the Holy Father gave him his niece in marriage? And yet, when I come to think of it, how could you have heard about it? You were in prison at the time through the good offices of your friend Edward. Oh, it was a little affair that would have made much less stir had it not been for the fellow's alliances. This Jourdain, a Gascon lord, had committed a few minor misdeeds, such as robbery, homicide, rape, deflowering virgins and a little buggery with the young men into the bargain. The King, at the request of Pope John, agreed to pardon him, and even restored his property to him on a promise of reform. Reform? Jourdain returned to his fief and we soon heard that he had begun all over again, and worse than ever, that he was keeping thieves, murderers and other bad hats about him, who plundered priests and laymen for his benefit. A King's sergeant, carrying his lilied staff, was sent to arrest him. Do you know how Jourdain received the sergeant? He had him seized, beaten with the royal staff and, just to complete things, impaled on it, of which the man died.'

Robert uttered a loud laugh that made the window-panes rattle in their leads. How gaily Monseigneur of Artois laughed, and how, in his heart of hearts, he approved, even envied, except for his sad end, Messire Jourdain de l'Isle. He would have liked to have had him for a friend.

'One really does not know which was the greater crime,' he went on, 'to have killed an officer of the King, or to have befouled the lilies with a sergeant's guts! For his deserts, my lord Jourdain was judged worthy to be strung up to the gibbet at Montfaucon. He was taken there with great ceremony, being dragged at the horse's tail, and was hanged in the robes with which his uncle, the Pope, had presented him. You can still see him in them should you happen to pass that way. They have become a little too big for him now.'

And Robert began laughing again, his head thrown back, his thumbs in his belt. His amusement was so sincere and infectious that Roger Mortimer began laughing too. And Valois was laughing, and his son Philippe. The courtiers at the farther end of the room gazed at them with curiosity.

One of the blessings of our lot is to be ignorant of our end. And these four great barons were right to seize any opportunity to be amused; for one of them would be dead within two years; and another had but seven years to wait, almost to the day, to be dragged to execution in his turn at the horse's tail through the streets of a town.

Laughing together had made them feel more friendly towards each other. Mortimer suddenly had the feeling that he had been admitted to Valois's inner circle of power, and felt a little more at ease. He glanced sympathetically at Monseigneur Charles's face; it was a broad, high-coloured face, the face of a man who ate too much and whom the duties of his position deprived of the opportunity of taking enough exercise. Mortimer had not seen Valois since various meetings long ago: once in England during the celebrations for Queen Isabella's marriage, and a second time, in 1313, when he had accompanied the English sovereigns to Paris to pay their first homage. And all this, which seemed but yesterday, was already in the distant past. Monseigneur of Valois, who had been a young man then, had since become this massive and imposing personage; and Mortimer himself had lived, on the best expectation of life, half his allotted span, if God willed that he should not be killed in battle, drowned at sea or die by the axe of Edward's executioner. To have reached the age of thirty-seven was already a long span of life, particularly when you were surrounded by so many jealousies and enemies, when you had risked your life in tournaments and in war, and spent eighteen months in the dungeons of the Tower. Clearly, he must not waste his time, nor neglect opportunities for adventure. The idea of a crusade was beginning to interest Roger Mortimer after all.

'And when will your ships sail, Monseigneur?' he asked.

'In eighteen months' time, I think,' replied Valois, 'I shall send a third embassy to Avignon to make a definite arrangement about the subsidies, the bulls of indulgences, and the order of battle.'

'It will be a splendid expedition, Monseigneur of Mortimer, in which the people one sees about at courts, who talk so much and so valiantly of war, will be able to show what they can do outside the tournament ground,' said Philippe of Valois, who had so far not uttered a word and now blushed a little.

Charles of Valois's eldest son was already imagining the swelling sails of galleys, landings on distant shores, the banners, the knights, the shock of the heavy French cavalry charging the Infidel, the Crescent trampled beneath the horses' hooves, Saracen girls captured in the secret depths of palaces and beautiful naked slaves in chains. And nothing was going to prevent Philippe of Valois from slaking his desires on those buxom wenches. His wide nostrils were already distending. For Jeanne the Lame would remain in France. He loved his wife, of course, but could not help trembling in her presence, for her jealousy burst out into furious scenes whenever he so much as looked at another woman's breast. Oh, this sister of Marguerite of Burgundy had a far from easy character! And, indeed, it can so happen that one may love one's wife and yet be impelled by the forces of nature to desire other women. It would need a crusade at least for tall Philippe to dare to deceive his lame wife.

Mortimer sat up a little straighter and pulled at his black tunic. He wanted to turn the conversation to his own affairs, which had nothing to do with the crusade.

'Monseigneur,' he said to Charles of Valois, 'you can count on me to march in your ranks, but I have come also to ask of you . . .'

The word was said. The ex-Justiciar of Ireland had uttered that word without which no petitioner can hope to receive anything and without which no powerful man accords his support. To ask, to seek, to pray . . . But there was no need for him to say anything more.

'I know, I know,' replied Charles of Valois; 'my son-in-law, Robert, has informed me. You want me to plead your case with King Edward. Well, my loyal friend . . .'

Because he had 'asked,' he had suddenly become a friend.

'Well, I shall not do it, for it would serve no purpose, except to expose me to further insult. Do you know the answer your King Edward sent me by the Count de Bouville? Yes, you must of course be aware of it. And when the licence for the marriage had already been asked of the Holy Father! What sort of figure does he make me cut? And do you really expect me, after that, to ask him to restore your lands to you, give you back your titles, and dismiss, for the one implies the other, those shameless Despensers of his?'

'And at the same time, to restore to Queen Isabella . . .'

'My poor niece!' cried Valois. 'I know, my loyal friend, I know it all. Do you think that I or the King of France can make King Edward change both his morals and his ministers? Nevertheless, you must be aware that he sent the Bishop of Rochester to demand that we hand you over. And we refused. We refused even to give the Bishop audience. This is the first affront I have been able to offer Edward in exchange for his. We are linked to each other, Monseigneur of Mortimer, by the outrages that have been inflicted on us. And if either of us has an opportunity of revenge, I can promise you, my dear Lord, that we shall avenge ourselves jointly.'

Mortimer, though he gave no sign, felt an overwhelming despair. The audience, from which Robert of Artois had promised him such wonderful results – 'My father-in-law Charles can do anything; if he likes you, and he undoubtedly will, you can be sure of gaining the day; if necessary he'll bring the Pope in on your side . . .' – seemed to be over. And what had it achieved? Nothing at all. Merely the promise of some vague command in the land of the Saracens, in eighteen months' time. Roger Mortimer was already considering leaving Paris and going to see the Pope; and if he could get nothing out of him, then he would go to the Emperor of Germany. Oh, how bitter were the disappointments of exile. His uncle of Chirk had forewarned him.

It was then that Robert of Artois broke the somewhat embarrassed silence by saying: 'Charles, why should we not create the opportunity for the revenge of which you spoke just now?'

He was the only man at court who called the Count of Valois by his Christian name, having maintained the habit from the time they were mere cousins; besides, his size, strength and general truculence gave him rights no one else would have dared assume.

'Robert is right,' said Philippe of Valois. 'One might, for instance, invite King Edward to the crusade, and then . . .'

A vague gesture completed his thought. Tall Philippe was clearly of an imaginative turn. He could see them all crossing a ford, or better still riding across the desert; they would meet a band of the Infidel, they would let Edward lead a charge and then coldly abandon him into the hands of the Saracens. That would be a fine revenge.

'Never!' cried Charles of Valois. 'Never will Edward join his banners to mine! Besides, can one even think of him as a Christian prince? Indeed, it's only the Saracens who have such morals as his!'

In spite of Valois's indignation, Mortimer felt a certain anxiety. He knew only too well what the speeches of princes were worth, and how the enemies of yesterday became reconciled tomorrow, even if only hypocritically, when it was in their interest to do so. If it occurred to Monseigneur of

Valois, so as to increase the size of his crusade, to invite Edward, and if Edward pretended to accept . . .

'Even if you did invite him, Monseigneur,' Mortimer said, 'there's very little likelihood of King Edward responding to your invitation; he likes wrestling but hates arms, and it was not he, I can promise you, who defeated me at Shrewsbury, but Thomas of Lancaster's bad tactics. Edward would plead, and with reason, the danger he is in from the Scots.'

'But I want the Scots in my crusade!' said Valois.

Robert of Artois was knocking his huge fists impatiently together. He was utterly indifferent to the crusade and, to tell the truth, had no wish to go on it. To begin with, he was always seasick. He would undertake anything on shore, but not at sea; a new-born babe would be better at it than he was. Besides, his thoughts were concerned in the first place with the recovery of his county of Artois, and to go and wander about the ends of the earth for five years was unlikely to benefit his affairs. The throne of Constantinople was no part of his inheritance, and to find himself one day governing some desert island amid forgotten seas had no attraction for him. He had no interest in the spice trade, nor any need to go and capture Saracen women; Paris was overflowing with houris at fifty sols and of bourgeoises for even less; and Madame de Beaumont, his wife, the daughter of Monseigneur of Valois, closed her eyes to all his infidelities. It was therefore in Robert's interest to postpone the date of the crusade as long as possible and, while pretending enthusiasm for it, to do his best to delay it. He had a plan in mind, and it was not for nothing he had brought Roger Mortimer to see his father-in-law.

'I wonder, Charles,' he said, 'whether it is really wise to leave the kingdom of France deprived of its men for so long and, without either its nobility or your hand at the helm, at the mercy of the King of England, who has given so much evidence of his ill-will towards us.'

'The castles will be provisioned, Robert; and we shall leave sufficient garrisons,' Valois replied.

'But without the nobility and most of the knights, and without you, I repeat, who are our one great general, who will defend the kingdom in our absence? The Constable, who is nearly seventy-five and can only remain in the saddle by a miracle? Our King Charles? If Edward, as Lord Mortimer tells us, does not much care for war, our dear cousin is still less skilled in it. Indeed, if it comes to that, what can he do except show himself fresh and smiling to the people? It would be folly to leave the field open to Edward's sly tricks without having first weakened him by a defeat.'

'Then let's help the Scots,' suggested Philippe of Valois. 'Let's land on their coasts and support their war. For my part, I'm ready to do so.'

Robert of Artois looked down so as not to show what he was thinking. There'd be a pretty mess if brave Philippe took command of an expedition to Scotland. The heir to the Valois had already shown his capacity in Italy, where he had been sent to support the Papal Legate against the Visconti of Milan. Philippe had arrived proudly with his banners, and had then allowed himself to be so imposed on and out-manœuvred by Galeazzo Visconti that he had, in fact, yielded everything while believing himself victorious, and had come home without even having engaged in a skirmish. One needed to beware above all of any enterprise in which he was engaged. None of which prevented Philippe of Valois being Robert's best and closest friend, as well as his brother-in-law. But, indeed, you can think what you like of your friends, provided you don't tell them.

Roger Mortimer had paled a little on hearing Philippe of Valois's suggestion. For if he was King Edward's adversary and enemy, England was nevertheless still his country.

'For the moment,' he said, 'the Scots are being more or less peaceful; they appear to be respecting the treaty they imposed on Edward a year ago.'

'But, really,' said Robert, 'to get to Scotland you have to cross the sea. Let's keep our ships for the crusade. But we have better grounds on which to defy that bugger Edward. He has failed to render homage for Aquitaine. If we forced him to come and defend his rights to his duchy in France, and then went and crushed him we should, in the first place, all be avenged and, in the second, he'd stay quiet enough during our absence.'

Valois was fiddling with his rings and reflecting. Once again Robert was showing himself to be a wise counsellor. Robert's suggestion was still vague, but already Valois was visualizing its implications. Aquitaine was far from unknown territory to him; he had campaigned there – his first, great and victorious campaign – in 1294.

'It would undoubtedly be good training for our knights, who have not been properly to war for a long time now,' he said; 'and also an opportunity of trying out this gunpowder artillery the Italians are beginning to make use of and which our old friend Tolomei offers to supply us with. And the King of France can certainly sequester the Duchy of Aquitaine owing to the default in rendering homage for it.'

He thought for a moment.

'But it won't necessarily lead to a real campaign,' he went on. 'As usual, there'll be negotiations; it'll become a matter for parliaments and embassies. And eventually the homage will be rendered with a bad grace. It's not really a completely safe pretext.'

Robert of Artois sat down again, his elbows on his knees, his fists supporting his chin.

'We can find a more sure pretext than a mere failure to render homage,' he said. 'I have no need to inform you, Cousin Mortimer, of all the difficulties, quarrels and battles to which Aquitaine has given rise since Duchess Alienor, having made her first husband, our King Louis VII, so notorious a cuckold that their marriage was dissolved, took her wanton body and her duchy to your King Henry II of England. Nor need I tell you of the treaty with which our good King Saint Louis, who did his best to put things on an equitable basis, tried to put a term to a hundred years of war.[15] But equity goes for nothing in settlements between kingdoms. The treaty Monseigneur Saint Louis concluded with Henry III Plantagenet, in the Year of Grace 1259, was so confused that a cat couldn't have found her kittens in it. Even the Seneschal de Joinville, your wife's great-uncle, Cousin Mortimer, who was devoted to the sainted King, advised him not to sign it. Indeed, we have to admit frankly that the treaty was a piece of folly.'

Robert felt like adding: 'As was also everything else Saint Louis did, for he was undoubtedly the most disastrous king we ever had. What with his ruinous crusades, his botched treaties, and his moral laws in which what is black in one passage is discovered to be white in another . . . Oh, how much happier France would have been had she been spared that reign! And yet, since Saint Louis's death, everyone regrets him, for their recollection is at fault; they remember only how he dealt out justice under an oak and, through listening to the lies of bumpkins, wasted the time he should have been devoting to the kingdom.'

He went on: 'Since the death of Saint Louis, there has been nothing but disputes, arguments, treaties concluded and broken, homage paid with reservations, hearings by Parliament, plaintiffs non-suited or condemned, rebellions in those lands and then further prosecutions. But when you, Charles, were sent by your brother Philip the Fair into Aquitaine,' Robert asked, turning to Valois, 'and so effectively restored order there, what were the actual motives given for your expedition?'

'Serious rioting in Bayonne, where French and English sailors had come to blows and shed blood.'

'Very well!' cried Robert. 'We must organize an occasion for more rioting like that of Bayonne. We must take steps to see that somewhere or other the subjects of the two Kings come to serious blows and that a few people get killed. And I believe I know the very place for it.'

He pointed his huge forefinger at them and went on: 'In the Treaty of Paris, confirmed by the peace of 1303, and reviewed by the jurists of Périgueux in the year 1311, the case of certain lordships, which are called privileged, has always been reserved, for though they lie within the borders of

Aquitaine, they owe direct allegiance to the King of France. And these lordships themselves have dependencies, vassal territories, in Aquitaine, but it has never been definitely decided whether these dependencies are subject to the King of France or to the Duke of Aquitaine. You see the point?'

'I do,' said Monseigneur of Valois.

His son, Philippe, did not see it. He opened wide blue eyes and his failure to understand was so obvious that his father explained: 'It's quite simple, my boy. Suppose I gave you, as if it were a fief, the whole of this house, but reserved to myself the use and free disposal of this room in which we are now sitting. And this room has, as a dependency, the ante-room which controls this door. Which of us enjoys rights over the ante-room and is responsible for its furnishing and cleaning? The whole plan,' Valois added, turning back to Robert, 'depends on being able to arrange action of sufficient importance to compel Edward to make a rejoinder.'

'There's a very suitable dependency,' the giant replied, 'in the lands of Saint-Sardos, which appertain to the Priory of Sarlat in the diocese of Périgueux. Their status was argued when Philip the Fair agreed to a Treaty of Association with the Prior of Sarlat, which made the King of France co-lord of that lordship. Edward I appealed to the Parliament of Paris, but nothing was decided.[16] If the King of France, as co-lord of Sarlat, builds a castle in the dependency of Saint-Sardos and puts into it a strong garrison threatening the surrounding territory, what does the King of England, as Duke of Aquitaine, do about it? He must clearly give orders to his Seneschal to oppose it, and will want to station troops there himself. And the first time a couple of soldiers meet, or an officer of the King is maltreated or even insulted . . .'

Robert spread wide his great hands as if the result was obvious. And Monseigneur of Valois, in his blue, gold-embroidered, velvet robes, rose from his throne. He could already see himself in the saddle, at the head of his banners; he would leave for Guyenne where, thirty years ago, he had won a great victory for the King of France.

'I congratulate you, Brother,' cried Philippe of Valois, 'on the fact that so distinguished a knight as you are should also have as great a knowledge of procedure as a lawyer.'

'Oh, there's no great merit attached to that, you know, Brother. It's not from any particular liking that I've been led to inquire into the laws of France and the edicts of Parliament; it's due to my lawsuit about Artois. And since, so far, it has been no use to me, let it at least be some use to my friends,' said Robert of Artois, bowing slightly to Roger Mortimer, as if this whole great affair was being organized entirely for his benefit.

'Your coming has been of great assistance to us, my lord,' said Charles of Valois, 'for our causes are linked, and we shall not fail to ask you most strictly for your counsel throughout this enterprise, which may God protect!'

Mortimer felt disconcerted and embarrassed. He had done nothing and suggested nothing; but his mere presence seemed to have occasioned the others to give concrete form to their secret aspirations. And now he would be required to take part in a war against his own country; and he had no choice in the matter.

And so, if God so willed it, the French were going to make war in France against the French subjects of the King of

England, with the support of a great English baron, and money furnished by the Pope for the freeing of Armenia from the Turks.

5

A Time of Waiting

THE END OF THE autumn passed, then winter, spring and the beginning of summer. Roger Mortimer saw Paris in all the four seasons of the year. He saw mud accumulating in its narrow streets, snow covering the great roofs of the abbeys and the fields of Saint-Germain, then the buds opening on the trees by the banks of the Seine, and the sun shining on the square tower of the Louvre, on the round Tower of Nesle and on the pointed steeple of the Sainte-Chapelle.

An exile has to wait. It is his role, one might think, almost his function. He has to wait for the bad times to pass; he has to wait till the people of the country in which he has taken refuge finish arranging their own affairs so as to have time at last to concern themselves with his. After his first days in exile, when his misfortunes excite curiosity and everyone wants to secure him as if he were a rare animal on exhibition, his presence soon becomes wearisome, embarrassing, a mute reproach even. One cannot be concerned with his affairs all the time; after all, he is the petitioner, so let him be patient.

So Roger Mortimer waited, as he had waited two months in Picardy, when staying with his cousin Jean de Fiennes, for the French Court to return to Paris, as he had waited for Monseigneur of Valois to find time among all his other tasks to give him audience. And now he was waiting for the war in Guyenne with which his destiny seemed to be unavoidably involved.

Oh, Monseigneur of Valois had not delayed in giving his orders! The officers of the King of France, as Robert had advised, had begun to mark out the foundations of a castle at Saint-Sardos, in the disputed dependencies of the lordship of Sarlat; but a castle is not built in a day, nor even in three months, and the people of the King of England had not seemed unduly concerned, at least to start with. It was a matter of waiting for an incident to occur.

Roger Mortimer devoted his leisure to exploring the capital, which he had seen only on a brief visit ten years earlier, and to discovering the French people whom he knew but little. How powerful and populous a nation it was, and how very different from England! On both sides of the Channel it was generally believed that the two nations were very similar because their nobility derived from the same source; but what disparities there were when you looked closer. The whole population of the kingdom of England, which numbered two million souls, did not amount to a tenth of the total of the King of France's subjects. The French numbered approximately twenty-two million. Paris alone had three hundred thousand inhabitants, while London had but forty thousand.[17] And what a seething mass of people there were in the streets, how active trade and industry were, what huge sums of money changed hands. To become aware of it, one had only to take a walk across the Pont-au-Change or along the quay of the goldsmiths, and listen to all the little hammers beating gold in the back shops; or walk, holding one's nose a little, through the butchers' district behind the Châtelet, where the flayers and tripe-sellers worked; or go down the Rue Saint-Denis, where the mercers' shops were; or go and inspect the stuffs in the great drapers' market; while big business was conducted in the comparative silence of the Rue des Lombards, which Mortimer now knew well.

Nearly three hundred and fifty guilds and corporations regulated and controlled the conduct of these trades; each had its laws, customs and Feast Days, and there was practically no day in the year on which, after Mass had been heard and a conference held in the parlour, a great banquet was not given for the Masters and Companions. Sometimes it was the Hatters, sometimes the Candlemakers, sometimes the Tanners. On the hill of Sainte-Geneviève a whole population of clerics and doctors in hoods argued in Latin, and the echoes of their controversies over apologetics or the principles of Aristotle furnished the seed for discussions throughout the whole of Christendom.

The great barons and prelates, as well as many foreign sovereigns, maintained houses in the city where they held a sort of court. The nobility frequented the streets of the Cité, the Mercers' Gallery in the Royal Palace, and the neighbourhood of the town houses of Valois, Navarre, Artois, Burgundy and Savoy. Each of these houses was a sort of permanent agency for the great fiefs; in them were concentrated the interests of each province. And the city was ceaselessly growing, pushing out its suburbs into the gardens and fields beyond the walls of Philip Augustus, which were now beginning to disappear, swamped by the new building.

If you went a little way out of Paris, you saw that the countryside was prosperous. Mere drovers and swineherds often possessed a vineyard or field of their own. Women employed in tilling the land, or indeed in other trades, never worked on Saturday afternoons for which they were however paid; moreover, almost everywhere, work ceased on Saturdays at the third ringing for vespers. The large number of religious feast days were all holidays, as were the feast days of the Corporations. And yet these people complained. But what were their principal grievances? Tithes and taxes, of course, as in every country in every period, and the fact that they always had someone over them to whom they belonged. They had the feeling that they were always working for someone else's benefit, and that they could never dispose freely either of themselves or the fruits of their labour. In spite of the decrees of Philippe V, which had indeed been insufficiently observed, there were still many more serfs in France than there were in England, where most peasants were free men, bound moreover to equip themselves for service in the army, and had a form of representation in the Royal Parliament. This made the fact that the people of England had demanded charters from their sovereigns easier to understand.

On the other hand, the nobility of France was not divided like England's; there were, of course, many sworn enemies over matters of personal interest, such as the Count of Artois and his aunt Mahaut; there were clans and parties; but the whole nobility made common front when it was a question of the general interest or the defence of the realm. The conception of the nation was clearer and claimed greater adherence.

At this period the real similarity between the two countries lay in the persons of their kings. Both in London and in Paris the crown had devolved on a weak man, incapable of that true concern for the public good without which a prince is but a prince in name.

Mortimer had been presented to the King of France and had seen him on several occasions; he had been able to form no high opinion of this man of twenty-nine, whom the lords were accustomed to call Charles the Fair and the people Charles the Fool because, though in face and figure he resembled his father closely enough, he had not an ounce of brains behind his noble appearance.

'Have you found suitable lodgings, my lord Mortimer? Is your wife with you? Oh, how you must miss her! How many children has she borne you?'

This was practically the sum of the King's conversation with the exile. And on each occasion he had asked him once again: 'Is your wife with you? How many children has she borne you?' having forgotten the answers between two audiences. His preoccupations seemed to be entirely domestic and uxorious. His unfortunate marriage to Blanche of Burgundy, from which he had retained a scar, had been dissolved by an annulment in which he himself had not appeared in the best light. Monseigneur of Valois had immediately married him off to Marie of Luxemburg, the young sister of the King of Bohemia with whom Valois, at that particular moment, wished to come to an understanding over the kingdom of Arles. And now Marie of Luxemburg was pregnant, and Charles the Fair fussed over her in a rather silly way.

The King's incompetence did not, however, prevent France from taking a hand in the affairs of the whole world. The Council governed in the King's name, and Monseigneur of Valois in the name of the Council; nothing, so it appeared, could be done without France having decided on it. She was at this time giving continual advice to the papacy, and the great courier, Robin Cuisse-Maria, who earned eight livres and some deniers – a real fortune – for making the journey to Avignon, was constantly occupied carrying dispatches, requisitioning his horses from the monasteries on the way. And it was the same with regard to all the courts, those of Naples, Aragon and Germany. For the affairs of Germany were being closely watched, and Charles of Valois and his friend Jean of Luxemburg had worked hard to get the Pope to excommunicate the Emperor, Ludwig of Bavaria, so that the crown of the Holy Roman Empire might be offered – to whom, indeed? To Monseigneur of Valois himself, of course! This was an old dream with which he was infatuated. Whenever the throne of the Holy Roman Empire had been vacant, or made vacant, Monseigneur of Valois had put himself forward as a candidate. At the same time, the preparations for the crusade were being pushed forward, and it had to be recognized that, could the crusade be led by the Emperor, it would make a great impression on the Infidel, and on Christians, too, for that matter.

There was also trouble with Flanders, which was always causing the Crown anxiety, whether the people were rebelling against their Count because he was loyal to the King of France, or whether the Count himself rose against the King to satisfy his people. And then, too, there was concern over England, and Roger Mortimer was now summoned by Valois whenever this subject was in question.

Mortimer had taken lodgings near Robert of Artois's house, in the Rue Saint-Germain-des-Prés, opposite the Navarre house. Gerard de Alspaye, who had been with him since his escape from the Tower, was in charge of his household, in which Ogle, the barber, held the position of butler. The household had been increased by a few refugees who had also been compelled to go into exile owing to the enmity of the Despensers. In particular, there was John Maltravers, an English lord belonging to Mortimer's party and, like Mortimer himself, a descendant of a companion of the Conqueror. He had been declared a King's enemy. Maltravers had a long, dark face with straight, lank hair, and huge teeth; he looked like his horse. He was not the most agreeable of companions and was inclined to make people start with an abrupt, neighing laugh, which generally appeared quite motiveless. But you do not choose your friends in exile; common misfortune forces them on you. Mortimer learnt from Maltravers that his wife had been transferred to Skipton Castle in the county of York, her sole attendants being her lady, her equerry, a laundress, a footman and a page, and that she received only thirteen shillings and four deniers a week on which to keep herself and her people; it might almost have been imprisonment.

As for Queen Isabella, her lot became increasingly difficult from day to day. The Despensers plundered, despoiled and humiliated her with a patient perfection of cruelty. 'I have nothing left of my own but my life,' she sent word to Mortimer, 'and I much fear they are preparing to take that from me. Hasten my brother to my defence.'

But the King of France – 'Is your wife with you? Have you any sons?' – had no opinion apart from Monseigneur of Valois's, and Valois was putting all decision off till he had seen the results of the action he had taken in Aquitaine. But suppose the Despensers assassinated the Queen meanwhile?

'They won't dare,' Valois replied.

Mortimer went to get news from the banker, Tolomei, through whose good offices he carried on his correspondence with the other side of the Channel. The Lombards had a better postal service than the Court, and their travellers were cleverer at concealing messages. The correspondence between Mortimer and Bishop Orleton was therefore fairly regular.

The Bishop of Hereford had paid dearly for organizing Mortimer's escape; but he had courage and was standing up to the King. As the first English bishop ever to be arraigned before a lay court of justice, he refused to answer his accusers, and in this he was supported by all the archbishops and bishops in the Kingdom, who saw their privileges threatened. Edward had pursued the prosecution, had Orleton found guilty and ordered the confiscation of his property. The King had also written to the Pope and demanded the Bishop's dethronement as a rebel; it was essential that Monseigneur of Valois should make representations to John XXII to prevent this measure being taken, for its inevitable result would be to bring Orleton to the scaffold.

As far as Henry Crouchback was concerned, the situation was somewhat confused. For Edward had made him Earl of Lancaster in March, and had returned to him both the titles and the properties of his brother, who had been beheaded, including the great castle of Kenilworth. And then, almost immediately afterwards, the King had found a letter of friendship and encouragement he had written to Orleton, and had accused Crouchback of high treason.

'And your King still obstinately refuses to pay us. Since you frequently see Messeigneurs of Valois and Artois and are their friend,' said Tolomei, 'make sure you remind them, my lord, of those gunpowder engines with which they have been experimenting in Italy and which must be of great use in besieging towns. My nephew in Siena and the Bardi in Florence can undertake to supply them. As pieces of artillery, they are much easier to place in position than those great catapults with cross-beams, and they do more damage. Monseigneur of Valois should equip his crusade with them – if he ever undertakes it.'

To begin with, the women had taken considerable interest in Mortimer, in this high personage with such strange ways, who was always dressed in austere and mysterious black, and who was continually biting the white scar on his lower lip. They made him repeat the story of his escape over and over again, and, as he recounted it, exquisite bosoms tended to heave beneath white and transparent linen bodices. His grave, rather hoarse voice, that had so unexpected an intonation on certain words, was calculated to touch the heart-free. On several occasions, Robert of Artois had tried to impel the English lord into arms that asked for nothing better than to open to him. He had also suggested to Mortimer that, if his tastes tended more towards the lower classes, he could procure for him women of easy virtue to distract him from his cares. But Mortimer had yielded to none of these temptations, so much so that, since he gave but little appearance of being inordinately strait-laced, people began wondering to what this apparent virtue might be due, and whether it was not that he shared the morals of his King.

Indeed, no one guessed the truth, which was simply that the man, who had wagered his safety on a raven's death, had staked a reversal of fortune in his favour on mere chastity. He had sworn an oath not to touch a woman before he had returned to the land of England and had recovered his titles and his power. It was a knightly oath, such as a Lancelot or an Amadis, some companion of King Arthur, might have made. But, as time went on, Roger Mortimer had to admit that he had been rather hasty in making such an oath, and that it contributed not a little to his depression.

At last good news came from Aquitaine. The Seneschal of the King of England in Guyenne, Messire Basset, who was all the more solicitous for his authority because his name gave rise to laughter, began to take alarm at the castle that was being built at Saint-Sardos. He saw in it both the usurpation of the rights of his master, the King of England, and a personal insult. Assembling a few troops, he suddenly entered Saint-Sardos, pillaged the town, arrested the officers in charge of the work and hanged them from gallows which, since they bore lilies on escutcheons, marked the King of France's sovereignty over the dependency. Messire Ralph Basset did not act alone in this expedition; several lords of the region had joined in with him.

As soon as Robert of Artois heard what had happened, he called for Mortimer and took him to Charles of Valois. Monseigneur of Artois was beside himself with joy and pride; he laughed even louder than usual and gave his friends playful taps that sent them rebounding against the walls. At last the opportunity was at hand, born of his fertile brain!

The affair was immediately discussed in the Privy Council; the usual representations were made, and the men who were guilty of the sack of Saint-Sardos were summoned to appear before the Parliament of Toulouse. Would they present themselves, plead guilty to their crime and make submission? It was very much feared that they might.

By good fortune, one of them, and only one, Raymond Bernard de Montpezat, refused to surrender to the summons. No more was needed. The rebel was condemned by default, his property decreed to be confiscated, and Jean de Roye, who had succeeded Pierre-Hector de Galard as Grand Master of the Cross-Bowmen, was sent into Guyenne with a small escort to seize both the Lord of Montpezat and his property, and see to the dismantling of his castle. But it was the Lord of Montpezat who had the better of it, for he took the royal officer prisoner and demanded a ransom for him. King Edward had nothing to do with the matter, but the turn of events aggravated the case, and Robert of Artois exulted. For a Grand Master of Cross-Bowmen was not the man to be taken prisoner without serious consequences.

Further protests were made, and now direct to the King of England, supported by a threat to confiscate the duchy. Early in April the Earl of Kent, half-brother to King Edward, accompanied by the Archbishop of Dublin, came to propose to Charles IV that their differences might be settled by remitting Edward's duty to pay homage. Mortimer, who saw Kent during his visit (their relations were perfectly courteous though the circumstances were far from easy), assured him of the utter uselessness of the proposal. The young Earl of Kent was indeed perfectly aware of it, and had embarked on his mission only with reluctance. He departed with the King of France's refusal, which had been transmitted to him with some contempt by Charles of Valois. It looked as if the war, which Robert of Artois had invented, might be on the point of breaking out.

But, at this very moment, the new Queen, Marie of Luxemburg, died suddenly at Issoudun, having been brought to bed before her time of a stillborn child.

War could not be made during a period of mourning; moreover, King Charles was so despondent that he was almost incapable of presiding over his Council. As a husband, fate appeared to be decidedly against him. He had been first deceived and now was a widower. Monseigneur of Valois had to lay everything else aside to set about finding the King a third wife. For the King had become anxious and ill-tempered, and indeed blamed everyone but himself for the fact that there was no heir to the throne. His father had arranged his first marriage, his uncle the second; and neither seemed to have been very successful.

But it was not so easy now to find princesses who were

prepared to marry into the family of France, which people were beginning to say was pursued by bad luck.

Charles of Valois would have been delighted to give his nephew one of his remaining daughters, had their ages been suitable; but unfortunately even the eldest, the daughter who had been formerly proposed for the heir-apparent of England, was no more than ten years old. And Charles the Fair was far from being prepared to await in patience either the recovery of the comfort of his nights or the assuring of the succession.

And Roger Mortimer had to wait until a wife had been found for the King.

But Charles IV had another cousin-german, the daughter of Monseigneur Louis of Évreux, now dead, and sister of Philippe of Évreux, who had been married to Jeanne of Navarre, the supposed bastard of Marguerite of Burgundy. Though lacking in beauty, this Jeanne of Évreux had a good figure and, above all, was of an age to become a mother. Monseigneur of Valois, who was longing to resolve the difficulty, encouraged the whole Court to influence Charles in favour of this marriage. Three months after the death of Marie of Luxemburg, a new licence was asked of the Pope. And Robert of Artois, son-in-law to Charles of Valois, who was the King's uncle, himself became uncle by marriage to the sovereign who was already his cousin, since Jeanne of Évreux was the daughter of his late sister Marguerite of Artois.

The marriage took place on July 5. Four days earlier, Charles had decided on the confiscation of Aquitaine and Ponthieu for rebellion and failure to render homage. Pope John XXII, since he considered it his duty to intervene whenever a conflict developed between sovereigns, wrote to

King Edward and pressed him to come to render homage so that at least one of the points in dispute might be resolved. But the French army was already on the march and assembling at Orléans, while a fleet was being equipped in the ports to attack the English coast.

In the meantime, the King of England had ordered levies to be made in Aquitaine, and Messire Ralph Basset was assembling his banners; the Earl of Kent was on his way back to France, but this time by sea all the way, to take up the post of Lieutenant in the duchy, to which he had been appointed by his half-brother.

Was war about to break out? Not at all. Monseigneur of Valois had to go to Bar-sur-Aube to meet Leopold of Hapsburg about the elections to the Holy Roman Empire, and conclude a treaty by which Hapsburg undertook not to come forward as a candidate, in return for a sum of money and various pensions and revenues in the event of Valois being elected Emperor. Roger Mortimer still had to wait.

Finally, on August 1, in a crushing heat that boiled the knights in their armour as if in so many saucepans, Charles of Valois, stout, resplendent, a crest on his helmet and a surcoat of gold over his mail, had himself hoisted into the saddle. Among his entourage were his second son, the Count of Alençon, his nephew Philippe of Évreux, the King's new brother-in-law, the Constable Gaucher de Châtillon, Roger Mortimer, and finally Robert of Artois who, mounted on a horse in keeping with his own size, could overlook the whole army.

Was Monseigneur of Valois as he left for this campaign, his second in Guyenne, a campaign he had himself desired, decided on and almost invented, pleased and happy or merely satisfied? He was none of these things. His mood was peculiarly morose, because Charles IV had refused to sign his commission as the King's Lieutenant in Aquitaine. If anyone had a right to that title, was it not Charles of Valois? And what sort of figure did he cut, when the Earl of Kent, that young whippersnapper – and his nephew into the bargain – had been appointed to the Lieutenancy by King Edward?

One might well wonder what was passing through Charles the Fair's mind, and what reasons he had for his intransigent obstinacy in refusing what was so clearly necessary, when he was normally incapable of making up his mind about anything at all. Indeed – and Valois had no hesitation in discussing it with his companions – was this crowned fool, this ninny, worth all the trouble one took to govern his kingdom for him? Would he one day also have to be provided with an heir?

The old Constable Gaucher de Châtillon, who was theoretically in command of the army since Valois had no official commission, was screwing up his saurian eyes beneath his old-fashioned helm. He was rather deaf, but at seventy-four still looked well on horseback.

Roger Mortimer had bought his arms from Tolomei. His hard, bright eyes, the colour of new steel, gleamed beneath his raised visor. Since, through his King's fault, he was marching against his own country, he wore a surcoat of black velvet as a sign of mourning. He would never forget the date on which they were setting out; it was 1 August 1324, the Feast of St Peter ad Vincula, and it was a year to the very day since he had escaped from the Tower of London.

6

The Bombards

THE RINGING OF THE tocsin surprised young Edmund, Earl of Kent, as he was lying on the flagstones of a room in the castle, trying vainly to get cool. He had half-undressed and was wearing only cloth breeches as he lay there with outspread arms, motionless and overcome by the Bordeaux summer. His favourite greyhound lay panting beside him.

The dog was the first to hear the tocsin. It rose on its front legs, pointed with its nose, and laid its quivering ears back. The young Earl of Kent woke out of his doze, stretched himself, and suddenly realized that this huge clangour came from the bells of La Réole which were all wildly ringing. In an instant he was on his feet, had seized the thin cambric shirt he had thrown over a chair, and had hastily put it on.

But already there was a sound of footsteps hurrying towards his door. Messire Ralph Basset, the Seneschal, came in, followed by some local lords, the Lord of Bergerac, the Barons of Budos and Mauvezin, and the Lord of Montpezat on whose account – at least he thought so and took pride in it – the war had broken out.

The Seneschal Basset was a very short man indeed; and the young Earl of Kent was surprised by his lack of inches each time he saw him. Moreover, he was as round as a barrel, for he had a prodigious appetite, and was always on the verge of losing his temper, which made his neck swell and his eyes pop.

The greyhound disliked the Seneschal and growled whenever it saw him.

'Is it a fire or the French, Messire Seneschal?' asked the Earl of Kent.

'The French, the French, Monseigneur!' cried the Seneschal, almost shocked by the question. 'Come and look; you can already make them out.'

The Earl of Kent bent to gaze into a tin mirror and put his fair curls straight about his ears; then he followed the Seneschal. In his white shirt, open across his chest and falling loose over his belt, with neither boots nor spurs, and his head bare, he gave a curious impression of grace and intrepidity, also perhaps of a certain lack of responsibility, among these armed barons in their iron mail.

As he emerged from the keep, the huge clangour of the bells took him by surprise and the bright August sun dazzled him. The greyhound started howling.

They went up to the top of the Thomasse Tower, the great round tower which had been built by Richard Cœur de Lion. Indeed, what has that ancestor of his not built? The outer fortifications of the Tower of London, Château Gaillard, the Castle of La Réole . . .

The wide Garonne flowed sparkling at the foot of the almost precipitous hill, its course meandering across the great fertile plain which was bounded by the distant blue line of the Agenois hills.

'I can't make anything out,' said the Earl of Kent, who was expecting to see the French vanguard on the outskirts of the town.

'Yes, look there, Monseigneur!' someone shouted above the noise of the tocsin. 'By the river, upstream, towards Sainte-Bazeille!'

Screwing up his eyes and shading them with his hand, the Earl of Kent was finally able to make out a glittering ribbon advancing parallel to the river. He was told it was the reflection of the sun on breastplates and horse-armour.

The din of the bells was still making the air quiver. The ringers' arms must have been exhausted. Below, the population of the town was hurrying to and fro, swarming in the streets and particularly about the Town Hall. How small men seemed when observed from the battlements of a citadel! Mere insects. Frightened peasants were crowding down the roads leading to the town, some dragging a cow along, some driving goats before them, some goading their ox-teams. Everyone was flying from the fields; and soon the people from the neighbouring villages would start arriving, their belongings on their backs or heaped in carts. And the whole crowd of them would have to find what lodging they could in a town already over-populated by the troops and knights of Guyenne.

'We shall be unable to make any proper estimate of the numbers of the French for another two hours, and they won't be under the walls before nightfall,' the Seneschal said.

'Oh, it's a bad time of year for making war,' said the Lord of Bergerac peevishly, for he had had to fly before the French advance from Sainte-Foy-la-Grande a few days earlier.

'Why is it a bad time of year?' asked the Earl of Kent, pointing to the clear sky and the smiling countryside below.

It was rather hot, of course, but wasn't that better than rain and mud? Had these people of Aquitaine been in the Scottish wars, they might have complained less.

'Because it's the grape harvest, Monseigneur,' said the Lord of Montpezat. 'The villeins will be aghast to see their vines trampled underfoot, and they'll blame us. The Count of Valois knows very well what he's doing; he did the same in 1294; ravaged the whole country to wear it down the more quickly.'

The Earl of Kent shrugged his shoulders. The Bordeaux country would not be affected by the loss of a few barrels, and war or no war, one would still be able to go on drinking claret. An unexpected little breeze was blowing about the top of the Thomasse Tower; it entered the young prince's open shirt and played agreeably over his skin. How marvellous it felt merely to be alive!

The Earl of Kent placed his elbows on the warm stone of the battlements and allowed himself to dream. At twenty-three, he was the King's Lieutenant for the whole duchy, that is to say invested with all the royal powers, justice, war, finance. In his own person he was the King himself. It was he who said: 'I will it' and who was obeyed. He could give the order: 'Hang him!' Not that he was thinking of giving any such order, but he had the power to do so. And then, above all, he was far from England, far from the Court, far from his half-brother and his whims, angers and suspicions, far from the Despensers, with whom he had of necessity to pretend to be on good terms, though he hated them. Here he was on his own, his own master, and master of all he surveyed. An army was coming to meet him, but he would charge it and defeat it, there could be no doubt of that. An astrologer had told him that he would accomplish his greatest actions and achieve renown between the ages of twenty-four and twenty-six. His childhood dreams were suddenly coming true. A great plain, an army, sovereign power . . . No, indeed, he had never felt happier to be alive in his life. His head was swimming a little with an intoxication which was entirely due to his own feelings and to the breeze playing over his chest, the vastness of the horizon . . .

'Your orders, Monseigneur?' asked Messire Basset, who was becoming impatient.

The Earl of Kent turned and looked at the little Seneschal with a shade of haughty astonishment.

'My orders?' he repeated. 'Have the *busines*[18] sounded, of course, Messire Seneschal, and get your people to horse. We shall go out to meet them and charge.'

'But what with, Monseigneur?'

'Good God, with our troops, Basset!'

'Monseigneur, we have barely two hundred knights here, and there are more than fifteen hundred coming against us according to the figures in our possession. Is that not correct, Messire de Bergerac?'

Reginald de Pons de Bergerac nodded agreement. The little Seneschal's neck was redder and more swollen than ever; he was aghast and on the verge of exploding at such imprudence.

'Have we no news of reinforcements?' asked the Earl of Kent.

'No, Monseigneur, still nothing. The King your brother, if you will forgive my saying so, is letting us down badly.'

They had been waiting for these long-heralded reinforcements from England for four weeks. And the Constable of Bordeaux, who had troops, made a pretext of their failure to arrive for not moving himself, for he had received an order from King Edward to march when the reinforcements had disembarked. The young Earl of Kent was not so much a sovereign as it might appear.

Owing to the delay and the consequent lack of men – who could tell if the promised reinforcements had ever been shipped? – they had been unable to prevent Monseigneur of Valois strolling across the countryside, from Agen to Marmande and from Bergerac to Duras, as if in a pleasure park. And now that uncle Valois was in sight, with his long ribbon of steel, there was still nothing that could be done about it.

'Is that also your advice, Montpezat?' asked the Earl of Kent.

'I fear so, Monseigneur, I very much fear so,' replied the Lord of Montpezat, chewing his black moustaches.

For he was obsessed with a longing for revenge. As a reprisal for his disobedience, Valois had ordered his castle to be demolished.

'And you, Bergerac?' Kent asked again.

'It makes me weep with rage,' said Pons de Bergerac with

that strong, sing-song accent that was common to all the minor lords of the region.

Edmund of Kent did not bother to ask the Barons of Budos and Fargues de Mauvezin for their opinions; for they could speak neither French nor English, but only Gascon, and Kent could not understand a word they said. In any case, their expressions were sufficient answer.

'Very well then, close the gates, Messire Seneschal, and make dispositions for a siege. And when the reinforcements do arrive, they'll take the French in the rear, and perhaps that will be better still,' said the Earl of Kent, trying to console himself.

He scratched his greyhound's forehead with the tips of his fingers, and then leaned on the warm stone again to watch the valley. There was an old saying: 'Who holds La Réole holds Guyenne.' They would hold out as long as was necessary.

For an army too easy an advance is almost as exhausting as a retreat. Having met no resistance to bring it to a halt, even if only for a day, to draw breath, the French army had been marching unceasingly for more than three weeks, to be precise for twenty-five days. The great host, with its banners, knights, squires, archers, wagons, forges and cookers, with the merchants and brothel-keepers in its train, extended over a league of the plain. Its horses were wither-galled, and every few minutes one of them cast a shoe. Many of the knights had had to give up wearing their armour which, aided by the heat, had given them sores and boils at the joints. The footmen were wearily dragging their heavy nailed boots. Moreover, the fine black plums of Agen, which looked ripe enough on the trees, had violently purged the thirsty, pilfering soldiers. They were continually leaving the column to lower their breeches by the roadside.

The Constable Gaucher de Châtillon slept as much as he could on his horse. He had trained himself to do this through nearly fifty years of the profession of arms and eight wars or campaigns.

'I shall sleep a little,' he would say to his two squires.

Adjusting their horses' pace to his, they placed themselves on each side of the Constable, so as to prop him up should he slip sideways; and the old leader, his back well supported by the cantle, snored inside his helm.

Robert of Artois, though he sweated, grew no thinner; for twenty yards around he diffused the stench of a wild beast. He had made a friend of one of the English in Mortimer's train, the tall Baron Maltravers, who looked like a horse, and he had even offered him a place in his banner because he was a great gambler and ready to handle the dice-box at every halt.

Charles of Valois's ill-humour was not improving. Surrounded by his son Alençon, his nephew Évreux, the two Marshals Mathieu de Trye and Jean des Barres, and his cousin Alfonso of Spain, he spent his time swearing at everything, at the intolerable climate, the stuffiness of the nights and the furnace of the days, at the flies, at the greasy food. The wine they served him was but thin stuff and fit for rustics, though they were in a country famous for its wines, were they not? Where did these people hide their good cakes? The eggs tasted bad and the milk was sour. Monseigneur of Valois sometimes woke up in the morning feeling sick and for several days past he had been suffering from a dull pain in the left shoulder which worried him. And then the footmen marched so slowly. Oh, if one could make war with the chivalry alone! And then, had he been right to take the advice of Tolomei, supported though it was by Robert of Artois, and drag these huge bombards on their wooden carriages all the way from Castelsarrasin, instead of relying on the catapults and perriers to which he was accustomed? For though they might take longer to put in position, they had the great advantage of being transported in pieces.

'I seemed to be condemned to hot suns,' he said. 'My first campaign, when I was fifteen years old, was fought in the burning heat of your bare Aragon, of which I was once king for a time, Cousin Alfonso, and against your grandfather.'

He was talking to Alfonso of Spain, heir to the throne of Aragon, reminding him, perhaps not very tactfully, of the enmity that had divided their respective families. But he could do so with impunity, for Alfonso was very easy-going, and ready to do anything to please; he was prepared to go on the crusade since he had been asked to do so, and in the meantime to train himself for the crusade by fighting the English.

'I shall never forget the capture of Gerona,' Valois went on. 'What an oven that was! The Cardinal de Cholet, since he had no crown available for my coronation, crowned me with his hat. I was stifled under that huge red piece of felt. Yes, I was fifteen years old. If my noble father, King Philippe the Bold, had not died of the fever he contracted in those parts on his way home . . .'

Talking of his father made him feel gloomy. He was

thinking that he had died at forty. His elder brother, Philip the Fair, had died at forty-six, and his half-brother, Louis of Évreux, at forty-three. And he himself had turned fifty-four in March! He had clearly shown that he was the most robust member of the family. But how many more years would Providence permit him?

'And Campania, Romagna and Tuscany, those are hot countries for you,' he went on. 'I marched through the whole of Italy, in midsummer, from Naples up to Siena and Florence, to chase out the Ghibellines some – let me see, it was in 1301 – twenty-three years ago. And even here, in Guyenne in the year 1294, it was summer. It always is summer. But when you have to fight in Flanders, it's always winter and you're up to your thighs in mud.'

'You know, Charles, it'll be hotter still on the crusade,' Robert of Artois said sarcastically. 'Do you see us invading the Egyptian Sudan? It seems vines are not much cultivated in those parts. We shall have to drink the sand.'

'Oh, the crusade, the crusade . . .' Valois replied with weary irritation. 'How can one even tell whether the crusade will ever take place with all the obstacles people put in my way? It's all very well to devote one's life to the service of the kingdom and the Church, but in the end one grows weary of expending all one's strength for such ungrateful people.'

The ungrateful people were in the first place Pope John XXII, who was still reluctant to grant the subsidies, almost as if he really wished to discourage the expedition; but above all King Charles IV, who had not only failed to send the commission for the lieutenancy to Charles of Valois, a dereliction which was now becoming offensive, but had also taken advantage of his uncle's absence to put himself forward as a candidate for the Empire. And the Pope, of course, had given him his official support. And so all Valois's splendid arrangements with Leopold of Hapsburg had fallen to the ground. King Charles was considered a fool and, in fact, was one; but on occasion he was competent enough to deal a foul blow. Valois had received the news that very day, August 25. It was an unsatisfactory Feast of Saint Louis, to say the least. He was in such a bad temper and so busy chasing the flies from his face, that he had forgotten to look at the landscape. He saw La Réole only when they were before it, within four or five bowshots.

La Réole stood on a rocky spur above the Garonne, but was dominated by a circle of green hills. Etched against the pale sky, enclosed within her ramparts of fine yellow stone, now turning gold in the setting sun, with her steeples, her castle's turrets, and the high roof of her Town Hall with its open belfry, and all her crowded roofs of red tiles, she resembled the miniatures of Jerusalem you can find in Books of Hours. A pretty town. Furthermore, owing to the height on which La Réole was set, she was an ideal stronghold. The Earl of Kent had made no error in shutting himself up within her walls. She would be no easy fortress to take.

The army had come to a halt, awaiting orders. But Monseigneur of Valois issued none. He was sulking. Let the Constable and the Marshals take what decisions seemed good to them. Since he was not the King's Lieutenant and had no power, he refused to take any responsibility.

'Come, Alfonso, let us go and refresh ourselves,' he said to his Spanish cousin.

Waking up, the Constable twisted his head inside his helm and stuck out an ear to hear what the leaders of his banners were saying to him. He sent the Count of Boulogne to reconnoitre. Boulogne returned an hour later, having ridden round the town by the hills. All the gates were shut, and the garrison showed no signs of making a sortie. It was therefore decided to make camp where they were, and the banners selected their areas pretty much as they liked. The vines, their branches trailing between trees and tall vine-props, made agreeably sheltered tunnels. The army was exhausted and fell asleep in the clear twilight as the first stars appeared.

The young Earl of Kent was unable to resist the temptation and, after a sleepless night, of which he spent the waking hours playing *trémerel*[19] with his equerries, he sent for Seneschal Basset, ordered him to summon his knights to arms and, before dawn, without sound of trumpet, left the town by a sally-port.

The French, snoring among the vines, wakened only when the galloping Gascon knights were among them. They looked up in astonishment only to lower their heads again as they saw the charging hooves go by. Edmund of Kent and his companions had it all their own way among the sleeping host; they hewed with their swords, struck with their maces and their leaded flails at naked ribs and legs, unprotected by greaves or breastplates. There was a cracking of bones as they drove a path, leaving screams in their wake, through the French camp. Some of the great lords' tents collapsed. But soon a loud voice was heard above the hubbub shouting:

'Rally to Châtillon!' And the Constable's banner – gules, three pales vair, in chief or, a dragon for crest, and supporting lions – was floating in the rising sun. Old Gaucher had prudently made his own vassal knights camp a little in the rear, and now came to the rescue. Cries of 'Artois to the fore!' and 'Rally to Valois!' responded from either hand. Only half-equipped, some on horseback and some on foot, the knights hurled themselves on the enemy.

The camp was too big and too scattered, and the French knights too numerous, to enable the Earl of Kent to pursue his ravages for long. The Gascons soon became aware of a pincer-movement being mounted against them. Kent had only just time to turn aside and retreat at a gallop to the gates of La Réole behind which he could take refuge. Then, having complimented his followers, he took off his armour and went to bed, his honour vindicated.

The French camp was echoing with the groaning of the wounded; consternation reigned. Among the dead, who numbered about sixty, were Jean des Barres, one of the Marshals, and the Count of Boulogne, who had made the reconnaissance the evening before. It was much deplored that these two lords, both valiant warriors, should have met so sudden and so absurd an end. Slaughtered on awakening!

But Kent's prowess inspired respect. Charles of Valois himself who, the evening before, had been asserting that he would make mincemeat of the young man, if he encountered him in the lists, had now changed his opinion and almost took pride in saying: 'Well, Messeigneurs, after all he's my nephew, don't forget that!'

Forgetting the wounds to his vanity, his physical ills and

the heat of the season, he set himself, when sufficiently magnificent funeral honours had been rendered to the Marshal des Barres, to prepare the siege of the town. And in this he displayed singular activity and competence for, though he was excessively vain, he was none the less a very remarkable soldier.

All the roads leading to La Réole were cut, and the whole region controlled by posts set up in depth. Entrenchments, gabions, and other earthworks were undertaken within a short distance of the walls to give cover to the archers. While, in the most suitable places, the army began constructing emplacements for the bombards. It also started to build platforms for the cross-bowmen. Monseigneur of Valois seemed to be everywhere, inspecting, encouraging and issuing orders. To the rear, the knights had set up their round tents, from the summits of which floated their banners. Charles of Valois's tent, placed in a position from which it could dominate both the camp and the beleaguered town, was a veritable palace of tapestried hangings. The whole camp was situated in a huge amphitheatre under the flank of the hills.

On August 30 Valois at last received his commission as the King's Lieutenant. His mood changed at once, and from then on he seemed to have no doubt that the war was as good as won.

Two days later, Mathieu de Trye, the surviving Marshal, Pierre de Cugnières and Alfonso of Spain, preceded by sounding *busines* and the white flag of envoys, advanced to the foot of the walls of La Réole to summon the Earl of Kent, on the order of the most high and puissant Lord Charles, Count of Valois, Lieutenant of the King of France in Gascony and Aquitaine, to yield and surrender into their hands the duchy in its entirety, in default of loyalty and the rendering of homage due.

To which Seneschal Basset, who had to stand on tiptoe to look over the battlements, replied, on the order of Edmund, Earl of Kent, Lieutenant of the King of England in Gascony and Aquitaine, that the summons could not be accepted, and that the Earl would not leave the town, nor hand over the duchy, unless he were dislodged by force.

Now that a state of siege had been declared in accordance with the rules, each side went to its tasks.

Monseigneur of Valois put to work the thirty miners lent him by the Bishop of Metz. They were to tunnel underground galleries beneath the walls and place in them barrels of powder which would later be exploded. Engineer Hugues, who belonged to the Duke of Lorraine, guaranteed miraculous results from this operation. The walls would burst open like a flower in spring.

But the besieged, becoming aware of the muffled sounds of tunnelling, put tanks of water on the ramparts. Whenever they saw the surface of the water ripple, they knew the French were digging a sap below. They dug saps from their side too, but at night, for the Lorraine miners worked by day. One morning, the two galleries met and an appalling butchery took place underground by the dim light of lanterns. The survivors emerged covered with sweat, black dust and blood, their eyes as wild with horror as if they had returned from Hell.

But now the firing platforms were ready and Monseigneur of Valois decided to use the bombards.

They were huge tubes of thick bronze bound with iron hoops, mounted on wooden wheelless carriages. Ten horses were needed to move each one of these monsters, and twenty men to load, aim and fire it. Each was surrounded with a sort of box-like structure of heavy beams to protect the gunners should the bombard explode.

These engines, which came from Pisa, had been delivered first to the Seneschal of Languedoc, who had sent them on to Castelsarrasin and Agen. The Italian crews called them *bombarda* because of the noise they made.

All the great lords and the commanders of banners were assembled to see the bombards work. The Constable Gaucher shrugged his shoulders and said with a growl that he did not believe in the destructive effects of these engines. Why place your trust in such new-fangled things, when you could use good mangonels, trebuchets and perriers, which had proved their worth over the centuries? What need had he, Châtillon, of the founders of Lombardy to reduce the towns he had taken? Wars were won by valour and the strength of men's arms, not by having recourse to the powders of alchemists which stank rather too much of the Devil's sulphur.

Beside each bombard the gunners lit a brazier and set an iron rod to become red-hot. Then, having loaded the bombard by the muzzle, introducing the powder with huge spoons of beaten iron, followed by a wad of tow and then a huge stone ball weighing approximately a hundred pounds, they placed a little powder on the top of the breech in a groove which communicated with the charge inside by a touch-hole.

The spectators were asked to withdraw to a distance of

fifty paces. The gunners lay down with their hands over their ears; only one remained standing by each bombard to set fire to the powder with the long iron rod which had been heated in the brazier. As soon as they had done so, they threw themselves to the ground and lay flat against the beams built round the carriages.

Red flames gushed forth and the ground shook. The noise rolled down the valley of the Garonne and was heard from Marmande to Langon.

The whole air about the bombards turned black with smoke. The back ends of them had sunk into the light soil with the recoil. The Constable was coughing, spitting and swearing. When the dust had dissipated a little, it was discovered that one of the balls had fallen among the French; it was a wonder no one had been killed. Nevertheless, it could be seen that a roof in the town had been holed.

'A great deal of noise for very little damage,' said the Constable. 'With the old ballisters with weights and slings, all the balls would have reached their target without one's being asphyxiated into the bargain.'

In the meantime, within La Réole, no one could at first understand why a great cascade of tiles should suddenly have fallen into the street from the roof of Master Delpuch, the notary. Nor could the people make out where the thunderclap that reached their ears a moment later came from, since there was not a cloud in the sky. But then Master Delpuch came rushing out of his house, shouting that a huge stone ball had fallen into his kitchen.

Then the population ran to the ramparts only to discover that there were none of those great engines which were the normal equipment for sieges in the French camp. At the second salvo, which was less well aimed, the balls starred the walls, and the defenders were forced to the conclusion that the noise and the projectiles came from the long tubes lying on the hillside with a cloud of smoke hanging over them. They were seized with panic, and the women rushed to the churches to pray against these inventions of the Devil.

The first cannon-shot in a Western war had been fired.[20]

On the morning of September 22 the Earl of Kent was asked to receive Messires Ramon de Labison, Jean de Miral, Imbert Esclau, the brothers Doat and Barsan de Pins, the Notary Hélie de Malenat and all six jurats of La Réole together with several burgesses who were accompanying them. The jurats presented to the Lieutenant of the King of England a long list of grievances, and in a tone that was far from being one of submission and respect. The town was without food, water or roofs. The bottoms of the cisterns were showing, the floors of the granaries were being swept, and the population could no longer stand the hail of balls which had fallen on it every quarter of an hour for more than three weeks now. People had been killed in their beds and children crushed in the streets. The hospital was full to overflowing with sick and wounded. The dead were lying in heaps in the crypts of the churches. The steeple of the church of Saint Peter had been hit and the bells had fallen with a sound like the last trump, which was clear proof that God was not supporting the English cause. Moreover, the time for the grape-harvest had come, at least in the vineyards the French had not ravaged, and the grapes could not be left to rot on the vines. The population, encouraged by the landowners and merchants, was ready to rise in revolt and fight the soldiers of the Seneschal, if necessary, to force the surrender of the town.

While the jurats were talking, a ball whistled through the air and they heard the sound of a roof caving in. The Earl of Kent's greyhound began howling. Its master silenced it with weary irritation.

Edmund of Kent had known for several days past that he would have to surrender. He had continued his obstinate resistance for no valid reason. His few troops were exhausted by the siege and in no condition to repulse an assault. To attempt another sortie against an adversary who was now solidly entrenched would have been mere folly. And now the townspeople of La Réole were threatening rebellion.

Kent turned to Seneschal Basset.

'Do you still believe in reinforcements from Bordeaux, Messire Ralph?' he asked.

It was not the Seneschal, but Kent himself who had believed, against all the evidence, in the arrival of these promised reinforcements, who were to take Charles of Valois's army in the rear.

Ralph Basset was at the end of his tether and had no hesitation in accusing King Edward and his Despensers of having let the defenders of La Réole down to a degree that amounted to a betrayal.

The Lords of Bergerac, Budos and Montpezat looked no happier. No one felt like dying for a king who showed such little concern for his most faithful servants. Loyalty seemed to be far too ill-rewarded.

'Have you a white flag, Messire Seneschal?' asked the Earl

of Kent. 'Very well, have it hoisted on the top of the castle.'

A few minutes later the bombards fell silent; and there reigned over the French camp that profound stillness of surprise which tends to greet an event that has been much longed for. Envoys emerged from La Réole and were conducted to the tent of Marshal de Trye, who informed them of the general terms of surrender. The town, of course, would be handed over; but the Earl of Kent must also sign and proclaim the handing over of the whole duchy to the Lieutenant of the King of France. There would be no pillage nor prisoners taken, merely hostages and an indemnity to be fixed later. Furthermore, the Count of Valois invited the Earl of Kent to dinner.

A great feast was prepared in the tent embroidered with the lilies of France in which Monseigneur had been living for nearly a month. The Earl of Kent arrived in his best suit of armour, but pale and doing his best to conceal beneath an air of dignity his humiliation and despair. He was accompanied by the Seneschal Basset and a number of Gascon lords.

The two Royal Lieutenants, conqueror and conquered, conversed with a certain coolness, though calling each other 'Monseigneur my Nephew' and 'Monseigneur my Uncle', as if even war could not break family ties.

Monseigneur of Valois made the Earl of Kent sit opposite him at dinner. The Gascon knights began gorging themselves as they had had no chance of doing for many weeks.

Everyone did his best to be courteous and compliment the adversary on his valour as if it were question merely of a tournament. The Earl of Kent was congratulated on his spirited sortie, which had cost the French a marshal. Kent replied by showing great admiration for his uncle's dispositions for the siege and his use of the bombards.

'Listen, Messire Constable, and all of you, Messeigneurs,' cried Valois, 'to what my noble nephew says! Without our bombards the town could have held out for four months! Remember that, all of you!'

Kent and Mortimer watched each other across the platters, goblets and flagons.

As soon as the banquet was over, the principal leaders went into conference to negotiate the act of surrender, which had numerous articles. Kent was, in fact, prepared to yield on every point, with the exception of certain clauses, of which one cast a doubt on the legitimacy of the King of England's power and another placed Seneschal Basset and the Lord of Montpezat at the head of the list of hostages. For since these last had arrested and hanged officers of the King of France, their fate would be only too certain. But Valois insisted that the Seneschal and the man responsible for the rebellion at Saint-Sardos should be handed over to him.

Roger Mortimer was present at the negotiations. He suggested he should have a private conversation with the Earl of Kent, but the Constable opposed it. You really could not allow the terms of an armistice to be negotiated by a deserter from the opposing camp! But Robert of Artois and Charles of Valois trusted Mortimer. So the two Englishmen went apart into a corner of the tent.

'Are you really anxious, my lord, to return to England at once?' Mortimer asked.

Kent made no reply.

'Are you so desirous of confronting King Edward, your

brother, with whose fits of passion and injustice you are so familiar?' Mortimer went on. 'He'll reproach you with a defeat for which the Despensers are alone responsible. You must be aware, my lord, that you have been betrayed. We have known all along that you were promised reinforcements were on the way to you, when in fact they had never even been embarked. And the order given the Seneschal of Bordeaux not to come to your assistance before the reinforcements arrived – reinforcements that, in fact, did not exist – was surely nothing but a betrayal? You need not be surprised to find me well-informed, for I owe it merely to the Lombard bankers. And have you not asked yourself the reason for so criminal a negligence towards you? Do you not see the object of it?'

Kent still remained silent, his head inclined a little to one side, gazing at his fingernails.

'Had you won this war, you would have been a danger to the Despensers, my lord,' Mortimer went on, 'and would have achieved too important a position in the kingdom. They have quite naturally preferred to subject you to the discredit of a defeat, even at the price of Aquitaine, which has but little importance for men who have no care but to steal the baronies of the Marches one after the other. Do you not realize that my rebellion of three years ago was for England against the King, or perhaps for the King against himself? How do you know that you will not be accused of criminal negligence and immediately cast into prison on your arrival home? You are still young, my lord, and have no idea of what those wicked men are capable.'

Kent smoothed his fair curls back behind his ears and

replied at last: 'I'm beginning to know it, my lord, and to my cost.'

'Would you be entirely reluctant to offer yourself as the first hostage, on the guarantee, of course, that you would be treated as a prince? Since Aquitaine is now lost, and I fear for ever, our duty is to save the kingdom itself, and we can do that best from here.'

The young man looked at Mortimer in surprise, but he was already half-prepared to consent.

'But two hours ago,' he said, 'I was still the Lieutenant of my brother the King, and are you asking me so soon to join a rebellion?'

'Without its being apparent, my lord, without its being apparent. Great decisions are made in a few seconds.'

'How many seconds do you give me?'

'There is no need, my lord. You have already made your decision.'

Roger Mortimer scored no little success when young Edmund, Earl of Kent, came back to the council table and announced that he was prepared to offer himself as the senior hostage.

Mortimer leaned towards him and said: 'And now we must work to save your cousin and sister-in-law, the Queen. She deserves our love and can be of the greatest help to us.'

PART TWO

ISABELLA IN LOVE

I

Dinner with Pope John

THE CHURCH OF Saint Agricola had recently been entirely rebuilt. The cathedral of the Doms, the church of the Minorites, and those of the Predicant Friars and the Augustinians had been enlarged and renovated. The Hospitallers of Saint John of Jerusalem had built themselves a magnificent commandery. Beyond the Place au Change a new chapel to Saint Anthony was rising, and the foundations for a future church of Saint Didier were being dug.

The Count de Bouville had been going about Avignon for a week. He no longer recognized it, nor could he find in it a single reminder of the past. Every time he went out, he was surprised and amazed. How could a town have changed its appearance so completely in eight years?

For it was not only churches that had risen from the earth or acquired new façades, raising on every hand spires, arches, rose-windows, and traceries of white stone which the winter sunlight tinged with gold while the wind from the Rhône sang through them.

On every hand princes' and prelates' palaces, communal buildings, rich burgesses' houses, offices of Lombard Companies, shops and warehouses were building. On all sides the patient, incessant sound of masons' hammers seemed to patter like rain; the millions of little taps of metal on soft stone by which capitals are built. Constantly traversed by the torches which preceded the cardinals even in daylight, the swarming, lively, busy crowd trampled the sawdust, the stonedust and the rubbish. The embroidered shoes of power being soiled by the dust of building is the symbol of a period of wealth.

No, indeed, Hugues de Bouville no longer recognized the place. Not only were his eyes filled with the dust of building by the mistral but they were constantly being dazzled. The shops, which all boasted of being suppliers to the Holy Father, the Pope, or to their Eminences of his Sacred College, were full of the most sumptuous merchandise on earth, the thickest velvets, silks, cloth of gold and the richest braid, sacerdotal jewels, pectoral crosses, croziers, rings, ciboriums, monstrances, patens, as well as eating platters, spoons, goblets and tankards, engraved with the papal or with cardinals' arms, were heaped on the counters of Tauro the Sienese, of Merchant Corboli and of Master Cachette, the silversmiths.

Painters were needed to decorate all these naves, ceilings, cloisters and audience chambers; the three Pierres, Pierre du Puy, Pierre de Camelère and Pierre Gaudrac, with the assistance of their innumerable pupils, were spreading gold, azure and carmine as they depicted the signs of the Zodiac round scenes from the two Testaments. Sculptors were needed and Master Macciolo of Spoleto was carving effigies of the saints in oak and walnut which he would then paint or cover with gold. And in the streets everyone bowed low to a man who, though preceded by no torches, was always escorted by an imposing following carrying measuring-rods and huge plans on rolls of parchment; he was Messire Guillaume de Coucouron, the chief of all the papal architects, who had been rebuilding Avignon since the year 1317 at the fabulous cost of five thousand gold florins.

The women of this religious metropolis were more beautifully dressed than those of anywhere else in the world. To watch them come out of Mass, walk through the streets, visit the shops, hold court in the middle of the street itself, shivering and laughing in their furred cloaks, among assiduous lords and knowing clerics, was an enchantment to the eye. Some of these ladies had no hesitation in being seen walking on the arm even of a canon or a bishop, and the two skirts swept the white dust in harmonious accord.

The Church's Treasury enabled every human activity to prosper. It had been necessary to construct new brothels and extend the prostitutes' quarter, for all the monks, novices, clerics, deacons and sub-deacons who haunted Avignon were not necessarily saints. The town magistrates had posted up strict regulations: 'Prostitutes and procuresses are forbidden to live in the better streets, to wear the same ornaments as respectable women, to wear veils in public or to touch with the hand bread and fruit on the stalls on pain of being obliged to buy the goods they have so touched. Married courtesans are expelled from the town and will be summoned to appear before the magistrates should they enter it.' But, despite the regulations, the courtesans dressed in the finest clothes, bought the best fruit, walked in the aristocratic streets and had no difficulty in marrying, so prosperous and sought-after were they. They gazed with assurance at the so-called respectable women who behaved no better than they did, for the only difference between them was that chance had given them lovers of higher rank.

And it was not only Avignon but all the neighbouring countryside that was being transformed. On the farther side of the bridge of Saint-Bénézet, on the Villeneuve bank, Cardinal Arnaud de Via, a nephew of the Pope, was building an enormous collegiate church; and Philip the Fair's tower was already being called 'the old tower' because it was thirty years old. But would any of all this have existed but for Philip the Fair, who in times past had imposed Avignon on the papacy as its headquarters?[21] At Bédarrides, Châteauneuf and Noves, the Pope's builders were raising churches and castles out of the earth.

Bouville could not help taking a certain personal pride in all this. For it was in part due to him that the present Pope had been elected. Indeed, it was he, Bouville, who eight or even nine years ago now, after an exhausting chase in pursuit of the cardinals who were scattered all over the countryside between Carpentras and Orange, had discovered Cardinal Duèze, given him funds for his electoral campaign and sent his name to Paris as that of the best candidate for France. In fact, Duèze, who was already the candidate of the King of Naples, had taken great care to let himself be discovered. But it is the habit of ambassadors to believe themselves solely responsible for the outcome of their missions when they are successful. And Bouville, on his way to the banquet Pope John XXII was giving in his honour, stuck out his stomach – though he imagined he was throwing out his chest – shook his white hair over his fur collar and spoke rather loudly to his equerries as he passed through the streets of Avignon.

In any case, one thing appeared to be quite settled: the Holy See would not return to Italy. There was now an end to the illusions that Clement V had prudently allowed to be entertained during his pontificate. The Roman patricians might well conspire against John XXII and threaten that, if he did not return to the Eternal City, they would create a schism by electing another pope who would occupy the true throne of Saint Peter.[22] The one-time burgess of Cahors had answered the Roman princes by conferring but one hat on them among the sixteen cardinals he had created since his enthronement. All the other hats had gone to Frenchmen.

'You see, Messire Count,' Pope John had said to Bouville, a few days earlier, at the first audience he had granted him, speaking in that hoarsely whispering voice with which he controlled Christendom in such a masterful way, 'you see, Messire Count, one must govern with one's friends and against one's enemies. Princes who spend their time and their strength trying to win over their adversaries create only discontent among their true supporters while acquiring false friends, who are always ready to betray them.'

To be convinced of the Pope's intention to remain in France, it was necessary only to look at the castle he had built by incorporating the old Bishop's Palace and which now dominated the town with its towers, battlements and machicolations. The interior was divided into spacious cloisters, reception rooms, and splendidly decorated apartments under blue ceilings strewn with stars like the sky.[23] There were two ushers on the first door, two on the second, five on the third, and fourteen for the other doors. The Palace Marshal had under his orders forty couriers and sixty-three sergeants-at-arms. This was no temporary establishment.

And to discover with whom Pope John intended ruling, Bouville had merely to look at the dignitaries who came to take their places at the long table gleaming with gold and silver plate in the banqueting-hall, which was hung with silk tapestries.

The Cardinal-Archbishop of Avignon was called Arnaud de Via; he was the son of a sister of the Pope. The Cardinal-Chancellor of the Roman Church, that is to say the Prime Minister of Christendom, a tall, stout man, who looked well in his purple, was Gaucelin Duèze, the son of Pierre Duèze, that brother of the Pope whom King Philippe V had ennobled. And then there were a nephew of the Pope, Cardinal de la Motte-Fressange, and a cousin of the Pope, Cardinal Raymond Le Roux. Another nephew of the Pope, Pierre de Vicy, controlled the papal household and its expenses, and was in charge of the two stewards, the four cellarers, the masters of the stables and the farriery, the six grooms of the chamber, the thirty chaplains, the sixteen confessors for visiting pilgrims, the bellringers, the sweepers, the water-carriers, the laundresses, the physicians, the apothecaries and the barbers.

Cardinal Bertrand du Pouget was certainly not the least of the personages present at the papal table. He was the perambulating Papal Legate in Italy, and it was whispered of him – but of whom were things not whispered here? – that he was a natural son Jacques Duèze had had when, so far from thinking he would ever become pope, he was not yet a prelate, chancellor to the King of Naples, nor even a doctor or a cleric, and had not indeed thought of leaving his native Cahors, though already past his fortieth year!

All Pope John's relations, down to cousins once removed, were lodged in his palace and shared his repasts; two of them even lived in the private *entresol* underneath the dining-room. They had all been given posts among the hundred noble knights, one as the Dispenser of Charity, another as Master of the Apostolic Chamber, who administered all the ecclesiastical income, the annates, tithes, subsidies, death duties and taxes from the Sacred Penitential. The Court consisted of more than four hundred persons and its annual expenses amounted to over four thousand florins.

When, eight years earlier, the Conclave at Lyons had raised to the throne of Saint Peter an exhausted and fragile old man, who, so it was expected and indeed hoped, would give up the ghost the following week, the papal treasury had been empty. But during these eight years, this little old man, who looked like a feather blown by the wind, had administered so well the Church's finances, had taxed so successfully the adulterers, the sodomites and the incestuous, the thieves and the criminals, the bad priests and the bishops guilty of violence, had sold abbeys for such good prices and had so cleverly organized all the resources of ecclesiastical property, that he had been able to build a town and acquire the greatest income in the world. He might well afford to feed his family and govern through it. Nor was he niggardly with charity to the poor and gifts to the rich. He presented his visitors with jewels and holy medals of gold, which were furnished by his usual supplier, the Jew Boncœur.

Buried, rather than seated, in an armchair with an immensely high back, his feet resting on two thick cushions covered with gold silk, Pope John presided over his long table, which had something of the dual quality of a consistory and a family dinner-party. Bouville, sitting on his right, watched him with fascination. How the Holy Father had changed since his election! Not in physical appearance: time no longer had power to alter that thin, pointed face, so wrinkled and mobile, its head covered with a fur-edged skull-cap, its eyes small and mouse-like, lacking both eyelashes and eyebrows, and its extraordinarily little mouth, whose upper lip tended to disappear behind a toothless gum. John XXII carried his eighty years more easily than many people their fifty; his hands were proof of it: smooth and the skin hardly parchmenty, the joints were still perfectly flexible. It was rather in his whole demeanour, in his tone of voice and conversation, that the transformation had taken place. This man, who had originally owed his cardinal's hat to forging a royal signature, and his tiara to two years of secret intrigue, to electoral corruption, and to a month's simulation of incurable disease, seemed to have acquired a new personality through the mere aura of the supreme pontificate. Having started with almost nothing at all and having reached the summit of human ambitions with nothing more to desire or obtain for himself personally, all the strength and redoubtable mental machinery that had elevated him to his present position could now be employed, in complete detachment, for the sole good of the Church such as he conceived it to be. And what energy he expended! How many there were among those who had elected him, thinking he was on the point of death or would allow the Curia to govern in his name, who repented it now! John XXII led them a hard life. Indeed, this little man was a great sovereign of the Church.

He dealt with everything, decided everything. He had not hesitated in the previous March to excommunicate the Emperor of Germany, Ludwig of Bavaria, and, at the same time, to remove him from his throne and thereby open the succession to the Holy Roman Empire about which the King of France and the Count of Valois were so concerned. He intervened in all the differences between the princes of Christendom, reminding them, as was consonant with his mission as universal pastor, of their duty to keep the peace. He had recently been considering the war in Aquitaine and had settled, during the audiences he had given Bouville, the course he intended to pursue.

The sovereigns of France and England would be asked to prolong the truce signed by the Earl of Kent at La Réole, which was due to expire in this very month of December. Monseigneur of Valois would make no use of the four hundred men-at-arms and the thousand cross-bowmen King Charles IV had recently sent to him at Bergerac as reinforcements. But King Edward would be urgently invited to come and render homage to the King of France with the least possible delay. The two sovereigns would free the Gascon lords they were respectively detaining and would show them no severity for having taken the enemy's part. Finally, the

Pope intended writing to Queen Isabella to adjure her to do all she could to re-establish good relations between her husband and her brother. Pope John had no more illusions than had Bouville as to the unhappy Queen's influence. But the mere fact of the Holy Father writing to her was bound to restore her credit to some extent and might make her enemies hesitate to ill-treat her further. And then John XXII would suggest her coming to Paris on a mission of conciliation, there to preside over the drawing up of a treaty which would leave England only a small coastal strip of the Duchy of Aquitaine which would include Saintes, Bordeaux, Dax and Bayonne. Thus the political ambitions of the Count of Valois, the machinations of Robert of Artois and the secret wishes of Roger Mortimer were to receive from the Holy Father a significant impulse towards their accomplishment.

Bouville, having thus fulfilled the first part of his mission with success, could devote himself to the richly and delectably spiced stewed eels with which his silver bowl had been filled.

'We get our eels from the Lake of Martigues,' Pope John remarked to Bouville. 'Do you like them?'

Fat Bouville's mouth was so full that he could reply only by assuming an expression of delighted astonishment.

The papal cuisine was luxurious, and even the Friday menus were rare feasts. Fresh tunny fish, Norwegian cod, lampreys and sturgeons, prepared in twenty different ways and accompanied by twenty different sauces, succeeded each other in dish after gleaming dish. The wine of Arbois flowed like gold into the goblets. The growths of Burgundy, the Lot or the Rhône accompanied the cheeses.

For his part, the Holy Father contented himself with nibbling with his gums at a spoonful of pike pâté and sipping at a goblet of milk. He had taken it into his head that the Pope should eat nothing but white food.

Bouville had been charged by Monseigneur of Valois to deal with another problem, and a more delicate one: the matter of the crusade, which seemed to have fallen somewhat into the background, for John XXII had said no word about it during their interviews. He had, nevertheless, to make up his mind to broach it. It is a rule that ambassadors should never approach thorny questions direct; and Bouville believed he was being subtle when he said: 'Most Holy Father, the Court of France noted with much interest the Council of Valladolid, held two years ago by your Legate, at which it was decreed that priests must give up their concubines . . .'

'Under pain, if they did not do so,' said Pope John in his rapid, whispering voice, 'of being deprived after two months of a third part of the yield of their benefices, and two months later of another third, and two months after that to be deprived of it all. Indeed, Messire Count, men are sinners even if they be priests, and we know very well that we shall not succeed in suppressing all sin. But at least those who are obstinate in wrongdoing will fill our coffers, and the money can be put to good use. And many will avoid making their scandals public.'

'And so bishops will cease attending in person the christenings and weddings of their illegitimate children, as they are all too inclined to do.'

Having said this, Bouville suddenly blushed. It was perhaps

not very tactful to talk of illegitimate children in the presence of the Cardinal du Pouget. He had been tactless, very tactless. But no one appeared to have noticed it. So Bouville hurried on: 'But, Holy Father, on what grounds is a more severe punishment decreed for priests whose concubines are not Christian?'

'The reason is a perfectly simple one, Messire Count,' replied Pope John. 'The decree is aimed at Spain where there are many Moors and where priests find it only too easy to acquire mistresses, for there is nothing to keep them from fornicating with the tonsured.'

He turned slightly in his great chair and his thin lips parted in a brief smile. He had quickly understood to what the other was leading up by turning the conversation to the Moors. And now he waited, at once mistrustful and amused, while Messire de Bouville drank a draught of wine to give himself courage and assumed an expression of unconcern before saying: 'It is clear, most Holy Father, that the Council made wise decisions which will be of the greatest use to us during the crusade. For we shall have many priests and chaplains in our armies when they advance into Moorish territory; it would be most unfortunate if they set an example of misconduct.'

Bouville breathed more easily, the word 'crusade' had been uttered.

Pope John screwed up his eyes and joined the tips of his fingers together.

'It would be equally unfortunate,' he replied calmly, 'if a similar licence should proliferate among the Christian nations while their armies are busy overseas. For it is a well-known fact, Messire Count, that when the armies are fighting in distant lands, and the most valiant combatants have been drained from the peoples, every sort of vice flourishes in the kingdoms as if, their strength being far away, the respect due to the laws of God had departed with it. Wars are always great occasions of sin. Is Monseigneur of Valois still as determined as ever on this crusade with which he wishes to honour our pontificate?'

'Well, most Holy Father, the emissaries from Lesser Armenia . . .'

'I know, I know,' said Pope John, tapping his little fingers together. 'It was I who sent the emissaries to Monseigneur of Valois.'

'We hear from all sources that the Moors on the coasts . . .'

'I know. I get the same reports as Monseigneur of Valois.'

All conversation had ceased at the great table. Bishop Pierre de Mortemart, who was accompanying Bouville on his mission, and who it was said would be made a cardinal at the next preferment, was listening, as were all the nephews and cousins, the prelates and dignitaries. The spoons scraped the plates as silently as if they were of velvet. The Pope's whisper, so singularly assured yet so lacking in tone, was difficult to catch, and one needed to be very accustomed to it to do so at any distance.

'Monseigneur of Valois, for whom I have a most paternal affection, has persuaded us to consent to the tithe; but until now this tithe has been used by him merely for the purposes of acquiring Aquitaine and supporting his candidature to the Holy Roman Empire. These are most noble enterprises, but they cannot be termed crusades. I am not at all sure that I shall consent to renew the tithe next year, and still less, Messire Count, that I shall agree to the supplementary subsidies that are being asked of me for the expedition.'

Bouville took the blow hard. If that was all he could report on his return to Paris, Charles of Valois would be very angry indeed.

'Most Holy Father,' he replied as coldly as he could, 'both the Count of Valois and King Charles imagined that you were sensible of the honour Christendom would derive . . .'

'The honour of Christendom, my dear son, consists in living at peace,' interrupted the Pope, lightly tapping Bouville's hand.

How the Holy Father had changed. In the old days he had always allowed people to finish their remarks, even if he had understood what they were driving at from the first word they uttered. Now he interrupted; he was too busy to wait for matters he already knew about to be explained to him. But Bouville, who had prepared his plan of attack, went on: 'Is it not our duty to bring the Infidel to the true Faith and to go to fight heresy among them?'

'Heresy? Heresy, Bouville?' replied Pope John in an indignant whisper. 'Let our first care be to extirpate the heresy flourishing among our own peoples and be less anxious to go and lance the abscess on the face of our neighbour when leprosy is corroding our own. Heresy is my business, and I think I understand well enough how to chastise it. My tribunals are functioning, and I need the help of all my priests, as indeed I do that of all the princes of Christendom, to track it down. If the chivalry of Europe takes the road to the Orient, the Devil will have a free hand in France, Spain and Italy!

For how long now have the Cathari, the Albigenses and the Spirituels been quiet? Why have I split up the big diocese of Toulouse, which was their haunt, and created sixteen new bishoprics in the Languedoc? And the *pastoureaux*, whose bands came even as far as this but a few years ago, were they not incited by heresy? Such ills cannot be extirpated in a single generation. You have to await the sons of the grandsons to have done with it.'

All the prelates present could bear witness to the severity with which John XXII persecuted heresy. If they were commanded to be easy on the minor sins of human nature, out of consideration for the finances, the faggots on the other hand flamed high when it was a question of spiritual error. Indeed, the whole of Christendom was repeating the words of the monk Bernard Délicieux, a Franciscan, who had attacked the Dominican Inquisition and had even had the audacity to come to preach in Avignon itself, which had earned him imprisonment for life. 'Even Saint Peter and Saint Paul themselves,' he had said, 'could not prove their innocence of heresy, if they returned to this world and were accused by the Inquisitors.'

But, at the same time, the Holy Father could not help advocating certain strange ideas, the offspring of his lively intelligence, which, emitted from the summit of the pontifical throne, created a considerable stir among the doctors of the theological faculties. He had, for instance, pronounced against the Immaculate Conception of the Virgin Mary, which was not of course a dogma, but of which the principle was generally admitted. The most he would concede was that the Lord had purified the Virgin before her birth, but at a moment which, so he declared, was difficult to determine precisely. On the other hand, he would admit of no doubt concerning her Assumption. Moreover, John XXII did not believe in the Beatific Vision, in any case until the day of the Last Judgment, and thereby denied there could, as yet, be a single soul in Paradise or, consequently, in Hell.

For many theologians such theses exhaled at least the ghost of an odour of sulphur. But, sitting at this very table, was a tall Cistercian named Jacques Fournier, the son of a baker of Foix, in Ariège, one-time Abbot of Fontfroide and Bishop of Pamiers, who was known as 'the White Cardinal' because of the colour of his habit, and who, singled out by the Pope to become his closest confidant, employed all the resources of his talent for apologetics to support and justify the Holy Father's more daring propositions.[24]

The Pope went on: 'Don't worry too much, Messire Count, about the heresy of the Moors. Protect our coasts against their ships by all means, but leave them to the Judgment of Almighty God, for, after all, they too are His creatures and, no doubt, He has some design concerning them. Can any of us know what fate is in store for souls that have never been touched by the Grace of the Revelation?'

'I presume they go to Hell,' said Bouville ingenuously.

'Hell, Hell,' the frail Pope whispered, shrugging his shoulders. 'Do not talk of things concerning which you know nothing. Moreover, don't tell me – for we're much too old friends, Bouville – that it is for the salvation of the Infidel Monseigneur of Valois is asking for twelve hundred thousand livres of subsidy from my treasury, of which three hundred thousand are for himself. In any case, I very well know that the Count of Valois no longer has any great enthusiasm for his crusade.'

'To be honest, Most Holy Father,' said Bouville, hesitating a little, 'without of course being as well informed as you are, it seems to me nevertheless that . . .'

'Oh, what a very unskilful ambassador,' thought Pope John. 'If I were in his place, I'd allow it to be believed that Valois had already assembled his banners, and I'd stand out for no less than three hundred thousand livres.'

When he had let Bouville flounder long enough, he said: 'Tell Monseigneur of Valois that the Holy Father renounces the crusade; and, knowing that Monseigneur is a most obedient son and a most excellent Christian, he will obey for the good of Holy Church herself.'

Bouville was very unhappy indeed. It was true that everyone was inclined to give up the crusade, but not quite like this, in a couple of words, without discussion.

'I have no doubt, Most Holy Father,' Bouville replied, 'that Monseigneur of Valois will obey you; but he has already personally assumed very great liabilities.'

'How much does Monseigneur of Valois require not to suffer too much from these liabilities he has assumed?'

'I do not know, Most Holy Father,' said Bouville, blushing pink. 'Monseigneur of Valois has given me no instruction in the matter.'

'Oh, yes, indeed I know him well enough to be sure he foresaw this. How much?'

'He has already advanced a great sum to the knights of his own fiefs so that they might equip their banners . . .'

'How much?'

'He has been experimenting with this new gunpowder artillery . . .'

'How much, Bouville?'

'He has signed very considerable orders for weapons of all kinds . . .'

'I'm no soldier, Messire, and I'm not asking you for the number of cross-bows. I merely want to know what figure Monseigneur of Valois requires as compensation.'

But he was amused to see Bouville in such difficulties. And Bouville himself could not help smiling to see all his stratagems pierced like a sieve. There was no doubt he would have to give the figure. Whispering as softly as the Pope himself, he murmured: 'One hundred thousand livres.'

John XXII shook his head and said: 'That is no more than Count Charles's customary and unreasonable demand. I seem to remember that, on a certain occasion, the Florentines had to pay him even more to free themselves of the help he had brought them. It cost the Sienese a little less to persuade him to consent to leave their city. And, on another occasion, the King of Anjou had to disgorge a very similar sum in gratitude for assistance for which he had never asked. It's a method of financing oneself as good as another, no doubt. Do you know, Bouville, your Valois is no more than a bandit. Very well, take him back the good news. We'll give him his hundred thousand livres, together with our apostolic blessing.'

On the whole, the Pope was glad to get out of it at the price. And Bouville was delighted that his mission was so suddenly accomplished. To have to bargain with the Sovereign Pontiff as if he were a Lombard merchant would have been really too painful. But the Holy Father made gestures of this kind, which were not perhaps precisely those of generosity, but rather a sound estimate of the price he must pay for power.

'Do you remember, Messire Count,' went on the Pope, 'the time you brought me five thousand livres from the Count of Valois to this very town, to assure the election of a French cardinal by the Conclave? Indeed, that was money invested at a high rate of interest!'

Bouville was always sentimental about the past. He remembered the misty field in the country to the north of Avignon, near Pontet, and the curious conversation they had had, sitting together on a low wall.

'Yes, I remember, Most Holy Father,' he said. 'Do you know that, when I saw you approaching, never having seen you before, I thought I had been deceived and that you were no cardinal, but merely a very young priest whom some prelate had disguised to send in his place?'

The compliment made Pope John smile. He, too, remembered well.

'And that young Italian,' he asked, 'that little Sienese, who worked in a bank and was with you at the time, the boy whom you later sent to me at Lyons, where he served me so well during the Conclave, young Guccio Baglioni, what's happened to him? I have always thought I'd see him again. He's the only one who ever did me a service in the past who has not come forward to ask me some favour or preferment.'

'I don't know, Most Holy Father, I really don't know. He went back to his native Italy. I have had no news of him, either.'

But Bouville looked a little flustered as he answered, and the Pope noticed it.

'If I remember correctly, there was some unfortunate business about a marriage, or a false marriage, with a daughter of the nobility, whom he had made a mother. Her brothers were persecuting him. Wasn't that it?'

Indeed, the Holy Father remembered it all very well. What a memory he had!

'I'm really very surprised,' went on Pope John, 'that being a protégé both of yours and mine, as well as being professionally engaged in finance, he has not profited by the circumstances to make his fortune. He begot child. Was it born? Did it live?'

'Yes, yes, it was born,' Bouville said hastily. 'It's living somewhere in the country with its mother.'

He was looking more and more embarrassed.

'Someone told me – now who was it?' went on the Pope, '– that the girl was wet-nurse to the little posthumous king born to Madame Clémence of Hungary during the regency of the Count of Poitiers. Is that right?'

'Yes, indeed, Most Holy Father, I believe that was the girl.'

The thousands of tiny wrinkles that furrowed the Pope's face seemed to quiver.

'What do you mean, you believe it? Were you not Curator of Madame Clémence's stomach? And beside her when she had the misfortune to lose her son? You really should know who the wet-nurse was?'

Bouville had turned purple. He should have been more careful and realized that, when the Holy Father mentioned the name of Guccio Baglioni, there was an underlying intention behind it, and a rather cleverer one than when he himself had mentioned the Council of Valladolid and the Moors of Spain in order to broach the question of the crusade. In the first place, the Holy Father must certainly have news of Guccio, since the Tolomei of Siena were one of his bankers.

The Pope's little grey eyes never left those of Bouville, and the questioning went on: 'Madame Mahaut of Artois was involved in a trial, was she not? And you must have been a witness? What was the real truth of that affair, my dear Messire Count?'

'Oh, nothing more than what the court brought to light, Most Holy Father. Mere spiteful gossip, of which Madame Mahaut wished to clear herself.'

The repast had come to an end and the noble pages, handing round the ewers and basins, were pouring water over the diners' fingers. Two noble knights came forward to pull the Pope's chair back.

'Messire Count,' he said, 'it has been a great joy to me to see you once more. I do not know, in view of my great age, whether this joy will be accorded me again . . .'

Bouville, who had risen to his feet, breathed more easily. The moment to say goodbye seemed to have arrived and there would be an end to the interrogation.

'But,' went on the Pope, 'before you leave, I would like to grant you the greatest favour that it lies in my power to give a Christian. I shall hear your confession myself. Come with me to my room.'

2

The Holy Father's Penance

'SINS OF THE FLESH? Naturally, since you're a man. Sins of gluttony? One has only to look at you; you're fat. Sins of pride? You're a great lord. But your very position obliges you to be attentive to your devotions; so you confess all these sins, which are the common basis of human nature, and are regularly absolved of them before you approach the Holy Table.'

It was a strange confession in which the Vicar of Christ both asked the questions and answered them. From time to time his whispering voice was drowned by the cries of birds, for the Pope kept a chained parrot in his room and there were parakeets, canaries, and those little red birds from the islands, called cardinals, fluttering about in an aviary.

The floor of the room was of painted squares on which had been laid Spanish rugs. The walls and the chairs were covered in green; the bed-hangings and the curtains at the windows were of green linen. And against this leafy, woodland colour, the birds showed up bright as flowers.[25] In a corner was a bathroom with a marble bath. Next door was the wardrobe, where huge cupboards contained white habits, red capes and embroidered robes, and beyond that again was the study.

As fat Bouville entered the room, he had made to kneel, but the Holy Father had put him into one of the green chairs near himself. Indeed, no penitent could have been treated with greater consideration. Philip the Fair's ex-Chamberlain was at once surprised and relieved for, great dignitary that he was, he had feared having to make a real confession, and to the Sovereign Pontiff, of all the dust, the dross, the mean desires and the nasty actions of a life, of all the dregs that fall to the bottom of the soul through the days and the years. But the Holy Father seemed to consider these kinds of sins to be trifles or, at least, to be within the competence of humbler priests than himself. But on leaving the table, Bouville had not noticed the glances exchanged between Cardinal Gaucelin Duèze, Cardinal du Pouget and Jacques Fournier, the 'White Cardinal'. They were well acquainted with this particular stratagem of Pope John, the post-prandial confession, which he used so as to be able to talk in real privacy to an important guest, and by which he gained knowledge of many state secrets. Who could resist this sudden offer, as flattering as it was terrifying? Everything – surprise, religious awe and the beginnings of the digestive process – was calculated to break down intellectual resistance.

'All that matters,' went on the Pope, 'is that a man should have behaved well in that particular station to which God has called him in this world, and it is in this matter that his sins are visited on him most severely. You, my son, have been chamberlain to a king and entrusted with most important missions under three others. Have you always been truly conscientious in the performance of your duties and responsibilities?'

'I think, Father, Most Holy Father I mean, that I have performed my tasks with zeal, and have been to the best of my ability a loyal servant to my suzerains . . .'

He broke off, realizing suddenly that he was hardly there to utter his own eulogy. Changing his tone, he went on: 'I must accuse myself of having failed in certain missions in which I might have succeeded. The fact is, Most Holy Father, I have not always been clever enough, and I have sometimes realized, only when it was too late, that I have made mistakes.'

'It is no sin to be a little slow-witted. It can happen to us all and, indeed, is the precise opposite of malice prepense. But have you committed on the occasion of your missions, or because of your missions, such grave sins as homicide, or bearing false witness?'

Bouville shook his head in denial.

But the little grey eyes, lacking both eyelashes and eyebrows, gazed luminously and fixedly at Bouville out of that wrinkled face.

'Are you quite certain? Here, my dear son, is the opportunity for the complete purification of your soul! You have never borne false witness – never?' asked the Pope.

Again Bouville felt ill at ease. What lay behind this persistence? The parrot uttered a raucous cry from its perch, and Bouville started.

'Indeed, Most Holy Father, there is one thing weighing on my mind, though I do not really know whether it is a sin, nor which sin's name to give it. I have not myself committed homicide, I swear it, but I was unable once to prevent it. And, afterwards, I was compelled to bear false witness; but I could not act otherwise.'

'Tell me about it, Bouville,' said the Pope.

But it was now the Pope's turn to adopt a more suitable tone: 'Confess to me this secret that weighs on you so much, my dear son.'

'It certainly does weigh on me,' Bouville said, 'and even more so since the death of my dear wife Marguerite, with whom I shared it. I often think that, should I die, without having entrusted it to anyone . . .'

Tears suddenly sprang to his eyes.

'Why have I never thought of confiding it to you before, Most Holy Father? As I was saying, I am often slow-witted. It was after the death of King Louis X, the eldest son of my master, Philip the Fair . . .'

Bouville glanced at the Pope and already felt comforted. At last he was going to be able to discharge his conscience of the burden it had borne for eight years. It had undoubtedly been the worst moment of his life and remorse still lay heavily on his mind. Of course, he must confess the whole thing to the Pope!

And now Bouville began to talk more easily. He recounted how, having been appointed the Curator of Queen Clémence's stomach after the death of her husband, Louis Hutin, he had feared that the Countess Mahaut of Artois would make an attempt on the lives both of the Queen and the child she was carrying. It was at the time when Monseigneur Philippe of Poitiers, the late King's brother, was manoeuvring for the Regency against the Count of Valois and the Duke of Burgundy.

At the recollection, John XXII raised his eyes to the painted beams of the ceiling, and his thin face looked thoughtful for a moment. For it was he himself who had announced the death of his brother to Philippe of Poitiers, having learned it from the young Lombard, Baglioni. Oh, the Count of Poitiers had managed things very well, both with regard to the Conclave and the Regency! It had all been arranged that June morning in 1316, at Lyons, in the house of Consul Varay.

So Bouville had feared that the Countess of Artois would commit a crime, another crime, since it was common gossip that she had murdered Louis Hutin by poison. And she had had every reason to hate him, moreover, for he had just confiscated her county. But she had also had very good reason, after his death, to wish for the success of the Count of Poitiers, for she was his mother-in-law. If he became King, she was certain of holding her possessions. The one obstacle in her way was the child the Queen was carrying. The child who was born and was a male.

'Unhappy Queen Clémence,' said the Pope.

Mahaut of Artois had arranged to be appointed godmother. In this capacity it was her duty to carry the new little King to the ceremony of presentation to the barons. Bouville had been certain, as had Madame de Bouville, that if the terrible Mahaut intended committing a crime, she would do so without hesitation during the ceremony, for it was the only occasion she would have of carrying the child in her arms. Bouville and his wife had therefore decided to hide the royal infant during those hours, and to substitute for him the wet-nurse's son, who was but a few days older. Under the state swaddling clothes, no one would notice the substitution, for no one had as yet seen Queen Clémence's child, not even herself, for she was suffering from a serious fever and almost at the point of death.

'And indeed,' said Bouville, 'Countess Mahaut smeared poison over the child's mouth and nose after I had handed him to her, and he died in convulsions in the presence of the barons. It was this innocent little creature I delivered over to death. And the crime was accomplished so smoothly and so quickly, and I was so perturbed, that it never occurred to me to cry out at once, and in public: "This is a lie!" And then it was too late. How could I explain?'

The Pope was leaning forward a little, his hands clasped over his robe, losing not a word of the story.

'What happened to the other child, the little King, Bouville? What did you do with him?'

'He is alive, Most Holy Father, he is alive! My late wife and I confided him to the wet-nurse. And, indeed, we had considerable difficulty. The unfortunate woman hated us both, as you can well imagine, and was groaning in her anguish. With mingled threats and appeals we made her swear on the Gospel to look after the little King as if he were her own child, and never to reveal what had happened to anyone at all, even in the confessional.'

'Oh, oh,' murmured the Holy Father.

'And so little King John, the real King of France, is being brought up in a manor in the Île-de-France, without his or anyone else's knowing who he really is, apart from the woman who passes for his mother and myself.'

'And who is this woman?'

'She is Marie de Cressay, the woman the young Lombard, Guccio Baglioni, was in love with.'

Everything was now clear to the Holy Father.

'And does Baglioni know nothing about it?'

'Nothing, I'm sure of it, Most Holy Father. For the Cressay woman refused ever to see him again, as we had ordered her, so as to keep her oath. Besides, it all happened very quickly, and the boy set out at once for Italy. He thinks his son is still alive. He gets news of him from time to time through his uncle, the banker Tolomei.'

'But why, Bouville, since you had proof of the crime, and it should have been easy enough to bring it home to her, did you not denounce the Countess Mahaut? When I think,' added Pope John, 'that she was sending her chancellor to me, at that very time, to try to persuade me to support her cause against her nephew Robert . . .'

It suddenly occurred to the Pope that Robert of Artois, the rowdy giant, the sower of discord, the assassin even – for it seemed more than likely he had had a hand in the murder of Marguerite of Burgundy at Château Gaillard – Robert of Artois, the great baron of France, the black sheep, was nevertheless more worthy perhaps, when all was said and done, than his cruel aunt, and that he possibly had some right on his side in his fight against her. What a world of wolves these sovereign courts were. It was the same in every kingdom. And was it to govern, to pacify and to direct this sort of flock that God had inspired him, a poor little burgess of Cahors, with the great ambition of attaining to the tiara which, indeed, he now wore and sometimes felt to be a trifle heavy?

'I kept silent, Most Holy Father,' Bouville went on, 'largely on the advice of my late wife. As I had let the opportune moment of confounding the murderess go by, my late wife pointed out with some truth that, if we revealed what had happened, Mahaut would turn furiously on the little King and on us too. Therefore, if we wanted to save him, and ourselves as well, we had to let her believe her crime had been successful. I therefore took the wet-nurse's child to the Abbey of Saint-Denis that he might be buried among the kings.'

The Pope was thinking.

'Therefore, the accusations made against Madame Mahaut in the lawsuit that took place the next year were well-founded?' he asked.

'Indeed they were, Most Holy Father, indeed they were. Monseigneur Robert was able, through his cousin, Messire Jean de Fiennes, to lay his hands on a poisoner, a sorceress, named Isabelle de Férienne, who had given to a lady-in-waiting of Countess Mahaut the poison she used to kill first King Louis, then the child who was presented to the barons. This Isabelle de Férienne, together with her son Jean, was brought to Paris to give evidence against Mahaut, You can imagine how this suited Monseigneur Robert's book! Their depositions were taken, and it clearly appeared that they had supplied the Countess, for they had previously given her the philtre by which she boasted of having reconciled her daughter Jeanne to her son-in-law, the Count of Poitiers.'

'Magic and sorcery! You could have had the Countess burnt,' whispered the Pope.

'But not at that time, Most Holy Father, not at that time. For the Count of Poitiers had become King and was giving

Madame Mahaut such protection that, in my heart of hearts, I am sure he had been her accomplice, at least in the second crime.'

The Pope's narrow face seemed to crumple even more beneath his furred skull-cap. These last words had pained him. For he had been fond of King Philippe V, to whom he owed his tiara, and with whom he had always been in perfect accord over all state matters.

'But God's punishment fell on them both,' Bouville went on, 'for within a year they had both lost their sole male heir. The Countess's only son died at the age of seventeen. And young King Philippe lost his at only a few months old, and he never had another. But the Countess put up a clever defence against the accusations brought against her. She pleaded the irregularity of the procedure before Parliament; and the disqualification of her accusers, for, she maintained, her rank as a peer of France rendered her liable to be tried only by the Chamber of Barons. However, to establish her innocence, so she said, she besought her son-in-law – it was a fine scene of public hypocrisy – to have the inquiry continued so as to give her the opportunity of confounding her enemies. The Férienne sorceress and her son were heard again, but after being put to the question. They were in no very good state, and were covered in blood. They retracted completely, declared that their earlier accusations were lies and maintained that they had been persuaded to bring them by favours, prayers, promises and also by violence to their persons, instigated, according to the records of the Clerk of the Court, by a person whose name should not at present be mentioned; which was equivalent to naming Monseigneur Robert of

Artois. Then King Philippe the Long sat in the seat of justice himself and made all his family and relations and all the intimates of his late brother appear before him: the Count of Valois, the Count of Évreux, Monseigneur of Bourbon, Monseigneur Gaucher, the Constable, Monseigneur de Beaumont, the Master of the Household, and Queen Clémence herself, asking them on their oath whether they knew or believed that King Louis and his son, Jean, had died any but a natural death. Since no proof could be produced, the hearing was being held in public, and the Countess Mahaut was sitting beside the King, everyone declared, though in many cases against their private convictions, that these deaths had been due to natural causes.'

'But, no doubt, you were summoned to appear yourself?'

Fat Bouville hung his head.

'I bore false witness, Most Holy Father,' he said. 'But what else could I do when the whole Court, the peers, the King's uncles, the privy servants, and the widowed Queen herself all certified Madame Mahaut's innocence on oath? I should then have been accused of lying and perjury; and I should have been sent to swing at Montfaucon.'

He seemed so unhappy, so cast down, so sad, that one could suddenly see in that plump and fleshy face the features of the little boy he had been half a century before. The Pope was moved to compassion.

'Calm yourself, Bouville,' he said, leaning towards him and putting his hand on his shoulder. 'And don't reproach yourself with having done wrong. God set you a problem that was a little heavy for you. I will take your secret on myself. Only the future can tell whether you did the right thing. You wanted to save a life that had been confided to you as part of the responsibilities of your position, and you saved it. You might have endangered many other lives had you spoken.'

'Oh, Most Holy Father, indeed I feel much calmer now,' said the ex-Chamberlain. 'But what will happen to the little hidden King? What should be done about him?'

'Wait and do nothing. I'll think about it and let you know. Go in peace, Bouville. As for Monseigneur of Valois, he can have his hundred thousand livres, but not a florin more. And let him stop bothering me about his crusade, and come to an agreement with England.'

Bouville knelt, raised the Pope's hand effusively to his lips, got to his feet, and backed towards the door, since it appeared the audience was over.

The Pope recalled him with a gesture.

'Bouville, what about your absolution? Don't you want it?'

A moment later Pope John was alone and walking up and down his study with little tripping steps. The wind from the Rhône was blowing under the doors and wailing through the fine new palace. The parakeets were chirping in the aviary. The embers in the brazier in the corner of the room had turned dull. John XXII was confronted with one of the most difficult problems he had known since his election. The real King of France was an unknown child, hidden away in the courtyard of a manor. Only two people in the world, or three now, knew of it. Fear prevented the two first from talking. And now that he himself knew, what was he to do about it, when two kings had already succeeded to the throne of France, two kings duly crowned and anointed with the holy oil, thought they were in fact nothing but usurpers? Oh, yes indeed, it was a grave matter, nearly as grave as the excommunication of the Emperor of Germany. What should he do? Reveal the whole affair? It would throw France and, in her wake, a great part of Europe into the most appalling dynastic turmoil. Once again, here were the seeds of war.

There was also another consideration that decided him to keep silent, and it had to do with the memory of King Philippe the Long. Yes, John XXII had been very fond of that young man, and had helped him as much as he could. Indeed, he had been the only sovereign he had ever admired or to whom he was grateful. To tarnish his memory was to tarnish John XXII at the same time; for, without Philippe the Long, would he ever have become Pope? And now dear Philippe was revealed to have been a criminal, or at least the accomplice of a criminal. But was it for Pope John, for Jacques Duèze, to throw the first stone? Did he not owe both his hat and his tiara to the grossest frauds? And suppose, to assure his election, he had had to allow a murder to be committed?

'Lord, Lord, I thank Thee for having spared me that temptation. But am I worthy of being charged with the care of Thy creatures? And suppose the wet-nurse talked one day, what would happen then? Could one ever trust a woman's tongue? Lord, it would be merciful, if Thou wouldst sometimes enlighten me! I have given Bouville absolution, but the penance is for me.'

He collapsed on to the green cushion of his prie-dieu and remained there a long time, his face hidden in his hands.

3

The Road to Paris

HOW THE FRENCH ROADS rang out clear beneath the horses' hooves! What happy music the crunching gravel made! And the air she was breathing, the soft, sunlit morning air, how wonderfully scented it was, what a marvellous savour it had! The buds were beginning to open, and little, tender, green, crinkled leaves stretched out across the road to caress the travellers' brows. No doubt the grass of the banks and fields of the Île-de-France was not so thick or rich as English grass, but for Queen Isabella it was the grass of freedom and, indeed, of hope.

Her white mare's mane swung to the rhythm of its paces. A litter, carried by two mules, was following a few yards behind. But the Queen was too happy and too impatient to tolerate being enclosed in such a conveyance. She preferred to ride her hack and to set a faster pace; she would have liked to jump the hedge and gallop away across the grass.

Boulogne, where she had been married fifteen years earlier

in the Church of Notre-Dame, Montreuil, Abbeville and Beauvais had formed the stages of her journey. She had spent the preceding night at Maubuisson, near Pontoise, in the royal manor where she had seen her father, Philip the Fair, for the last time. Her journey had been almost a pilgrimage through the past. It was as if she were journeying back through the stages of her life, as if fifteen years were being abolished, so that she could make a new start.

'Your brother Charles would no doubt have taken her back,' Robert of Artois was saying, as he rode beside Isabella. 'And he would have imposed her on us as Queen, so much did he regret her and so little could he make up his mind to find a new wife.'

Of whom was Robert talking? Oh yes, of Blanche of Burgundy. Her memory had been evoked by Maubuisson where, a little while ago, a cavalcade consisting of Henri de Sully, Jean de Roye, the Earl of Kent, Roger Mortimer and Robert of Artois himself, together with a whole company of lords, had come to greet the traveller. Isabella had felt considerable pleasure at being treated like a Queen again.

'I really believe Charles derived a secret pleasure from contemplating the horns of cuckoldom she had set on his brow,' Robert went on. 'Unfortunately, or rather fortunately, the sweet Blanche, a year before Charles became King, got herself pregnant in prison by her gaoler. Those daughters of Mahaut are such damned hot pieces they'd set a bundle of tow on fire at five yards.'

The giant was riding on the Queen's left, on the sunny side, and was mounted on a huge, dappled percheron; he cast his shadow over the Queen. She was urging her hack forward, trying to keep in the sun. Robert talked and talked, delighted to have met her again, giving rein to his naturally trivial nature, and trying at the same time, during these first leagues, to renew the links of cousinship and old friendship. Isabella had not seen him for eleven years; she found him less changed than she had expected. His voice was still the same, and so was that odour of a great eater of venison which his body emitted in the heat of the march and the breeze blew in gusts about him. His hands were red and hairy to the nails, his expression malicious even when he tried to make it amiable, and his paunch bulged over his belt as if he had swallowed a bell. But the assurance of his speech and gestures was less feigned than it had been, for it had now become part of his nature; the lines that framed his mouth were cut deeper in the fat.

'And Mahaut, my bitch of an aunt, has had to resign herself to the annulment of her daughter's marriage. Oh, not without a struggle and bearing false witness before the bishops! But she was finally confounded. For once, Cousin Charles was obstinate. Because of the business with the gaoler and the pregnancy. And once that weak-kneed creature sticks his toes in about something, you can't move him. There were any number of questions asked during the annulment case. They even salvaged from its dust the dispensation, granted by Clement V, allowing Charles to marry a relation but without specifying a name. But what member of our families ever married anyone but a cousin or a niece? So then, Monseigneur Jean de Marigny most cleverly turned to the question of a spiritual relationship. Was not Mahaut Charles's godmother? Of course, she denied it and said she had attended the baptism only as an assistant and unofficial godmother.[26] Then everyone, barons, stewards, valets, priests, choristers and townsmen of Creil, where the baptism took place, gave evidence that she had held the child to hand it to Charles of Valois, and that no mistake was possible in view of the fact that she was the tallest woman in the chapel, indeed taller by a head than anyone else. What a liar she is!'

Isabella compelled herself to listen, but her attention was really focused on herself and on a curious contact which, a little while before, had moved her. How surprising a man's hair felt when it was suddenly brought in touch with your fingers.

The Queen glanced up at Roger Mortimer, who had placed himself on her right with a sort of natural authority, as if he were her protector and guardian. She looked at the thick curls emerging from under his black hat. You would never have thought his hair could be so silky to the touch.

It had happened by chance at the very first moment of their meeting. Isabella had been surprised to see Mortimer appear beside the Earl of Kent. So in France the rebel, fugitive and outlaw – for Edward had, of course, deprived him of all his rights, titles and property – rode beside the King of England's brother and seemed even to take precedence over him. The members of the English escort had looked at each other in astonishment.

And Mortimer had jumped from his horse and hurried over to the Queen to kiss the hem of her dress; but the hack had moved and Roger's lips had lightly touched Isabella's knee, while she had mechanically put out her hand and rested it on the bare head of the friend she had regained. And now, as they rode along the road, its surface striped with the shadows of the branches overhead, the silky contact of his hair was still with her, as perceptible as if it were enclosed within her velvet glove.

'But the most serious grounds for pronouncing the marriage annulled, besides the fact that the contracting parties were not of canon age for copulating, nor indeed physically capable of doing so, were discovered in the fact that your brother Charles, when he was married, lacked the discernment to select a wife suited to his rank, or the ability to express a preference, in view of the fact that he was incapable, simple and imbecile, and that the contract was consequently invalid. *Inhabilis, simplex et imbecillus!* And everyone, from your uncle Valois to the last chambermaid, were at one in agreeing that he was all that, and the best proof of it was that the late Queen his mother had herself thought him so stupid that she had nicknamed him "the Goose"! Forgive me, Cousin, for talking of your brother like this, but after all he's the King we've got over us. A pleasant companion however in other respects, and with a handsome face, but with not much spirit about him. You'll realize that one has to govern in his stead and that you mustn't expect too much of him.'

From Isabella's left came Robert of Artois's inexhaustible voice and his wild-beast odour. From her right Isabella felt Roger Mortimer's eyes resting on her with a disturbing persistence. From time to time she looked up at his flint-coloured eyes, his clean-cut features and the deep cleft in his chin, at his tall, shapely figure sitting so erect in the saddle. She was surprised she had no memory of the white scar marking his lower lip.

'Are you still as chaste as ever, my fair Cousin?' Robert of Artois suddenly asked her.

Queen Isabella blushed and raised her eyes furtively to Roger Mortimer, as if the question had already made her, in some inexplicable way, feel a little guilty towards him.

'Indeed, I've been forced to be,' she replied.

'Do you remember our interview in London, Cousin?'

She blushed deeper still. Of what was he reminding her, and what would Mortimer think? It had been nothing but a moment of forlornness when saying goodbye; there had not even been so much as a kiss; she had merely leaned her forehead against a man's chest in search of refuge. Did Robert still remember it after eleven years? She felt flattered, but not in the least moved. Had he mistaken what had been but a moment of dismay for an avowal of love? Yet, perhaps, on that day, but on that day only, had she not been Queen, and had he not been in such a hurry to leave in order to denounce the Burgundy girls . . .

'Well, if you do take it into your head to change your habits . . .' said Robert gallantly. 'Whenever I think of you, I always have the feeling of a debt I've never collected . . .'

He broke off suddenly, having met Mortimer's eyes and seen in them the glance of a man ready to draw his sword if he heard another word. The Queen saw the challenge and, to keep herself in countenance, stroked the white mane of her mare. Dear Mortimer, how noble and chivalrous he was! And how good it was to breathe the air of France, and how pretty the road was, with its alternating sunlight and shade!

There was an ironical half-smile on Robert of Artois's fat cheeks. As for the debt – he had thought the expression delicate enough – he must think no more of it. He felt sure that Mortimer loved Queen Isabella and that Isabella loved Mortimer.

Other people are generally aware of our love before we realize it ourselves.

'Ah, well,' he thought, 'my good cousin will amuse herself with this Knight Templar.'

4
King Charles

IT HAD TAKEN ABOUT a quarter of an hour to cross the town from the gates to the Palace of the Cité. There were tears in Queen Isabella's eyes when she set foot in the courtyard of that palace she had seen her father build, and which had already begun to acquire something of the patina of time. The black stains on the stone where the gutters emptied had not been there when Isabella had set out from this very place to become Queen.

The doors were thrown open at the top of the grand staircase, and Isabella could not help expecting to see the imposing, icy, sovereign features of King Philip the Fair. How often in the past she had gazed at her father standing at the top of these very stairs preparing to go down into his city.

The young man who now appeared, wearing a short tunic, his well-turned legs in neat white hose, followed by his chamberlains, much resembled the great dead monarch in figure and feature, but his person radiated neither strength nor majesty. He was but a pale copy, a plaster cast taken from an effigy. And yet, because the shade of the Iron King stood behind this spiritless personage, because the Crown of France was incarnate in him, as well as the headship of the family, Isabella tried three or four times to kneel to him; and each time her brother took her by the hand, raised her, and said: 'Welcome, sweet sister, welcome.'

Having forced her to rise, and still holding her by the hand, he led her through the galleries to the large private apartment, where he normally sat, asking the Queen for news of her journey: had she been properly received at Boulogne by the Captain of the town?

He sent to make sure that the chamberlains were attending to the luggage, warning them not to drop the chests.

'Because the cloth crumples,' he explained, 'and I noticed on my last journey to Languedoc, what a state my robes got into.'

Was he trying to hide his emotion or his embarrassment by fussing over such things?

When they had sat down, Charles the Fair said: 'Well, and how are things with you, my dear sister?'

'Poorly, Brother,' she replied.

'And what is the reason for your journey?'

Isabella could not help looking painfully surprised. Did her brother really not know what was going on? Robert of Artois, who had entered the Palace with the leaders of the escort, making his spurs ring on the flagstones as if he were at home, gave Isabella a look which implied: 'What did I tell you?'

'Brother, I have come to negotiate a treaty with you, which

must be ratified if our two kingdoms are to stop harming one another.'

Charles the Fair looked thoughtful for a moment, as if he were taking time to reflect. In fact, he was thinking of nothing in particular. As during the audiences he had granted Mortimer, or indeed anyone else for that matter, he asked questions and paid no attention to the answers.

'The treaty,' he said at last; 'yes, I'm prepared to receive homage from your husband, Edward. You'll discuss it with our Uncle Charles, to whom I've given authority to deal with the matter. Were you seasick? Do you know, I've never been on the sea? It has always seemed to me a most impressive expanse of water.'

They had to wait till he had uttered a few more trivialities of this order before they could present the Bishop of Norwich, who was to conduct the negotiations, and Lord de Cromwell, who commanded the English escort. He greeted them with courtesy but clearly would never remember who they were.

Charles IV was doubtless little stupider than thousands of men of his age in the kingdom, who harrowed their fields the wrong way, broke the shuttles of their looms, or perpetrated errors in their accounts when selling wax and tallow. What was so unfortunate was that he was the King and had so very few of the right qualities.

'I have also come, Brother,' said Isabella, 'to request your help and to place myself under your protection, for all my possessions have been taken from me, even the county of Cornwall, which was settled on me by England in my marriage contract.'

'You will explain your grievances to our Uncle Charles; he

is a wise counsellor, and I shall approve anything he decides for your advantage, Sister. I will take you to your rooms.'

Charles IV left the assembly to show his sister the apartments that had been set aside for her: a suite of five rooms with a private staircase.

'For the ordinary comings and goings of your household,' he thought it proper to explain.

He drew her attention to the fact that the furniture had been refurbished, that he had placed various objects in the rooms that had belonged to their parents, in particular a reliquary which their mother, Queen Jeanne of Navarre, had always kept by her bed; it contained a tooth of Saint Louis in a sort of miniature cathedral of silver-gilt. The figured tapestries with which the walls were hung were new, and he drew her attention to them. He showed all the cares of a good housewife; he fingered the material of the counterpane and besought his sister not to hesitate to ask for all the embers she might need to warm her bed. No one could have been more attentive or more affable.

'As for the lodgings of your suite, Messire de Mortimer will arrange matters with my chamberlains. I want everyone to be comfortable.'

He had uttered Mortimer's name without any particular intention, merely because, when English affairs were in question, his name was frequently mentioned to him. It seemed to him, therefore, quite natural that Mortimer should be in charge of the Queen of England's household. He had quite clearly forgotten that the King of England was asking for his head.

He went on with his tour of the apartments, straightening

the fold of a hanging here, checking the inside fastening of a shutter there. And then, suddenly coming to a halt, he leaned forward, clasped his hands behind his back, and said: 'We have not been very happy in our marriages, Sister. I had hoped to be better served by God in the person of my dear Marie of Luxemburg than I was with Blanche . . .'

From the brief glance he gave her, Isabella realized he still felt a vague resentment at the part she had played in bringing to light the misconduct of his first wife.

'And then death took Marie from me, together with the heir to the throne she was about to bring into the world. After that, they made me marry our cousin of Évreux whom you will see presently; she is an amiable wife who loves me well, I think. But we were married in July last; and now we're in March, and she shows no sign of being pregnant. I must talk to you of matters which one can only mention to a sister. Even with that wicked husband of yours, who has no liking for your sex, you have nevertheless had four children. Whereas, I with my three wives . . . And yet, I assure you, I perform my conjugal duties most frequently, and take pleasure in them. What then, Sister? Do you believe in this curse my people say hangs over our race and our house?'

Isabella looked sadly at him. He had suddenly become rather touching as he voiced the troubles that weighed on his mind and were no doubt his constant anxiety. But the most humble gardener would not have expressed himself differently when complaining of his misfortunes or the barrenness of his wife. What did this poor King want? An heir to his throne or a child in his house?

And, similarly, what was there royal about Jeanne of

Évreux, who came to greet Isabella a few moments later? Her face was rather weak and her expression docile; it was clear that she was humbly aware of her status as third wife; that she had been selected from among the nearest relations merely because France needed a Queen and the courts of Europe seemed reluctant to provide one. She was sad. She constantly watched her husband's face for signs of that obsession she knew so well, which no doubt was the sole subject of their nocturnal conversations.

Isabella found the real King in Charles of Valois. He hurried to the Palace as soon as he heard that his niece had arrived, clasped her in his arms and kissed her on both cheeks. Isabella realized at once that it was in those arms the real power resided, and nowhere else.

Supper did not last long. Gathered about the sovereigns were the Counts of Valois, Artois and their wives, the Earl of Kent, the Bishop of Norwich, and Roger Mortimer. King Charles the Fair liked to go to bed early.

The English all met afterwards to confer in Queen Isabella's apartment. When they eventually left, Mortimer was the last at the door. Isabella detained him. For merely a moment, so she said. She had a message to give him.

5

The Cross of Blood

THEY WERE UNCONSCIOUS of the passing of time. The liqueur wine, scented with rosemary, roses and pomegranate, had sunk more than halfway down the crystal flask; the fire had burnt low in the hearth.

They had not even heard the cries of the night-watchman which arose hour by hour in the distance throughout the night. They could not stop talking, particularly the Queen who, for the first time in many years, had no need to fear that a spy was concealed behind the arras to report every word she uttered. She could not have said whether she had ever confided so freely in anyone before; she had forgotten even the memory of freedom. And she could not remember ever having talked to a man who listened with so much interest, replied so intelligently, and gave her such generous attention. They had days and days before them in which to talk, and yet they could not make up their minds to stop and part till tomorrow. Theirs was an orgy of confidences. They had so much to discuss: the state of the kingdoms, the treaty of peace, the Pope's letters, their common enemies, and Mortimer recounted his imprisonment, escape and exile, and the Queen told him of her harassments, and of the latest outrages the Despensers had inflicted on her.

Isabella intended remaining in France till Edward came in person to render homage. This was the advice Orleton had given her at a secret interview between London and Dover.

'You cannot return to England, Madame, before the Despensers have been driven out,' Mortimer said. 'You cannot and you must not.'

'Their object in persecuting me so cruelly these last months is perfectly clear. They were trying to provoke me to some foolish act of rebellion so that they might accuse me of high treason and shut me up in some convent or remote castle as they have your wife.'

'Poor dear Jeanne,' said Mortimer; 'she has suffered much on my account.'

And he went over to put a log on the fire.

She has been such a great help to me,' Isabella went on. 'And it was she who taught me to know what kind of man you are. On many a night I made her sleep beside me for I was so afraid they would assassinate me. And she talked to me of you, always of you. I know you better than you realize, my lord.'

For a moment it seemed as if they were both waiting for something, and they were a little embarrassed too. Mortimer was leaning towards the fire and its glow illuminated his deeply cleft chin and thick eyebrows.

'Had it not been for this war in Aquitaine,' continued the Queen, 'and the letters from the Pope, and this mission to my brother, I am sure something terrible would have happened to me.'

'I knew it was the only way, Madame. Believe me, I had no liking for a war against the kingdom. If I consented to take part in running it and appear as a traitor – for to rebel to defend one's rights is one thing, but to go over to the enemy's camp is another –'

He had the campaign in Aquitaine very much on his mind and wanted to exonerate himself.

'It – it was because I knew there was no hope of saving you except by weakening King Edward. And it was I who conceived the idea of your mission to France, Madame. I worked for it unceasingly till it was finally agreed and you were here.'

There was a deep vibrant note in Mortimer's voice. Isabella half-closed her eyes. She mechanically pushed back one of the blonde tresses that framed her face like the handles of an amphora.

'What's that scar on your lip? I never noticed it before,' she said.

'A present from your husband, Madame, a mark he left on me so that I should never forget him, when the men of his party threw me down in my armour at Shrewsbury where I was unlucky. And unlucky, Madame, less because I lost the battle, risked death and endured prison, than because I failed in my dream of coming to you that evening, carrying the heads of the Despensers, to do homage for the battle I had fought for your sake.'

This was not the whole truth; the safeguarding of his estates and prerogatives had weighed at least as heavily in the military decisions taken by the Baron of the Marches as had the service of the Queen. But, at this moment, he was sincerely persuaded he had acted only on her behalf. And Isabella believed it too; she had so much wanted to believe it. She had so longed for the day when her cause would have a champion. And now here was that champion, sitting beside her, with his long and slender hand that had held the sword, and on his face the slight but indelible mark of a wound incurred for her. In his black clothes, he seemed to her to have come straight out of some romance of chivalry.

'Do you remember, friend Mortimer . . .'

She had dropped the 'my lord' and Mortimer felt greater joy at it than if he had been victorious at Shrewsbury.

'. . . do you remember the lay of the Knight of Graëlent?'

He knitted his thick brows. Graëlent? It was a name he had heard; but he could not remember the story.

'It's in a book by Marie of France, which was stolen from me, like everything else,' Isabella went on. 'Graëlent was so strong and so splendidly loyal a knight, and his renown so great, that the Queen at that time fell in love with him without knowing him; and having sent for him, the first words she said to him when he appeared before her were: "Friend Graëlent, I have never loved my husband, but I love you as much as it is possible to love, and I am yours."'

She was astonished at her own audacity, and that her memory should furnish her with words so exactly appropriate to her own feelings. For some seconds the sound of her own voice seemed to be echoing in her ears. She waited, anxious, troubled, embarrassed and ardent, for this new Graëlent's reply.

'Can I now tell her I love her?' Roger Mortimer wondered, as if there were anything else to say. But there are lists in which the bravest of warriors prove themselves singularly clumsy.

'Have you ever loved King Edward?' he asked.

And they both felt equally disappointed, as if they had missed an irretrievable opportunity. Was it really necessary to mention Edward at this moment? The Queen sat up a little in her chair.

'I thought I loved him,' she said. 'I forced myself to it like a girl going to her wedding with all the proper emotions; but I soon realized what sort of a man I had been married to. And now I hate him, and with so strong a hatred that it can die only with me, or with him. Do you know that for long years I thought my body could inspire nothing but repulsion, and that Edward's disgust for me was due to some physical fault of mine? And do you know I even still sometimes think so? Do you know, friend Mortimer, since I am admitting everything to you – besides, your wife knows it all – that in fifteen years Edward has entered my bed no more than twenty times, and then only on days appointed both by his astrologer and my physician? On the last occasion we had relations, when my youngest daughter was conceived, he insisted that Hugh the Younger should accompany him to my bed, and he fondled and caressed him before he was able to accomplish his conjugal act, telling me that I should love Hugh like himself, since they were so united that they were but one. It was then I threatened to write to the Pope.'

Mortimer turned scarlet with anger. Honour and love were both equally offended. Edward was utterly unworthy to be king. When would they be able to cry to all his vassals: 'See who is your suzerain and before whom you have knelt and paid homage! Take back your sworn allegiance!' And when there were so many unfaithful wives in the world, why should that man have a wife of such extraordinary virtue that she had respected his honour in spite of everything? Would he not have deserved it if she had dishonoured him with everyone who came along? But had she been completely faithful? Had no secret love lightened that desperate loneliness?

'And have you never sought the arms of another?' he asked in a voice of sombre jealousy, in that tone of voice which, so touching and moving at the awakening of love, becomes so wearying at the end of a love affair.

'Never,' she said.

'Not even with your cousin, the Count of Artois, who seemed this morning to be showing you with considerable frankness that he was attracted to you?'

She shrugged her shoulders.

'You know my cousin Robert; all's one that comes to his net. Queen or whore, it's all the same to him. One day long ago, at Westminster, I told him of my loneliness and, as we stood in a window embrasure, he offered to console me. That was all. Besides, didn't you hear him say: "Are you still as chaste as ever, my fair Cousin?" No, dear Mortimer, my heart is desolate and free, and very weary of being so.'

'Oh, Madame, it is so long now that I have not dared tell you that you were the only woman in my thoughts!' cried Mortimer.

'Is that true, sweet friend? Is it so long?'

'I think, Madame, that it dates from the very first time I saw you. But I believe I realized it only one day at Windsor when tears came to your eyes for some shame King Edward had put on you. But you were distant; not so much because of your crown, but because you were protected by that aloofness of demeanour you have always maintained. And then Lady Jeanne was with you, always talking to you, but an obstacle to my approaching you. Shall I tell you that when I was in prison there was no morning or evening I did not think of you, and that the first question I asked when I escaped from the Tower . . .'

'I know, friend Roger, I know; Bishop Orleton told me. And it made me happy to think I had given money from my privy purse to help you towards freedom; not because of the gold, which was nothing, but because of the risk which was great. Your escape increased my troubles . . .'

He bowed very low, knelt almost, to show his gratitude.

'Do you know, Madame,' he said, his voice graver yet, 'that when I set foot in France, I made a vow to wear nothing but black till I could return to England, and to touch no woman till I had freed you and seen you again?'

He was slightly altering the original terms of his vow and confusing, in the service of his love, the Queen and the kingdom. But in Isabella's eyes he was but the more like Graëlent, Perceval and Lancelot.

'And have you kept your vow?' she asked.

'Can you doubt it?'

She thanked him with a smile, with tears swimming in her great blue eyes, and with an outstretched hand, a fragile hand that sought refuge like a bird in the tall baron's. Their fingers opened, crossed, interlaced.

'Clasp them,' Isabella murmured. 'Clasp them hard, my friend. For me, too, it has been a long time.'

She fell silent a moment and then went on: 'Do you think we would be right? I have plighted my troth to my husband, wicked though he is. And you, for your part, have a wife who is without reproach. We have contracted alliances before God. And I have been so hard on the sins of others.'

Was she seeking protection against herself, or did she wish him to take the sin on himself?

He got to his feet.

'Neither you nor I, my Queen, were married of our own free choice. We have uttered vows, but not towards people we chose for ourselves. We obeyed decisions made by our families, not the wishes of our own hearts. To people like us, made for each other as we are . . .'

He fell silent. A love that fears to declare itself can lead to strange actions indeed; and desire can take the most circuitous ways to assert its rights. Mortimer was standing in front of Isabella, though their hands were still clasped in each other's.

'Shall we make a vow of blood-brotherhood, my Queen?' he went on. 'Shall we mingle our blood so that I may always be your support and you always my lady?'

His voice was quivering under the influence of this strange and sudden inspiration; and the trembling had communicated itself to the Queen's shoulders. For there were sorcery, passion and faith, all divine and diabolical things, and all that was chivalrous and carnal in what he was proposing. It was the blood-bond of brothers-in-arms and of legendary lovers, the bond the Templars had brought back from the Orient in the crusades, the bond of love that united the unhappy wife to the lover of her choice, and sometimes even in the presence of the husband on condition their love remained chaste, or at least was held to be so. It was the oath of the body, more powerful than that of words; and it could not be broken, disavowed or annulled. Those who pronounced it became more united than identical twins; what each possessed belonged to the other; they had to protect each other at all times and might not survive each other. 'They must be blood-brothers . . .' people whispered of certain couples with a shiver of fear and envy.[27]

'I can ask everything of you?' said Isabella in a low voice.

He replied by lowering his lids over his flint-coloured eyes.

'I put myself in your hands,' he said. 'You can ask of me anything you wish. You can give me as much of yourself as you want. My love will be what you desire it to be. I could lie naked beside you naked, and never touch you if you forbade it.'

The reality of their love did not lie in this, but it was a sort of rite of honour they owed themselves in conformity with accepted tradition. A lover bound himself to show his strength of spirit and the force of his respect. He submitted himself to ordeal by courtesy, but its duration was subject to his mistress's decision; it depended on her whether it should last for ever or cease forthwith. The knight, who was to be armed, remained standing in prayer all night, his arms lying beside him, and swore to defend the widow and the orphan, but, as soon as his spurs had been buckled on and he had gone to the wars, he pillaged and raped, and used his sword to make widows and orphans by the hundred amid houses in flames.

'Do you agree, my Queen?' he said.

It was her turn to answer by lowering her lids. They had neither of them ever been blood-brothers, nor ever seen anyone so made. They had to invent their own ceremony.

'Shall it be the finger, the forehead or the heart?' Mortimer asked.

They could prick their fingers, let their blood drip to mingle in a glass and each drink in turn. They could make incisions on their foreheads at the hair-line and, standing brow to brow, exchange their thoughts.

'The heart,' Isabella replied.

It was the answer he had hoped for.

Somewhere in the neighbourhood a cock crowed and its cry tore apart the silence of the night. Isabella thought that the day about to break would be the first of spring.

Roger Mortimer undid his tunic and let it fall to the ground; he tore off his shirt. He stood there with his muscular chest bared to Isabella's gaze.

The Queen unlaced her bodice; with a supple movement of the shoulders she drew her slender white arms from the sleeves and uncovered her breasts with their rosy nipples; four maternities had not impaired them; her gesture was proudly decisive, almost defiant.

Mortimer drew his dagger from his belt. Isabella withdrew the long pearl-headed pin that held her tresses in place, and the handles of the amphora fell softly down. Without taking his eyes from the Queen's, Mortimer gashed his skin with a firm hand; the blood ran in a little red rivulet over the sparse chestnut hair of his chest. Isabella did the same to herself with the pin, near the left breast, and a bead of blood came out like the juice of a fruit. The fear of pain, rather than the pain itself, for an instant twisted the corners of her mouth. Then they moved towards each other across the three feet that separated them. She placed her breast against the man's tall torso, rising on her toes so that the two wounds might meet. They each felt the contact of the other's body for the first time, and the warm blood that now belonged to them both.

'Dearest,' she said, 'I give you my heart and take yours by which I live.'

'Dearest,' he replied, 'I take it and promise to keep it in place of my own.'

They did not move apart, prolonging indefinitely this strange kiss between lips that had been voluntarily opened in their breasts. Their hearts beat with the same quick and violent rhythm, seeming to reverberate from one to the other. The three years of chastity on his side and the fifteen on hers of waiting for love made the room reel about them.

'Hold me tight, dearest,' she murmured.

Her mouth rose towards the white scar that marked Mortimer's lip, and her little carnivore's teeth opened to bite.

The English rebel, the escaped prisoner from the Tower of London, the great Baron of the Welsh Marches, the former Justiciar of Ireland, Roger Mortimer, Baron of Wigmore, who had been Queen Isabella's lover for two hours past, had just left in triumphant happiness, his head full of dreams, by the private staircase.

The Queen was not sleepy. Perhaps she would feel tired later; for the moment she was dazzled and astounded, as if a comet were aglow within her. She gazed with tremulous gratitude at the huge and ravaged bed. She was savouring her astonishment at a happiness she had never known before. She had never realized that one might have to crush one's mouth against a shoulder to stifle a cry. She had opened the painted shutters and was standing by the window. Dawn was breaking in misty enchantment over Paris. Had she really arrived only yesterday evening? Had she ever lived before this night? Was it really this same city she had known in her childhood? The world had suddenly come to birth.

The Seine was flowing grey at the foot of the Palace, and over there, on the farther bank, stood the old Tower of Nesle. Isabella suddenly remembered her sister-in-law Marguerite of Burgundy. And a great horror seized on her. 'What have I done?' she thought. 'What have I done? Had I but known!'

All women in love, in every part of the world and since the beginning of time, were her sisters, were women elect. The dead Marguerite, who had cried to her after the sentence at Maubuisson: 'I have known a pleasure that is worth all the crowns of the world, and I regret nothing!' How often had Isabella thought of that cry without understanding it! But this morning, in this new springtime, having known a man's strength and the joy of taking and being taken, she understood at last. 'I would certainly never denounce her today!' she thought. And suddenly she felt shame and remorse for the act of royal justice she had instigated long ago, as though it were the one sin she had ever committed.

6

The Happy Year of 1325

For Queen Isabella, the spring of 1325 was an enchantment. She marvelled at the sunny mornings shining on the roofs of the city; thousands of birds twittered in the gardens; the bells of all the churches, convents and monasteries, even the great bourdon of Notre-Dame, seemed to be ringing out hours of happiness. The nights were scented with lilac under a starry sky.

Each day brought its meed of pleasure: jousts, feasts, tournaments, hunts and picnics. An atmosphere of prosperity lay over the capital, and there was a great urge for amusement. There was profuse expenditure on public pleasures, even though the Treasury accounts showed a deficit for the last year of thirteen thousand, six hundred livres, due, as everyone was agreed, to the war in Aquitaine. But to obtain the necessary funds the Bishops of Rouen, Langres and Lisieux had been fined respectively twelve, fifteen and fifty thousand livres, for using violence against their chapters or the King's men; and thus these too authoritarian prelates had more than made up for the military deficit. And then the Lombards had been summoned once again to repurchase their rights as burgesses.

In this way the luxury of the Court was maintained; and everyone hastened to take a part in the diversions, for the prime pleasure which consists of showing oneself off to others. And as it was with the nobility, so it was also with the bourgeoisie and even with the common people, for everyone was spending rather more than he could afford on the mere pleasures of life. There are, every now and then, years of this sort, when Fate seems to smile and to be affording a rest and a respite amid times of affliction. People buy and sell what are called unnecessary luxuries, as if it could ever be unnecessary to adorn oneself, to charm, to conquer, to lay claim to the right to love, to taste the rare fruits of human ingenuity and to profit by all that Providence and nature have given man for his pleasure in the exceptional place to which he has attained in the world.

Of course people complained, but not so much of being destitute as of being unable to satisfy all their desires. People complained of being less rich than the richest, of having less than those who had everything. The weather was exceptionally clement, business miraculously prosperous. The crusade had been given up; there was no longer talk of raising an army nor of devaluing the livre to the angel; the Privy Council was concerned with the conservation of fish in the rivers; and the fishermen with rod and line who occupied both banks of the Seine were warming themselves in the gentle May sunshine.

Love was in the air that spring. There were more weddings, and more little bastards too, than for a long time past. The girls were courted and happy, the boys boastful and enterprising. Travellers' eyes were not wide enough to take in all the marvels of the city, nor their throats large enough to savour all the wine poured out for them in the hostelries, nor their nights long enough to enjoy all the pleasures offered them.

Oh, how that spring would live in the memory! Of course, there were diseases and deaths, mothers carrying new-born children to the cemetery, paralytics, cuckolded husbands complaining of a decline in morals, burgled shopkeepers accusing the Watch of neglecting its duty, men ruined from too great a thirst for pleasure or simply from mere heedlessness, fires that left families homeless, and crimes here and there; but these things were due to the common mischances of life, not to the fault of the King and his Council.

Indeed, it was a blessing, and due only to a happy and fleeting concatenation of events, to be alive in 1325, to be young or, at least, still active, or merely to possess good health. And it was grave folly not to appreciate to the full what God was giving, and not to thank Him for it. How much more greatly would the people of Paris have soured that spring of 1325, had they guessed what was in store for them! It was a fairy story, which children conceived between lavender-scented sheets during those wonderful months would find it hard to credit when one day they were told of it. 1325! The great days! And how very soon that year would come to be known as the 'good times'.

And what of Queen Isabella? The Queen of England

seemed to unite in her person all the magic and all the joy. People turned as she went by, not only because she was the Queen of England and the daughter of the great King, whose financial decrees, burnings at the stake, and terrible prosecutions were now forgotten and only the laws that had brought peace and strength to the realm remembered, but because she was beautiful and seemed immeasurably happy.

Among the people it was said that she would have worn the crown better than her brother, Charles the Fool, a charming prince but very weak, and they wondered whether Philippe the Long's law which set women aside from the throne was a sound one. The English were very stupid to make so charming a Queen suffer so much.

At thirty-three, Isabella's beauty was unrivalled by that of any young girl, however fresh she might be. The most renowned beauties among the young women of France seemed to retreat into the shade when Queen Isabella passed by. And all the young ladies dreamed of resembling her and took her as their model, copying her dresses, her gestures, her high-piled tresses, her way of looking at you and smiling.

A woman in love is characterized by the way she walks, even seen from the back; Isabella's shoulders and hips, every step she took, all expressed her happiness. She was nearly always accompanied by Roger Mortimer who, since the Queen's arrival, had made a sudden conquest of the town. People who the year before had thought him gloomy and proud, rather too arrogant for an exile, who had detected a certain censure in his virtuous air, suddenly discovered in Mortimer a man not only of admirably high character but of great charm. They ceased to think his black clothes, which were relieved only by a few silver clasps, lugubrious and now saw them as the elegant affectation of a man who was in mourning for his lost country.

Though he had no official position about the Queen, which would have constituted too overt a provocation to King Edward, Mortimer in fact led the negotiations. The Bishop of Norwich submitted to his ascendancy; John de Cromwell did not hesitate to declare that the Baron of Wigmore had been treated unjustly and that it was folly on the part of the sovereign to have alienated so meritorious a lord; the Earl of Kent had struck up a definite friendship with Mortimer and could decide nothing without his advice. And Mortimer received much evidence from England which went to prove that he was now looked on as the real leader of the opposition to the party of the Despensers.

It was generally known and admitted that Mortimer remained with the Queen after supper, for she required his counsel, so she said. And every night, as he came out of Isabella's apartments, he found Ogle, the ex-barber of the Tower of London, now promoted to the position of butler, sleeping on a chest as he waited for his master. Mortimer shook him by the shoulder and they stepped over the servants asleep on the stone floors of the corridors, who never even raised the skirts of their coats from their faces, so accustomed had they become to these familiar footsteps.

Mortimer went home to his lodgings in Saint-Germain-des-Prés, to be welcomed by the fair, pink-complexioned and attentive Alspaye, whom he believed – how ingenuous lovers are! – to be the only man who knew of his royal liaison. He breathed the fresh dawn air triumphantly.

It was now settled that the Queen would not return to England until he could do so himself. The bond between them, renewed day by day and night by night, was becoming closer and more firmly knit; and the little white scar on Isabella's breast, to which he ritually placed his lips before leaving her, remained the visible sign of the fusion of their wills.

Though a woman may be a queen, her lover is always her master; Isabella of England, who was capable of facing alone marital discord, the King's betrayals, the hatred of a court, trembled long when Mortimer put his hand on her shoulder, felt her heart dissolve when he left her room, and took candles to the churches to thank God for having given her so wonderful a sin. When Mortimer was absent, even for an hour, she enthroned him in the forefront of her thoughts, and talked to him in a low voice. Each morning, when she awakened, before calling her women, she slid across the bed to the place her lover had left. A midwife had taught her certain secrets useful to ladies who seek their pleasure outside marriage. And it was whispered in Court circles, though no one saw offence in it, because it seemed only just amends on the part of Fate, that Queen Isabella was in love, as one might have said she was in the country, or better still, in raptures.

The treaty, whose preliminaries had been dragging on for some time, was at last signed on May 31 between Isabella and her brother, with the reluctant agreement of Edward, who was to recover his domain of Aquitaine, but shorn of Agenais and Bazadais, that is to say of those districts which the French Army had occupied the previous year, and this only in consideration of an indemnity of sixty thousand livres. Valois had been inflexible on that point. It had required no less than the mediation of papal envoys to reach this agreement, which was still subject to the express condition that Edward should come and render homage, and this he was clearly reluctant to do, not now merely from considerations of prestige, but from motives of safety. It was agreed therefore to resort to a subterfuge which seemed to satisfy everyone. A date would be appointed for his rendering homage; then, at the last minute, Edward would pretend to be ill, which indeed would scarcely be a lie, for whenever there was now any question of his setting foot in France, he was attacked by all the symptoms of extreme anxiety; he turned pale, grew short of breath, felt his heart beat to an irregular rhythm, and had to lie down, panting, for an hour. He would therefore make over to his eldest son, the young Edward, the titles and estates of the Duke of Aquitaine, and would send him to take the oath in his place.

Everyone thought himself the gainer by this arrangement. Edward escaped the necessity of making a terrifying journey. The Despensers avoided the danger of losing their hold over the King. The Queen would recover her favourite son, for, involved though she was in her love affair, she suffered from being separated from him. And Mortimer foresaw the support to his future plans to be derived from the presence of the heir to the throne in the Queen's party.

This party was continually growing, and in France itself. Edward was surprised that several of his barons, in this late spring, should have found it necessary to visit their French possessions, and he was even more disturbed by the fact that none of them returned. On the other hand, the Despensers had a number of spies in Paris who kept Edward informed about the attitude of the Earl of Kent, the presence of Maltravers in Mortimer's household, and generally about the opposition party which was gravitating to the Court of France about the Queen. Officially the correspondence between husband and wife was still courteous, and Isabella addressed Edward as 'sweetheart' in the long letters she wrote explaining the slowness of the negotiations. But Edward had given orders to the admirals and sheriffs of the ports to intercept all messengers, no matter who they might be, carrying letters sent to anyone by the Queen, the Bishop of Norwich or members of their entourage. These messengers were to be sent to the King under safe escort. But was it possible to arrest all the Lombards who travelled about with letters of exchange?

One day in Paris, when Roger Mortimer was walking in the Temple quarter, accompanied only by Alspaye and Ogle, he was grazed by a block of stone falling from a building under construction. He was saved from being crushed to death only by the noise the block made as it hit a plank in the scaffolding. At the time he thought it merely an accident; but three days later, as he was coming from Robert of Artois's house, a ladder fell in front of his horse. Mortimer went to seek advice from Tolomei, who knew the secrets of Paris better than anyone. The Sienese sent for one of the leaders of the Companion Masons of the Temple who had kept their privileges in spite of the dispersal of the Knights of the Order. And the attempts on Mortimer's life ceased. Indeed, from then on, as soon as the workmen saw the black-clothed English lord, they saluted him with raised caps from their scaffoldings. Nevertheless, Mortimer took to having a stronger escort and had his wine tested with a narwhal's horn as a precaution against poison. The vagabonds in Robert of Artois's pay were told to keep their eyes and ears open. The dangers threatening Mortimer merely increased Queen Isabella's love for him.

And then suddenly, at the beginning of August, a little before the time arranged for the English homage, Monseigneur of Valois, whose power was now so firmly based that he was generally referred to as 'the second King', suddenly collapsed, at the age of fifty-five.

For several weeks, he had been extremely irascible, losing his temper about everything and nothing; in particular, he had flown into a great rage, which had frightened his entourage, on receiving an unexpected proposal from King Edward that they should marry their youngest children, Louis of Valois and Jane of England, who were both about seven years old. Had Edward realized too late the blunder he had made two years ago by refusing his eldest son in marriage, and did he think he was going to win Valois over by this offer and detach him from the Queen's party? Monseigneur Charles, reacting somewhat eccentrically perhaps, had taken this proposal as another insult, and had become so enraged that he had broken every object on his table, which was very abnormal behaviour in him. At the same time he had shown a feverish impatience in his approach to the work of government, had complained of the slowness of Parliament in ratifying decrees, and had argued with Mille de Noyers about the accounts produced by the Exchequer; and had then complained of the exhaustion all these duties caused him.

One morning in Council, as he was about to sign an act, he let the goose-quill fall as it was being handed to him, and it spattered ink over the blue robe he was wearing. He bent as if to pick up the quill and was unable to raise himself; his hand hung down by his leg and his fingers had turned stiff as marble. He was surprised by the silence all about him, and did not realize he was falling out of his chair.

They picked him up. His eyes were fixed in their sockets, turned up towards the left, his mouth was twisted to the same side, and he was unconscious. His face was very red, almost purple, and they hastily summoned a physician to bleed him. As had happened to his brother, Philip the Fair, eleven years earlier, he had been stricken in the head, in the mysterious mechanism of the will. They thought he was dying and, when they got him back to his house, the huge household was thrown into the tragic bustle of mourning.

However, after a few days, during which he seemed to be alive more by the fact of breathing than by any consciousness of mind, he recovered a sort of semi-existence. His power of speech returned, though it was hesitant, badly articulated, stumbled over certain words, and lacked all the fluency and force that had previously distinguished it. His right leg was paralysed, as was the hand that had dropped the goose-quill.

Sitting motionless in a chair, oppressed with heat from the coverings with which it was considered proper to stifle him, the former King of Aragon and Emperor of Constantinople, the Count of Romagna, the Peer of France, the perpetual candidate to the Holy Roman Empire, the tyrant of Florence, the conqueror of Aquitaine, the assembler of crusades, suddenly realized that all the honours a man may reap count for nothing when his body is in process of dissolution. He who since childhood had had no anxiety but to acquire the goods of the earth, suddenly became aware of other cares. He demanded to be taken to his manor of Perray, near Rambouillet, to which he had seldom gone but which had now suddenly become dear to him by one of those eccentric longings the sick have for places where they believe they may recover their health.

The similarity of his disease to that which had struck down his elder brother obsessed his mind which, though it had become less energetic, was still as clear as ever. He sought in his past deeds the reason for this punishment the Almighty had inflicted on him. Become weak, he turned pious. He thought of the Day of Judgment. But the proud easily persuade themselves of a clear conscience; Valois found almost nothing with which to reproach himself. In all his campaigns, in all the pillages and massacres he had ordered, in all the extortions he had imposed on provinces he had conquered or delivered, he considered that he had always used his powers, both as general and prince, for the good. Only one memory caused him remorse, only one action seemed to him to be the possible cause of his present expiation, one name alone hung on his lips when he examined his career: Marigny. For, indeed, he had never really hated anyone, except Marigny. In the case of all those others whom he had ill-treated, punished, tortured, sent to their deaths, he had never acted except out of a conviction that it was for the general good, which he confused with his own ambitions. But the case of Marigny had really been a matter of private hatred. When accusing Marigny, he had deliberately lied; he had borne false witness against him; and he had organized false depositions. He had shrunk from no baseness in order to send the former Prime Minister, Coadjutor and Rector of the Kingdom, who had then been younger than he himself was now, to swing at Montfaucon. There had been no other reason for this except his desire for vengeance, the rancour he felt at seeing, day after day, another enjoy greater power in France than he did himself.

And now, sitting in the courtyard of his manor of Perray, looking at the birds flying past and watching his grooms bring out the beautiful horses he would never ride again, Valois had begun – the word surprised him, but there was no other – had begun to *love* Marigny, to love his memory. He would have liked his enemy to be still alive so that he might be reconciled to him and talk to him of the many things they had both known and experienced and about which they had quarrelled so much. He missed his elder brother, Philip the Fair, his brother Louis of Évreux, and even his two first wives, less than his old rival; and at moments, when he thought no one was looking, he might have been surprised muttering a few phrases of a conversation with a dead man.

Every day he sent one of his chamberlains to distribute a bag of money in charity to the poor of a Paris district, parish by parish; and the chamberlains were ordered to say as they placed the coins in the filthy hands: 'Pray, good people, pray God for Monseigneur Enguerrand de Marigny and for Monseigneur Charles of Valois.' He believed he might earn the Divine Mercy if his name were coupled with that of his victim in the same prayers. And the people of Paris were much surprised that the powerful and magnificent Lord of

Valois should desire his name to be mentioned after that of the man whom he had once proclaimed responsible for all the misfortunes of the realm and had had hanged in chains from a gibbet.

In the Council the power had passed to Robert of Artois who, owing to the illness of his father-in-law, now suddenly found himself promoted to the first rank. The giant frequently galloped down the road to Perray, in company with Philippe of Valois, to go to ask the sick man's advice. For everyone was aware, and Artois first of all, of the gap that had suddenly been opened in the direction of the affairs of France. Of course Monseigneur of Valois had often passed for a bungler, had indeed often made decisions without having given them enough thought, and had governed by instinct rather than principle; but from having moved from Court to Court, from Paris to Spain and from Spain to Naples, from having supported the interests of the Holy Father in Tuscany, from having taken part in all the campaigns in Flanders, from having intrigued for the Empire and from having sat for more than thirty years in the Councils of four kings of France, he had acquired a habit of placing the problems of the realm within the framework of the affairs of Europe. It was a mental process that took place almost automatically.

Robert of Artois, who was a stickler for custom and procedure, had not such wide views. Also, people said of the Count of Valois that he was 'the last', though they could not have explained precisely what they meant by this, unless it was that he was the last representative of the grand manner of administering the world, which would doubtless disappear with him.

King Charles the Fair seemed quite indifferent and journeyed from Orléans to Saint-Maixent and to Châteauneuf-sur-Loire, still waiting for his third wife to announce the happy news that she was pregnant.

Queen Isabella had become, so to speak, mistress of the palace in Paris, and held a sort of second English Court there.

The date of the homage had been fixed for August 30. Edward therefore waited for the last week in the month to set out on his journey and pretend to fall ill at Sandown Abbey, near Dover. The Bishop of Winchester was then sent to Paris to certify under oath, if need be, though he was not asked to do so, the truth of the excuse, and to suggest the substitution of the son for the father, it being understood that Prince Edward, who had been made Duke of Aquitaine and Count of Ponthieu, would bring the promised sixty thousand livres.

On September 16 the young prince arrived, but accompanied by the Bishop of Oxford and above all by Walter Stapledon, Bishop of Exeter and Lord Treasurer. In selecting Stapledon, who was one of the most active and violent partisans of the Despenser party, and also the cleverest, most cunning and among the most hated of his entourage, King Edward emphasized not only the fact that he had no intention of changing his policy but that he mistrusted everything that was going forward in Paris. The Bishop of Exeter's mission was not solely that of an escort.

The very day of their arrival, and almost at the very moment Queen Isabella was clasping her son in her arms, it was learned that Monseigneur of Valois had had a relapse and that it was to be expected God would take him to Himself at any moment. Everyone, the family, the great dignitaries, the barons who were in Paris, the English envoys, immediately hurried to Perray, except the indifferent Charles the Fair, who was superintending a few interior alterations at Vincennes which he had ordered Painfetiz, his architect, to undertake.

And the people of France continued to enjoy the happy year of 1325.

7

Each Prince who Dies . . .

To those who had not seen him during these last weeks Monseigneur of Valois seemed to have changed terribly. In the first place, everyone was used to seeing him always with some form of head-dress, whether it was a large crown glittering with precious stones on days of state, or an embroidered velvet cap whose long scalloped crest fell to his shoulder, or again one of those caps of maintenance with a gold coronet about it which he wore within doors. For the first time he appeared bareheaded, and his hair was fair, mingled with white and faded with age, while illness had taken the twist out of his long curls, which now hung lifelessly down his cheeks and over the pillows. That he should have grown so thin was startling enough, when one considered how stout and ruddy he had been, but it was less so than the contorted immobility of one side of his face and the twisted mouth from which a servant was continually wiping away the saliva, or than the dull fixity of his eyes. The gold-embroidered sheets, the blue hangings sewn with lilies which hung draped like a baldachin over the bed-head, merely served to emphasize the dying man's physical decay.

And before receiving the crowd of people who were now pressing into the room, he had asked for a looking-glass and for a moment had studied that face which, only two months ago, had dominated kings and nations. What did prestige and the power of his name matter to him now? Where were all the ambitions he had pursued so long? And what satisfaction was there in always walking with one's head held high while other people bowed, since within that head, the day before yesterday, there had taken place so shattering a fall into the dark void? And what was the use of the hand whose back and palm servants, grooms and vassals had hurried so assiduously to kiss, now that it lay dead beside him? And the other hand, which he could still control, and which he would use in a little while for the last time to sign the will he was about to dictate – if a left hand would lend itself to writing – did it belong to him any more than the signet ring with which he sealed his orders and which would be slipped from his finger after his death? Had anything ever really belonged to him?

His right leg, which was completely paralysed, seemed already to have been taken from him. And at times he felt a sort of empty chasm in his chest.

Man is a thinking individual who acts on other men and transforms the world. And then, suddenly, the individual disintegrates, falls apart, and then what is the world, and what are other men? At this moment, the important thing for Monseigneur of Valois was no longer titles, possessions, crowns, kingdoms, the exercise of power, or the primacy of his own person among the living. The emblems of his lineage, the acquisition of wealth, even the heirs of his blood whom he saw assembled about him, none of these was of any account in his lustreless eyes. The important things were the September air, the leaves, still green but beginning to turn, which he could see through the open windows, but above all the air, the air he breathed with such difficulty and which was engulfed in that chasm which seemed to lie deep within his chest. As long as he could feel the air entering his throat, the world would continue to exist with himself as its centre, but a frail centre now, like the last flicker of a candle-flame. And then everything would cease to be, or rather everything would continue to be, but in an utter darkness and a terrifying silence, as a cathedral still exists when the last candle has been put out.

Valois thought of the great deaths in his family. He could hear again the words of Philip the Fair: 'See what the world is worth. Here lies the King of France!' He remembered those of his nephew, Philippe the Long: 'Look on your Sovereign Lord; there is none among you, however poor he may be, with whom I would not exchange my lot!' At the time, he had heard these words without understanding them; but now he knew what the princes of his family had felt at the moment of passing into the tomb. There were no other words in which to express it, and those who still had time to live could not understand it. Each man who dies is the poorest man in the world.

And when all was dissolved, destroyed and extinguished, when the cathedral was filled with shadows, what would that poorest of men discover on the other side? Would he find what he had been taught by religion? Yet what were those teachings but immense and alarming uncertainties? Would he be brought before a Judgment Seat; and what was the face of the Judge like? And in what scales would all the actions of his life be weighed? What punishment could be inflicted on a being who no longer existed? Punishment . . . What punishment? Perhaps the punishment consisted in being conscious at the moment of crossing the dark wall.

Charles of Valois could not put aside the thought that Enguerrand de Marigny had also been conscious, indeed even more completely conscious, for he was a man in good health and at the height of his powers, who was not dying of the rupture of some secret cog in the human mechanism, but by another's will. For him it had not been the last flicker of a single candle, but all the flames blown out at once.

The very same marshals, dignitaries and great officers who had accompanied Marigny to the scaffold were here now, standing round his bed, filling the whole room, overflowing into the next room beyond the door, and they had that very same look of men who were leading one of their number to his last heartbeat, strangers to the death they were watching, participants in a future from which the condemned man was eliminated.

Oh, he would have given all the crowns of Byzantium, all the thrones of Germany, all the sceptres and all the gold from ransoms for one look, just one, in which he did not feel himself *eliminated*. Sorrow, compassion, regret, horror, and the sadness of memories: all these might be seen in the circle of multi-coloured eyes surrounding the bed of a dying prince.

But every one of these emotions was simply a proof of his elimination.

Valois looked at his eldest son, Philippe, the tall fellow with the big nose, standing beside him under the baldachin, who tomorrow, or one day soon, or perhaps even in a minute's time, would be the only, the real Count of Valois, the living Valois; tall Philippe was sad, as was proper, and was holding the hand of his wife, Jeanne of Burgundy, the Lame; but he was also being careful to adopt the right attitude because of the future before him, and he seemed to be saying to those present: 'Look, it's my father who's dying!' And from those features, of which he was the source and the progenitor, Valois was wiped out.

And the other sons: Charles of Alençon who avoided catching the dying man's eye, and turned slowly away when their glances met; and young Louis, who was frightened, seemed indeed almost ill with fear because this was the first deathbed he had ever attended. And his daughters, several of whom were present: the Countess of Hainaut, who from time to time made a sign to the servant whose duty it was to wipe his mouth, and her younger sister, the Countess of Blois, and a little farther away the Countess of Beaumont beside her giant husband Robert of Artois, both standing in a group with Queen Isabella of England and the young Duke of Aquitaine, the boy with the long eyelashes, behaving as well as if he was in church, who would have but this one memory of his great-uncle Valois.

It seemed to Valois as if they were plotting together over there, preparing a future from which he would also be eliminated.

If he turned his head to the other side of the bed, it was to see standing there, upright, competent, like a woman who has seen many people die and is already a widow, Mahaut de Châtillon-Saint-Pol, his third wife. Gaucher de Châtillon, the old Constable, with his saurian head and his seventy-seven years, was in process of winning another victory; he was watching a man twenty years his junior die before him.

Étienne de Mornay and Jean de Cherchemont, both former chancellors of Charles of Valois before becoming in turn Chancellors of France, Mille de Noyers, the lawyer and Master of the Exchequer, Robert Bertrand, the Knight of the Green Lion, and lately appointed a marshal, Brother Thomas de Bourges, his confessor, and Jean de Torpo, his physician, were all there to help him, each in accordance with his function. But who could help a man to die? Hugues de Bouville wiped away a tear. But for what was fat Bouville weeping if it were not for his own lost youth, the imminence of old age and the passing of his own life?

Indeed, a dying prince was a poorer man than the poorest serf in his kingdom. For the poor serf had not to die in public; his wife and children could deceive him as to the imminence of death; he was surrounded by no pomp foretelling his end; nor was he obliged to draw up, when *in extremis*, the affidavit of his own demise. And indeed that was what they were all waiting for, all these high personages assembled. For what, after all, was a will but an avowal drawn up by oneself of one's own death? It was a document concerned with other people's futures. The secretary was waiting, his inkpot in place on his writing-board, his parchment and pen ready. So be it. He must begin, or rather finish. It was not so much the effort of mind that was so great but the effort of renouncement. A will should begin like a prayer.

'In the Name of the Father, the Son and the Holy Ghost . . .'

Charles of Valois had spoken. Everyone thought he was praying.

'Write, friend,' he said to the secretary. 'Can't you hear that I'm dictating? I, Charles . . .'

He stopped, because it gave him a painful and frightening sensation to hear his own voice uttering his own name for the last time. Was not a name the very symbol of a man's existence and of his individuality? Valois would have liked to stop there, because nothing else interested him any more. But there were all those eyes fixed on him. For the last time he must act, and for others from whom he already felt himself so profoundly separated.

'I, Charles, son of the King of France, Count of Valois, Alençon, Chartres and Anjou, make known to all concerned that I, being sound in mind, though ill in body . . .'

Though his utterance was slightly embarrassed and his tongue stumbled over certain words, often the simplest, his mental machinery, that had always been accustomed to formulate his wishes in words, apparently continued to function normally. But to the dying man it seemed as if he himself was his only audience. He was in the middle of a river; his voice was speaking to the bank he was leaving; he trembled at the thought of what would happen when he reached the farther side.

'. . . and asking God's mercy, while in fear and dread of His Judgment, I order by these presents the disposal of myself and my possessions, and make my last will and testament in the manner hereinafter written. In the first place I resign my soul into the keeping of our Lord Jesus Christ and His merciful Mother and all His Saints . . .'

On a sign from the Countess of Hainaut the servant wiped away the saliva which was dribbling from the corner of his mouth. All private conversation had ceased and everyone was trying to avoid even the rustling of clothes. Those present seemed utterly astonished that this inert and feeble body, crippled by illness, should still be able to think so clearly and even be fastidious in the choice of language.

Gaucher de Châtillon murmured to his neighbours: 'He won't die today.'

Jean de Torpo, one of the physicians, shook his head doubtfully. In his opinion Monseigneur Charles would not see another dawn. But Gaucher went on: 'I've seen many of them, I've seen many of them . . . I tell you there's still life in that body . . .'

The Countess of Hainaut put her finger to her lips and prayed the Constable to be silent; Gaucher was deaf and did not realize how loud he whispered.

Valois continued his dictation: 'I wish my body to be buried in the Church of the Minorites in Paris, between the tombs of my two first wives . . .'

His eyes sought the face of his third wife, the living one, the future widow Mahaut de Châtillon. Three wives, and a whole life had been lived . . . And it was Catherine, the second, whom he had loved the most, perhaps because of her mythical crown of Constantinople. Catherine had been a beauty, well worthy to bear her legendary title. Valois was astonished that his unhappy body, half-paralysed and on the very verge of annihilation, should still retain a vague and diffused quivering of the old desires that transmitted life. And so he would lie beside her, beside the Empress, and on the other side he would have his first wife, the daughter of the King of Naples, both dust for such a long time now. How strange that the memory of a desire should remain when the body which was its object no longer exists! And what of the Resurrection? But there was his third wife, the wife he was looking at now, who had been a good companion to him too. He must leave her something.

'Item, I desire my heart to be placed in the town and place which my wife Mahaut de Saint-Pol elects for her burial; and my entrails in the Abbey of Chaâlis, the right to divide my body having been granted me by a Bull of our Most Holy Father, the Pope . . .' He hesitated in a vain endeavour to remember the date, and added: '. . . previously.'[28]

How proud he had been of this authorization, which was given only to kings, to distribute his body as saints were divided up into relics! He had insisted on being treated as a king even in the tomb. But now he was thinking of the Resurrection, the only hope left to those on the verge of the final step. If the teachings of religion were true, how would the Resurrection affect him? His entrails at Chaâlis, his heart wherever Mahaut de Saint-Pol chose, and his body in the church in Paris, would he rise up before Catherine and Marguerite with an empty breast and a stomach filled with straw and sewn up with hemp? There must be some other arrangement, something the human mind was incapable of conceiving. Would there be a press of bodies and eyes, like that which was now about his bed? What wild confusion there would be, if all ancestors and all descendants rose up together, and all murderers face to face with their victims, and all mistresses, and all the betrayed. Would Marigny rise up before him?

'Item, I leave to the Abbey of Chaâlis sixty livres tournois to celebrate my birthday . . .'

Once again the napkin wiped his chin. For nearly a quarter of an hour he detailed all the churches, abbeys and pious foundations in his fiefs to which he desired to leave here a hundred livres, there fifty, there a hundred and twenty, and there a lily to embellish a shrine. The enumeration was monotonous, except to himself for whom each name represented a steeple, a village, a town of which for a few hours more, or even days perhaps, he would still be the lord, and some particular and personal memory of it. The thoughts of those present wandered, as they did at Mass when the service was too long. Only Jeanne the Lame, who found it painful to stand for so long on her short leg, listened attentively. She was adding and calculating. At every figure she looked at her husband, Philippe of Valois, and her face, though far from naturally ugly, was made hideous by the avarice of her thoughts. These legacies would all have to be paid out of their inheritance! Philippe was frowning too.

In the meantime, the English clan was standing by the windows and plotting again. Queen Isabella was anxious, though the concern on her face might have been thought due to the circumstances. In face she was extremely worried. In the first place, because Mortimer was not there; and she never felt really safe, or indeed really alive, when he was not near her. And in the second, she felt that she was constantly watched and spied on by Stapledon, the Bishop of Exeter, who had come unbidden to Perray on the grounds that it was his duty to escort the young Duke of Aquitaine everywhere. This man, who was Edward's evil genius, was bound to cause disaster wherever he might be, or at the very least serious trouble. Isabella pulled Robert of Artois by the sleeve to make him bend his ear down to her.

'Beware of Exeter,' she whispered, 'that thin Bishop standing over there biting his thumb. I'm very anxious, Cousin. My last letter from Orleton had been opened and the seal glued on again.'

They could hear Charles of Valois's voice saying: 'Item, I bequeath to my wife, the Countess, the ruby which my daughter of Blois gave me. Item, I bequeath to her the embroidered cloth which belonged to my mother, Queen Marie . . .'

Though everyone's mind had wandered during the pious bequests, all eyes grew brighter now that it was a question of the jewels. The Countess of Blois raised her eyebrows and showed a certain disappointment. Her father might well have returned to her the ruby she had given him, instead of leaving it to his wife.

'Item, the reliquary of Saint Edward in my possession . . .'

Hearing the name of Saint Edward, the young Prince Edward of England raised his long lashes and tried to catch his mother's eye. But no, the reliquary went also to Mahaut de Châtillon. And Isabella thought that Uncle Charles might well have left it to his great-nephew who was present.

'Item, I leave to Philippe, my eldest son, a ruby and all my arms and harness, except a coat of mail which is of Acre work, and the sword with which the Lord of Harcourt fought, both of which I leave to Charles, my second son. Item, to my daughter of Burgundy, the wife of Philippe my son, the finest of all my emeralds.'

The lame woman's cheeks turned a little red, and she thanked him with an inclination of the head which seemed almost indecent. You could be sure that she would have the emeralds examined by an expert jeweller to make certain which of them was the finest.

'Item, to Charles my second son, all my horses and palfreys, my gold chalice, a silver bowl and a missal.'

Charles of Alençon began stupidly weeping, as if he had only become aware of the fact that his father was dying, and of the sorrow he felt at it, at the very moment the dying man mentioned him by name.

'Item, I leave to Louis, my third son, all my silver plate . . .'

The child clung to Mahaut de Châtillon's skirts; she tenderly stroked his forehead.

'Item, I will and command that all that remains of my funeral trappings be sold to pay for prayers for my soul . . . Item, that my wardrobe be distributed to my body-servants . . .'

There was a discreet stir by the open windows and heads leaned out. Three litters were entering the courtyard of the manor, which had been strewn with straw to deaden the sound of horses' hooves. From a great litter, decorated with gilded carvings and curtains embroidered with representations of the castles of Artois, the huge and monumental Countess Mahaut, her hair now grey beneath her veil, alighted, as did her daughter, the Dowager Queen Jeanne of Burgundy, the widow of Philippe the Long. The Countess was also accompanied by her Chancellor, Canon Thierry d'Hirson, and her lady-in-waiting, Béatrice, the Canon's niece. Mahaut had come from her Castle of Conflans, near Vincennes, which she rarely left in these days which were so hostile to her.

The second litter, which was all white, was that of the Dowager Queen Clémence of Hungary, widow of Louis Hutin.

From the third and more modest litter, which had plain curtains of black leather, emerged with some difficulty, and assisted by only two servants, Messer Spinello Tolomei, Captain-General of the Lombard Companies of Paris.

And so, through the corridors of the manor, came two former Queens of France, young women of the same age: they were both thirty-two and one had succeeded the other on the throne. They were dressed all in white, which was the custom for widowed queens. They were both fair and beautiful, particularly Queen Clémence, and indeed they looked rather like twin sisters. Behind them, a head and shoulders taller, came the redoubtable Countess Mahaut who, as everyone knew, though they lacked the courage to say so, had killed the husband of one of these queens so that the husband of the other might reign. And then, behind again, dragging a leg, his stomach to the fore, his white hair sparse over his collar and the crow's-feet of time on his cheeks, came old Tolomei, who had been involved, more or less closely, in every intrigue. And because age is in itself ennobling, because money is the real source of power in the world, because

Monseigneur of Valois could not in the past have married the Empress of Constantinople without him, and because without Tolomei the Court of France could not have sent Bouville to fetch Queen Clémence from Naples, nor Robert of Artois have undertaken his lawsuits, nor married the daughter of the Count of Valois, and because without Tolomei the Queen of England could not have been here with her son, the old Lombard, who had seen so much and learnt so much and had kept so many secrets, was treated with that respect which is normally reserved only for princes.

Everyone moved aside and backed against the walls to free the doorway. Bouville trembled when Mahaut's skirts brushed against his stomach.

Isabella and Robert of Artois looked at each other questioningly. Did Tolomei's and Mahaut's simultaneous arrival mean that the old Tuscan fox was working also for their adversaries? But Tolomei reassured his clients with a discreet smile. There was no more to their joint arrival than could be explained by the chances of the road.

Mahaut's entrance embarrassed everyone. It was as if the beams of the ceiling had suddenly become lower. Valois stopped dictating when he saw his old giantess of an enemy appear, driving the two white widows before her, as if they were a couple of ewe lambs she was taking out to pasture. And then Valois saw Tolomei, and his unparalysed hand, on which glittered the ruby that was to pass to the finger of his eldest son, waved in front of his face as he said: 'Marigny, Marigny . . .'

Everyone thought his mind was wandering. But not at all; the sight of Tolomei had merely reminded him of their common enemy. Without the help of the Lombards, Valois could never have triumphed over the Coadjutor.

Then the huge Mahaut of Artois was heard to say: 'God will forgive you, Charles, for your repentance is sincere.'

'The bitch!' said Robert of Artois, loud enough for those about him to hear. 'She, of all people, dares to speak of remorse!'

Charles of Valois paid no attention to the Countess of Artois and signed to the Lombard to come near. The old Sienese went to the bedside, raised the paralysed hand and kissed it. But Valois did not feel the kiss.

'We are praying for your recovery, Monseigneur,' said Tolomei.

Recovery! It was the only word of comfort Valois had heard from any of these people for whom his death appeared to be no more than a formality! Recovery! Was the banker saying that merely out of kindness or did he really believe in it? They looked at each other and, in Tolomei's single open eye, that dark and cunning eye, the dying man saw something like an expression of complicity. Here, at last, was one eye from which he was not eliminated!

'Item, item,' went on Valois, levelling his forefinger at the secretary, 'I will and command that all my debt be paid by my children.'

This was indeed a splendid bequest he was making Tolomei with these words, a more valuable one than all the rubies and all the reliquaries. And Philippe of Valois, Charles of Alençon, Jeanne the Lame and the Countess of Blois all looked equally disconcerted. How right the Lombard had been to come!

'Item, to Aubert de Villepion, my chamberlain, the sum of

two hundred livres tournois; to Jean de Cherchemont, who was my chancellor before being that of France, a similar sum; to Pierre de Montguillon, my equerry . . .'

And now once more Monseigneur of Valois was in the thrall of that spirit of largesse which had cost him so dear throughout his life. Acting the prince to the last gasp, he was recompensing those who had served him. Two hundred or three hundred livres were not in themselves great sums but, when multiplied by forty or fifty and added to the pious bequests, all the Pope's gold, which had already been considerably diminished, could not suffice. Nor would a year's revenues from the whole Valois appanage. Charles clearly intended to be prodigal even after his death.

Mahaut went over to the English group. She greeted Isabella with a glance in which gleamed an old hatred, smiled at the little Prince Edward as if she wanted to bite him, and at last looked at Robert.

'My dear Nephew, how grievous this must be to you; he was a real father to you . . .' she said in a low voice.

'And it must be a terrible shock to you, Aunt,' he replied in the same tone. 'After all, he is the same age as yourself, or very near it. You cannot have many more years to live . . .'

People were coming and going at the back of the room. Isabella suddenly noticed that the Bishop of Exeter had disappeared; or rather that he was in process of disappearing, for she saw him going out through the door, with that proud, unctuous and gliding motion so common among ecclesiastics when moving through a crowd; and he was in company with Canon d'Hirson, Mahaut's chancellor. And the giantess was also watching them going out together, and each woman realized that the other was aware of what was taking place.

Isabella was anxiously wondering. What could Stapledon, her enemy's envoy, have to say to the Countess's chancellor? And how did they know each other, since Stapledon had arrived only yesterday? It was perfectly clear that the English spies had been in contact with Mahaut. Indeed, it was only to be expected. 'She has every reason to want to avenge herself on me and destroy me,' thought Isabella. 'After all, I denounced her daughters. Oh, how I wish Roger were here! Why did I not insist on his coming?'

The two priests had found no difficulty in meeting. Canon d'Hirson had had Edward's envoy pointed out to him.

'Reverendissimus sanctissimusque Exeteris episcopus?' he asked him. 'Ego canonicus et comitissae Artesiensis cancellarius sum.'*

They had been instructed to meet at the first opportunity. And this opportunity had arisen here. And now, sitting side by side in a window embrasure at the end of a corridor, their beads in their hands, they conversed in Latin, as if they were making the responses to the prayers for the dying.

Canon d'Hirson had a copy of a very interesting letter addressed to Queen Isabella from a certain English bishop who signed himself 'O'. The letter had been stolen from an Italian businessman while he was sleeping in an inn in Artois. Bishop 'O' advised the Queen not to come back for the present, but to gather as many partisans in France as she

---

* Very reverend and most saintly Bishop of Exeter? I am a Canon and chancellor to the Countess of Artois.

could, to assemble a thousand knights and land with them in England to chase out the Despensers and that wicked Bishop Stapledon. Thierry d'Hirson had the copy on him. Would Monseigneur Stapledon care to have it? A paper passed from the Canon's cloak to the Bishop, who cast an eye on it and recognized the clever, succinct style of Adam Orleton. If, he added, Roger Mortimer took command of this expedition, the whole English nobility would rally to him within a few days.

Bishop Stapledon gnawed at a corner of his thumb.

'Ille baro de Mortuo Mari concubinus Isabellae reginae aperte est,'* said Thierry d'Hirson.

Did the Bishop want proof of it? Hirson could give him whatever proof he might require. It would be enough to question the servants, have the comings and goings at the Palace of the Cité watched, or merely ask the familiars of the Court what they thought.

Stapledon concealed the letter in his robe, under his pectoral cross.

The crowd was beginning to leave the bedroom. Monseigneur of Valois had named the executors of his will. His great seal, bearing the lilies and surrounded with the inscription: 'Caroli regis Franciae filii, comitis Valesi et Andegaviae',† had been impressed in the wax poured on to the ribbons hanging from the document.

'Monseigneur, may I present to your high and saintly person my niece Béatrice, lady-in-waiting to the Countess?'

---

* Baron Mortimer is living here in open concubinage with Queen Isabella.

† Of Charles, son of the King of France, Count of Valois and Anjou.

said Thierry d'Hirson to Stapledon, indicating a beautiful dark girl, with liquid eyes and swaying hips, who was approaching them.

Béatrice d'Hirson kissed the Bishop's ring; then her uncle whispered a few words to her. She went back to the Countess Mahaut and murmured in her ear: 'It is done, Madame.'

And Mahaut, who was still standing near Isabella, put out her great hand and stroked young Prince Edward's forehead.

Then everyone went back to Paris. Robert of Artois and the Chancellor because they had to attend to government matters. Tolomei because he had business. And Mahaut because, now that her revenge was in train, she had nothing more to do here. Isabella because she wanted to see Mortimer. The widowed Queens because nobody could find room to put them up. Even Philippe of Valois had to go back to Paris for administrative matters concerning the great county of which he was already the *de facto* lord.

There remained beside the dying man only his third wife, his eldest daughter, the Countess of Hainaut, his younger children and his personal servants. Scarcely more people than there would have been round the deathbed of some little provincial knight, although Valois's name and actions had concerned the world from the Atlantic to the Bosporus.

And next day Monseigneur Charles of Valois was still breathing, and the following day too. The Constable Gaucher had been right; there was still life in that broken body.

The whole Court during these days went to Vincennes for the homage that young Prince Edward, Duke of Aquitaine, was to render to his uncle, Charles the Fair.

Then, in Paris, a brick fell from a scaffolding very close to

Bishop Stapledon's head; after which a footbridge gave way under the prelate's mule, while he happened to be following it on foot. And again, one morning, as he was leaving his lodgings at the hour of early Mass, he found himself in a narrow street face to face with Gerard de Alspaye, the ex-Lieutenant of the Tower of London, and barber Ogle. The two men seemed to be out simply for a stroll. But did people leave home at that hour of the morning merely to listen to the birds singing? A little silent group of men was standing in the mouth of an alley and, among them, Stapledon thought he recognized the long horse-face of Baron Maltravers. A convoy of market-gardeners, which was crowding the street at that moment, gave the Bishop the opportunity to hurry back to his own door. That very night, saying goodbye to no one, he took the road to Boulogne, where he embarked secretly.

And he took with him, not only the copy of Orleton's letter, but ample evidence against Queen Isabella, Mortimer, the Earl of Kent and all the lords who formed their entourage.

In his manor in the Île-de-France, a league distant from Rambouillet, Charles of Valois, abandoned by nearly everyone, and withdrawn into his own body as if he were already in the tomb, was still alive. He, who had been called the second King of France, no longer paid attention to anything except the air which entered his lungs with an irregular rhythm and, from time to time, with agonizing pauses. And he was to continue breathing this air, which was life to all God's creatures, for long weeks to come, indeed until December.

PART THREE

THE DISINHERITED KING

I

The Hostile Spouses

Queen Isabella had been living in France for eight months; she had learnt what freedom meant and had found love. And she had forgotten her husband, King Edward. He no longer held a place in her thoughts, except in a rather abstract way, as if he were a tiresome legacy left by some older Isabella now defunct; he had passed into the dead zones of her memory. She could no longer remember, when she tried to do so to exacerbate her resentment, even the smell of her husband's body or the exact colour of his eyes. She could recapture only the vague, fluid outline of his over-long chin and blond beard, and the disagreeable movement of his back. Though memory might be proving evasive, hatred on the other hand remained tenaciously present.

Bishop Stapledon's hurried return to London confirmed all Edward's fears and showed him how urgent it was that he should make his wife return to England. And yet he realized he must act cunningly and, as Hugh the Elder said, lull the she-wolf if he wanted her to return to her lair. For some weeks, therefore, Edward's letters were those of a loving husband regretting his wife's absence. The Despensers also played their part in this duplicity by addressing protestations of devotion to the Queen and joining their supplications to those of the King that she should afford them the joy of her early return. Edward also told the Bishop of Winchester to use his influence with the Queen.

But on December 1 everything changed. On that day Edward flew into one of his sudden, hysterical rages, which were so un-royal and yet afforded him the illusion of authority. The Bishop of Winchester had just given him the Queen's answer; she refused to return to England for fear of Hugh the Younger and she had also informed the King of France, her brother, of the fear she had of him. No more was necessary. The letters Edward dictated at Westminster, during five continuous hours, were to cause the Courts of Europe considerable stupefaction.

But first he wrote to the Queen. There was no question of 'sweetheart' now.

'Madame,' wrote Edward, 'we have often asked you, both before the homage and after, that for the great desire we have that you should be with us and the great unease we suffer due to your long absence, you should come to us as quickly as possible and without making any more excuses.

'Before the homage you were excused by reason of the furtherance of the business; but since then you have informed us through the Honourable Father, the Bishop of Winchester, that you will not come, through fear and mistrust of Hugh the Despenser, which astonishes us greatly; for both you with regard to him and he with regard to you have always praised each other in my presence, and in particular on your departure, by special promises and other proofs of confident friendship, and also by your letters to him which he has shown us.

'We know for a fact, and you must know it equally, Madame, that the said Hugh has always done all he could to maintain our honour; and you know too that he has never done you any harm since you have been my wife, except, and by chance, on one single occasion, and through your own fault, if you remember.

'It would much displease us, now that the homage has been rendered to our very dear brother the King of France and we are in such friendly relations with him, that you, whom we sent for peace, should be the cause of any coldness between us and for false reasons.

'That is why we ask you, and charge you, and order you, that you should cease making excuses and feigning pretexts, and should return to us with all haste.

'As for your expenses, when you have returned as a wife should to her lord, we will order them in such manner that you will lack nothing and in no way be dishonoured.

'We also wish and command that you make our very dear son Edward come to us as quickly as possible, for we have a great desire to see him and speak to him.

'The Honourable Father in God Wautier, Bishop of Exeter,[29] has told us that some of our banished enemies, who are with you, sought him out to do him bodily harm if they had had the time to do so, and that, to escape such perils, he hastened back to us because of the loyalty and allegiance he owes us. We tell you this so that you may understand that the said Bishop, when he left you so suddenly, did so for no other reason.

'Given at Westminster the First Day of December, 1325.

'Edward'

If his anger broke out in the first part of the letter, to be followed by lies, the venom was very cleverly placed at the end.

Another and shorter letter was addressed to the young Duke of Aquitaine.

'Most dear son, though you are young and tender in age, remember well what we charged you with and ordered you to do on your departure from us at Dover, and what you then replied, for which we were most grateful to you, and do not go beyond or contravene in any way what we then said to you.

'And since all is done and your homage is received, present yourself to our very dear brother, the King of France, your uncle, and take leave of him, and come to us in the company of our very dear wife, the Queen, your mother, if she comes at once.

'But if she does not come, come yourself at once and do not remain longer; for we have a great desire to see you and talk with you; and do not in any circumstances fail to do this, either because of your mother or anyone else. With our blessing.'

The repetitions and the irritation manifest in the ill-constructed sentences showed that the writing of the letters had not been confided to the Chancellor or a secretary but was the work of the King himself. One could almost hear Edward's voice dictating. Charles IV, the Fair, was not forgotten. The letter Edward sent him repeated almost phrase by phrase the points he had made in his letter to the Queen.

'You will have heard from people you can trust that our wife, the Queen of England, dare not come to us through fear for her life and the mistrust she has of Hugh the Despenser. Of course, beloved brother, she had no need to mistrust him nor any other man living in our kingdom; for, by God, neither Hugh nor any other living man in our territory wishes her ill, and, if we discovered such existed, we would punish him in such a way that he would be an example to others, which we have sufficient power to do, thank God.

'That is why, very dear and beloved brother, we particularly pray you, for your honour and our own, and that of our said wife, that you should do everything in your power to see that she comes to us as quickly as possible; we are much chagrined to be deprived of her company, a thing which we would never have allowed had it not been for the great trust and confidence we have in you and in your good faith that she would return when we wished.'

Edward also demanded the return of his son and denounced the attempts at assassination made on the Bishop of Exeter which he attributed to 'the enemies and outlaws over there'.

Undoubtedly, his anger on that first day of December must have been great and the vaults of Westminster have echoed long to his furious shouting. For Edward also wrote to the same purpose and in the same tone to the Archbishops of Rheims and Rouen, to Jean de Marigny, Bishop of Beauvais, to the Bishops of Langres and Laon, all peers spiritual, to the Dukes of Burgundy and Brittany, as well as to the Counts of Valois and Flanders, peers temporal, to the Abbot of Saint-Denis, to Louis of Clermont-Bourbon, the Great Chamberlain, to Robert of Artois, to Mille de Noyers, Master of the Exchequer, and to the Constable Gaucher de Châtillon.

The fact that Mahaut was the only peer of France who was excepted from this correspondence was proof enough of her relations with Edward and that she already knew enough about the affair to make it unnecessary to write to her officially about it.[30]

When Robert opened his letter he was overjoyed, and went off laughing and slapping his thighs to his cousin of England. It was exactly the sort of situation that was calculated to delight him. So poor Edward was sending couriers to the four corners of the realm to tell everyone of his marital difficulties, defend his little catamite and announce publicly that he was unable to make his wife come home! How unfortunate the lords of England were, what a sorry King they had, and how weak were the hands that had inherited the sceptre of William the Conqueror! Nothing so ridiculous as this had occurred since the quarrels of Louis the Pious and Alienor of Aquitaine.

'Turn him into a proper cuckold, Cousin,' cried Robert, 'and make no bones about it. Let your Edward's horns grow so long that he has to bend double to get through the doors of his castles. Isn't that what he deserves, Cousin Roger?'

And he gaily slapped Mortimer on the back.

Edward, in his fury, had also decided on reprisals, and had confiscated the property of his half-brother the Earl of Kent and that of Lord de Cromwell, the commander of Isabella's escort. But he had done even worse than that: he had sealed a decree by which he made himself 'Governor and Administrator' of the fiefs of his son, the Duke of Aquitaine, and was demanding in his name the lost territory. It was tantamount to repudiating both the treaty negotiated by his wife and the homage rendered by his son.

'Let him, let him!' said Robert of Artois. 'We'll just go and take his duchy from him again, or rather what remains of it, for one can say that the half of it is only uncovered at low tide. And since two campaigns haven't taught the wretched fellow his duty, we'll mount a third against him. The cross-bows for the crusade are beginning to rust!'

But there was no need to raise an army or send the Constable, whose joints were becoming stiff with age; the two Marshals, at the head of the permanent garrisons, would be strong enough to deal with the Gascon lords in the Bordelais who were still weak or foolish enough to remain loyal to the King of England. It was becoming almost a habit. And each time there were fewer adversaries.

Edward's letter was one of the last Charles of Valois read, one of the last echoes of the great affairs of the world that reached him.

Monseigneur Charles died in the middle of this month of December; his obsequies were as pompous as his life had been. The whole house of Valois, and seeing its members in procession one could the better realize how numerous and important it was, the whole family of France, all the dignitaries, most of the peers, the widowed Queens, Parliament, the Exchequer, the Constable, the doctors of the University, the Corporations of Paris, the vassals of the fiefs of appanage and the clergy of the churches and abbeys mentioned in the will accompanied the body, now very light by reason of illness and embalming, of the most turbulent man of his time to the Church of the Minorites so that he might lie between his first two wives.

It was his fate to have missed, by less than three years, becoming King of France, since Charles IV, his nephew, who had no son, and who was now following his coffin, had no more than that to live.

The entrails of the great Charles of Valois were taken to the Abbey of Chaâlis and his heart, enclosed in an urn, handed over to his third wife to await the time when she herself would have a tomb.

And then a great cold fell over the kingdom, as if the bones of this prince, from the mere fact of being placed in the earth, had suddenly made the whole of France freeze. People of those times would have no difficulty in recollecting the year of his death; they would merely have to say: 'It was at the time of the great frost.'

The Seine was entirely covered with ice; you could cross its minor tributaries, such as the stream of the Grange Batelière, on foot; the wells were frozen, and water had to be drawn from the cisterns not with buckets but with axes. The bark of the trees cracked in the gardens; there were elms split to the heart. The gates of Paris suffered much damage, for the cold fissured even the stone. Birds of all kinds, such as jays and magpies, which were never normally seen in towns, were searching for food in the cobbled streets. The price of peat doubled and there were no furs left in the shops, not a moleskin nor a miniver, nor even a mere sheepskin. In the poorer districts many old people and children died. Travellers' feet froze in their boots; the couriers' hands were blue when they delivered their dispatches. All river traffic had ceased. The troops sent to Guyenne, if unwise enough to remove their gloves, peeled the skin from their hands off on their weapons. Urchins amused themselves by persuading village idiots to put their tongues on to the blade of an axe. But what was to remain most impressed on people's memories was the extraordinary sense of silence because life seemed to have come to a stop.

At Court the New Year was celebrated rather quietly, partly because of mourning and partly because of the frost. Nevertheless, there was mistletoe and the usual presents were exchanged. On the accounts of the past year the Treasury would show a surplus of seventy-three thousand livres[31] – sixty thousand being derived from the Treaty of Aquitaine – of which Robert of Artois persuaded the King to credit him with eight thousand livres. It was indeed only fair, since Robert had been ruling the kingdom on behalf of his cousin for the last six months. He mounted an expedition in Guyenne, where the French arms scored a rapid victory since they found practically no English opposition. The local lords, at the mercy once again of the anger of the suzerain in Paris against his vassal in London, began to regret having been born Gascons. God would have done better by them had he given them lands in some other duchy.

Edward, ruined, in debt and unable to get any more credit, had been unable to send troops to defend his fief; but he sent ships to bring back his wife. She had written to the Bishop of

Winchester, so that he might communicate her letter to the whole English clergy:

'Neither you nor others of good understanding must believe that we have left the company of our lord without grave and reasonable cause and without our being in bodily peril from the said Hugh, who has our said lord under his dominion as well as all our kingdom and who wishes to dishonour us, of which we are most certain from having suffered it. So long as Hugh remains as at present, with our husband under his sway, we cannot return to the Kingdom of England without exposing our life and that of our very dear son to the danger of death.'

This letter crossed the new orders Edward sent the sheriffs of the coastal counties at the beginning of February. He informed them that the Queen and his son, the Duke of Aquitaine, whom he had sent to France to establish peace, had, under the influence of the traitor and rebel Mortimer, made alliance with the enemies of the King and the kingdom, and that should the Queen or the Duke of Aquitaine disembark from such ships as he, the King, had sent to France, his will was that they should be courteously received, but only if they arrived with good intentions; should they, however, disembark from foreign ships and show that they were bent on a course contrary to his wishes, the order was to spare only the Queen and Prince Edward, and to treat everyone else who landed as a rebel.

To gain time, Isabella got her son to write to the King that she was ill and in no condition to travel.

But in the month of March, when King Edward had learnt that his wife was enjoying herself going about in Paris, he had another attack of epistolatory fury. It seemed to be a cyclic disease that attacked him every three months.

Edward II wrote to the young Duke of Aquitaine as follows:

'On false pretexts our wife, your mother, has withdrawn herself from us because of our dear and faithful Hugh the Despenser, who had always served us so well and so loyally; but you can see, and everyone else can see, that she has openly and notoriously, departing from her duty and to the prejudice of our Crown, taken to herself Mortimer, the traitor and our mortal enemy, as he has been proved, attested and judged in full Parliament, and keeps company with him at home and abroad, in despite of us, our Crown and the rights of our realm. And she does even worse, if it be possible, by keeping you in company of our said enemy before the whole world, in very great dishonour and villainy, and in prejudice of the laws and usages of the Realm of England which it is your sovereign duty to safeguard and uphold.'

At the same time, he wrote to Charles IV:

'If your sister loved and desired to be in our company, as she lyingly told you, if your Grace will excuse the expression, she would not have left us on the pretext of furthering peace and friendship between us and you, which I believed in all good faith when I sent her to you. But really, very dear brother, we perceive clearly enough that she does not love us, and the reason she gives, concerning our dear kinsman Hugh the Despenser, is feigned. We think she must be out of her mind when, so overtly and notoriously, she retains in her counsels the traitor and our mortal enemy Mortimer, and is in company with this wicked man both at home and abroad.

You might also see, very dear brother, that she corrects her behaviour and conducts herself as she should for the honour of all her relations. Have the goodness to let us know what you intend to do, in accordance with God, good sense and good faith, and without regard to the caprices of women or other desires.'

Letters to the same effect were sent out once again in all directions, to peers, dignitaries, prelates, even to the Pope himself. The English sovereigns were each denouncing the other's lover in public, and this double affair of two couples consisting of three men and one woman vastly entertained the courts of Europe.

Discretion was now no longer possible to the lovers in Paris. Rather than seek to conceal things, Isabella and Mortimer lived openly together, and appeared on every occasion in each other's company. That the Earl of Kent and his wife, who had joined him, were on intimate terms with the adulterous couple seemed to constitute a sort of guarantee. Why should anyone be more concerned for the honour of the King of England than his own half-brother seemed to be? Indeed, Edward's letters had done no more than confirm the evidence of a liaison which everyone accepted as an accomplished and immutable fact. And all the unfaithful wives thought there must be some special forgiveness for queens and that Isabella was very lucky to have a bugger for a husband.

But there was a shortage of money. No funds now reached the emigrants, whose property had all been confiscated. And the little English Court in Paris lived entirely on loans from the Lombards.

At the end of March they had to summon old Tolomei

once again. He came to see Queen Isabella, accompanied by Signor Boccaccio, who had on him her account with the Bardi. The Queen and Mortimer received him most affably and explained their need for more money. With equal affability, and many expressions of regret, Messer Spinello Tolomei refused. He had good arguments to support his case; he opened his big black book and showed them the figures. Messire de Alspaye, Lord de Cromwell, Queen Isabella – as he turned the page, Tolomei bowed low – the Earl of Kent and the Countess – another bow – Lord Maltravers, Mortimer . . . And then, on four consecutive pages, the debts of King Edward himself . . .

Roger Mortimer protested: King Edward's account was no concern of theirs.

'But my lord,' said Tolomei, 'as far as we're concerned all the English debts are lumped together. I am grieved to have to refuse you, greatly grieved, and to have to disappoint so beautiful a lady as Madame the Queen; but it is really asking too much of me to expect from me what I no longer possess and you have had. This great fortune we are supposed to own is made up of nothing but debts. My whole wealth, my lord, consists of your debts. Consider, Madame,' he went on, turning to the Queen, 'consider, Madame, the situation of us poor Lombards, who are always being threatened, and always having to pay each new king the dues customary on a happy accession. And, alas, how many we have had to pay in the last twelve years! And then under every king our right of citizenship is withdrawn so that we must repurchase it at a high fee, and sometimes even twice over if the reign be a long one. Yet, look at what we do for the kingdoms! England has cost our companies a hundred and seventy thousand livres, the expenses of her coronations, her wars and her rebellions, Madame. Think of my age. I should have retired long ago, had I not to be ceaselessly going to and fro recovering these debts which we need to assist other purposes. We are called avaricious, greedy for what is due to us, yet no one considers the risks we take in lending everyone money and enabling the princes of this world to carry on their affairs. Priests are concerned with the lower classes, with giving alms to beggars and opening hospitals for the unfortunate; but we are concerned with the difficulties of the great.'

His age gave him the right to express himself in this way, and the gentleness of his tone was such that it was impossible to take offence at what he said. And all the time he was talking, his half-open eye was fixed on a jewel shining at the Queen's neck and which his book showed Mortimer had bought on credit.

'How did our business begin? Why do we exist? No one remembers it now,' he went on. 'Our Italian banks were created during the crusades because lords and travellers disliked carrying gold on the unsafe roads, where people were always being robbed, or even in the camps which were not peopled only by honest men. And there were also ransoms to pay. So that we should transport the gold on their account and at our risk, the lords, and particularly those of England, pledged the revenues of their fiefs to us. But when we presented ourselves in these fiefs with our accounts, thinking that the seal of a great baron was a sufficient guarantee, we were not paid. So then we appealed to the kings, who were prepared to guarantee their vassals' debts provided we lent money to them too; and this is how our resources came to be laid out among the kingdoms. No, Madame, to my great sorrow and regret, this time I cannot.'

The Earl of Kent who was present at the conversation said: 'All right, Messer Tolomei. We shall have to go to one of the other companies.'

Tolomei smiled. Did this fair young man, sitting there with his legs crossed and casually stroking a greyhound's head, really think he could take his custom elsewhere? In his long career Tolomei had heard that phrase a thousand times and more. What a terrible threat!

'My lord, when it is a question of such great borrowers as you royal personages, you must realize that all our companies are informed, and that the credit which I must regretfully refuse you will not be granted you by any other company. Messer Boccaccio, whom you see here with me, represents the Bardi interests. Ask him. For, Madame' – and Tolomei turned back to the Queen – 'this total of indebtedness has become very vexatious owing to the fact that none of it is covered by any guarantee. In the circumstances of your present relations with the King of England, he will most certainly not guarantee your debts. Nor you his, I imagine. Unless, of course, you do intend taking them over? If that were the case, then I think we might still perhaps be able to help you.'

And he closed his left eye completely, clasped his hands over his stomach and waited.

Isabella understood very little about finance. She looked at Roger Mortimer. What did the banker intend by these last words? After all the talk, what did this sudden overture mean?

'Make yourself a little clearer, Messer Tolomei,' she said.

'Madame,' went on the banker, 'your cause is good and your husband's far from pretty. The whole of Christendom knows of his wicked treatment of you, of the morals that blacken his life and of the bad government he inflicts on his subjects through his detestable counsellors. On the other hand, Madame, you are loved for your kindness, and I guarantee that there is no lack of good knights in France and elsewhere who would be ready to raise their banners for you and restore you to your place in your kingdom, even if it meant turning your husband, the King of England, off his throne.'

'Messer Tolomei,' cried the Earl of Kent, 'does it mean nothing to you that my brother, detestable though he may be, has been crowned?'

'My lord, my lord,' replied Tolomei, 'kings are really only such by the consent of their subjects. And you have at hand another king to give to the people of England, the young Duke of Aquitaine, who seems to show great sense for his age. I have seen too much of human passions not to recognize those that cannot be altered and lead the most powerful princes to disaster. King Edward will not rid himself of Despenser; but, on the other hand, England is perfectly prepared to acclaim any sovereign presented to her in exchange for the bad king she has and the wicked men who surround him. No doubt you will argue, Madame, that the knights who come forward to fight for your cause will be expensive to pay; they will have to be furnished with harness, food and their pleasures. But we Lombards, who can no longer face the prospect of supporting your exile, could still face the prospect of supporting your army, if Lord Mortimer, whose valour is known to all, would undertake to lead it, and if, of course, we had your guarantee that you would take over Messire Edward's debts and liquidate them on your success.'

The proposal could not have been more clearly put. The Lombard Companies were offering to back the wife against the husband, the son against the father, the lover against the legitimate husband. Mortimer was not so surprised as might have been expected, nor indeed did he pretend to be when he replied: 'The difficulty, Messer Tolomei, is to assemble these banners. You can't do it in a cellar. Where can we muster a thousand knights in our pay? In what country? We cannot ask King Charles, however well disposed he may be towards his sister, Madame the Queen, to allow us to assemble them in France.'

There was a certain connivance between the old Sienese and Edward's former prisoner.

'Has not the young Duke of Aquitaine,' said Tolomei, 'received as his personal property the county of Ponthieu, which came to him from Madame the Queen, and is not Ponthieu opposite England, and next to the county of Artois where Monseigneur Robert, though he is not its present holder, has many partisans, as you well know, my lord, since you took refuge there after your escape?'

'Ponthieu ...' repeated the Queen thoughtfully. 'What is your opinion, dear Mortimer?'

Though there was only a verbal agreement, it was nevertheless a bond. Tolomei was prepared to give the Queen and her lover a small credit at once so that they might deal with immediate necessities and leave straightway for Ponthieu to organize the expedition. And then, in May, he would supply the major part of the funds. Why May? Could he not make it an earlier date?

Tolomei was planning things in his mind. He was thinking that, together with the Bardi, he had a debt to recover from the Pope, and that he would ask Guccio, who was in Siena, to go to Avignon, since the Pope had happened to let him know, through a Bardi traveller, that he would like to see the young man again. And advantage must be taken of the Pope's benevolence. It would also be an opportunity, and perhaps the last, for Tolomei to see once again the nephew he missed so much.

And there was a flicker of amusement in the banker's thoughts. For, like Valois over the crusade and Robert of Artois over Aquitaine, the Lombard was thinking: 'It's the Pope who'll pay for England.' But when he had calculated the time it would take Boccaccio, who was about to set out for Italy, to reach Siena, and the time it would take Guccio to travel from Siena to Avignon, do his business there, and come on to Paris, he said: 'In May, Madame, in May; and may God prosper your affairs.'

And thus began the war of incompatible loves which was to make the destiny of nations totter.

2

The Return to Neauphle

WAS THE BANKING HOUSE at Neauphle really so small, the church beyond the little market-square so low, and the road winding up towards Cressay, Thoiry and Septeuil so narrow? Or was it Guccio who had grown bigger, not in inches of course, for the body grows no taller after the age of twenty, but bigger in mind and in importance, as if his eyes had become used to vaster spaces and his sense of the place he held in the world had expanded?

Nine years had gone by! The façade, the trees, the steeple, all suddenly made him feel nine years younger. Or, on the other hand perhaps, older by all the time that had elapsed.

Guccio had instinctively bent his head, as he had in the past, when he went through the low door that separated the two rooms of business on the ground floor of this branch of the Tolomei bank. His hand had instinctively sought the handrope on the oak pillar round which the corkscrew staircase was built as he went up to his old room. And so it was here that he had loved, as never before and never since!

The tiny room under the eaves was redolent of the countryside and of the past. How could so small a room have contained so great a love? Beyond the window, which was barely more than a loophole, the landscape was unchanged. It was the beginning of May and the trees were in blossom as they had been when he had left nine years ago. Why did trees in blossom arouse so intense an emotion, and why should the snow that dropped from cherry-trees or lay, tinged with pink, under apple-trees seem to fall from the heart? Between the branches that curved upwards like arms he could see the roof of the stable from which he had fled on the arrival of the brothers Cressay. How frightened he had been that night!

He turned to the tin mirror, which still stood in the same place on the chest. At the memory of his weaknesses, every man tends to reassure himself by staring at his own face, forgetting that the signs of strength he detects in it impress only himself, and that it was before others he showed weakness. The grey reflection on the polished metal showed Guccio the likeness of a dark-complexioned young man of thirty, with a deep line between the eyebrows, and two dark eyes with which he was not wholly displeased, for they had already seen many and varied landscapes, mountain snows and ocean waves, and they had aroused desire in women's hearts, and met the gaze of kings and princes.

'Guccio Baglioni, my friend, why did you not go on with the career you began so well? You travelled from Siena to Paris, from Paris to London, from London to Naples and then to Lyons and to Avignon; you carried messages for Queen Isabella, treasure for cardinals, and a demand for the hand in marriage of Queen Clémence. During two fabulous years you lived and journeyed among the great of this world, charged with their interests and their secrets. And you were barely twenty! And all you did succeeded. The proof of it lies in the welcome you receive everywhere after nine years' absence, and in the memories you left behind you and the friendship you inspired. And, in the first place, with the Holy Father himself. As soon as he saw you on a matter of business, the Sovereign Pontiff, from the elevation of the throne of Saint Peter, and though beset by so many tasks, showed an interest in your fate and fortune; he remembered even that you had had a son in the past, was concerned to learn that you had been deprived of your child, and devoted several of his precious minutes to giving you advice. "A son should be brought up by his father," he said; and he furnished you with a papal messenger's safe-conduct, the surest there is. And then Bouville! Bouville, whom you went to see, bearing Pope John's blessing, and who treated you as a long-awaited friend, wept on seeing you, and gave you one of his own sergeants-at-arms to accompany you on your journey, as well as a letter, sealed with his own seal, addressed to the brothers Cressay, so that you should be allowed to see your son.'

And thus it was that the highest personages took notice of Guccio, and, so he thought, without any interested motive, but simply because he could inspire them with feelings of friendliness, owing, no doubt, both to his intelligence and his particular way of conducting himself in the presence of the great of this world, which was simply a natural gift he happened to possess.

Oh, why had he not persevered? He could so easily have

become one of the great Lombards, as powerful among the nations as princes, such as Macci dei Macci, the real keeper of the Royal Treasury of France, or perhaps like Frescobaldi in England, who had access to the Chancellor of the Exchequer without having to be announced.

After all, was it too late? In his heart of hearts, Guccio felt he was his uncle's superior and capable of an even more remarkable success. For good Uncle Spinello, if you looked at it objectively, was engaged very largely in purely short-term business. He had become Captain-General of the Lombards of Paris mostly because of his seniority and the fact that his colleagues knew they could trust him. He had common sense, of course, and indeed a certain cunning, but no very great ambition, nor any great talent to justify it. Guccio could look at these things quite impartially, now that he had grown out of the age of illusions and felt himself to be a man of sound judgment. Yes, he had been wrong over the deplorable affair of the child born to Marie de Cressay. That had been the cause of it all. And then his fear – and this he had to admit – of being beaten to death by Marie's brothers!

For long months afterwards, his thoughts had been full of nothing but this unhappy event. He had been a prey to disappointed love, to despondency, to shame at seeing his friends and patrons after so inglorious an episode, and to dreams of revenge. He had been obsessed by these thoughts while beginning a new life in Siena, where no one knew anything of his unhappy adventure in France, except what he might care to tell them. Oh, she did not know, that ungrateful Marie, she did not know the great destiny she had destroyed by refusing to elope with him. How often he had thought bitterly of it in Italy. But now he was going to avenge himself.

And suppose Marie suddenly declared she still loved him, had been waiting loyally for him and that an appalling misunderstanding had been the only cause of their separation? Yes, suppose that was the case? Guccio knew he would yield at once, would forget his wrongs as soon as he had given them expression and would take Marie de Cressay back to Siena, to the family palace on the Piazza Tolomei, to show his beautiful wife off to his fellow-citizens. And he would show Marie the new city, which was smaller than Paris or London of course, but could rival them in beauty, with its Municipio only recently completed, of which the great Simone Martini was at this very moment finishing the interior, and with its black and white cathedral which would be the most beautiful in Tuscany, once its façade was done. Oh, the joys of sharing what one loved with a beloved wife! But what was he doing dreaming in front of a tin mirror, when he ought to be hurrying to Cressay and turning her surprise to his advantage?

But then he began to think. The bitterness he had nursed for nine years could not be forgotten all at once, nor indeed the fear that had driven him from this very garden. In the first place, it was his son he wanted above all. Perhaps he had better send the sergeant-at-arms down with the Count de Bouville's letter; the demand would carry more weight. And then, after nine years, was Marie still as beautiful? Would he still be as proud of appearing with her on his arm?

Guccio believed he had now attained to maturity, reached the age at which one acted from reason. Yet, even if there was now a line between his eyebrows, he was still the same man, the same mixture of cunning and ingenuousness, pride and romantic dreams. For in truth the years have little effect on our nature and age does not free us of our faults. We lose our hair more quickly than our weaknesses.

She had dreamed of its happening for nine years, hoped for it, feared it, prayed God each day to bring it about and prayed the Virgin to spare it her; evening after evening, morning after morning, she had prepared what she would say if it occurred, she had murmured to herself every answer she could think of to all the questions she could imagine; she had thought of a hundred, a thousand ways in which it might come about. It had come about. And now she did not know how to meet the situation.

For that morning Marie de Cressay's maid, who in the old days had been the confidante of her happiness and her tragedy, came to her room and whispered to her that Guccio Baglioni was back. He had been seen to arrive in the village of Neauphle; he had the retinue of a lord and several of the King's sergeants as his escort; he seemed to be a messenger from the Pope. This was the popular gossip which, as it so often does, bore some relation to the truth, because a single detail had awakened local curiosity: the urchins in the market-square had stared open-mouthed at the yellow leather harness embroidered with the keys of Saint Peter, which was indeed a present from the Pope to his banker's nephew, and that harness had set the whole village speculating.

And now the maid stood there breathless, her eyes bright with emotion and her cheeks red. Marie de Cressay had no idea what she ought or indeed would do.

She said: 'Give me my dress.'

She said it at once and without thinking, but the maid understood. For Marie had very few dresses, and the dress she was asking for could only be the one that had been made long ago out of the beautiful piece of silk Guccio had brought her as a present. Every week it was taken out of the chest, carefully brushed, ironed, aired, sometimes wept over, and never worn.

Guccio might appear at any moment. Had the maid seen him? No. She was merely repeating the gossip which was going from house to house. Perhaps he was already on the way! If Marie had only had a whole day in which to prepare for his arrival. She had had nine years, but they were all reduced now to a single instant.

What did it matter that the water was cold with which she washed her breast, stomach and arms, while the servant turned away, surprised at her mistress's sudden immodesty, though she could not resist a glance at the beautiful body which had been deprived so pitifully of a man for so long. She could not help being a little jealous at seeing how full and firm it had remained, like a fine plant in the sun, though the breasts were heavier than in the old days and sagged a little on to the chest, the thighs were not quite so smooth, and maternity had marked the stomach with a few small lines. So the bodies of noble girls spoiled too. Less than those of servants, of course. But they spoiled nevertheless, and it was God's justice in making all His creatures the same.

Marie had difficulty getting into her dress. Had the material shrunk from being unused so long, or had Marie grown stouter? It was more perhaps that the shape of her body had altered, as if the curves and contours were no longer in the same places. She had changed. She knew that the fair down was thicker on her lip, and that the freckles, due to her open-air life in the fields, had spread over her face. Her hair, that mass of golden hair whose braids must be so hurriedly plaited, was neither as soft nor as gleaming as it once had been.

But now Marie had donned her party dress, which was a bit tight at the armholes; and her hands, reddened by housework, emerged from the green silk sleeves, empty hands, empty of all the nine years that had suddenly been abolished.

What had she done with all those years that now seemed but a sigh of time?

She had lived on her memories. She had drawn daily nourishment from those few months of love and happiness, as if from a harvest that had been too quickly garnered. She had crushed each moment of that past in the mill of her memory. A thousand times over she had seen the young Lombard come to claim his debt and drive away the wicked Provost, caught his first glance, and relived their first walk together. A thousand times over she had repeated her vow in the dark, silent chapel before the unknown monk. A thousand times over she had discovered her pregnancy. A thousand times over she had been dragged violently from the convent in the Faubourg Saint-Marcel and taken in a closed litter, clasping her new-born child to her breast, to the royal Castle of Vincennes. A thousand times over she had seen her child dressed in the royal swaddling clothes, and then brought back to her dead. And it was still a dagger in her heart. And she still hated the Countess de Bouville even though she was dead, and she hoped she was suffering all the torments of Hell. A thousand times over she had been made to swear on the Bible to keep the little King of France, not to reveal the terrible secrets of the Court even in the confessional, and never to see Guccio again. And a thousand times over she had asked herself: 'Why should this have happened to me?'

She had asked it of the great dumb blue sky of August days, of the winter nights she spent shivering alone between coarse sheets, of the hopeless dawns, and of the evenings of eventless days. Why?

She had asked it of the linen she counted for the laundry, of the sauces she stirred on the kitchen fire, of the meat she put in the salting-tub, and of the stream that ran below the manor, on whose banks the people picked jonquils and irises on the mornings of religious processions.

At moments she had hated Guccio, hated him for existing and for having passed through her life like a tempestuous wind through a house with open doors; and then she had immediately reproached herself for the thought as if it were a blasphemy.

In turn she had looked on herself as a great sinner on whom the Almighty had imposed this perpetual expiation, as a martyr, as a sort of saint expressly designated by the Divine Will to save the Crown of France, Saint Louis's succession and the whole realm in the person of this little child who had been confided to her care. And it was like this that you could go mad, little by little, without those about you being aware of it.

She had only occasionally heard news of the one man she had ever loved, of her husband whom no one would recognize as such, and then only from a few words dropped by the employee at the bank to her maid. Guccio was alive.

That was all she knew. How she suffered from imagining him, or rather being unable to imagine him, in a distant country, in a strange town, and to think that perhaps he had married again. The Lombards had no such great respect for a vow as all that. And now Guccio was only a quarter of a league away. But had he really come back for her sake? Or merely to deal with some matter at the bank? That would be the most terrible thing of all: that he should be so near and not for her sake. But could she blame him even for this, since it was she herself who had refused to see him nine years ago, so harshly told him he must never see her again, and without being able to reveal the reason for her cruelty. And suddenly she cried, 'The child!'

For Guccio would want to see the little boy he believed his. It must surely be for that he had come?

Jeannot was out in the meadow – she could see it from the window – down by the Mauldre, the stream which was bordered with yellow irises and too shallow for there to be any danger of his drowning, playing with the groom's youngest son, the wheelwright's two boys and the miller's daughter, who was round as a ball. He had mud on his knees and face, and even in the lock of fair hair that lay in a curl across his forehead. He had strong, rosy legs and was shouting at the top of his voice. People thought him a little bastard, a child of sin, and treated him as such.

But why did not Marie's brothers, the peasants on the estate and the people of Neauphle see that Jeannot had nothing of that golden, almost auburn fairness that was his mother's and less still of Guccio's dark, almost gingerbread complexion? How could they fail to notice that he was a real little Capet, with his broad face, pale blue eyes set a little too far apart, his chin that would grow strong, and his straw-like fairness? King Philip the Fair was his grandfather. It was extraordinary how people shut their eyes so firmly to everything but the preconceived ideas they had of people and of things.

When Marie had suggested to her brothers that Jeannot should be sent to the monks of a neighbouring Augustinian monastery to be taught to write, they had merely shrugged their shoulders.

'We can read a little and it's not much good to us. We can't write and it wouldn't be any use to us if we could,' the eldest replied. 'Why do you want Jeannot to know more than we do? It's all very well for priests to study, but you can't even make him a priest since he's a bastard.'

Down among the irises in the meadow the child was sulkily following the servant who had been sent to fetch him. With a pole in his hand, he had been playing at being a knight, and had almost broken through the defences of a shed where wicked men were holding the miller's daughter prisoner.

And at this moment Marie's brothers, Jeannot's uncles, though they did not know they were only false uncles, came in from inspecting their fields. They were dusty, smelt of horses' sweat and their nails were black. Pierre, the elder, was already like what his father had been; his stomach bulged over his belt, his beard was shaggy, his teeth rotten and the two eye-teeth missing. He was hoping for a war in which he could make his name; and whenever he heard talk of England or the Empire, he would declare that the King had only to raise an army and everyone would see what the chivalry could do. He had not, however, been dubbed knight; but he might perhaps become one in the course of a campaign. His only experience of war had been in Louis Hutin's Muddy Host, for he had not been summoned to the expedition into Aquitaine. He had had a moment of hope on learning of Monseigneur Charles of Valois's proposed crusade; but then Monseigneur Charles had died. Oh, that was the baron God should have given them for king!

Jean de Cressay, the younger, was both thinner and paler, but paid no greater attention to his appearance. His life was a mixture of indifference and routine. Neither of them had married. Their sister had kept house for them since the death of their mother, Dame Eliabel; and they had thus someone to look after the kitchen and the linen, and someone, too, with whom they could lose their temper from time to time, and more easily indeed than they would have dared to do with a wife. Should their breeches have a tear in them, they could always blame Marie for the fact that they had been unable to find suitable wives because of the shame she had brought on the family.

Nevertheless, they lived in modest ease thanks to the pension that Count de Bouville regularly sent their sister on the pretext that she had been a royal wet-nurse, and thanks also to the presents in kind the banker Tolomei continued sending the child he believed to be his great-nephew. Marie's sin had therefore been of considerable advantage to the two brothers.

Jean knew a widow in Montfort-l'Amaury and visited her from time to time; and on those days he dressed himself up with a rather guilty air. Pierre preferred to hunt his own land,

and felt himself quite a seigneur, and at little cost, because a number of children in the neighbouring villages had already begun to resemble him. But what did honour to a son of the nobility was dishonourable in a daughter of the nobility; this was an accepted fact, which was not open to discussion.

Pierre and Jean were much surprised to find their sister wearing her silk dress and Jeannot stamping with rage because he was being washed. Was it by any chance a feast day they had forgotten?

'Guccio is in Neauphle,' Marie said.

And she took a hasty step backwards, because Pierre was quite capable of slapping her face.

But Pierre did nothing. He merely stared at Marie. And Jean did the same. They both stood there, their arms dangling, like men whose minds were incapable of grasping the unexpected. Guccio had come back. It was an important piece of news and it took them several minutes to absorb it. What new problems was it likely to create? They had to admit they had liked Guccio very well, when he had been their hunting companion and had brought them hawks from Milan; but this was before they had realized the fellow was making love to their sister practically under their noses. Then, when Dame Eliabel had discovered that her daughter was sinfully pregnant, they had wanted to kill him. But they had regretted their violence when they had visited the banker Tolomei in his house in Paris, and had realized, too late, that if their sister married a rich Lombard it would be less of a dishonour than to keep her at home as the mother of a fatherless child.

However, they had little time to consider the news, for the sergeant-at-arms, in the livery of the Count de Bouville, trotting along on a great bay horse, and wearing a coat of blue cloth scalloped about the thighs, rode in to the manor's courtyard, which was at once crowded with astonished onlookers. The peasants doffed their caps; children's heads appeared in the doorways; the women wiped their hands on their aprons.

The sergeant had come to deliver two messages to the Sire Pierre, one from Guccio and the other from the Count de Bouville himself. Pierre de Cressay assumed the important and haughty expression of a man receiving a letter. He frowned, pursed his lips behind his beard and loudly ordered that the messenger should be given to eat and drink, just as if he had ridden fifteen leagues. Then he went aside with his brother to read the letters. And, indeed, the two of them were not too many. They had even to summon Marie, who was more skilled in interpreting the letters of the alphabet.

And Marie began to tremble, tremble, tremble.

'We cannot understand it, Messire. Our sister began trembling as if Satan himself had appeared before her. And she utterly refused to see you. Then she burst into tears.'

The two Cressay brothers were much embarrassed. They had had their boots cleaned, and Jean had donned the tunic he normally wore only when visiting his widow in Montfort. They were standing looking abashed and rather uncertain of themselves in the back room of the branch bank of Neauphle, while Guccio contemplated them rather sourly and did not even ask them to sit down.

Two hours before, when they had received the letters, they had imagined they could do good business over their sister's departure and the recognition of her marriage. A thousand livres cash down was what they intended asking. A Lombard could well afford that much. But Marie had destroyed their hopes by her strange attitude and her determination not to see Guccio.

'We tried to reason with her, and indeed much to our own disadvantage; for, if she left us, we should miss her very much, since she does all the housekeeping. But, when it comes to it, we really do understand that, if you have come back to ask for her after so long a time, it must be because she really is your wife, even though the marriage took place in secret. Besides, much time has passed.'

The bearded brother was spokesman and he was getting a bit mixed up. His younger brother contented himself with nodding approval.

'We frankly admit,' went on Pierre de Cressay, 'that we made a mistake when we refused you our sister. But it was not us so much as our mother – may God keep her! – who had decided against it. A gentleman should recognize his errors, and if our sister Marie acted without our consent, we were partly to blame. All that should be wiped out. Time is the master of us all. But now it is she who refuses to see you; and yet I swear to God that she has no other man in mind. That I do know. But I really don't understand what it's all about any more. Our sister's got an odd mentality, hasn't she, Jean?'

Jean de Cressay nodded.

For Guccio it was a splendid revenge to have these two men standing there stammeringly repentant, when they had once come sword in hand in the middle of the night to kill him, and had obliged him to leave France. Now they wanted to give him their sister more than anything else in the world. A little more and they would be praying him to take the bull by the horns, come to Cressay, impose his will and stand out for his rights as a husband.

But they misunderstood Guccio and his easily offended pride. He cared nothing for the two idiots. Only Marie mattered to him; and Marie was repulsing him when he was there so close to her, and had come prepared to forget all the injuries of the past. Did these people exist merely to humiliate him every time they met?

'Monseigneur de Bouville must have thought she might behave like this,' said the bearded brother, 'for he says in his letter: "If Dame Marie, as is very likely, refuses to see the Seigneur Guccio . . ." Do you know why he should have written like that?'

'No, I don't,' replied Guccio. 'But she must have made her position with regard to me perfectly clear to Messire de Bouville for him to be so sure of it.'

'And yet she has no other man in mind,' repeated the bearded brother.

Guccio was getting angry. His dark eyebrows contracted about the vertical line that marked his forehead. This time he really had the right to act towards Marie without scruple. She should be paid for her cruelty with even greater cruelty.

'What about my son?' he asked.

'He's here. We brought him with us.'

In the next room the child, who was inscribed on the list of kings and whom the whole of France thought had died nine years ago, was watching the clerk doing his accounts and playing with a goose-quill. Jean de Cressay opened the door.

'Jeannot, come here,' he said.

Guccio, interested in his own reactions, managed to summon up a little emotion. 'My son, I'm going to see my son,' he thought. In fact he really felt nothing at all. And yet he had so often longed for this moment. But he had not expected the heavy little countryman's footsteps he heard approaching.

The boy came in. He was wearing short breeches and a linen smock; his rebellious lock of hair lay askew on his pale forehead. A real little peasant.

For a moment the three men were embarrassed, and the child was well aware of it. Pierre pushed him towards Guccio.

'Jeannot, this is . . .'

He had to say something, tell Jeannot who Guccio was. And what else could he tell him but the truth?

'This is your father.'

Guccio had foolishly expected transports, open arms, tears. Little Jeannot looked up at him with astonished blue eyes.

'But I was told my father was dead,' he said.

This was a shock to Guccio; he suddenly felt furiously angry.

'Not at all, not at all,' Jean de Cressay interrupted hastily. 'He was travelling and couldn't send news. Isn't that right, friend Guccio?'

'I wonder how many lies they've brought him up on?' Guccio thought. 'Patience, I must have patience. How wicked to tell him his father was dead!' And since he had to say something, he said: 'How very fair he is.'

'Yes, exactly like our uncle Pierre, the brother of our late father, whose name I bear,' replied the bearded brother.

'Jeannot, come to me, come,' said Guccio.

The boy obeyed, but his rough little hand seemed ill at ease in Guccio's and he wiped his cheek after being kissed.

'I'd like to have him for a few days,' Guccio went on, 'to take him to see my uncle Tolomei, who wants to make his acquaintance.'

And, as he said this, Guccio automatically closed his left eye, like Tolomei.

Jeannot looked at him with his mouth open. What a lot of uncles there were! Everyone always seemed to be talking of uncles.

'I've got an uncle in Paris who sends me presents,' he said in a clear voice.

'He's the one we're going to visit. If your uncles have no objection. You see nothing against it, do you?' Guccio asked.

'Of course not,' replied Pierre de Cressay. 'Monseigneur de Bouville mentions it in his letter and tells us to permit it.'

It was obvious that the Cressays never did anything without Bouville's permission.

The bearded brother was already thinking of the presents the banker was bound to give his great-nephew. He might reasonably expect a purse of gold, which would be particularly welcome since a murrain had fallen on the livestock this year. And – who could tell? – the banker was old and might well intend mentioning the child in his will.

Guccio was already savouring his vengeance. But had vengeance ever consoled for lost love?

It was Guccio's horse and the Pope's harness that first attracted the boy. He had never seen so fine a mount. He also stared with a mixture of curiosity and admiration at the clothes this father who had fallen to him from the skies was wearing. He gazed at the skin-tight breeches that had no single crease at the knee, the boots of dark, supple leather, and the short travelling coat of a curiously shot material, leaf-brown in colour, closed high in front by a line of small buttons held in loops, and with a little hood that fell back from the neck.

The Count de Bouville's sergeant-at-arms was much more brightly and splendidly dressed in his azure-blue coat gleaming in the sunshine, with its braided scallops at wrist and thigh and its lordly coat of arms embroidered on the breast. But the boy had realized at once that it was Guccio who gave the sergeant orders, and he was lost in admiration for a father who spoke as a master to someone so resplendently clothed.

They had already ridden some four leagues. In the inn at Saint-Nom-la-Bretèche where they halted, Guccio, in a naturally authoritarian voice, ordered an omelette with herbs, a capon roasted on the spit, and a cream cheese. And wine. The alacrity displayed by the servants still further increased Jeannot's respect for him.

'Why do you speak differently from us, Messire?' he asked. 'You don't pronounce your words in the same way we do.'

Guccio was rather hurt at this remark from his own son about his Tuscan accent.

'Because I come from Siena, in Italy, which is my country,' he replied proudly. 'And you will become a Sienese too, a free citizen of a town in which we are powerful. And now don't call me Messire, but *Padre*.'

'*Padre*,' the boy repeated docilely.

Then Guccio, the sergeant and the boy sat down to their

meal. And while they were waiting for the omelette, Guccio began to teach Jeannot the names of common objects in his own tongue.

'*Tavola*,' he said, putting his hand on the edge of the table, '*bottiglia*,' picking up a bottle, '*vino* . . .'

He felt rather embarrassed by the boy's presence, and found it difficult to be himself; he was paralysed by the fear of being unable to make himself loved, and also of being unable to love. Though he kept on saying to himself 'This is my son,' he felt nothing except a profound hostility to the people who had brought him up.

Jeannot had never drunk wine before. At Cressay they drank only cider, or even skimmed milk like peasants. He drank a few mouthfuls. He was accustomed to the omelette and the cream cheese, but the roast capon made it like a feast day. He enjoyed this meal taken on the road in the middle of the afternoon. He was not frightened, and the excitement of the adventure made him forget to think of his mother. He had been told he would see her again in a few days' time. The names Paris and Siena meant little to him and he had no precise idea of how far away they were. Next Saturday he would be back beside the Mauldre and would be able to say to the miller's daughter and the wheelwright's sons: 'I am Sienese.' Nor would he have to explain matters, since they knew even less about these things than he did.

When they had swallowed their last mouthful, wiped their daggers on pieces of bread and replaced them at their belts, they remounted their horses. Guccio lifted the boy and placed him in front of him across the saddle-bow.[32]

The heavy meal and above all the wine, which he had now

tasted for the first time, had made the child drowsy. Before they had gone half a league, he fell asleep, indifferent to the jolting of the trotting horse.

There is nothing so moving as a sleeping child, particularly during the day, when adults are awake and about their business. Guccio held the jolting, swaying, abandoned little body steady. It was already quite heavy. He instinctively caressed with his chin the fair hair that seemed to be seeking shelter against him and drew his arm closer about the boy, as if to make the little, round, drowsy head lie even closer against his chest. There was a smell of childhood about the little sleeping body. And suddenly Guccio felt himself to be really a father, and proud of it, and tears misted his eyes.

'Jeannot, my Jeannot, my Giannino,' he murmured, putting his lips to the warm, silky hair.

He had reined his horse back into a walk and signed to the sergeant to do likewise, so as not to wake the boy and at the same time to prolong his own happiness. What did it matter when they arrived? Tomorrow Giannino would wake up in the house in the Rue des Lombards, which would seem a palace to him; servants would fuss over him, wash him, dress him like a little lord, and a fairy-tale life would begin for him.

Marie de Cressay refolded the now useless dress under the eyes of her silent but disappointed maid. For the maid had also dreamed of a different life to which she would follow her mistress, and there was a certain reproof in her attitude.

But Marie had stopped trembling and her eyes were dry; she had made her decision. She had only a few days to wait, a week at most. This morning she had been taken unawares; it was those nine years in which she had turned the same thoughts over and over in her mind which had made her so nervous and afraid and induced her to give so absurd an answer, so crazy a refusal.

It was because she had been thinking only of the oath Madame de Bouville – that wicked woman – had made her swear so long ago; and of her threats: 'If you insist on seeing this man again . . . it will be his death.'

But the years had gone by. Two kings had succeeded to the throne and no one had ever uttered a word. And Madame de Bouville was dead. Besides, did that terrible oath agree with the laws of God? Was it not a sin to prevent a human being avowing her spiritual troubles to her confessor? Even nuns could be relieved of their vows. Surely no one had the right to separate a wife from her husband? That was not Christian either. And the Count de Bouville was not a bishop, nor indeed was he anything like so terrifying as his wife had been.

Marie ought to have thought of all these things this morning; she should have realized that she could not live without Guccio, that her place was beside him, and that when Guccio came to fetch her nothing in the world – oaths taken in the past, the secrets of the Crown, the fear of what men might do, or even the punishment of God, were it to be inflicted – ought to prevent her going with him.

She would not lie to Guccio. A man who still loved you after nine years, had taken no other woman, and had come back to look for you, had a loyal and upright heart, like a knight who surmounted every ordeal. Such a man could share a secret and keep it. Besides, what right had she to lie to him, to let him believe his son was alive and that he was clasping him in his arms, when it was not true?

Marie would explain to Guccio that their child, their first-born – for, in her thoughts, the dead child was already only their first-born – had been given and exchanged by a tragic concatenation of events to save the life of the real King of France. And she would ask Guccio to share her oath. Together they would bring up the little posthumous Jean, who had reigned during the first five days of his life, until the day came when the barons sought him out to give him back his crown. And the other children they would have would be like real brothers to the King of France one day. If things could all go wrong through the agency of a blind Fate, why should they not also go right?

All this Marie would explain to Guccio, when he came back in a few days' time, next week, and brought Jeannot with him, as had been agreed with her brothers.

And then their happiness, which had been so long deferred, could really begin. And if all joy on earth had to be paid for by an equal weight of suffering, then they would both have earned all their future happiness in advance. Would Guccio want to live at Cressay? Clearly not. In Paris? It would be dangerous for little Jean and they must not defy the Count de Bouville from too close at hand, after all. They would go to Italy. Guccio would take her to that country of which she knew nothing but the beautiful cloth it produced and its clever goldsmiths' work. She already loved Italy because the man God had selected for her came from that country. Marie was already travelling in her thoughts beside her recovered husband. In a week's time everything would be all right; she had only a week to wait.

Alas, in love, it is not enough to have the same desires; they must also be expressed at the same time.

3

The Queen in the Temple

For a boy of nine whose whole horizon, since he had been of an age to remember, had been limited by a stream, manure pits and village roofs, the discovery of Paris could be no other than an enchantment. But how could this discovery be described when it was made under the aegis of a father who was so proud of his son, who positively gloried in him, and who had him dressed, curled, bathed and anointed, who took him to the best shops, stuffed him with sweetmeats, bought him embroidered shoes and a purse to wear at his belt with real money in it? Jeannot, or Giannino, was having a wonderful time.

And then there were all the fine houses to which his father took him. For Guccio, on a variety of pretexts, and sometimes on none at all, was making the round of his old acquaintances, merely to be able to say proudly: 'My son!' and show off this miracle, this unique splendour to the world: a little boy who said: '*Padre mio*' with an Île-de-France accent.

If people showed surprise at Giannino's fairness, Guccio mentioned his mother who was of noble family; and on these occasions he would assume an expression of pretended discretion, which was indeed redolent both of indiscretion and of that boastfully mysterious air with which Italians feign silence about their conquests. And thus all the Lombards in Paris, the Peruzzi, the Boccanegra, the Macci, the Albizzi, the Frescobaldi, the Scamozzi, and Signor Boccaccio himself were in the know.

Uncle Tolomei, one eye open, the other closed, his stomach larger than ever and his leg trailing, took a considerable part in all this display. Oh, if only Guccio could come and live in Paris again under his roof, together with little Giannino, how happy the old Lombard would be for the rest of his days.

But it was an impossible dream. For in that case the child would have to be surrendered to his other family, according to promise, and they would be able to see him only from time to time. But why would not that silly, stubborn Marie de Cressay agree to the regularization of the marriage? Why would she not live with her husband now that everyone was in agreement? Tolomei, though he hated travelling anywhere nowadays, offered to go to Neauphle and make a last attempt.

'But it's I who no longer want anything to do with her, Uncle,' declared Guccio. 'I won't have my honour flouted. Besides, what pleasure would there be in living with a woman who no longer loves me?'

'Are you quite sure of that?'

There was one sign, and one only, which made Guccio a little uncertain of the answer to that question. He had found about Giannino's neck the little reliquary Queen Clémence had once given him when he was in the Hôtel-Dieu at Marseilles, and which he in turn had given Marie once when she was very ill.

'My mother took it from her neck and put it round mine when my uncles brought me to you that morning,' the boy explained.

But could he rely on so slender an indication as this, on a gesture that might well have a purely religious significance?

And then the Count de Bouville had been categorical.

'If you want to keep the child, you must take him to Siena, and the sooner the better,' he had said to Guccio.

The interview had taken place at the former Great Chamberlain's house, behind the Pré-aux-Clercs. Bouville was walking in his garden which was enclosed by walls. Tears came to his eyes when he saw Giannino. He had kissed the little boy's hand before kissing his cheek and, gazing at him, looking him up and down from head to foot, he had murmured: 'A real little prince, a real little prince!'

And as he talked he wiped the tears from his eyes. Guccio was astonished by such evident emotion in a man who had held such high positions, and he was touched by it, taking it for a token of friendship for himself.

'A real little prince, as you say, Messire,' Guccio had replied happily; 'and it's surprising enough when you think that he has seen nothing of life but the country and that his mother, after all, is really only a peasant.'

Bouville nodded his head. Yes, yes, it really was very surprising.

'You can't do better than take him with you. Besides, haven't you the august approval of the Holy Father? I shall give you two sergeants to accompany you to the frontier of the kingdom, so that no harm shall come to you, or to . . . this child.'

He seemed to find it difficult to say: 'your son'.

'Goodbye, my little prince,' he said, embracing Giannino once more. 'Shall I ever see you again?'

And then he had walked quickly away, because the tears were welling to his eyes again. The child was really too painfully like the great King Philip the Fair.

'Are we going back to Cressay?' Giannino asked on the morning of May 11, when he saw the travelling-trunks being packed and a great commotion in the house announcing a journey.

He did not seem particularly impatient to return to the manor.

'No, my son,' replied Guccio; 'we're going to Siena first.'

'Is my mother coming with us?'

'No, not at present; she'll join us later.'

The boy seemed satisfied. It occurred to Guccio that after hearing lies about his father for nine years, Giannino was now entering on a further period of years in which he would hear lies about his mother. But what else could he do? Perhaps one day he would have to let him believe his mother was dead.

There was still one visit to make before leaving; the most fascinating if not the most important. He must pay his respects to Queen Clémence of Hungary.

'Where is Hungary?' the boy asked.

'Very far away, towards the east. It takes weeks of travelling to get there. Very few people have ever been there.'

'But why does Queen Clémence live in Paris if she is Queen of Hungary?'

'She has never been Queen of Hungary, Giannino; her father was King of Hungary, but she was Queen of France.'

'Then she's the wife of Charles the Fool?'

No, the King's wife was Madame of Évreux, who was being crowned that very day; and later on they would go to the royal palace to have a look at the ceremony in the Sainte-Chapelle, so that Giannino might leave with a last memory more splendid than all the rest. Guccio, who was normally so impatient, grew neither weary nor bored explaining to the young mind things that seemed self-evident but indeed were not so unless you had known them always. For this was how you learned about the great world.

But then who was this Queen Clémence they were going to see? And how did Guccio know her?

From the Rue des Lombards to the Temple, by way of the Rue de la Verrerie, was not very far to walk. On the way Guccio told the boy how he had gone to Naples with the Count de Bouville – 'the fat lord, you know, whom we visited the other day and who kissed you' – to ask for this Princess's hand in marriage to King Louis X, who was now dead. And how he, Guccio, had been with Madame Clémence in the ship that had brought them to France, and how she had nearly been drowned in a great storm before they reached Marseilles.

'And that reliquary you're wearing round your neck was given me by her in gratitude for having saved her from drowning.'

And then, when Queen Clémence had had a son, Giannino's mother had been chosen as wet-nurse.

'My mother has never told me anything about it,' the boy said in surprise. 'So she knew Madame Clémence too?'

All this seemed very complicated. Giannino would have liked to know whether Naples was in Hungary. But then passers-by were jostling them; a phrase hung unfinished in the air; a water-carrier interrupted a reply. It was very difficult for the boy to make sense of the story. And in twenty or thirty years' time he would say: 'My father told me about these things, one day, in Paris, when we were walking up the Rue du Temple, but I was very young; he told me that I was the foster-brother of King Jean the Posthumous . . .'

Giannino knew very well what a foster-brother was. He had often heard them spoken of at Cressay; the country was full of foster-brothers. But foster-brother to a king? That gave one food for thought. For a king was a tall, strong man with a crown on his head. It had never occurred to him that kings had foster-brothers, or might be little children who died at five days old.

'My mother has never told me anything about it,' he repeated.

And he began to blame his mother for concealing so many astonishing things from him.

'And why is the place we're going to called the Temple?'

'Because of the Templars.'

'Oh, yes, I know. They used to spit on the Cross, worship the head of a cat, and poison the wells so as to keep all the money in the kingdom.'

He had heard about this from the wheelwright's son, who had got his information from his father, who had got it from God knew where. It was not easy for Guccio, among all the crowd and in such a short time, to explain to his son that the truth was a little more complex. And the boy could not understand why the Queen they were going to see should be living with such wicked people.

'They no longer live there, *figlio mio*. They no longer exist; it's the Grand Master's old house.

'Master Jacques de Molay? Was that he?'

'You must ward off the evil eye with your fingers, my boy, when you utter that name. The Templars were suppressed, burnt or driven out, and the King seized the Temple which was their house.'

'Which king?'

Among so many kings, poor Giannino was all at sea.

'Philip the Fair.'

'Did you ever see King Philip the Fair?'

The boy had heard talk of this terrifying king who was now so highly respected; but it was all part of those shadowy times before he was born. And Guccio was touched.

'Of course,' he thought, 'he wasn't born then; to him it's all as remote as Saint Louis.'

And now they had to walk even slower because of the crowd, and he said: 'Yes, I saw him. Indeed, I nearly knocked him down in one of these very streets because of two greyhounds I was taking for a walk on a lead. It was the day I arrived in Paris twelve years ago.'

And time seemed to flow back over him like a huge wave, submerging him before breaking. A froth of days lay all about him. He was already a man recounting his memories.

'So you see,' he went on, 'the house of the Templars became the property of King Philip the Fair, and afterwards of King Louis, and afterwards of King Philippe the Long, who preceded the present King. And King Philippe the Long gave the Temple to Queen Clémence in exchange for the Castle of Vincennes which she had inherited by the will of her husband King Louis.'[33]

'*Padre mio*, I want a waffle.'

He had noticed a delicious smell of waffles coming from a stall, and his interest in these kings who succeeded each other all too rapidly and exchanged their houses suddenly vanished. He already knew, too, that to begin by saying '*Padre mio*' was a sure way of getting what he wanted; but it didn't work this time.

'No, on the way back; you'll only make yourself dirty. And remember what I told you. Don't talk to the Queen unless she talks to you; and kneel to kiss her hand.'

'Like in church?'

'No, not like in church. Look, I'll show you, or at least I'll explain, because I find difficulty in doing it owing to my wounded leg.'

They were an odd sight for the passers-by, the short dark foreigner and the fair boy practising going down on their knees in a doorway.

'And then you must get up quickly; but don't jostle the Queen.'

The Temple had been much altered since the days of Messire de Molay; and indeed had been split up. Queen Clémence's residence consisted only of the great square tower with its four turrets and a few secondary lodgings, buildings and stables round the huge paved courtyard, and the garden behind. The rest of the commandery, the lodgings of the knights, the armouries, and the workshops of the companions, cut off by high walls, had been put to other uses. And the huge courtyard, where several hundred men could be paraded, seemed now deserted and dead. The state litter with its white curtains, which was waiting to take Queen Clémence to the coronation, looked like a ship that had arrived in error or distress in some disused port. Though there were a few grooms and footmen standing around the litter, the whole house had an atmosphere of silence and desuetude.

Guccio and Giannino entered the tower of the Temple by the very same door from which Jacques de Molay had come from his dungeon, twelve years before, to be taken to the place of execution.[34] The rooms had been redecorated; but, in spite of the tapestries and splendid works of art in ivory, silver and gold, the heavy vaults and narrow windows, the walls deadening all sound, and indeed the very proportions of his warriors' residence, all made it far from a suitable habitation for a woman, particularly for a woman of only thirty-two. It all seemed designed for those rough men who wore a sword over their robe, and who had at one time assured the total supremacy of Christendom within the frontiers of the old Roman Empire. For a young widow the Temple seemed a prison.

Madame Clémence did not keep her visitors waiting long. She appeared, already dressed for the ceremony she was to attend, wearing a white dress, with a bodice of veiling across her breast, a royal cloak hanging from her shoulders and a gold crown on her head. She looked a true Queen, like those depicted in church windows. Giannino thought queens dressed like this every day of their lives. Beautiful, fair, magnificent and distant, her eyes a little absent, Clémence of Hungary smiled conventionally, with that smile a Queen, who has neither power nor realm, owes it to herself to give people who approach her.

This dead woman without a tomb, who had to fill her too long days with useless occupations, collected pieces of goldsmiths' work, and this was the only interest she had in the world, or indeed pretended to have.

The audience was rather disappointing for Guccio, who had expected some display of emotion, but not for the boy, who saw before him a saint out of Heaven in a mantle of stars.

Madame of Hungary asked all the proper questions that form the basis for the conversation of sovereigns who have nothing to say. For all Guccio's attempts to turn the conversation to their common memories, to Naples and the storm, the Queen evaded him. For, in fact, all memories were painful to her and she thrust them from her. And when Guccio, trying to attract her attention to Giannino, said he was 'the foster-brother of your son, Madame', her beautiful face turned almost hard. A Queen did not weep in public. But it was too great cruelty, though unconscious, to show her a fair, fresh, living child of the same age as hers would have been, and one, moreover, who had sucked the same milk.

The voice of their common blood was silent, only the voice of misfortune was alive. And the day, perhaps, was not very well chosen, for Clémence was going to attend the coronation of the third Queen of France since herself. Out of politeness, she forced herself to ask: 'What will this pretty boy do when he's grown up?'

'He will be a banker, Madame; at least I hope so, like his father and all his ancestors.'

Like all his ancestors. Queen Clémence was in the presence of her son. She did not know it. She never would know it.

She imagined Guccio had come to claim a debt or ask payment for some gold cup or jewel she had bought from his uncle. She was so used to tradesmen's demands. She was surprised when she realized that this young man had come merely to visit her. Were there still people who came to pay their respects and wanted nothing from her, neither money nor services?

Guccio told the boy to show the Queen the reliquary he was wearing round his neck. The Queen had forgotten, and Guccio had to remind her of the Hôtel-Dieu in Marseilles, where she had given it to him. 'This young man was once in love with me,' she thought.

It was the illusory consolation of a woman whose love-life had ended too soon and who grasped at any evidence of an emotion she might once have aroused, even when that emotion was so tenuous that the man who showed it was not even aware of it himself.

She bent down to kiss the boy. But Giannino immediately fell on his knees again and kissed her hand.

She looked round, almost automatically, for a present to give him and, seeing a silver-gilt box, handed it to the boy, saying, 'I am sure you like comfits? Take this comfit-box, and may God keep you.'

It was time to set out for the ceremony. She got into her

litter, and ordered the white curtains to be closed. She was suddenly devastated by an intolerable sense of unhappiness that seemed to emanate from her whole body, from her breasts, legs and stomach, from that whole useless beauty which was hers. At last she could weep.

In the Rue du Temple there was a considerable crowd all moving the same way, towards the Seine and the Cité, to see what they could of the coronation, though they would doubtless see little more than themselves.

Guccio took Giannino by the hand and followed the white litter, as if he were part of the Queen's escort. In this way they were able to cross the Pont-au-Change, enter the courtyard of the Palace, and watch the great lords going into the Sainte-Chapelle, wearing their state robes. Guccio recognized most of them and could tell the boy their names: the Countess Mahaut of Artois, still taller in her coronet; Count Robert, her nephew, who was even taller still; Monseigneur Philippe of Valois, now a Peer of France, with his lame wife beside him; and Madame Jeanne of Burgundy, the other widowed Queen. But who were this young couple, some eighteen and fifteen years of age, who were following them? Guccio asked his neighbours. He was told they were Madame Jeanne of Navarre and her husband, Philippe of Évreux. Indeed, you had to get used to the changes life brought about. The daughter of Marguerite of Burgundy was fifteen years old, and now she was married, after all the dynastic dramas that had been caused by her presumed bastardy.

The crush was so great that Guccio had had to hoist Giannino on to his shoulders; the little devil weighed a ton.

And then Queen Isabella of England came by, having

returned expressly from Ponthieu. Guccio thought her astonishingly little altered since he had seen her long ago at Westminster, when he had delivered to her a message from Count Robert. Though he had thought of her as being taller than she was. Beside her walked her son, young Edward of Aquitaine. And everyone craned their necks because the train of the boy's ducal mantle was borne by Roger Mortimer, as if he were the Prince's Great Chamberlain or tutor. It was an audacious thing to do. Perhaps only Madame Isabella would have dared show such defiance before the peers, bishops and all the others who had received letters from her cuckolded husband. Roger Mortimer wore an air of triumph, which was only surpassed by that of King Charles the Fair, whom no one had ever seen looking so happy before. The Queen of France, so it was whispered, was two months gone at last. And her official coronation, which had been deferred till now, was by way of being a reward.

Giannino suddenly lent down to Guccio's ear and said: '*Padre mio*, the fat lord who kissed me in his garden the other day is there, looking at me.'

What a confused and disturbing succession of thoughts passed through good Bouville's mind as from amid the press of dignitaries he saw the real King of France, whom all the world thought in his tomb at Saint-Denis, perched on the shoulders of a Lombard banker, while the wife of his second successor was being crowned.

And that very afternoon, on the road to Dijon, the pleasantest and safest for Italy, two of that same Count de Bouville's sergeants-at-arms were escorting the Sienese traveller accompanied by the fair boy. Guccio Baglioni thought he was carrying off his son; in fact, he was kidnapping the true and legitimate King of France. And this secret was known by no one save an august old man in a room in Avignon filled with the cries of birds, a former Chamberlain in his garden in the Pré-aux-Clercs, and a despairing young woman in a meadow in the Île-de-France. The widowed Queen in the Temple would continue to have Masses said for a dead child.

4
The Council at Chaâlis

THE LATE JUNE sky had cleared after the storm. In the royal apartments of the Abbey of Chaâlis, that Cistercian establishment founded by the Capets in which the entrails of Charles of Valois had been deposited a few months ago,[35] the candles were smoking and mingling the smell of wax with the scent of the earth after rain and the odour of incense that lingered about all religious houses. Insects escaping the storm had come in through the arched windows and were fluttering round the flames.

It was a melancholy evening. The expressions of all those present were thoughtful, sullen or bored. The tapestries that hung over the bare stone walls of the vaulted chamber were already old; they were strewn with lilies and followed the pattern in general use in the royal residences. There were some ten people assembled about Charles IV: Count Robert of Artois, Count Philippe of Valois, the Bishop of Beauvais, Jean de Marigny, a Peer of the Realm, the Chancellor Jean de

Cherchemont, Count Louis of Bourbon, the Lame, the Great Chamberlain, and the Constable Gaucher de Châtillon. The last had lost his eldest son the previous year, and it seemed to have aged him at a single blow. He now really looked every one of his seventy-six years; and he was getting increasingly deaf, which he attributed to the bombards which had been let off in his ear at the siege of La Réole.

A few women had been admitted because it was a family matter that had to be dealt with this evening. There were the three Jeannes, who were the first ladies of the kingdom; Madame Jeanne of Évreux, the Queen, Madame Jeanne of Valois, Robert's wife – who was called the Countess of Beaumont, in accordance with her husband's official title, though the latter, from habit, was still referred to as Monseigneur of Artois – and then Jeanne of Burgundy, the wicked, avaricious granddaughter of Saint Louis, who was lame like her cousin of Bourbon, and was the wife of Philippe of Valois.

And then Mahaut, a Mahaut with grey hair and dressed in black and purple, heavy of bust, buttock, arm and shoulder, colossal. People often seemed to grow shorter with age, but not Mahaut. During these last months she had become an old giantess, and was even more impressive than as a young giantess. It was the first time in a very long while that the Countess of Artois had appeared at Court without a coronet on her head for the ceremonies at which her rank as a Peer of the Realm compelled her attendance. It was the first time, since the death of her son-in-law, Philippe the Long, that she had been seen at a Council.

She had arrived at Chaâlis arrayed in mourning like a walking catafalque, draped like a church in Passion week. In fact, her daughter Blanche had recently died in the Abbey of Maubuisson to which she had finally been admitted, after first being transferred from Château Gaillard to a less forbidding residence near Coutances, a privilege Mahaut had obtained for her in exchange for the annulment of her marriage. But Blanche had not profited much by this amelioration of her lot. She had died only a few months after entering the convent, exhausted by the long years of imprisonment and by the terrible winter nights in the fortress at Andelys. She had died of emaciation, coughing and misfortune, at the age of thirty, wearing a nun's veil and almost mad. And all this for one year of love, if indeed her adventure with Gautier d'Aunay could be called love; all this because she had allowed herself to be drawn into imitating the pleasures of her sister-in-law, Marguerite of Burgundy, and at the age of eighteen, when she scarcely knew what she was doing.

The woman who would at this moment have been Queen of France, the only woman Charles the Fair had ever really loved, had thus died at the very moment she had at last achieved a relative peace. And King Charles the Fair, in whom her death aroused so many painful memories, was sad, and though his third wife knew very well what he was thinking of, she pretended not to notice it.

And Mahaut had seized the opportunity this death afforded her. She had come, unbidden and unannounced, as if, a sorrowing mother, she was responding merely to the dictates of her heart, and desired to present her condolences to the unhappy former husband; and they had fallen into each other's arms. Mahaut had placed her mustachioed lips to her former son-in-law's cheeks; Charles, with a childish gesture, had rested his brow on that monumental shoulder and had shed a few tears among the giantess's hearse-like draperies. And thus, as so often, human relations were changed by the passage of death and the obliteration of the springs of resentment.

But Mahaut knew very well what she was doing by hurrying to Chaâlis; and her nephew Robert was fretting. He smiled at her, they smiled at each other, they called each other 'my good aunt' and 'my dear nephew' and both showed that 'proper love between relations' to which they had bound themselves by the Treaty of 1318. They hated each other. They would have done their best to kill each other had they ever found themselves alone in the same room. The real reason for Mahaut's coming – she had not said so, but Robert was well aware of it – was because of a letter she had received. Indeed, everyone present had received a similar letter, with merely a few minor variations: Philippe of Valois, Jean de Marigny, the Constable, and the King – above all the King.

Beyond the windows the clear night was spangled with stars. Here were eleven people of the highest importance, sitting in a circle under the arched ceiling, between the pillars with their carved capitals, and they felt insufficient. They were unable to persuade themselves they had any real power.

The King, weak in character and limited in understanding, had moreover no immediate family and no personal servants. Who were these princes and dignitaries assembled about him this evening? Cousins or councillors inherited from his father or his uncle. Not one of them was really his, created by him and bound to him. His father had had three sons and two brothers sitting in his Council; and even on days when there were quarrels, days when the late Monseigneur of Valois stormed at everyone, they remained family rows. Louis the Hutin had had two brothers and two uncles; Philippe the Long, the same two uncles, who supported him in their diverse ways, as well as a brother, Charles himself. But the survivor had almost no one. His Council gave the irresistible impression of the end of a dynasty; the only hope of a continuation of the line, of a direct succession, was asleep in the womb of that silent woman who, neither particularly pretty nor ugly, was standing beside Charles with her hands clasped, knowing well that as Queen she was merely a replacement.

The letter, the notorious letter they were now considering, was dated June 19, at Westminster. The Chancellor held it in his hand, and the green wax of the broken seal was peeling from the parchment.

'The matter that has caused King Edward such great anger appears to be that Monseigneur Mortimer carried the train of the Duke of Aquitaine's mantle at Madame the Queen's coronation. And, naturally, the fact that his personal enemy should have been appointed to his son's entourage with such a considerable mark of dignity can be felt by our Lord Edward only as a personal affront.'

It was Monseigneur Jean de Marigny who was speaking in that suave, melodious, well-modulated voice of his, which he accompanied from time to time with a gesture of his fine hands, on which gleamed his bishop's amethyst. His three superimposed robes were of thin cloth, as was suited to the season, and the outer robe, which was shortest, fell in elegant folds. They were impregnated with that particular scent with which Monseigneur de Marigny liked to anoint himself on coming from the bath or the sweating-room; a bishop rarely smelled so fine. His face seemed to have no weaknesses and his eyebrows made a horizontal line each side of his straight nose. If the sculptor reproduced his features accurately, Monseigneur de Marigny would make a handsome effigy for the cover of his tomb; but that would be a long time hence, for he was still young. He had known how to profit by his brother's position as Coadjutor to the Iron King, and had also correctly judged the right moment at which to betray that brother. Indeed, he had succeeded in surmounting with ease those vicissitudes which occurred when reigns changed, and had gone from one see to another, ultimately to attain, at the age of forty, the distinction of being a Peer Spiritual and a member of the King's Council.

'Cherchemont,' said King Charles to his Chancellor, 'read again that passage in which our brother Edward complains about Messire de Mortimer.'

Jean de Cherchemont unfolded the parchment, held it under a candle, mumbling a little as he searched for the passage, and read: 'The adherence of our wife and our son to our notoriously known traitors and mortal enemies, in particular the said traitor, Mortimer, who carried at Paris the train of our son, in public, during the solemnization of the coronation of our very dear sister, your wife, the Queen of France, at the last Pentecost, with such great shame and vexation to us.'

Bishop Marigny leaned towards Constable Gaucher and murmured: 'That's an ill-written letter, and his Latin's worse still.'

The Constable had not heard very well; he contented himself with muttering: 'An unnatural sodomite!'

'Cherchemont,' went on the King, 'have we any right to refuse the request of our brother of England when he asks us to put a term to his wife's sojourn?'

The way Charles the Fair addressed his Chancellor, instead of turning, as he normally did, to Robert of Artois, who was at once his senior Councillor and his uncle by marriage, proved that for once he had a plan in mind.

Both because he was not absolutely sure of the King's intentions and because he feared to offend Monseigneur Robert of Artois, who was so powerful, Jean de Cherchemont, before answering, took refuge in the end of the letter as if he required to reconsider the last lines before giving his advice.

'And this is why, very dear Brother,' read the Chancellor, 'we pray you once more, as affectionately and as much from the heart as we can, that in this thing we desire above all others, you will listen to our requests and carry them out with good will, and soon, to the profit and honour of our mutual relations; and so that we shall not be dishonoured . . .'

Jean de Marigny shook his head and sighed. Such awkward and uneven prose pained him. Nevertheless, however badly the letter might be written, its meaning was clear enough.

The Countess Mahaut of Artois remained silent; she was taking care not to express her triumph too soon, and her grey eyes glittered in the light of the candles. Her secret accusations made last autumn and her intrigues with the Bishop of Exeter had now borne ripe fruit at the beginning of summer, and fit to pick.

'It would seem clear, Sire,' the Chancellor made up his mind to say at last, since no one had helped him out by intervening, 'it seems clear, Sire, that, in accordance with the laws both of the Church and the kingdoms, King Edward must somehow or other be satisfied. He is demanding his wife . . .'

Jean de Cherchemont was a priest, as his position required, and he turned to Bishop Marigny, seeking his support with a look.

'Our Holy Father the Pope has sent us a message in that sense by Bishop Thibaud de Châtillon,' said Charles the Fair.

For Edward had gone so far as to write to Pope John XXII and had sent him copies of all the correspondence dealing with his matrimonial difficulties. And what could Pope John do, except reply that a wife should live with her husband?

'It would seem, therefore, that Madame my sister must leave for the country of her marriage,' added Charles the Fair.

He looked at no one while he said this, but dropped his eyes to his embroidered shoes. A candelabra which stood above his chair lit up his forehead, which suddenly had something of the stubborn expression of his brother, the Hutin.

'Sire Charles,' said Robert of Artois, 'to oblige Madame Isabella to return to England is to hand her over bound hand and foot to the Despensers. Was it not because she feared assassination that she came to seek refuge with you? How much greater the danger will be now.'

'Really, Sire my Cousin, you cannot . . .' said tall Philippe of Valois, who was always prepared to adopt Robert's point of view.

But his wife, Jeanne of Burgundy, pulled him by the sleeve, and he stopped short; and, had it not been night, he would undoubtedly have been seen to blush.

Robert of Artois had seen the gesture and was aware of the reason for Philippe's sudden silence; he had also noticed the glance exchanged between Mahaut and the young Countess of Valois. Had he had the chance, he would have wrung the lame woman's neck.

'My sister may have exaggerated the danger,' the King went on. 'These Despensers do not appear to be so wicked as she has made out. I have received a number of most polite letters from them, which go far to show they desire my friendship . . .'

'And you have had presents from them, too, fine goldsmith's work,' cried Robert, getting to his feet, and all the candle-flames flickered and the shadows wavered over their faces. 'Sire Charles, my beloved Cousin, have you changed your opinion of these people who declared war on you, and are like he-goats to a goat in their relationship with your brother-in-law, for three silver-gilt sauce-boats lacking to your sideboard? We have all received presents from them; am I not right, Monseigneur de Beauvais, and you Cherchemont, and you Philippe? An agent, and I can give you his name, he's called Arnold, received a few months ago five casks of silver, to the value of five thousand marks sterling, with instructions to use it in making friends for the Earl of Gloucester in the Council of the King of France. These presents cost the Despensers nothing, for they are easily paid for out of the revenues of the county of Cornwall which they seized from your sister. That, Sire, is what you must know and remember.

And what loyalty can you expect from men who dress up as women to serve the vices of their master? Do not forget what they are, and what is at the bottom of their power.'

And Robert could not resist making an obscene remark: 'Bottom,' he said, 'would appear to be the right word!'

But his laugh got no response except from the Constable. In the old days the Constable had had no love for Robert of Artois, and he had given sufficient proof of this in helping Philippe the Long, when he was Regent, to defeat the giant and put him in prison. But for some time past, old Gaucher had discovered good qualities in Robert, largely because of his voice, which was the only one which he could hear without an effort.

There were few partisans of Queen Isabella present this evening. The Chancellor was indifferent, or rather he was intent on keeping his appointment which depended on favour; he would support the majority. Queen Jeanne, who had few thoughts on the subject, was also indifferent. Her main concern was to avoid any emotion which might interfere with her pregnancy. She was Robert of Artois's niece, and could not but be sensible of his authority, his height and his assurance; but she was anxious to show what a good wife she was, and was therefore ready to condemn on principle all wives who became a cause of scandal.

The Constable was on the whole in favour of Isabella. Mainly because he loathed Edward of England on account of his morals, his incompetent government of his kingdom, and his refusal to pay homage. In general, he did not like the English; but he had to admit that Roger Mortimer had rendered good service; and it would be cowardly to abandon him now. And old Gaucher did not mind saying so and declaring also that Isabella had a good deal of excuse.

'To hell with it, she's a woman, and her husband's not a man. The chief fault's his.'

Monseigneur de Marigny, raising his voice a little, replied that Queen Isabella might well be forgiven, and that he, for his part, was prepared to give her absolution; but Madame Isabella's error, her great error, was to have made her sin public; a Queen should not set an example of adultery.

'Oh yes, that's quite right,' said Gaucher. 'There was no need for them to attend every ceremony hand in hand and share the same bed, as it's said they do.'

On that point he agreed with the Bishop. The Constable and the prelate were therefore on Queen Isabella's side, but with considerable reservations, and, as far as the Constable was concerned, that was as far as his thoughts on the subject went. He began thinking of the College of Romance Languages he had founded near his Castle of Châtillon-sur-Seine where he would be at this moment if he had not been summoned to deal with this business. He would console himself later on by going to listen to the monks chanting the midnight office, a strange pleasure perhaps for a man who was becoming deaf; but there it was, Gaucher could hear better amid a noise. Besides, this soldier had a taste for the arts; not so unusual a predilection.

The Countess of Beaumont, a pretty young woman whose mouth was always smiling though her eyes were not, was much amused. How was this giant she had been given as a husband, and who provided her with perpetual entertainment, to get out of the difficulty in which he found himself?

He would win, she knew he would win; Robert always won, and she would help him to win if she could, but not by committing herself in public.

Philippe of Valois, her half-brother, was wholly in favour of Madame of England, but he was prepared to betray her, because his wife, who hated Isabella, had made a scene about it before the Council, and would refuse herself to him this night and with a great deal of shouting and temper if he acted otherwise than as she had decided. And the long-nosed young man hesitated and stuttered in his anxiety.

Louis of Bourbon lacked courage. He was no longer sent into battle because he always ran away. He had no affection for Queen Isabella.

The King was weak, but capable of being stubborn, as on the occasion which everyone remembered when he had refused for a whole month to give Charles of Valois the commission of Royal Lieutenant in Aquitaine. He was ill-disposed towards his sister because Edward's absurd letters, by dint of repetition, had finally had their effect on him, and, above all, because Blanche was dead and he was thinking of the pitiless Isabella of twelve years ago. Except for her, he would never have known. And even had he known, he would have forgiven, had it not been for Isabella, so as to keep Blanche. Did it really deserve all the horror, all the scandal, all those days of agony, and such a death at the last? Betrayals in love are generally bearable to weak men so long as no one else knows of them.

The party of Isabella's real enemies consisted of two people only, Jeanne the Lame and Mahaut of Artois, but they were closely allied by their common hatred.

And so it turned out that Robert of Artois, the most powerful man after the King, and even, from many points of view, more important than the Sovereign, whose opinion always prevailed, who decided everything to do with the administration and dictated his orders to governors, bailiffs and seneschals, was suddenly alone in supporting his cousin's cause.

For such is the nature of influence at courts; it depends on a strange and fluctuating concatenation of states of mind, in which situations become insensibly transformed with the march of events and the sum of the interests at stake. And fortune carries within it the germs of misfortune. Not that Robert was threatened with misfortune; but Isabella was in real danger. She who, but a few months ago, was pitied, protected and admired, who was allowed every latitude and whose love affair was applauded as a splendid revenge, had now in the King's Council but one supporter of her sojourn in Paris. And yet, to compel her to return to England was no more nor less than to put her neck on the block in the Tower of London, and everyone knew it. But suddenly no one cared about her any more; her triumph had been too great. No one was prepared to compromise himself for her any longer, except Robert, but in his case it was a means of fighting Mahaut.

And now Mahaut took the initiative at last and launched her attack which had been long prepared.

'Sire, my dear Son, I know the love you have for your sister, which does you honour,' she said; 'but it must be admitted that Isabella is a wicked woman from whom we have all suffered or are suffering. Look at the example she has set your Court ever since she has been here. And to think that it is the same woman who in the past told so many lies about my daughters and the sister of Jeanne here present. When, at the time, I told your father – may God rest his soul! – that he was being deceived by his daughter, was I not right? She has wantonly sullied us all, because of the wicked thoughts she detected in the hearts of others when they were merely in her own, as she has now proved to us. Blanche who was pure, and who loved you to the last day of her life, as you know, has died of it this very week! She was innocent, my daughters were innocent.'

Mahaut's huge forefinger, which was as tough as a piece of wood, took Heaven to witness. And to please her ally of the moment she turned to Jeanne the Lame and said: 'Your sister was most certainly innocent, my poor Jeanne, and we have all suffered misfortunes from Isabella's calumnies, and my mother's heart has bled because of them.'

Had she been allowed to go on like this, she would no doubt have reduced the Council to tears. But Robert said: 'Your Blanche innocent? I should like to believe it, Aunt. But it really cannot have been the Holy Ghost who got her with child in prison.'

King Charles the Fair frowned nervously. Really, Cousin Robert had no business to remind people of that.

'It was despair that drove my little girl to it,' cried Mahaut angrily. 'What had my dove to lose, when she was dishonoured by calumny, imprisoned in a fortress and driven half-mad? I'd like to know who could withstand such treatment.'

'I've been in prison too, Aunt, at the time when your

son-in-law Philippe put me there at your behest. But that didn't make me put the gaoler's daughters in the family way nor, from despair, make use of the turnkey for wife, though these things seem to happen in our family!'

The Constable's interest in the discussion began to revive.

'And how do you know, Nephew, though you take such pleasure in sullying the memory of a dead woman, that my Blanche was not taken by force? After all, her cousin was strangled in the same prison,' she said, looking Robert straight in the eyes, 'so she may well have been raped. No, Sire my Son,' she went on, turning back to the King, 'since you have summoned me to your Council . . .'

'No one summoned you,' said Robert; 'you came of your own accord.'

But it was not so easy to interrupt the old giantess.

'I will give you this counsel which comes straight from a mother's heart, which has never ceased to beat for you, despite everything that may have estranged us. I say this to you, Sire Charles: expel your sister from France, for each time she has returned here some misfortune has befallen the Crown. The year you were dubbed knight with your brothers and my nephew Robert, who may well remember it, Maubuisson caught fire and we were all nearly burnt to death. The following year she brought such a scandal on us that we were all covered with infamy. A scandal which a good King's daughter, and a good sister to her brothers, even had there been any shadow of truth in it, ought to have kept quiet about, instead of spreading slander everywhere, with the help of I know whom. And again, in the time of your brother Philippe, when she came to Amiens that Edward might render homage, what happened? The *pastoureaux* ravaged the realm. And now that she's come back again, I positively tremble. For you are expecting a child, who one hopes will be a son, since you must give France a king; so I warn you, Sire my Son, to keep this harbinger of misfortune as far removed as possible from your wife's womb.'

She had indeed aimed the quarrel of her cross-bow with precision. But Robert was already making reply: 'And when our cousin the Hutin died, my good Aunt, where was Isabella then? Not in France, so far as I know. And when his son, the little Jean the Posthumous, died so suddenly in your arms, when you were holding him, my good Aunt, where was Isabella then? Had she visited Louis's room? Was she among the assembled barons? My memory may well be at fault, but I do not recollect her presence. Unless, of course, the deaths of those two Kings are not, in your view, to be counted among the misfortunes of the realm?'

Rascality was face to face with even greater rascality. It needed but another couple of words and they would be openly accusing each other of murder.

The Constable had known the family for nearly sixty years. He puckered his saurian eyes and said: 'Let us not stray from the point, Messeigneurs, but come back to the subject at issue.'

And there was a quality in his voice which somehow or other recalled the tones of the Iron King.

Charles the Fair passed his hand across his smooth brow and said: 'Suppose, to give Edward satisfaction, we expelled Messire Mortimer from the kingdom?'

Then Jeanne the Lame spoke. Her voice was precise but

low-pitched; nevertheless, after the great lowings of the two Artois bulls, she was listened to.

'It would be a waste of time and trouble,' she said. 'Do you really think our cousin will part from the man whose mistress she now is? She is devoted to him body and soul; she lives only for him. Either she will refuse to let him go, or she will go with him.'

Jeanne the Lame hated the Queen of England, not only because of the memory of Marguerite, her sister, but also because of this too great love Isabella was displaying to the whole of France. And yet Jeanne of Burgundy had no real need to complain; her tall Philippe loved her in every sense of the word, in spite of the fact that her legs were not of the same length. But the granddaughter of Saint Louis would have liked to be the only woman in the world who was loved. She hated the loves of others.

'We must come to a decision,' the Constable repeated.

He said this because it was growing late and because the women were talking much too much at this Council.

King Charles nodded approval, and then declared: 'Tomorrow morning, my sister will be taken to the port of Boulogne to be there embarked and returned to her legitimate husband under escort. I will it.'

He had said 'I will it' and everyone present stared at each other, for that phrase had emerged but rarely from the mouth of weak Charles.

'Cherchemont,' he added, 'you will prepare the commission for the escort and I will seal it with my lesser seal.'

There was no more to be said. For Charles the Fair was stubborn, and he was the King, and he sometimes remembered it; and the odd thing was that this usually occurred when he thought of his first wife, who had treated him so badly and whom he had loved so much.

The Countess Mahaut alone permitted herself to say: 'A wise decision, Sire my Son.'

And then they all separated without much in the way of effusive good-nights. They all felt they had been parties to a wicked deed. Chairs were pushed back, and everyone got to his feet to salute the departure of the King and Queen, who were the first to retire.

The Countess of Beaumont was disappointed. She had thought her husband, Robert, would win the day. She looked across at him and he signed to her to go to their room. He had still a word to say to Monseigneur de Marigny.

The Constable with a heavy step, Jeanne of Burgundy with a limping step, Louis of Bourbon limping too – how halt the descendants of Saint Louis were! – left the room. Tall Philippe followed his wife looking like a pointer that has failed to flush the game.

For a moment or two Robert of Artois spoke quietly to the Bishop of Beauvais, who gently rubbed his elegant hands together.

A moment later Robert was on his way back to his room by the cloister of the guest house. There was a shadow sitting between two pillars, a woman staring out into the night.

'Happy dreams, Monseigneur of Artois.'

The drawling, ironic voice belonged to the Countess Mahaut's lady-in-waiting, Béatrice d'Hirson, who was sitting there, apparently in a reverie, and awaiting what? Robert's coming of course; and he was well aware of it. She got to her feet, stretched herself, stood outlined under the arch, took a step forward, then another, her hips swaying and her dress trailing over the stone.

'What are you doing here, my fine wench?' said Robert.

She did not answer directly, but turned her face up to the stars and said: 'It's a beautiful night, and a pity to sleep alone. Sleep is slow in coming in such warm weather . . .'

Robert of Artois went close to her, gazed down into her long eyes that shone so defiantly in the dark, placed his huge hand on her buttocks – and then quickly withdrew it, shaking his fingers as if he had burned himself.

'My pretty Béatrice,' he cried laughing, 'be off to the pond and cool your bum, before you burst into flames!'

His coarseness of speech and gesture made Béatrice tremble. She had long been awaiting an opportunity to seduce the giant. For she knew that from then on Monseigneur Robert would be at the mercy of the Countess Mahaut, and she, Béatrice, would at long last have at least satisfied a desire. But it was not to be tonight.

Robert had more important things to do. He went to his apartments and entered the bedroom of the Countess, his wife. She sat up in bed. She was naked, for she always slept thus in summer. Robert, with the very same hand with which a moment before he had stroked Beatrice's bottom, automatically caressed a breast that indeed belonged to him by marriage; but it was merely a way of saying good night. The Countess of Beaumont was far from being excited by this caress, but she was amused by it; she was always amused by her giant of a husband and by wondering what was going on in his mind. Robert of Artois subsided into a chair. He stretched out his huge legs, raised them from time to time, and let them fall back, heels together.

'Aren't you coming to bed, Robert?'

'No, my dear, no. I'm even going to leave you for Paris shortly, as soon as these monks have stopped singing in their church.'

The Countess smiled.

'My dear, don't you think my sister of Hainaut might give Isabella asylum for a while to give her time to assemble her forces?'

'I was thinking that, my beautiful Countess, I was thinking just that.'

Madame of Beaumont was reassured; her husband was bound to win.

It was not so much Isabella's service that got Robert of Artois to horse that night as his hatred of Mahaut. The bitch wanted to oppose him, harm those he protected and recover her influence with the King, did she? She'd see who had the last word.

He went and shook his valet, Lormet, awake.

'Go and get three horses saddled. And warn my equerry and a sergeant-at-arms.'

'What about me?' asked Lormet.

'No, not you, you can go back to sleep.'

This was pure kindness on Robert's part. The years were beginning to weigh heavily on his old companion in misdeeds, who was at once bodyguard, strangler and nurse. Lormet was beginning to be short of breath and the mists of early morning did him no good. He grumbled. Since he wasn't needed what was the good of waking him? But he would have grumbled still more if he had had to go with them.

The horses were soon saddled; the equerry was yawning and the sergeant-at-arms getting into his equipment.

'To horse,' said Robert; 'this is going to be something of a ride.'

Sitting well down in the saddle, he kept to a walking pace as he left the Abbey by the farm and the out-buildings. Then, as soon as they reached the expanse of sand that stretched lonely and brightly gleaming amid the white birch trees under the night, a real landscape for fairies, he spurred his horse into a gallop. They went by Dammartin, Mitry, Aulnay and Saint-Ouen, a four hours' gallop with a few breaks to breathe their horses and one halt at an inn, which was open at night to serve market-gardeners' wagoners.

Dawn was not yet breaking when they reached the Palace of the Cité. The guard allowed the King's first councillor to pass in. Robert went straight up to the Queen's apartments, stepping over the sleeping servants in the corridors, crossed the women's room, while they squawked like frightened hens and cried: 'Madame! Madame!' But the giant had already passed on.

Roger Mortimer was in bed with the Queen. A night-light was burning in a corner of the room.

'And it's so that they may sleep in each other's arms that I've galloped through the night; and fast enough to take the skin off my arse!' Robert thought.

As soon as they had got over the first moment of surprise and the candles had been lit, all embarrassment was forgotten in the urgency of the moment.

Robert informed the two lovers as quickly as he could of what had been decided at Chaâlis and was being plotted against them. As he listened and asked questions, Mortimer was dressing in front of Robert of Artois with that complete naturalness which is usual among soldiers. Nor did the presence of his mistress appear to embarrass him; they were obviously quite used to living together.

'My advice to you, my friends, is to leave at once,' Robert said, 'and to go to the territory of the Empire where you will be out of danger. You must both go, and take young Edward with you, and perhaps Cromwell, Alspaye and Maltravers, but not too many, so as not to slow you down. You should make for Hainaut, and I'll send a courier on ahead of you. The good Count Guillaume and his brother Jean are both great and loyal lords, feared by their enemies, loved by their friends, of great good sense and of perfect honour. The Countess, my wife, will write to her sister on your behalf. It's the best refuge you can find at the moment. Our friend Kent, whom I shall warn, will join you by way of Ponthieu, to assemble the knights you have gathered there. And the rest is in God's hands. I'll see that Tolomei continues to send you funds; anyway, he can do nothing else now. Increase the numbers of your troops, do your best, and fight! Oh, if the Kingdom of France were not so important, and I could afford to leave my aunt's wickedness a free hand, I'd willingly go with you.'

'Turn your back, Cousin, I'm going to dress,' said Isabella.

'What, Cousin, no reward? Does that rascal Roger want to keep everything to himself?' said Robert, as he obeyed. 'The lucky dog!'

For once, his broad jokes did not seem shocking; indeed, there was something very reassuring about his ability to joke in a crisis. Though he was considered so wicked, he was capable of kindness; and his indecency of speech was sometimes merely a mask for a certain modesty of sentiment.

'I owe you my life, Robert,' Isabella said.

'One good turn deserves another, Cousin, one good turn deserves another! You never can tell!' he called over his shoulder.

He saw a bowl of fruit laid out on a table ready for the lovers; he seized a peach, took a great bite out of it, and the golden juice poured down his chin.

There was a hurrying to and fro in the corridors, equerries were running to the stables, messengers going off to the English lords who lodged in the town, and the women were quickly packing light travelling-trunks with what they needed; there was a great bustle and stir in all this part of the Palace.

'Don't go by Senlis,' said Robert, his mouth full of his twelfth peach. 'Our good Sire Charles is too close to it and might have you followed. Go by Beauvais and Amiens.'

Their goodbyes were hasty; dawn was just beginning to light up the steeple of the Sainte-Chapelle and the escort was waiting in the courtyard. Isabella went to the window; for a moment she was overwhelmed by emotion at the sight of the garden, the river and the nearness of the rumpled bed in which she had known the happiest time of her life. Fifteen months had passed since that first morning when she had breathed, on this very spot, that marvellous scent which spring broadcasts when one is in love. Roger Mortimer put his hand on her shoulder and the Queen's lips bent towards it.

Soon the horses' hooves were ringing out in the streets of the Cité, then on the Pont-au-Change and towards the north.

Monseigneur Robert of Artois went to his house. By the time the King heard of his sister's flight, she would have been out of reach for some time; and Mahaut would have to be bled and purged so as not to be choked by a flux of blood. 'Ah, my good bitch!' he thought. Now Robert could sleep, as heavily as an ox, till the bells rang out at noon.

PART FOUR

THE CRUEL INVASION

I

Harwich

THE SEAGULLS WERE CRYING and circling the ships' masts, searching for refuse thrown overboard. The fleet was approaching the port of Harwich, with its wooden mole and line of low houses, on the estuary into which flow the Orwell and the Stour.

Two of the smaller ships had already gone alongside and disembarked a company of archers to ensure that all was quiet in the neighbourhood; the coast did not appear to be guarded. There had been some slight confusion on the quay where the inhabitants, who had gathered to watch so many sail lying offshore, had fled when they saw the soldiers landing; but they had soon been reassured and the crowd gathered again.

The Queen's ship, wearing the long pennant embroidered with the lilies of France and the leopards of England at the peak, was steady on her course. Eighteen ships from Holland were following her. The crews, under the orders of the master mariners, were taking in sail; the long oars appeared along the ships' sides, like wing-feathers suddenly deployed, to assist in working the ships into port.

Standing on the sterncastle, the Queen of England, surrounded by her son Prince Edward, the Earl of Kent, Roger Mortimer, Messire Jean de Hainaut and several other English and Dutch lords, watched the working of the ships and the shores of her kingdom growing ever nearer.

For the first time since his escape Roger Mortimer was not dressed in black. He was not wearing a full suit of armour with a closed helm, but merely the harness for forays, a helmet without visor to which was attached the mail camail which hung down over neck and shoulders and a mail hauberk over which floated his surcoat of red and blue brocade, embroidered with his emblems.

The Queen was similarly attired, her fair slender face framed in steel; her skirt trailed to the ground but beneath it she was wearing greaves of mail like the men.

And young Prince Edward was also dressed for war. He had grown taller these last months and almost begun to look like a man. He was watching the seagulls which, so it seemed to him, were the same, and with the same hoarse cries and greedy beaks, as those that had attended the departure of the fleet from the mouth of the Meuse.

The birds reminded him of Holland. Indeed, everything, the grey sea, the grey sky with a few faint lines of pink, the quayside with its little brick houses, where they were soon to land, the green, rolling country with its lakes behind Harwich, all reminded him of the Dutch countryside and made him turn his thoughts back to Holland. But had he come to a desert of stones and sand under a flaming sky, he would still have thought, by contrast, of the landscapes of Brabant, Ostrevant and Hainaut which he had so recently left. The fact was that Monseigneur Edward, Duke of Aquitaine and heir to the throne of England, had fallen in love in Holland at the age of fourteen years and nine months.

And this was how it had come to pass and how these notable events came to be scored on young Prince Edward's memory.

When they had fled in such a hurry from Paris in the early hours of that morning when Monseigneur of Artois, shouting in his loud voice, had dragged them all from their beds, they had made all speed, travelling by forced marches, to the territory of the Empire; and one night they had reached the castle of Sire Eustache d'Aubercicourt, who together with his wife had extended a kindly and hospitable welcome to the little English company. And when he had seen to the comfort of their unexpected guests as best they could, Messire d'Aubercicourt had mounted his horse and gone off to inform the good Count Guillaume, whose wife was cousin-german to Queen Isabella, at his capital city of Valenciennes. And the following morning the Count's younger brother, Messire Jean de Hainaut, had come to see them.

Jean de Hainaut was an eccentric; not so much in his appearance, which was physically solid, with a round face set on a strong body, round eyes and a short, snub nose above a small fair moustache, but eccentric in the way he behaved. For, as soon as he came into the Queen's presence, and before he had even taken off his boots, he fell on one knee on the flagstones, and cried with his hand on his heart: 'Madame, here is your knight, ready to die for you even if the whole world fails you. And I shall do everything in my power, with the help of your friends, to take you and Monseigneur your son over the sea to your realm of England. And everyone I can collect will place his life at your service, and we shall have enough men-at-arms, if it please God.'

The Queen, to thank him for so sudden an expression of assistance, made to kneel before him; but Messire Jean de Hainaut prevented her by seizing her in his arms. Clasping her to him and breathing in her face, he went on: 'May it please God that the Queen of England shall never kneel to anyone. Comfort yourself, Madame, and your charming son also, for I shall keep my promise.'

Roger Mortimer was beginning to look a little glum, for he thought that Messire Jean de Hainaut was a little too eager to place his sword at ladies' service. Really, the man seemed to take himself for Lancelot of the Lake, for he had suddenly declared that he would not sleep the night under the same roof as the Queen for fear of compromising her, as if he were unaware of the fact that there were at least six great lords about her! He had beat a somewhat sanctimonious retreat to a neighbouring abbey, only to return early in the morning, after Mass and breakfast, to fetch the Queen and conduct the whole company to Valenciennes.

Count Guillaume the Good, his wife and their four daughters, who lived in a white castle, were excellent people. Their marriage was a happy one; it could be seen in their expressions and heard in every word they uttered. Young Prince Edward, who had suffered from childhood from the spectacle of the discord between his parents, looked with admiration at this united couple who were so kind in every way. How lucky the four young Princesses of Hainaut were to have been born into such a family!

Good Count Guillaume had offered his services to Queen Isabella, less eloquently however than had his brother and after making certain inquiries so as to be sure of not bringing down on himself the fury of the King of France, nor that of the Pope.

Messire Jean de Hainaut spared no effort. He wrote to all the knights of his acquaintance praying them to come in honour and friendship to join him in his enterprise and because of the vow he had made. He created such excitement in Hainaut, Brabant, Zeeland and Holland, that good Count Guillaume became anxious; Messire Jean was in process of raising the whole army of his states and all his chivalry. He therefore advised moderation; but the other would not hear of it.

'Messire my Brother,' he said, 'I have but one death to die, and that will be as God wills it, but I have promised this fair lady to take her to her kingdom, and this I shall do, even if I must die for it, for every knight is bound to give loyal assistance, and to the utmost of his power, to all ladies and maidens in sorrow and distress whenever they have need of it.'

Guillaume the Good was also concerned for his Treasury, for all these bannerets who were being set to polish up their armour would have to be paid; but on that score he was reassured by Roger Mortimer, who seemed to have enough money from the Lombard banks to maintain a thousand lances.

They therefore stayed three months at Valenciennes, living the life of the Court, while every day Jean de Hainaut announced that someone of importance had rallied to them, as it might be the Sire Michel de Ligne or the Sire de Sarre, or the Chevalier Oulfart de Ghistelles, or Perceval de Sémeries, or Sance de Boussoy.

They went in a family party on a pilgrimage to the church at Sebourg where were kept the relics of Saint Druon, which were much venerated since Count Guillaume's grandfather, Jean d'Avesnes, who was suffering pain from a stone, had gone to ask for a cure. In the presence of his whole Court and the people of the town, Count Jean d'Avesnes and Hainaut had knelt on the tomb and recited in a loud voice a prayer remarkable for its humility and faith; and hardly had he finished praying when he ejected from his body three stones each the size of a nut, and his pain had disappeared never to return.

Of Count Guillaume's four daughters, the second, Philippa, had immediately taken young Prince Edward's fancy. She was red-haired, chubby and covered with freckles, her face was wide and her stomach already conspicuous. She was a typical little Valois with a strong tinge of Brabant. It so happened that the two young people were perfectly matched in age; and everyone was surprised to see Prince Edward, who normally never spoke, going about as much as he could with the fat Philippa, and talking, talking, talking for hours on end. That he was attracted by her was evident to everyone. Silent people never can dissemble when they do abandon their silence.

And Queen Isabella and the Count of Hainaut had very

soon agreed to affiance their children since they showed such a great inclination towards each other. For Queen Isabella it was a means of cementing an alliance which alone could help her recover her throne of England, while the Count of Hainaut, as soon as it became clear that his daughter would one day become Queen across the sea, saw nothing but advantage in lending his knights.

In spite of the formal orders of King Edward II, who had forbidden his son to become affianced or to allow himself to be made affianced without his consent,[36] the necessary dispensations had already been asked of the Pope. It really seemed to be decreed by Destiny that Prince Edward should marry a Valois. His father, three years earlier, had refused one of the younger daughters of Monseigneur Charles for him, a fortunate refusal as it now turned out, since the young man could marry that same Monseigneur Charles's grand-daughter, with whom he was in love.

The expedition had at once taken on a new urgency for Prince Edward. For, if the invasion succeeded and his uncle of Kent and Roger Mortimer, with the assistance of his cousin of Hainaut, managed to expel the wicked Despensers and take their place beside the King, he would be forced to agree to the marriage.

Besides, people now talked openly in the boy's presence of his father's morals; he was horrified and aghast. How could a man, a knight, a king, behave in this way with a lord of his Court? The Prince determined, when it came to his turn to reign, never to tolerate such depravity among his barons, and with his Philippa he would show the whole world what a fine, loyal, true love of a man for a woman, of a king for a queen, could be. This fat, round, red-haired girl, who was already very feminine, and seemed to him the most beautiful girl in the world, had a reassuring effect on the Duke of Aquitaine.

It was, therefore, the right to love the boy was going to win, and this disguised the painful, if not odious, circumstance that he was marching to war against his own father.

Three months had consequently been spent in this happy manner, and they were without doubt the most agreeable Prince Edward had ever known.

The assembly of the Hennuyers, for this was the name by which the knights of Hainaut were known, had taken place at Dordrecht on the Meuse, a pretty town curiously intersected by canals and basins, where every street crossed a waterway, and ships from all the seas, as well as flat-bottomed barges without sails, which were used on the rivers, were moored even in front of the churches. It was a wealthy merchant city, where the lords walked about the quays, making their way between bales of wool and crates of spices, where the smell of fish, both fresh and salted, tainted the air about the markets, and in the streets of which watermen and dockers ate fine white soles, which could be bought at the stalls all hot from the frying-pan. And the inhabitants, when they came out of the huge brick cathedral after Mass, could go and gape idly at the great warlike array, such as had never before been seen, moored at the very foot of the houses. The swinging masts of the ships were taller than the roofs.

It had taken much time, effort and shouting to load the ships, which were as round as the clogs all Holland wore, with the equipment of the cavalry: cases of arms, chests of armour, food, kitchens, stoves and a farrier's shop, which would employ a hundred men, with its anvils, bellows and hammers. Then the great Flanders horses had to be embarked, those heavy chestnuts which, with their coats looking almost red under the sun, their paler, almost faded manes flowing, their large hooves covered with hair, and their huge, silky quarters, were proper mounts for knights. For, without tiring them, you could load them with a high-cantled saddle, heavy steel horse-armour, as well as a fully armed man, altogether some four hundred pounds to carry at a gallop.

There were a thousand or more of these horses, for Messire Jean de Hainaut had kept his word and assembled a thousand knights together with their squires, varlets and servants, making a total of 2,757 men on the pay-roll, according to the register kept by Gerard de Alspaye.

The sterncastles of the ships had been arranged to accommodate the most important lords.

They had set sail on the morning of September 22 so as to take advantage of the equinoctial currents and had spent a whole day navigating the Meuse before reaching their anchorage off the dykes of Holland. The seagulls had circled crying round the ships. Then, next day, they had set out to sea. The weather had seemed fine, but towards the end of the day the wind had become contrary and the ships had found difficulty in making headway against it; then the sea had got up, and the whole expedition had been very sick and very frightened. The knights vomited over the rail when they had the strength to reach it. The crews themselves had been far from happy, and the horses, tossed about in the deck stables, stank appallingly. The storm was even more terrifying by night than by day. The chaplains had set themselves to pray.

Messire Jean de Hainaut had shown great courage and alacrity in comforting Queen Isabella, indeed a little too much perhaps, for there are occasions when a man's attentiveness may be importunate to a lady. The Queen felt rather relieved when Messire de Hainaut also became seasick.

Roger Mortimer alone seemed unaffected by the storm; it is said that jealous men are never seasick. On the other hand, John Maltravers was in a pitiable state by the time dawn broke; his face was longer and more yellow than ever, his hair was hanging down over his ears and his surcoat was soiled; sitting with his legs spread wide against a coil of rope, he seemed to expect death with every wave.

At last, by the grace of Monseigneur Saint George, the sea had fallen, and everyone had been able to clean himself up a bit. The lookout men had seen the shores of England only a few miles south of where they had expected to make their landfall. Then the navigators had made for the port of Harwich, which they were now entering, and where the royal vessel, its oars shipped, was already coming alongside the wooden mole.

Young Prince Edward was staring dreamily about him through his long fair lashes, for everything he saw seemed red or pink and rounded, the clouds driven by the September breeze, the low, bellying sails of the last ships, the rumps of the Flanders chestnuts, the cheeks of Messire Jean de Hainaut, and they all reminded him invincibly of the Holland of his love.

As he set foot on the quay at Harwich, Roger Mortimer felt exactly like his ancestor who, two hundred and sixty years earlier, had disembarked on English soil beside the Conqueror. This was clear from his air, the tone of his voice and the way he took everything in hand.

He was sharing the command of the expedition on equal terms with Jean de Hainaut. This was reasonable, since Mortimer had to his account only his good cause, a few English lords and the Lombard money; while the other had provided the 2,757 fighting men. Nevertheless, Mortimer thought that Jean de Hainaut should devote himself exclusively to the management of his troops, while he himself would undertake the supreme direction of the operations. The Earl of Kent, for his part, did not appear eager to push himself forward; for if, in spite of the information they had received, part of the nobility remained loyal to King Edward, the King's troops would be commanded by the Earl of Norfolk, the Marshal of England, that is to say, Kent's own brother. And to rebel against a half-brother who is a bad king and twenty years your senior is one thing; but it is quite another to draw your sword against a beloved brother from whom you are separated in age by only a single year.

Mortimer, in search of information, had sent for the Mayor of Harwich. Did he know where the royal troops were? Where was the nearest castle which could shelter the Queen while the troops were being disembarked and the ships unloaded?

'We are here,' Mortimer told the Mayor, 'to help King Edward get rid of his bad councillors who are ruining the kingdom, and to restore the Queen to the position that is her due. We have, therefore, no intentions other than those which are in accord with the will of the barons and all the people of England.'

This was brief and clear, and Roger Mortimer was to repeat it at every halt, to explain the surprising arrival of a foreign army.

The Mayor, his white hair fluttering on each side of his skull, and trembling in his robe, not from cold, but from fear of his responsibilities, appeared to have no information. The King? It was said that he was in London, unless he was at Portsmouth. In any case a large fleet was to be gathered at Portsmouth, since orders had been received last month for every ship to assemble there to repel a French invasion; this explained why there were so few ships in the harbour.

At this Lord Mortimer showed considerable pride; particularly when he turned to Messire de Hainaut. For he had cleverly spread it abroad through agents that it was his intention to land on the south coast, and the trick had clearly succeeded. But Jean de Hainaut, on his side, could be proud of his Dutch sailors, who had held their course in spite of the storm.

The district was unguarded; the Mayor had no knowledge of any troop movements in the neighbourhood, nor had he received any orders for more than the usual coastal watch to be kept. A place to stay? The Mayor suggested Walton Abbey, about three leagues to the south, along the estuary. In his heart of hearts he very much wanted to get rid of the responsibility for lodging this company on to the monks.

An escort to protect the Queen had to be organized.

'I'll command it!' cried Jean de Hainaut.

'And who'll see to the disembarkation of your Hennuyers, Messire?' asked Mortimer. 'And how long will it take?'

'Three full days, before they'll be in marching order.

I'll leave my chief equerry, Philippe de Chasteaux, in charge.'

Mortimer's chief anxiety was concerning the secret messengers he had sent from Holland to Bishop Orleton and the Earl of Lancaster. Had contact been made with them, had they been warned in time, and where were they at this moment? No doubt he would be able to get information from the monks and could send couriers who, posting from monastery to monastery, would reach the two leaders of the internal resistance.

Authoritative and outwardly calm, Mortimer strode up and down Harwich High Street, which was lined with low houses, impatient to see the escort organized. He went down to the harbour to hurry on the disembarkation of the horses, and then returned to the Three Goblets where the Queen and Prince Edward were awaiting their horses. For several centuries to come the history of England was to pass through this street in which he was now walking.[37]

At last the escort was ready; the knights arrived, forming up four abreast and filling the whole width of the High Street. The grooms were running beside the horses fastening the last buckles of the horse-armour; the lances waved in front of the narrow windows; swords clattered against iron knee-caps.

The Queen was helped on to her palfrey, and then the ride began through the rolling country, with its thinly scattered trees, its tidal flats and rare thatched cottages. Behind low hedges, sheep with thick fleeces grazed round brackish pools. On the whole, a melancholy countryside with the sea-mist lying over the farther bank of the estuary. But the handful of Englishmen, Kent, Cromwell, Alspaye, and Maltravers himself, though he was still feeling far from well, gazed at the countryside and then looked at each other, tears shining in their eyes. This land was England!

And suddenly, owing to a cart-horse neighing through the half-door of its stable as the cavalcade went by, Roger Mortimer felt a sudden wave of emotion at being home again. The long-awaited joy, which had so far eluded him because of all the weighty matters he had on his mind and all the decisions he had to take, now suddenly overwhelmed him in the middle of the countryside because an English horse had neighed at the horses from Flanders.

Three years in exile abroad, three years of waiting and hoping. Mortimer remembered the night of his escape from the Tower, when wet through he had crossed the Thames in a boat to take horse on the farther bank. And now he was back, his coat of arms embroidered on his chest, and a thousand lances to do battle with him. He had come back as the lover of the Queen of whom he had dreamed so much in prison. Dreams sometimes came true, and then one could truly call oneself happy.

He turned to Queen Isabella with an expression of gratitude and complicity, towards that beautiful profile framed in steel mail from which the eyes shone out like sapphires. But Mortimer saw that Messire Jean de Hainaut, who was riding on the Queen's other side, was also looking at her, and his happiness immediately disappeared. He had a sudden feeling that he had already known this moment, that he was living it over again, and it disquieted him, for there are indeed few things more disturbing than the feeling that sometimes assails us of recognizing a road down which we have never been. And then he remembered the Paris road on that day when he had gone to welcome Isabella on her arrival, and Robert of Artois riding beside the Queen, as Jean de Hainaut was doing now. The similarity of his reaction had aroused in Mortimer this false sense of recognition.

And he heard the Queen say: 'Messire Jean, I owe you everything, and especially my being here.'

Isabella was also much moved at riding over the soil of her realm. But Mortimer scowled, and turned sombre, distant and abrupt during the rest of the journey; and he was still in the same state of mind when they reached the monks of Walton, where some of them were lodged in the Abbot's lodgings, some in the guest house, and the men-at-arms mostly in the barns. Indeed, so much was this so, that when Queen Isabella was alone with her lover that evening, she said: 'What has been the matter with you all afternoon, sweet Mortimer?'

'The fact, Madame, that I thought I had well served my Queen and my lover.'

'And who has said, my sweet Lord, that you have not done so?'

'I thought it was to me you owed your return to your kingdom, Madame.'

'And who has said that I do not owe it to you?'

'Yourself, Madame, yourself. You said so in my presence to Messire de Hainaut and thanked him for all that has been done.'

'Oh, Mortimer, my dear friend,' cried the Queen, 'what umbrage you take at the slightest word! What harm can there be in thanking people who have served you?'

'I take umbrage at the facts,' cried Mortimer. 'I take

umbrage at words as I take umbrage also at certain glances which I had hoped, in all loyalty, you owed only to me. You're a flirt, Madame, which I did not expect. You flirt!'

The Queen was tired. Three days on a rough sea, the anxieties of an adventurous landing and, on top of all the rest, a ride of four leagues, had been a sufficient ordeal. Were there many women who would have borne as much without ever a word of complaint nor even causing anyone a moment's anxiety? She was expecting compliments on her courage rather than jealous remonstrances.

'I ask you, my love, what flirtation?' she said impatiently. 'The chaste regard Messire de Hainaut has for me may be laughable but it comes from a kind heart; and don't forget we owe to it the troops we have with us. Allow me, therefore, without encouraging him, to make some little response; for you have only to compare the number of our English with his Hennuyers. It is also for your sake I smile at this man who irritates you so much.'

'One can always find excuses for behaving badly. Messire de Hainaut is serving you out of love, I admit it, but not to the point of refusing the gold he is paid for it. You have therefore no need to smile so tenderly at him. It humiliates me for your sake to see you descend from that high pedestal of purity on which I had placed you.'

'You did not seem hurt, dear Mortimer, the day I descended from that pedestal of purity into your arms.'

It was their first quarrel. Did it really have to take place on the very day for which they had longed so much and for which they had united all their efforts during the last three months?

'My love,' the Queen went on more gently, 'is not your anger due to the fact that I am now less far from my husband, and that our love will be less easy?'

Mortimer bowed his head, his rough eyebrows made a bar across his forehead.

'Indeed, Madame, I think that now you are on the soil of your kingdom, you must sleep alone.'

'That is what I was going to ask of you, dear love,' replied Isabella.

He left the room. He would not see his mistress's tears. Where were those happy nights of France?

In the corridor of the Abbot's lodgings, Mortimer found himself face to face with young Prince Edward. He was holding a candle and it lit up his thin white face. Was he there to spy on them?'

'Are you not going to sleep, my lord?' Mortimer said.

'No, I was looking for you, my lord, to ask you to send me your secretary. On this night of our return to the kingdom, I should like to send a letter to Madame Philippa.'

2

The Shining Hour

'To the most powerful and excellent Seigneur Guillaume, Count of Hainaut, Holland and Zeeland.

'My very dear and beloved Brother, I salute you in the name of God.

'We were still in process of organizing our banners round the port of Harwich, and the Queen was staying in Walton Abbey, when the good news reached us that Monseigneur Henry of Lancaster, who is cousin to King Edward and commonly called here Lord Crouchback, because his neck is all askew, was marching to meet us with a whole army of barons, knights and men-at-arms raised on their lands, and also with the Bishops of Hereford, Norwich and Lincoln, all to place themselves at the service of the Queen, my Lady Isabella. And Monseigneur of Norfolk, Marshal of England, has also declared his intention of doing the same together with his valiant troops.

'Our banners and those of the Lords of Lancaster and

Norfolk met at a place called Bury St Edmunds, where there happened to be a market in the streets that day.

'The meeting took place amid indescribable joy. The knights leapt from their horses, welcomed each other and embraced, Monseigneur of Kent and Monseigneur of Norfolk held each other breast to breast and shed tears like real brothers who had been separated for a long time, and my lord Mortimer was doing the same with my lord Bishop of Hereford, and Monseigneur Crouchback was kissing Prince Edward on both cheeks, and all running to the Queen's horse to welcome her and place their lips to the hem of her dress. Had I come to the Kingdom of England merely to see so much love and joy surrounding my Lady Isabella, I should have felt sufficiently repaid for my trouble. All the more since the people of Bury St Edmunds, abandoning their stalls of poultry and vegetables, joined in the general rejoicing, while people were continually arriving from the neighbouring countryside.

'The Queen presented me with great kindness and many compliments to all the English lords; and I had the distinction of having our thousand Dutch lances behind me, and I was proud, my much loved Brother, of the noble appearance our knights made before the foreign lords.

'Nor did the Queen fail to declare to all the members of her family and party that it was thanks to Lord Mortimer that she had been able to return so strongly supported; she praised his services highly and ordered that Lord Mortimer's opinion should prevail in all things. Besides, my Lady Isabella herself never issues a decree without having first consulted him. She loves him and shows it; but it can be only a chaste love, whatever the ready tongue of scandal may say, for she would take more care to dissimulate were it otherwise, and I also know full well, from the way she looks at me, that she could not make eyes at me as she does if her troth were plighted. I was rather afraid at Walton that their friendship, for some reason I do not know, had grown somewhat colder; but everything goes to show that it was nothing and that they are as united as ever, for which I am glad, since it is natural to love my Lady Isabella for all the good and fine qualities she has, and I would wish everyone to have the same love for her as I have myself.

'My lords Bishop brought sufficient funds with them, and promised that more would be collected in their dioceses, and this has reassured me as to the pay for our Hennuyers, for I feared that Lord Mortimer's Lombard subsidies would be too quickly exhausted. This all happened on the twenty-eighth day of September.

'From that place we set out on the march again, and it was a triumphal advance through the town of Newmarket, where there are many inns and lodgings, and the noble city of Cambridge, where everyone speaks Latin so that you wonder at it, and where there are as many priests in a single college as you could assemble in the whole of your Hainaut. The welcome of the people, as that of the lords, is everywhere sufficient proof that the King is not loved, and that his wicked councillors have made him hated and despised. Our banners are greeted with the cry of "Deliverance!"

'"*Nos Hennuyers ne s'ennuient pas,*" as Messire Henry Crouchback said and, as you can see, he speaks a graceful French. When this remark was repeated to me, I roared with laughter for a quarter of an hour on end, and I still laugh whenever I think of it. The English girls are gracious to our knights, which is a good thing to keep them in the proper humour for war. As for me, if I indulged in dalliance, I would be setting a bad example and lose the power a leader needs if he is to call his troops to order when necessary. Besides, the vow I made to my Lady Isabella forbids it, and if I broke it, the fortunes of our expedition might be imperilled. And if the nights fret me a little, our daily rides are nevertheless so long that sleep does not fail me. I think I shall get married when I return from this adventure.

'Talking of marriage, I must tell you, my dear Brother, and also my dear Sister, the Countess your wife, that my lord the young Prince Edward is still similarly disposed towards your daughter Philippa, that no single day goes by without his asking me for news of her, that all the leanings of his heart seem still to be directed towards her, that the betrothal which has been arranged is sound and advantageous, and that your daughter will, I am sure, always be happy. I have become very friendly with the young Prince Edward, who seems to admire me very much, though he speaks but little; he often remains silent as you have told me did the mighty King Philip the Fair, whose grandson he is. It may well be that he will one day become as great a sovereign as King Philip was, and perhaps even before the time he would normally have had to await his crown from God, if I am to believe what is said in the Council of the English barons.

'For King Edward has cut a sorry figure in face of these happenings. He was at Westminster when we disembarked, and at once took refuge in his Tower of London to put himself in safety; and he had the following announcement cried by all his sheriffs, who are governors of counties, throughout his kingdom, in all public places, squares, fairs and markets:

'"In view of the fact that Roger Mortimer and other traitors of the King and his Realm have made an armed landing at the head of foreign troops with the intention of destroying the Royal power, the King hereby commands his subjects to oppose them by every means in their power and to destroy them. Only the Queen, his son, and the Earl of Kent are to be spared. Everyone taking up arms against the invader will receive a high reward, and anyone bringing the body of Mortimer, or merely his head, to the King shall receive a reward of one thousand pounds sterling."

'No one has obeyed King Edward's orders; but they have been of great service to my lord Mortimer's authority by showing the high price that is set upon his life and designating him as our leader even more than he was before. The Queen has replied by promising two thousand pounds sterling to anyone bringing her the head of Hugh Despenser the Younger, placing that price upon the wrong that lord has done to her husband's love for her.

'The people of London have shown indifference to the safety of their King, who has remained stubborn in his errors to the end. It would have been wise of him to dispense with his Despenser, who bears such a suitable name, but King Edward has determined to keep him, saying that he has learnt from past experience, for similar circumstances once arose concerning Piers Gaveston, whom he agreed to send away, but that this had not prevented him being killed, while he, the King, had imposed on him a charter and a Council of

Commissioners, of whom he had had great difficulty in ridding himself. Despenser encouraged him in this opinion and, so it is said, they wept many tears on each other's breast, and Despenser even cried that he preferred to die on the breast of his King rather than live in safety and apart from him. And, indeed, it is to his advantage to say so, for that breast is his only rampart.

'And so, abandoned by everyone to their wicked love, their entourage consists now only of Despenser the Elder, the Earl of Arundel, who is a relation of Despenser, the Earl of Warenne, who is Arundel's brother-in-law, and finally of the Chancellor Baldock, who has no alternative but to remain loyal to the King for he is so generally hated that he would be torn to pieces wherever he might go.

'The King ceased to be satisfied with the safety of the Tower, and fled with his small following to raise an army in Wales after publishing, on the thirtieth day of September, the Bulls of excommunication the Holy Father the Pope had given him against his enemies. Do not be disturbed, beloved Brother, by this announcement if the news should have reached you; for the Bulls do not concern us; King Edward asked for them against the Scots, and no one has been taken in by this misuse of them. We are admitted by everyone to Communion as before, and the bishops are the first to do so.

'On flying so ignominiously from London, the King left the Government in the hands of Archbishop Reynolds, Bishop John de Stratford and Bishop Stapledon, Diocesan of Exeter and Treasurer to the Crown. But, faced with our rapid advance, Bishop Stratford came to make submission to Queen Isabella, while Archbishop Reynolds sent to ask for pardon from Kent where he had taken refuge. Only Bishop Stapledon remained therefore in London, thinking that by means of his thefts he could bribe a sufficient number of defenders. But the anger of the city rose against him and, when he did decide to fly, the populace pursued him, caught him, and killed him in the suburb of Cheapside, trampling his body till it was no longer recognizable.

'This happened on the fifteenth day of October while the Queen was at Wallingford, a town surrounded by ramparts of earth, where we delivered Messire Thomas de Berkeley who is brother-in-law to my lord Mortimer. When the Queen heard the news of Stapledon's end, she said there was no cause to weep the death of so wicked a man who had done her great wrong; and my lord Mortimer declared that all their enemies would be treated in the same manner.

'Two days before, in the city of Oxford, which has even more priests than the city of Cambridge, Messire Orleton, Bishop of Hereford, went into the pulpit before my Lady Isabella, the Duke of Aquitaine, the Earl of Kent and all the other lords, to deliver a great sermon on the text *"Doleo caput meum"*, from the sacred Book of Kings, to signify that the body of the kingdom of England suffered in its head and that it was there the remedy must be applied.

'This sermon made a profound impression on the whole congregation. It heard all the evils and harsh sufferings of the realm described and enumerated. And though, in an hour's sermon, Messire Orleton did not once mention the King by name, he was in everyone's mind as the cause of these misfortunes, and at the end the Bishop cried that both the lightning of Heaven and the swords of men must fall on the proud disturbers of the peace and the corrupters of kings. The said Monseigneur of Hereford is an extremely intelligent man, and I often have the honour of talking with him, though he generally seems to be in a hurry when he converses with me; but I always cull some clever remark from his lips. For instance, he said to me the other day: "Each one of us has his shining hour in the events of his century. On one occasion it may be Monseigneur of Kent, on another Monseigneur of Lancaster, some other on a previous occasion and yet another on a later, whom the event illumines because of the decisive part he plays in it. Thus is made the history of the world. And this actual moment, Messire de Hainaut, may well be your shining hour."

'Two days after the sermon, and as the result of the great effect it had on everyone, the Queen issued from Wallingford a proclamation against the Despensers, accusing them of having despoiled the Church and the Crown, unjustly put to death a great number of loyal subjects, disinherited, imprisoned and banished some of the greatest lords of the realm, oppressed widows and orphans, and crushed the people by taxes and extortions.

'At the same time we learnt that the King, who had first fled to take refuge in the town of Gloucester which belongs to Despenser the Younger, had gone to Westbury, and that his escort had split up. Despenser the Elder had retired to his city and castle of Bristol, to hold up our advance there, while the Earls of Arundel and Warenne had gone to their domains in Shropshire; this was so as to hold the Welsh Marches both in the north and the south, while the King, with Despenser the Younger and his Chancellor Baldock, went to raise an army in Wales. To tell the truth, we no longer know what has become of him. There is a rumour even of his having embarked for Ireland.

'While several English banners under the command of the Earl of Charlton set out for Shropshire to defy the Earl of Arundel, yesterday, the twenty-fourth day of October, precisely a month after our leaving Dordrecht, we entered without difficulty the town of Gloucester amid great acclamations. Today we are going to advance on Bristol, in which Despenser the Elder has shut himself up. I am to take command of the assault on this fortress and shall at last have the opportunity, which has so far been denied me owing to the fact that our advance has hardly been opposed, of doing battle for my Lady Isabella and of displaying my valour before her eyes. I shall kiss the pennant of Hainaut which floats from my lance before going into the attack.

'I confided my will to you, my dear and beloved Brother, before leaving, and I know of nothing which I wish to add to it or to alter. If I must die, you will know that I have done so without displeasure or regret, as a knight should in the noble defence of ladies and the unfortunate and oppressed, and for the honour of you and Madame, my dear sister, your wife, and of my nieces, your beloved daughters, whom God keep.

'Given at Gloucester the twenty-fifth day of October 1326.

'Jean.'

But Messire Jean de Hainaut had no need to display his valour the next day, and his very proper preparation of spirit was vain.

When he presented himself before Bristol in the morning,

banners flying and helms laced, the city had already decided to surrender and you could have taken it with a stick. The notables hurriedly sent envoys who were concerned only to know where the knights wished to be lodged, protested their attachment to the Queen and offered to surrender their lord, Hugh Despenser the Elder, on the spot, for he alone was to blame for the fact that they had not shown their good intentions earlier.

As soon as the gates of the city were opened, the knights took up their quarters in the fine houses of Bristol. Despenser the Elder was arrested in his castle and placed under the guard of four knights, while the Queen, the heir to the throne, and the principal barons took possession of his apartments. The Queen found there her three other children, whom Edward, when in flight, had left in Despenser's care. She was astonished to see how they had grown in twenty months and could not stop gazing at them and kissing them. She suddenly looked at Mortimer, as if this excess of joy might offend him, and murmured: 'I wish, my love, that God had granted they were born of you.'

At the instigation of the Earl of Lancaster, a Council was immediately assembled round the Queen, which included the Bishops of Hereford, Norwich, Lincoln, Ely and Winchester, the Archbishop of Dublin, the Earls of Norfolk and Kent, Roger Mortimer of Wigmore, Sir Thomas Wake, Sir William La Zouche d'Ashby, Robert de Montalt, Robert de Merle, Robert de Watteville and the Sire Henry de Beaumont.[38]

The Council derived its legal justification from the fact that King Edward was beyond the frontiers; whether he was in Wales or Ireland made no difference. It decided to proclaim young Prince Edward guardian and keeper of the realm in the sovereign's absence. The principal administrative posts were immediately redistributed and Adam Orleton, who was the intellectual leader of the rebellion, took most of them, in particular that of Lord Treasurer.

And, indeed, it was high time to make provision for the reorganization of the central authority. It was remarkable that during the whole month, when the King was in flight, his ministers dispersed, and England at the mercy of the Queen's and the barons' great expedition, the excise had continued functioning normally, the tax-collectors had gone on collecting taxes, the watch, in spite of everything, had maintained order in the towns and, taken all in all, ordinary life had pursued its normal course from a sort of habit of the social body.

And now the guardian of the realm, the provisional holder of sovereignty, was fifteen years old less one month. The decrees he would promulgate would be sealed with his private seal, since the seals of the realm had been carried away by the King and Chancellor Baldock. The young Prince's first act of government was to preside at the trial of Hugh Despenser the Elder that very day. The prosecution was in the hands of Sir Thomas Wake, a rugged old knight, who was Marshal of the Army.[39] He accused Hugh Despenser, Earl of Winchester, of being responsible for the execution of Thomas of Lancaster, for the death in the Tower of London of Roger Mortimer the Elder (for the old Lord of Chirk had not lived to see his nephew's triumphal return but had died in his dungeon a few weeks earlier), for the imprisonment, banishment, or death of many other lords, for the sequestration of the Queen's and the Earl of Kent's property, for the bad management of the affairs of the kingdom, for the defeats by the Scots and in the war in Aquitaine, all of which had been due to his disastrous advice and counsel. The same charges were later to be brought against all King Edward's councillors.

Wrinkled and bowed, his voice feeble, Hugh the Elder, who for so many years had feigned a tremulous self-effacement before the King's desires, now showed the energy of which he was capable. He had nothing more to lose and defended himself inch by inch.

Lost wars? They had been lost by the cowardice of the barons.[40] Executions and imprisonments? They had been punishments, decreed for traitors and rebels against the royal authority, lack of respect for which brought kingdoms to disaster. Sequestrations of fiefs and revenues had been decided on only to prevent enemies of the Crown raising men and money. And if he were to be accused of some plundering and spoliation, were the twenty-three manors, either his own property or that of his son, which Mortimer, Lancaster, Maltravers and Berkeley, all here present, had pillaged and burnt in 1321, before their defeat either at Shrewsbury or Boroughbridge, to count for nothing? He had merely reimbursed himself for the damage he had suffered and which he valued at forty thousand pounds, apart from the violence and cruelty of every kind committed against his people.

He finished his defence with these words addressed to the Queen: 'Oh, Madame, God owes us justice, and if we cannot have it in this age, He will owe it to us in the next world!'

Young Prince Edward raised his long lashes and listened

attentively. Hugh Despenser the Elder was condemned to be dragged through the streets, beheaded and his body hanged, to which he replied contemptuously: 'I see, my lords, that beheading and hanging are two different things for you, but for me they amount to but a single death!'

His behaviour, which much surprised those who had known him in other circumstances, went far to explain the great influence he had exercised. The obsequious courtier was no coward, nor the detestable minister a fool.

Prince Edward confirmed the sentence; but he was reflecting deeply and beginning silently to form views as to how a man destined to great responsibilities should behave. To listen before speaking, to inform yourself before judging, to understand before deciding, and to remember always that there were to be found in every man the springs both of the highest as well as the lowest actions: these, for a sovereign, were the first steps towards wisdom.

It was unusual to have to condemn a fellow-man to death before the age of fifteen. On his first day of power Edward of Aquitaine was receiving good training.

Old Despenser was tied by the feet to a horse's traces and dragged through the streets of Bristol. His tendons torn and his bones fractured, he was taken to the square in front of the castle and made to kneel before the block. His white hair was pulled forward to free his neck, and the executioner, wearing a red hood, raised the great sword and cut his head off. His body, spurting blood from the great arteries, was suspended by the armpits from a gibbet. The wrinkled, bloodstained head was placed beside it on a pike.

And all the knights who had sworn by Monseigneur Saint

George to defend ladies, maids, orphans and the oppressed, rejoiced with much laughter and gay talk at the spectacle of an old man's death.

3

Hereford

By All Saints' Day the new Court was installed at Hereford.

If, as Adam Orleton, the Bishop of that town, said, everyone in history has his shining hour, that hour was now his. After many vicissitudes, helping one of the greatest lords in the kingdom to escape, being brought to trial before Parliament and being saved by a coalition of his peers, and after preaching and encouraging rebellion, he was now returning in triumph to his bishopric, to which he had been provided in 1317, against the will of King Edward, and where he had conducted himself always as a great prelate.

And with what joy this little man, who was lacking in bodily grace, but possessed both physical and moral courage, dressed up in sacerdotal vestments, placed a mitre on his head and took his crozier in his hand, to process through the streets of this city for which he had done so much.

As soon as the royal party had taken possession of the

castle, which lay in the centre of the town on a bend of the Wye, Orleton could not rest till he had shown the Queen the buildings he had undertaken, and to begin with the great square tower, two stories high and pierced with huge arches, each angle surmounted with three bell-turrets, a low one on each side and a tall one dominating them, twelve spires in all mounting to the sky, which he had built over the centre of the cathedral, over the heart of the Cross. The November light gleamed on the rosy brick, its fresh colour preserved by the humidity, while round the building lay a huge, dark, well-tended lawn.

'Is it not the most beautiful tower in your kingdom, Madame?' asked Adam Orleton with the ingenuous pride of a builder, gazing up at the great hewn building, so pure in line, so restrained in decoration, which filled him with constant wonder. 'If it were only to have built this, I should be glad to have lived.'

Orleton's nobility derived, as they said, from Oxford rather than from armorial bearings. He was conscious of it, and wanted to justify the high position to which ambition allied to intelligence, and erudition even more than intrigue, had brought him. He knew himself to be superior to everyone about him.

He had reorganized the Cathedral library, in which stout volumes, arranged with their edges facing to the front, were bound to the shelves by chains with long forged links, so that they might not be stolen. There were nearly a thousand splendidly decorated and illuminated manuscripts, embodying five centuries of thought, faith and imagination, from the earliest translation of the Gospels into Saxon, the first pages still decorated with runic characters, to the most modern Latin dictionaries, as well as such volumes as *The Heavenly Hierarchy*, the works of Saint Jerome and Saint John Chrysostom, and those of the twelve minor prophets.

The Queen had also to admire the work in progress on the chapter-house, which was still under construction, and the famous map of the world painted by Richard de Bello, which had clearly been divinely inspired for it was already beginning to perform miracles.[41]

And so, for nearly a month, Hereford was the temporary capital of England. Mortimer was no less delighted than Orleton, since he recovered Wigmore Castle, which was only a few miles away, and was back so to speak in his own domains.

And, throughout this time, the search for the King went on.

A certain Rhys ap Owell, a Welsh knight, arrived one day with information that Edward II was hiding in an abbey on the coast of the county of Glamorgan, to which the ship he had taken in the hope of escaping to Ireland had been driven by contrary winds.

Jean de Hainaut immediately fell on his knees and offered to go and beard Madame Isabella's unfaithful husband in his Welsh lair. They had some difficulty in making him understand that it was impossible to confide the capture of the King to a foreigner, and that a member of the royal family was more suitable for the accomplishment of this painful duty. It was Henry Crouchback who had to take horse, which he did without much pleasure, to go and search the west coast, accompanied by Earl de la Zouche and Rhys ap Owell.

At about the same time the Earl of Charlton arrived from Shropshire where he had taken prisoner the Earl of Arundel, whom he now brought in chains. For Roger Mortimer this was a splendid revenge, for Edmund Fitzalan, Earl of Arundel, had received from the King a great part of his sequestered estates and also had conferred on him the title of Justiciar of Wales which had belonged to old Mortimer of Chirk.

Roger Mortimer contented himself with letting his enemy stand before him for a whole quarter of an hour without saying a word to him, merely looking him up and down, and savouring calmly the contemplation of a live enemy who would soon be a dead one.

The trial of Arundel as an enemy of the realm and on the same charges as had been preferred against Despenser the Elder was conducted without delay and his beheading gave the townspeople of Hereford and the troops stationed there an opportunity for merry-making.

It was noticed that the Queen and Roger Mortimer held each other's hands during the execution.

Young Prince Edward's fifteenth birthday had taken place three days earlier.

At last, on November 20, there was great news. King Edward had been taken by the Earl of Lancaster in the Cistercian Abbey of Neath, in the lower valley of the Tawe.

The King, his favourite and his Chancellor had been living hidden there for several weeks, wearing monks' habits. Edward had been spending his time, while waiting for a turn of fortune, working in the abbey's forge, a pastime which diverted his mind from too much thinking.

And it was here, standing naked to the waist with his habit

hanging down from his belt, his chest and beard lit up by the fire of the forge and his hands all among the sparks, while the Chancellor worked the bellows and Hugh the Younger, looking far from happy, handed him the tools, that Henry Crouchback found him. He stood in the doorway, his helmet almost touching his shoulder, and said: 'Sire, my Cousin, the time has now come when you must pay for your sins.'

The King dropped his hammer; the piece of metal he was forging glowed red on the anvil; and the sovereign of England, his tall white body trembling from head to foot, said: 'Cousin, Cousin, what will they do to me?'

'What the great ones of your realm may decide,' replied Crouchback.

And now Edward was waiting with his favourite and his Chancellor in the little fortified manor of Monmouth, some leagues from Hereford, where Lancaster had taken him and imprisoned him.

Adam Orleton, accompanied by his Archdeacon, Thomas Chandos, and the Great Chamberlain, William Blount, went immediately to Monmouth to demand the seal of the realm which Baldock still had in his possession.

When Orleton had explained his request, Edward seized the leather bag containing the seal from Baldock's belt, wrapped the laces round his wrist as if he wished to make a weapon of it, and cried: 'You traitor, you wicked bishop, if you want my seal, you shall take it from me by force and make it plain that a priest has raised his hand against his King!'

Destiny had undoubtedly designed Adam Orleton for the highest tasks. To remove the insignia of his power from a king's hands is no usual matter. Outfacing the angry athlete,

Orleton with his sloping shoulders and weak hands, with no other weapon than a light ivory-handled cane, replied: 'The handing over must be done of your own free will, and before witnesses. Sire Edward, are you going to compel your son, who is already keeper of the realm, to order his own sovereign's seal earlier than he expected to have to do? I can, however, forcibly seize the Lord Chancellor and Lord Despenser whom I have orders to bring to the Queen.'

At these words, Edward ceased being concerned about the seal and thought only of his beloved favourite. He removed the leather bag from his wrist and threw it to the Chamberlain William Blount, as if it had suddenly ceased to be an object of value. Opening wide his arms to Hugh, he cried: 'Oh, no, you won't take him from me!'

Hugh the Younger, emaciated, trembling, threw himself on the King's breast. His teeth chattered, he seemed about to swoon and he groaned: 'You see, it's your wife who has ordered this. It is she, that French she-wolf, who is the cause of it all. Oh, Edward, Edward, why did you marry her?'

Henry Crouchback, Orleton, Archdeacon Chandos and William Blount looked at the two men embracing and, though their passion was incomprehensible to them, they could not help recognizing that there was some appalling quality of grandeur about it.

In the end it was Crouchback who went up to them, took Despenser by the arm, and said: 'Come on, you must separate.' And he dragged him away.

'Goodbye, Hugh, goodbye!' cried Edward. 'My life's darling, my sweetest soul, I shall never see you again! They have taken everything from me!'

The tears were pouring down his blond beard.

Hugh Despenser was handed over to the knights of the escort who began by dressing him in a peasant's cloak of coarse cloth, on which they painted derisively the arms and emblems of the counties the King had given him. Then they bound his hands behind his back and hoisted him on to the smallest and wretchedest horse they could find, a rough, dwarf, scraggy, country screw. Hugh's legs were too long; he was forced either to draw them up or let his feet drag in the mud. In this way he was led through the towns and villages of Monmouthshire and Herefordshire, halting in the market-squares so that the people might mock him to their hearts' content. The trumpets sounded before the prisoner and a herald cried: 'Look, good people, look at the Earl of Gloucester, the Lord Chamberlain, look at the wicked man who has done such harm to the realm!'

The Chancellor, Robert de Baldock, was taken more discreetly, for the sake of the dignity of the Church, to the bishop's palace in London where he was imprisoned; as an archdeacon he could not be condemned to death.

All the hatred was therefore concentrated on Hugh Despenser, whom people still called the Younger though he was now nearly thirty-six years of age and his father was dead. He was quickly brought to trial in Hereford and his sentence, of which no one was in doubt, pronounced. But since he was held chiefly responsible for all the errors and misfortunes from which England had suffered, his execution was to have certain particular refinements.

On November 24 the stands were erected on an open space in front of the castle and the scaffold built high enough so that a numerous attendance should lose no detail of the execution. Queen Isabella sat in the first row of the largest stand, between Roger Mortimer and Prince Edward. It was drizzling.

The trumpets and *busines* sounded. Hugh the Younger was led out by the executioner's assistants and stripped of his clothes. When his long, wide-hipped, pigeon-breasted body appeared, white and completely naked, between the red-clothed executioners and above the pikes of the archers who surrounded the scaffold, a great coarse laugh rose from the crowd.

Queen Isabella leaned towards Mortimer and murmured: 'I wish Edward were here to see it.'

Her eyes bright, her little carnivore's teeth parted, her nails gripping the palm of her lover's hand, she was taking care to lose no detail of her vengeance.

Prince Edward was thinking: 'Is that really the man my father loved so much?' He had already attended two executions and knew he could hold out to the end without being sick.

The *busines* rang out again. Hugh was laid down on a horizontal Saint Andrew's cross and tied down by his arms and legs. The executioner was slowly sharpening a pointed knife, like a butcher's, on a hone, and testing the edge with his thumb. The crowd held its breath. Then an assistant came forward with a pair of pincers with which he seized the prisoner's penis. A wave of hysteria ran through the crowd; its stamping feet made the stands shake. And in spite of the noise everyone heard the cry Hugh uttered. A single, piercing cry that was suddenly broken off, as the blood spurted from him. The same operation was repeated on his testicles, but he was already unconscious, and the sad offal was thrown into a brazier of burning embers fanned by an assistant. An appalling stench of burning flesh rose from it. A herald, standing in front of the *busine*-blowers, announced that these things had been done 'because Despenser had been a sodomite, and had favoured the King in sodomy, and thereby had exiled the Queen from her bed'.

Then the executioner, selecting a longer and broader knife, ripped the chest across and the stomach lengthwise, as he might have done a pig; the pincers found the heart, that had barely ceased to beat, tore it from its place and it, too, was thrown into the brazier. The *busines* rang out and then the herald declared that 'Despenser had been a traitor and false in heart, and by his traitorous counsels had brought shame on the realm'.

The entrails were then removed from the stomach, unrolled and shaken, glistening, nacreous, and held up in front of the public because 'Despenser had fed upon the possessions both of the wealthy and of the poor'. And in their turn the entrails were transformed into the thick acrid smoke that mingled with the November drizzle.

After which the head was cut off, not with a blow from a sword, since it was hanging backwards between the arms of the cross, but detached with a knife, because 'Despenser had had the greatest barons of England beheaded and from his own head had come all the evil counsels'. Hugh Despenser's head was not burnt; the executioners set it aside to send to London, where it would be impaled at the entrance to the bridge.

And, finally, what remained of the long pale body was cut

into four quarters, an arm with its shoulder, the other arm also with its shoulder and the neck, and each leg with half the stomach, that they might be sent to the four greatest cities of the realm after London.

The crowd left the stands, relaxed, released and exhausted. Surely the pinnacle of cruelty had now been reached.

After each execution on their bloodstained path, Mortimer had found Queen Isabella more ardent in love than ever. But on the night following the execution of Hugh Despenser, her demands on him and the hysterical gratitude she expressed to him could not but disquiet him. To have hated the man who had taken her husband from her so much, she must surely once have loved Edward. And in Mortimer's suspicious mind a plan was born which he determined to put into effect, however long it might take him.

The next day Henry Crouchback, who had been appointed the King's gaoler, was ordered to take him to Kenilworth Castle and imprison him there. The Queen had not seen him again.

4

Vox Populi

'WHO DO YOU want for your king?'

This terrifying question on which depended the future of the nation was asked by Adam Orleton on 12 January 1327 in the great hall at Westminster, and the words echoed high among the beams in the roof.

'Who do you want for your king?'

For the last six days the English Parliament had been sitting, adjourning and sitting again. Adam Orleton, acting as Lord Chancellor, was leading the debates.

During its first session, a few weeks ago, Parliament had summoned the King to appear before it. Adam Orleton and John de Stratford, Bishop of Winchester, had gone to Kenilworth to present Edward II with the summons, and King Edward had refused to accept it.

He had refused to come and give an account of his actions to the lords, the bishops, and the members for boroughs and counties. Orleton had announced his reply to Parliament and no one could tell whether it was due to fear or contempt. But

Orleton was profoundly convinced, and had told Parliament of his conviction, that if the Queen were to be coerced into a reconciliation with her husband, it would mean her certain death.

And now the great question had been asked. And Orleton concluded his speech by counselling Parliament to adjourn till the following day so that the members might conscientiously consider their choice during the silence of the night. Tomorrow the House would determine whether it wished Edward II Plantagenet to retain the crown or whether it should pass to his eldest son, Edward, Duke of Aquitaine.

There was, however, not much silence for conscientious thought in the hubbub of London that night. The houses of the lords, the abbeys, the homes of the great merchants and the inns were to resound till dawn with the noise of passionate argument. All these barons, bishops, knights and squires, these representatives of boroughs selected by the sheriffs, were, in law, members of Parliament only by the King's appointment, and their function, in principle, was merely advisory. But now the sovereign was an incapable defaulter, a fugitive who had been apprehended outside his kingdom; and it was not the King who had summoned Parliament, but Parliament which had summoned its King, though he had refused to obey its orders. The supreme power was therefore for a moment, for a single night, in the hands of these men of disparate origins and unequal fortune, who came from every part of the country.

'Who do you want for your king?'

The question was a very real one, and even for those who had wished publicly for Edward II's early death, who had cried, at every scandal, at every new tax, at every war lost: 'May he die! May God deliver us from him!'

But now it was no longer a question of God intervening; everything depended on themselves, and they were suddenly aware of the importance of their collective will. Their wishes and their curses had been accomplished, and here was the sum of them. Could the Queen, even supported by her Hennuyers, have been able to seize the whole kingdom as she had done if the barons and the people had responded to the levy Edward had ordered?

But to depose a king and strip him for ever of his vested authority was an important action. Many members of Parliament were afraid of taking it because of the divine nature of the coronation and the royal majesty. Besides, the young Prince, for whom it was suggested they should vote, was very young. What was known of him, except that he was entirely in his mother's hands, who was entirely in the hands of Mortimer? And even if one respected, indeed admired the Baron of Wigmore, the former Justiciar and conqueror of Ireland, if his escape, exile and return, even his love affair, had made of him a legendary hero, and to many he appeared as a liberator, nevertheless his character, his hardness and his mercilessness were feared; already that severity in punishing, which he had shown during these last weeks, was being made a reproach to him, though he had but conformed to the people's will. Those who knew him well feared his ambition above all. Had he no secret desire to become king himself? As the Queen's lover, he was very close to the throne. There was some reluctance to invest him with the great power that would be his if Edward II were deposed. Indeed, there was much argument round the lamps and candles, over the pewter pots that were so frequently refilled with beer, till everyone went home exhausted to bed, without having really made up his mind.

The people of England, that night, were sovereign, but somewhat embarrassed at being so; they did not know to whom to hand over the exercise of that sovereignty.

History had taken a sudden step forward. Questions were being argued whose mere discussion was significant of the admission of new principles. A people does not forget such a precedent, nor a Parliament that it had exercised such power; a nation does not forget that, through its Parliament, it has had occasion to be the master of its destiny.

But the following morning, when Bishop Orleton took young Prince Edward by the hand, and presented him to the members assembled at Westminster, a great ovation rose echoing from wall to wall and up to the roof.

'We want him, we want him!'

Four bishops, among whom were those of London and York, protested and argued about the juridical problems of homage and the irrevocable nature of the coronation. But Archbishop Reynolds, to whom Edward II, before taking flight, had confided the Government, and who was now particularly anxious to prove the sincerity of his adherence to the new dispensation, cried: 'Vox populi, vox dei!'

And for a good quarter of an hour he preached on this text as if he were in the pulpit.

John de Stratford, Bishop of Winchester, drew up and read to Parliament six articles showing cause why Edward II Plantagenet should be deposed.

Primo: The King is incapable of governing. Throughout his reign he has been influenced by detestable counsellors.

Secundo: He has devoted all his time to employments and occupations unworthy of him and has neglected the affairs of the realm.

Tertio: He has lost Scotland, Ireland and half Guyenne.

Quarto: He has wronged the Church whose ministers he has imprisoned.

Quinto: He has imprisoned, exiled, disinherited, or condemned to a shameful death many of his great vassals.

Sexto: He has ruined the kingdom, and is incorrigible and incapable of amendment.

In the meantime the burgesses of London, who were both anxious and divided among themselves – had not their bishop declared against the dethronement? – were assembling in Guildhall. They were less easy to control than the representatives of the counties. Were they going to checkmate Parliament? Roger Mortimer, who was nothing by title and everything in fact, hurried to Guildhall, thanked the Londoners for their loyalty and guaranteed the maintenance of the customary liberties of the City. But in whose name, in the name of what, did he give this guarantee? In the name of a boy who was not yet King, who had indeed only just been accepted by acclamation. Nevertheless, Mortimer's prestige and personal authority had its effect on the London burgesses. He was already being called Lord Protector. But whose protector was he? The Prince's, the Queen's, the realm's? He was Lord Protector, and that was enough; he was the man chosen by events and into his hands everyone was prepared to place his own portion of power and judgment.

And then the unexpected happened. The young Prince, whom people already looked on as King, the pale boy with long eyelashes who had kept silence through all these events, and who, so one supposed, was thinking of nothing but Madame Philippa of Hainaut, suddenly declared to his mother, to the Lord Protector, to Orleton and the bishops, indeed to everyone about him, that he would never assume the crown without his father's consent and without the latter having written officially to proclaim his abdication.

There was utter stupefaction; everyone was aghast. Were all their efforts to come to nothing? Some were suspicious of the Queen. Had she perhaps brought pressure to bear secretly on her son, owing to one of those unforeseeable recurrences of affection to which women are prone? Or had there been some quarrel between her and the Lord Protector during the night in which every man was to consult his conscience?

But it was neither of these things. It was simply that this fifteen-year-old boy, completely on his own, had been reflecting on the importance of the legitimacy of power. He did not want to be looked on as a usurper, nor hold his crown by the will of Parliament which, since it had given it to him, might equally take it away. He insisted on the consent of his predecessor. It was not that he had any tender feelings towards his father; indeed, he had formed his own opinion about him. But then he formed his own opinion about everyone.

So many wicked things had been done in his presence over the years that he had been forced to begin forming his own opinions early. He knew that crime was not entirely on one side and innocence on the other. Of course, his father had made his mother suffer, had dishonoured her and despoiled her; but what sort of an example was his mother giving with Roger Mortimer now? Suppose one day, because of some fault he had committed, Madame Philippa acted thus? And all these barons and bishops, who were so ruthlessly opposed to King Edward today, were they not the very people who had governed with him? Norfolk and Kent, his young uncles, had been given and had accepted appointments; the Bishops of Winchester and Lincoln had carried on negotiations in King Edward's name. The Despensers had not been everywhere at once and, even if they gave the orders, they had not carried them out themselves. Who had taken the risk of refusing to obey? Cousin Lancaster Crouchback had undoubtedly had the courage to do so; and Roger Mortimer, too, who had paid for his rebellion by a long sojourn in prison. But, as opposed to these two, how many lackeys there were who had quickly changed sides and were eagerly seizing every opportunity to exculpate themselves.

Every other prince in the world would have been intoxicated at his age to see one of the great crowns of the world falling to his lot, and held out to him by so many hands. But he raised his long lashes, looked at them steadily, blushed a little at his audacity and held to his decision. Then Orleton summoned the Bishops of Winchester and Lincoln, as well as the Great Chamberlain William Blount, ordered the crown and sceptre to be brought from the Treasure House in the Tower, where they were kept, had them placed in a box on the pack-saddle of a mule and, taking his ceremonial vestments with him, set out on the road to Kenilworth to obtain the King's abdication.

5

Kenilworth

THE OUTER WALLS, which were built round the base of an extensive hill, enclosed gardens, meadows, stables and byres, a forge, barns and bakehouses, a mill, cisterns, the servants' lodgings and the soldiers' barracks; indeed, a whole village, which was almost larger than the village proper, the tiled roofs of whose cottages clustered close together outside. It was as if these cottages beyond the walls were inhabited by a different race of men from those who lived within the formidable castle that raised its red fortifications to the winter sky.

For Kenilworth had been built of a stone the colour of dried blood. It was one of those fabulous castles, dating back to the century after the Conquest, when a handful of Normans, the companions of William, had had to overawe a whole population with these huge fortresses built on hills.

The keep of Kenilworth, square and immensely high, reminded travellers from the Orient of the pylons of Egyptian temples.

The proportions of this enormous building were so great that large rooms were contained merely within the thickness of the walls; but the keep, on the other hand, could be entered only by a narrow staircase in which two people could barely walk abreast. Its red steps led to a door protected by a portcullis on the first floor. Within was a garden, or rather a grassy court, of some sixty feet square, open to the sky, but entirely contained within the keep.[42]

No military building could have been better conceived to withstand a siege. If the invader succeeded in breaching the outer wall, the defenders took refuge in the castle itself, behind a moat; and if the inner wall was breached, then the defenders would abandon the usual living-quarters, the great hall, the kitchens, the lords' chambers, the chapel, to the enemy, and retire into the keep built round the well of the green court which was sheltered by an enormous thickness of wall.

The King was living there as a prisoner. He knew Kenilworth well, for it had belonged to Thomas of Lancaster and had once served as a rallying centre for the rebellious barons. After Thomas had been beheaded, Edward had seized the castle and had lived in it himself during the winter of 1323, before giving it back to Henry Crouchback the following year, when he had returned to him all the Lancaster estates.

Henry III, Edward's grandfather, had in the past besieged Kenilworth for six months to recover it from the son of his brother-in-law, Simon de Montfort; and it was not to the military that it had fallen, but to famine, plague and excommunication.

At the beginning of the reign of Edward I, Roger Mortimer of Chirk, who had so recently died in prison, had been its constable, in the name of the first Earl of Lancaster, and had given his famous tournaments there. One of the towers on the outer wall, to Edward's exasperation, bore the name of Mortimer Tower. It stood there, a mockery and a defiance, in the centre of his daily view.

But King Edward II had still other memories of the district. Only four miles to the south, in Warwick Castle, whose white keep was visible from the summit of Kenilworth's red keep, Gaveston, his first lover, had been put to death by the barons. Had this neighbourhood changed the tenor of the King's thoughts? Edward seemed to have forgotten Hugh Despenser completely; on the other hand, he was obsessed by the memory of Piers Gaveston, and talked of him unceasingly to his gaoler, Henry of Lancaster.

Never had Edward and his cousin Crouchback lived so close together for so long, nor in such isolation. Never had Edward confided so much to the eldest member of his family. He had moments of considerable lucidity in which he judged himself dispassionately, and this sometimes astonished Lancaster, and touched him too. Lancaster was beginning to understand many things which seemed incomprehensible to the people of England.

It was Gaveston, Edward admitted, who had been responsible for, or at least the origin of, his first errors and of the deplorable path his life had taken.

'He loved me so much,' said the prisoner King; 'and at that time, young as I was, I was ready to believe anything and to trust myself entirely to so great a love.'

And even now he could not help being moved by the memory of the charm of that little Gascon knight who had risen from nothing, 'a mushroom sprouting in a night', as the barons said, and whom he had made Earl of Cornwall to the disgust of all the great lords of the realm.

'He wanted it so much!' Edward said.

And how splendidly insolent Piers had been; it was an insolence that delighted Edward. No king would have dared treat his great barons as his favourite did.

'Do you remember, Crouchback, how he used to call the Earl of Gloucester a bastard? And how he used to shout to the Earl of Warwick: "Go and lie down, you black dog!"'

'And how he insulted my brother by calling him a cuckold, which Thomas never forgave him, because it was true.'

Piers had been frightened of nothing. He had pillaged the Queen's jewels and thrown insults about as others distribute alms, because he was sure of the love of his King. He had had a greater effrontery than anyone in the world. Moreover, he had used his imagination in his diversions: he had stripped his pages naked, loaded their arms with pearls, rouged their lips, allowed them no more than a leafy frond for modest concealment, and had organized erotic pursuits through the woods. And then there had been his escapades in the low districts in the port of London, where he wrestled with the porters, for the fellow was strong, too. Oh, what splendid youthful years he had given the King!

'I thought I'd find all that again in Hugh, but my imagination endowed him with more than was there. You see, Crouchback, what made Hugh so different from Piers was the fact that he really did come from a family of great barons and he couldn't forget it. But had I not known Piers, I'm sure I should have been a very different King.'

During the interminable winter evenings, between games of chess, Henry Crouchback, his hair falling over his right shoulder, listened to the King's confessions. His reverses, the collapse of his power and his captivity had suddenly aged him; his athletic body seemed to have grown soft and his face become puffy, in particular the eyelids. And yet, such as he was, Edward still preserved a certain charm. He needed to be loved; that had been the great misfortune of his life. How sad it was that his loves had been so wicked and that he had sought consolation and loyalty from such evil hearts.

Crouchback had advised Edward to go to appear before his Parliament, but in vain. This weak King could show strength only in stubborn refusal.

'I know very well I've lost my throne, Henry,' he replied, 'but I shall not abdicate.'

Carried on a cushion, the crown and sceptre of England were moving slowly upwards, step by step, in the narrow staircase of the keep of Kenilworth. Behind, the mitres swayed and the jewels in the croziers glittered in the half-light. The Bishops, raising their embroidered robes above their ankles, were slowly hoisting themselves up the tower.

The King, seated on a chair which, because it was the only one, created something of the effect of a throne, was waiting at the end of the great hall, his head resting on his hand, his body bowed, between two of the pillars that supported the great arches which resembled those of a cathedral. Everything here was of colossal proportions. The pale January day, which entered through the high, narrow windows, was like twilight.

The Earl of Lancaster, with his head askew, was standing beside his cousin together with three attendants, who were not even the King's. The red walls, the red pillars and the red arches composed a tragic background for the end of a reign.

When Edward saw the crown and sceptre, which had been brought to him like this twenty years ago under the vaults of Westminster, appearing through the open double doors and advancing towards him across the huge spaces of the hall, he sat upright in his chair and his chin began quivering a little. He turned to look at his cousin of Lancaster, as if in search of his support, but Crouchback looked away, for this dumb entreaty was intolerable.

Then Orleton was standing before the King, Orleton whose every appearance for several weeks past had meant for Edward the forfeit of some part of his power. The King looked at the other Bishops and at the Great Chamberlain; he made an effort to maintain his dignity and asked: 'What have you to say to me, my lords?'

But the pale lips amid the blond beard could barely frame the words.

The Bishop of Winchester read the message by which Parliament summoned the King to sign his abdication together with a renunciation of homage from his vassals, to agree to the choice of his son, and to deliver up to the envoys the ritual insignia of sovereignty.

When the Bishop of Winchester had done, Edward was silent for a long moment. His whole attention seemed fixed on the crown. He was suffering, and his pain was so clearly physical, so profoundly marked on his features, that one might have doubted whether he was even thinking at all. Nevertheless, he said: 'You have the crown in your hands, my lords, and you have me at your mercy. Do therefore as you please, but you shall not do it with my consent.'

Then Adam Orleton took a step forward and said: 'Sire Edward, the people of England no longer want you for King and their Parliament has sent us to declare it to you. But Parliament accepts as King your eldest son, the Duke of Aquitaine, whom I have presented to it; but your son is not willing to accept the crown except with your consent. If you are therefore wilful in your refusal, the people will be free to choose and may well elect as their sovereign prince someone among the great men of the realm who most pleases them, and that king may not be of your lineage. You have brought too much trouble on the realm; and after all the harm you have done it, this is the one thing you can still do to give it peace.'

Once again Edward looked at Lancaster. In spite of the faintness he felt, the King had understood the warning contained in the bishop's words. If he did not agree to abdicate, Parliament, in its need to find a king, would certainly choose the leader of the rebellion, Roger Mortimer, who already possessed the Queen's heart. The King's face had taken on a curious and alarming hue; his chin was still quivering; his nostrils looked pinched.

'My lord Orleton is right,' said Crouchback. 'You must abdicate, Cousin, to bring peace back to England and so that the Plantagenets may continue to reign.'

Then Edward, who seemed incapable of speech, signed to

them to bring the crown near and he bowed his head as if he wished to wear it for a last time.

The Bishops looked at each other, knowing neither what to do nor how to do it, for this unexpected ceremony had no precedent in royal ritual. But the King's head was bowing lower and lower towards his knees.

'He's swooned!' suddenly cried Archdeacon Chandos who was carrying the cushion with the emblems of sovereignty.

Crouchback and Orleton hurried to the fainting Edward and caught him as his head was about to strike the flagstones.

They put him back in his chair, slapped his cheeks, and sent hurriedly for vinegar. At last he drew a deep breath, opened his eyes, looked about him, and then suddenly began to weep. The mysterious power with which the anointing and the mystic rites of the coronation imbue kings, and sometimes only to serve disastrous tendencies, had withdrawn itself from him. It was as if he had been exorcised of the quality of sovereignty.

He was heard to speak through his tears.

'I know, my lords, I know that it is through my own fault that I have fallen into such great misery, and I must resign myself to bear it. But I cannot help feeling a great sorrow at all this hatred from my people, whom I have never hated. I have offended you, I have not acted well. You are good, my lords, very good to preserve your devotion to my eldest son, to continue to love him and to want him for king. I shall therefore do as you wish. I renounce before you all my rights over the realm; I release all my vassals from the homage they have paid me and ask their pardon. Come near . . .'

And once again he signed for the emblems of sovereignty

to be brought to him. He took hold of the sceptre, and his arm dropped as if he had forgotten how much it weighed; he gave it to the Bishop of Winchester, saying: 'Forgive, my lord, forgive the wrongs I have done you.'

He extended his long white hands towards the cushion, raised the crown, put his lips to it as if it were a paten, and then, handing it to Adam Orleton, he said: 'Take it, my lord, to crown my son. And forgive me for the wrongs and injustices I have done you. May my people forgive me in my present misery. My lords, pray for me who am now nothing.'

Everyone was struck by the nobility of his words. Edward showed himself to be a King only at the moment he was ceasing to be one.

Then Sir William Blount, the Great Chamberlain, emerged from the shadows of the pillars, advanced between Edward and the Bishops, and broke across his knee the carved staff, which was the insignia of his office, to mark the fact that a reign was over, as he would have done before the body of a dead king that had been placed in its tomb.

6

The Camp-kettle War

'SEEING THAT SIR EDWARD, lately King of England, has by his own will and the general advice and assent of the prelates, earls, barons and other nobles, and that of all the population of the kingdom, resigned the government of the realm, and consented and willed that the government of the said realm pass to Sir Edward, his eldest son and heir, and that the latter should govern and be crowned King, on which account all the nobility have done homage, we proclaim and publish the peace of our Lord Sir Edward the son and order on his behalf that no one disturb the peace of our said Lord the King, for he will protect the rights of everyone in his said kingdom, both rich and poor, against whomsoever it may be. And if any have just cause or complaint against another, let him have resort to the law, and use neither force nor other violence.'

This proclamation was read on 24 January 1327 to the Parliament of England, and a Council of Regency was immediately appointed; the Queen presided over this Council of twelve members among whom were the Earls of Kent, Norfolk and Lancaster, the Marshal Sir Thomas Wake and, the most important of all, Roger Mortimer, Baron of Wigmore.

Edward III was crowned on Sunday, February 1, at Westminster. The day before, Henry Crouchback had armed the young King a knight together with the three elder sons of Roger Mortimer.

Lady Jeanne Mortimer, who had recovered both her liberty and her property, but lost her husband's love, was present. She dared not look at the Queen nor did the Queen dare look at her. Lady Jeanne suffered greatly from this betrayal by the two people in the world she had loved most and served best. Did fifteen years of attendance on Queen Isabella, of devotion, intimacy and shared risks, deserve such a reward? And did twenty-three years of marriage to Mortimer, to whom she had borne eleven children, deserve to come to an end like this? In this great upheaval, which was altering the destiny of the kingdom and giving her husband the highest power, Lady Jeanne, who had always been so loyal, found herself among the vanquished. And yet she could forgive, she could retire with dignity, precisely because the two people she most admired were concerned and because she understood that these two people were bound inevitably to fall in love as soon as Fate had brought them together.

After the coronation, the crowd was allowed to invade the Bishop of London's palace to kill the ex-Chancellor Robert de Baldock; and, the next week, Messire Jean de Hainaut received an income of one thousand marks sterling from the duty on wool and leather in the Port of London.

Messire Jean de Hainaut would have liked to stay longer at the Court of England. But he had promised to go to a great tournament at Condé-sur-l'Escault, where many princes, among them the King of Bohemia, were to meet. There would be jousting and parading and an opportunity to meet many beautiful women who had crossed Europe to watch the greatest knights compete; there would be dancing and flirting and feasting and masks. Messire Jean de Hainaut could not miss all that, nor the opportunity of shining in his plumed helm in the sanded lists. He agreed to take with him fifteen English knights who wanted to take part in the tournament.

In March the treaty was signed with France at last. It regularized the question of Aquitaine, and to England's great detriment. But could Mortimer make Edward III refuse the clauses that he himself had negotiated so that they might be imposed on Edward II? It was a legacy from a bad reign, and it had to be paid. Besides, Mortimer took little interest in Guyenne where he had no lands. At the moment his attention was concentrated, as it had been before his imprisonment, on Wales and the Welsh Marches.

The envoys he sent to Paris to ratify the treaty found King Charles IV very sad and cast down, for the child born to Jeanne of Évreux in the previous month of November had not only been a girl, when he had hoped for a boy, but had not lived two months.

Order was only just being restored in the kingdom of England, when the old King of Scotland, Robert the Bruce, who had caused Edward II so much trouble, though he was now old in years and suffered moreover from leprosy, sent on April 1, twelve days after Easter, a defiance to young Edward, informing him that he was about to invade his country.

Roger Mortimer's first reaction was to make ex-King Edward change his residence. It was only prudent. Moreover, Henry of Lancaster and his banners were needed with the army. And then, according to reports from Kenilworth, Lancaster seemed to be treating his prisoner too kindly, keeping but a lax guard over him and allowing him a certain amount of communication with the outside world. And the partisans of the Despensers had not all been executed, indeed far from it; in the first place the Earl of Warenne, more fortunate than his brother-in-law the Earl of Arundel, had managed to escape. Some had gone to earth in their manors or in friends' houses while waiting for the storm to blow over; others had fled the kingdom. It might even be that the defiance sent by the old King of Scotland had been inspired by them.

Moreover, the great popular enthusiasm with which the liberation had been welcomed was now beginning seriously to decrease. From the mere fact of having governed for six months, Roger Mortimer was already less beloved and less adulated; for there were still taxes to pay and people were still being sent to prison for failure to pay them. In the circles of power, people were beginning to reproach Mortimer with his too peremptory authority, which seemed to increase day by day, and with the great ambitions he was beginning to reveal. He had recovered all the estates which had been seized from him by the Earl of Arundel, and had added to them the county of Glamorgan as well as the greater part of Hugh the Younger's possessions. His three sons-in-law – for Mortimer already had three married daughters – Lord de Berkeley, the

Earl of Charlton and the Earl of Warwick, served to increase his territorial power. Having conferred on himself the appointment of Justiciar of Wales, which had been his uncle of Chirk's, as well as his uncle's lands, he was thinking of having himself created Earl of March, which would have given him a fabulous semi-independent principality in the west of the kingdom.

He had also managed to quarrel with Adam Orleton, who had been sent to Avignon to hasten the necessary dispensations for the marriage of the young King; and, since the Bishopric of Worcester happened to be vacant, Orleton had asked the Pope for this important diocese. Mortimer had taken offence that Orleton had not first asked his agreement, and had opposed the appointment. Edward II had behaved towards Orleton in exactly the same way over the see of Hereford.

It was natural that the Queen should also suffer from this decreasing popularity.

And now war had been declared, war with Scotland again. Nothing seemed to have changed. And the people had hoped for so much that they were bound to be disappointed. Suppose the armies were defeated and there was a conspiracy by which Edward II escaped, then the Scots, allies of the old Despenser party for the occasion, would have a King ready to replace on the throne and one who would undoubtedly be willing to surrender the northern provinces to them in exchange for his liberty and recovered power.[43]

During the night of April 3 the ex-King was awakened and asked to dress quickly. He found himself in the presence of a tall, bony, ungainly knight, with long yellow teeth, dark straight hair falling over his ears, and very much the appearance of a horse.

'Where are you taking me, Maltravers?' Edward asked in terror, recognizing a baron whom he had once ruined and banished, and who looked very like a murderer.

'I'm taking you to a place of greater security, Plantagenet; and so that the security shall be effective, you are not to know where you're going, and then there'll be no risk of your mentioning it.'

Maltravers had instructions to avoid the towns and not to linger on the road. On April 5, after a journey made entirely at a canter or indeed a gallop, and broken only by a single halt at an abbey near Gloucester, the ex-King reached Berkeley Castle, where his gaoler was one of Mortimer's sons-in-law.

The English army, summoned first to Newcastle for Ascension Day, finally assembled in the town of York at Pentecost. The Government of the kingdom had moved there, and Parliament held a session there, exactly as in the old days of the fallen King when the Scots invaded.

And soon Messire Jean de Hainaut and his Hennuyers arrived, for they had been called to the rescue. Once again, mounted on their big chestnut horses, and still in great excitement from the wonderful tournament of Condé-sur-l'Escaut, there appeared the Lords of Ligne, Enghien, Mons and Sarre, and Guillaume de Bailleul, Perceval de Sémeries, Sance de Boussoy, and Oulfart de Ghistelles, who had all carried the colours of Hainaut to success in the jousting, and Messires Thierry de Wallecourt, Rasses de Grez, Jean Pilastre and the three brothers Harlebeke under the banners of Brabant; and other Lords of Flanders, Cambrésis and Artois, and with them the sons of the Marquis de Juliers.

Jean de Hainaut had had no difficulty in assembling them at Condé. You just went from wars to jousts and from jousts to wars. My God, what fun it was!

Great festivities were held in York in honour of the Hennuyers' return. The best lodgings were given them; they were feasted and banqueted, with an abundance of meat and poultry. The wines of Gascony and the Rhine flowed from open barrels.

These festivities for the foreigners irritated the English archers, of whom there were some six thousand, among whom were many old soldiers of the Earl of Arundel, who had been beheaded.

One night a brawl, as often happens indeed in the ordinary way among troops in garrison, broke out over a game of dice between some English archers and the squires of a Brabant knight. The English, who were simply awaiting an opportunity, called their comrades to come and help; and all the archers rose to teach these continental cads a lesson; the Hennuyers ran to their billets for shelter. The knights, who had been feasting, were drawn into the streets by the noise and immediately set on by the English archers. They tried to take refuge in their billets, but could gain no entrance to them since their own men had barricaded the doors. And now, the flower of the nobility of Flanders was without arms or any means of defence. But it consisted of stout men. Messires Perceval de Sémeries, Fastres de Rues and Sance de Boussoy armed themselves with heavy pieces of oak they had found in a wheelwright's, put their backs to the wall and killed, between the three of them, some sixty archers belonging to the Bishop of Lincoln.

This minor quarrel between allies resulted in over three hundred dead.

The six thousand archers, forgetting all about the Scottish war, thought only of exterminating the Hennuyers. Messire Jean de Hainaut, who was both furious and outraged, determined to go home, if only the siege of his lines could be raised. In the end, after a few hangings, things calmed down. The English ladies, who had accompanied their husbands to the army, were particularly gracious to the Hainaut knights and pleaded with them to stay with tears in their eyes. The Hennuyers were then encamped half a league away from the rest of the army, and so a month went by during which they looked at each other like cats and dogs.

Finally the decision was taken to start campaigning. Young King Edward III, for this his first war, had under command eight thousand knights and thirty thousand footmen.

Most unfortunately the Scots proved elusive. The barbarians made war with neither baggage nor baggage-train. Their light troops needed no more than a flat stone at the saddle-bow and a small bag of flour; and on this they were able to live for several days, damping the flour in the burns and cooking it into cakes on the stones they heated in a fire. The Scots mocked the huge English army, made contact, skirmished and retreated, crossed and recrossed the rivers, drew the enemy into bogs, forests and narrow defiles. The English advanced at hazard between the Tyne and the Cheviot hills.

One day there was a considerable stir in some woods

through which the English were marching. The alarm was sounded. Everyone charged, visors down, targes at the ready, lances in rest, waiting for no one, father, brother or comrade, only to find, somewhat abashed, that a herd of deer were fleeing in terror from the clatter of their arms.

Supply was becoming difficult; there was no food to be found in the country except what was brought with considerable difficulty by a few merchants who sold their goods for ten times their value. The horses were lacking oats and forage. And then it rained without stopping for a whole week. Saddle-flaps began rotting under their riders' thighs; the horses cast their shoes in the mud; and the whole army was rusting. At night the knights had to cut branches with their swords to make themselves shelters. And the Scots were still proving elusive.

Sir Thomas Wake, the Marshal of the Army, was in despair. The Earl of Kent almost regretted La Réole; at least they had had fine weather there. Henry Crouchback had rheumatism in his neck. Mortimer was becoming increasingly bad-tempered and growing weary of going to and fro between the army and Yorkshire, where the Queen and the Government offices were lying. A hopelessness, giving rise to every kind of dissatisfaction, was beginning to take effect among the troops; they were talking of being betrayed.

One day, while the commanders of the banners were discussing angrily what had not been done and what ought to have been done, young King Edward III gathered a few squires of his own age together, and promised both a knighthood and lands worth a hundred pounds a year to anyone who could discover where the Scots army was. Some twenty boys, between fourteen and eighteen years of age, set out to scour the country. The first to return was Thomas de Rokesby; breathless and exhausted, he cried: 'Sire Edward, the Scots are four leagues from us among the hills and they have been there for a week. They have no more idea of where you are than you have of their position.'

Young Edward immediately had the trumpets sounded, assembled the army on what was known as 'the white moor', and ordered an advance against the Scots. The great men of the lists were astonished. But the noise this huge armoured force made as it advanced through the hills was heard afar off by Robert the Bruce's men. And when the knights of England and Hainaut reached the crest of a hill and were preparing to descend into the further valley, they suddenly saw the whole Scots army drawn up on foot in battle array with their arrows already slotted to their bow-strings. They stared at each other from a distance and did not dare come to battle, for the terrain was ill-suited to the launching of cavalry. They stared at each other for twenty-two days.

Since the Scots had apparently no intention of moving from a position that was so favourable to them, and the knights were disinclined to give battle on a terrain which prevented their proper deployment, the armies remained on either side of the crest, each waiting for the other to move. They contented themselves with skirmishing, generally by night, and with leaving these minor engagements to the infantry.

The most important action of this strange war, which was being fought between an octogenarian leper and a fifteen-year-old king, was carried out by the Scot James Douglas who, with two hundred horsemen of his clan, fell on the English camp one moonlit night, slaughtered everyone in his path and, to the cry of 'Douglas! Douglas!' succeeded in cutting three of the King's tent-ropes before retiring. After that night the English knights slept in their armour.

And then, one morning before dawn, two Scots scouts, who appeared to be watching the English army, were captured. It seemed almost as if they wanted to be taken. And when they were brought before the English King, they said: 'Sire, what do you seek here? We Scots have gone back to the mountains, and Sire Robert, our King, has told us to inform you of it, and also that he will make no more war against you this year, unless you pursue him.'

The English advanced carefully, fearing a trap, and found themselves suddenly face to face with four hundred camp-kettles for boiling meat hanging in a line. The Scots had left them there so as to travel light and make no noise during their retreat. They found, too, in a huge heap, five thousand worn rawhide boots. The Scots had changed their footgear before departing. There was not a living soul in the camp except five English prisoners who, completely naked and bound to posts, had had their legs broken by blows from cudgels.

To pursue the Scots through the mountains, over difficult country, in which the whole population was hostile to the English, and where the army, already exhausted, would have had to fight a war of ambushes for which it was not trained, was clearly pure folly. The campaign was declared at an end. The army returned to York and was disbanded.

Messire Jean de Hainaut had to take stock of his dead and

useless horses, and he presented a bill for fourteen thousand livres. Young King Edward had insufficient money in his Treasury, particularly since he had still to pay his own troops. So Messire Jean de Hainaut, making his usual grand gesture, guaranteed to his knights all the sums due to them from his future nephew.

During the course of the summer, Roger Mortimer, who had no interests in the north of the kingdom, concluded a treaty of peace. Edward III had to renounce all suzerainty over Scotland and to recognize Robert the Bruce as King of that country, which Edward II had always refused to do. Moreover, David Bruce, the son of Robert, married Jane of England, Queen Isabella's second daughter.

Had it really been worth depriving the former King, who was now living in seclusion at Berkeley Castle, of his powers for such a result as this?

7

The Grass Crown

DAWN WAS BREAKING red behind the Cotswold hills.

'The sun will soon be up, Sir John,' said Thomas Gournay, one of the two horsemen riding at the head of the escort.

'Yes, the sun will soon be up, my friend, and we haven't reached our halt yet,' replied John Maltravers, riding beside him, stirrup to stirrup.

'When day comes, people may well recognize our prisoner,' the first man replied.

'Yes, they may indeed, my friend, and that's precisely what we've got to avoid.'

They were talking in deliberately loud voices, so that the prisoner behind might hear.

Sir Thomas Gournay had reached Berkeley the day before, having ridden across half England to bring John Maltravers the latest orders from Roger Mortimer at York about the disposal of the fallen King.

Gournay was a man of singularly unprepossessing

appearance; his nose was short and flat, his lower teeth were longer than the rest, his face was blotchy and high in colour, covered with red hairs like a sow's hide; his too long hair curled like copper shavings under the edge of his steel helmet.

To assist Thomas Gournay, and also to some extent to keep an eye on him, Mortimer had given him Ogle, who had once been barber in the Tower of London.

As night was falling, at the hour when the peasants had eaten their suppers and were going to sleep, the little cavalcade had left Berkeley Castle and ridden south through the silent countryside and the dark villages. Maltravers and Gournay rode in front. The King was surrounded by a dozen soldiers under the command of a subaltern officer named Towurlee, a huge man with a small head whose intelligence was in inverse proportion to his physical strength which was considerable. But Towurlee was obedient and useful for tasks in which it was better not to ask oneself too many questions. Ogle brought up the rear, together with the monk William, who had never been looked on as among the best in his monastery. But he might be needed to give extreme unction.

All night the ex-King had been wondering in vain where he was being taken. And now dawn was breaking.

'How can one prevent a man being recognized?' Maltravers asked pointedly.

'Change his face, Sir John, I can see no other solution,' Gournay replied.

'You'd have to tar his face or black it with soot.'

'The peasants would think we were in company with a Moor.'

'But unfortunately we haven't any tar.

'We could shave him,' said Thomas Gournay, with a meaning wink.

'That's a good idea, my boy! And we've got a barber with us. Heaven's clearly on our side. Ogle, come here! Have you got your bowl and your razors with you?'

'Indeed I have, Sir John, at your service,' Ogle replied as he joined the two knights.

'Well, let's stop here. There's water in that stream.'

This had all been arranged the evening before. The little column came to a halt. Gournay and Ogle dismounted. Gournay had wide shoulders and very short bow legs. Ogle spread a cloth on the grassy bank, laid out the tools of his trade and began slowly sharpening a razor, while staring at the ex-King.

'What do you want with me? What are you going to do to me?' asked Edward II anxiously.

'We want you to alight from your steed, noble Sire, so that we can give you a new face. And here's a proper throne for you,' said Thomas Gournay flattening a mole-hill with the heel of his boot. 'Come on, sit down!'

Edward made to obey. But, as he seemed to hesitate a little, Gournay pushed him over and the soldiers of the escort burst out laughing.

'Stand round, my lads,' Gournay said.

The soldiers formed a circle and the huge Towurlee stood behind the King so as to push him down by the shoulders, should it be necessary.

Ogle went to fetch icy water from the stream.

'Wet his face well,' said Gournay.

The barber threw the whole contents of the bowl in the King's face. Then he put the razor roughly to the King's cheeks. Tufts of blond hair fell on the grass.

Maltravers was still on his horse and, sitting with his hands leaning on the pommel and his hair falling over his ears, he was watching the operation with evident satisfaction.

Between two strokes of the razor Edward cried: 'You're hurting! Couldn't you use hot water at least?'

'Hot water?' said Gournay. 'Particular, isn't he?'

And Ogle, pushing his round white face into the King's whispered in his ear: 'Did my lord Mortimer have hot water in his bowl when he was in the Tower of London?'

Then he continued his task with great strokes of the razor. Blood pearled on the skin. Edward began weeping with pain.

'Oh, look at the clever fellow,' cried Maltravers; 'he's discovered how to wet his cheeks with warm water!'

'Shall I shave the hair too, Sir Thomas?' Ogle asked.

'Of course, of course, the hair too,' Gournay replied.

From his forehead to the nape of the neck the locks fell under the razor.

Ten minutes later Ogle handed his victim a tin mirror, and the King stared with stupefaction at his real face which, at once childish and ageing, now appeared under a long narrow, naked skull. The long chin no longer concealed its weakness. Edward felt stripped and absurd, like a clipped dog.

'I don't recognize myself,' he said.

The men standing round him laughed again.

'That's all right then,' said Maltravers from his horse. 'If you can't recognize yourself, anyone looking for you will be still less likely to. That's what you get by trying to escape.'

For this was why the King was being moved. A few Welsh lords, led by a certain Rhys ap Gruffyd, had organized a conspiracy to rescue the King. But Mortimer had been warned of it. In the meantime, however, Edward, taking advantage of Thomas de Berkeley's negligence, had escaped from his prison one day. Maltravers had set off in pursuit and had recaptured him in the middle of a forest, running towards the water like a hunted stag. The King was trying to reach the Severn estuary in the hope of finding a boat. And now Maltravers was taking his revenge, for at the time he had been very much perturbed.

'Get up, Sire King; it's time we were moving on,' he said.

'Where are we going to halt?' Edward asked.

'Somewhere we can be sure you'll find no friends. Your sleep won't be disturbed. You can count on us to watch over you.'

Their journey lasted almost a week. They rode by night, and rested by day, either in a manor of which they could be sure, or in some shelter among the fields, some isolated barn. On the fifth morning, Edward saw the outline of a huge grey castle built on a hill. There was a gusty wind from the sea, fresh, damp and salt.

'It's Corfe!' Edward said. 'Is that where you're taking me?'

'Of course it's Corfe,' said Thomas Gournay. 'You seem to know the castles of your kingdom well.'

Edward uttered a cry of terror. His astrologer had once told him never to stay at Corfe, because it would be fatal to him. And, as a result, when he had journeyed in Dorset and

Devon, he had often passed Corfe, but had always obstinately refused to enter it.

Corfe Castle was older, larger and indeed more sinister than Kenilworth. Its giant keep dominated the whole surrounding countryside, the whole Purbeck peninsula. Some of its fortifications dated from before the Norman conquest. It had often been used as a prison, particularly by King John, who, a hundred and twenty years before, had ordered twenty-two French knights to be left there to starve to death. Corfe seemed specially dedicated to the commission of crime. The tragic stories about it dated back to the murder of a boy of fifteen, the other Edward II, called the Martyr, who belonged to the Saxon dynasty before the year one thousand.

The legend of his murder was still current in the surrounding countryside. This Saxon Edward, the son of King Edgar, whom he had succeeded, was hated by his stepmother, Queen Elfrida, his father's second wife. One day, when he had returned from hunting and was heated with the chase, while still on his horse, he raised a horn-cup of wine to his lips, and Queen Elfrida had struck him in the back with a dagger. Screaming with pain, the young King had spurred his horse and fled into the forest. Exhausted from loss of blood, he had soon fallen from the saddle; but he had caught his foot in the stirrup and his terrified horse had dragged him a long way, banging his head against the trees. Peasants had found his body by a trail of blood through the forest, and had buried him secretly. Then his grave had begun performing miracles, and King Edward had later been canonized.

The prisoner had the same name and the same number as that king of the other dynasty; and this coincidence, made more disturbing yet by the astrologer's prophecy, was well calculated to make Edward tremble. Was Corfe to be the scene of a second Edward's death?

'You must have a crown, noble Sire, with which to enter this fine castle,' said Maltravers. 'Towurlee, go and get some grass from that field!'

Maltravers made a crown of the handful of dry grass the giant brought back, and placed it on the King's shaven head. It was sharp enough to sink into the flesh.

'Now we'll go on, and you must forgive us for having no trumpets!'

A deep moat, a curtain wall, a drawbridge between two huge round towers, a green hill to climb, another fosse, another gate, another portcullis, and then more grassy slopes: turning round you could look down on the little houses in the village, with their roofs of flat, grey stone tiles. How could such small houses carry such heavy roofs?

'Go on!' cried Maltravers, giving Edward a blow with his fist in the small of the back.

The grass crown fell askew. The horses were moving forward through narrow, tortuous passages, paved with round cobbles, between huge, fantastic walls on whose summit crows were perched side by side making a black frieze along the grey stone, watching the column pass fifty feet below.

King Edward II was certain he was going to be killed. But there were many ways of putting a man to death.

Thomas Gournay and John Maltravers had no express orders to assassinate him, but rather to let him die. They therefore chose slow means. Twice a day Edward was given a disgusting gruel, while his guards crammed themselves in his presence with all kinds of delicious food. And yet the prisoner survived the disgusting food as he did the mockery and the blows. He was singularly robust in body and even in mind. Other men in his position might easily have lost their reason: he contented himself with complaining. But his very complaints were proof of the fact that he was sound in mind.

'Are my sins so heavy that they deserve neither pity nor relief? Have you lost all Christian charity, all kindness?' he said to his gaolers. 'Even if I am no longer a sovereign, I am still a father and a husband; what have my wife and children to fear from me now? Are they not satisfied with having taken from me everything I had?'

'And what complaint have you against your wife, Sire King? Has not Madame, the Queen, sent you fine clothes and kind letters, which we have read to you?'

'Rogues, rogues,' replied Edward, 'you have shown me the clothes but you have not given them to me. You're letting me rot away in this disgusting robe. And, as to the letters, why do you think that wicked woman has sent them, except to provide proof that she has shown me compassion? It is she, she and that wicked Mortimer who have given you orders to torture me. If it were not for her and that traitor, I am sure my children would hasten here to embrace me.'

'Your wife, the Queen, and your children,' replied Maltravers, 'are too afraid of your cruelty. They have suffered too much from your temper and your wickedness to want to come near you.'

'You can say what you like, you wicked man,' said the King, 'but the time will come when the tortures I am suffering will be avenged.'

And he began to weep, his denuded chin hidden in his arms. He wept, but he did not die.

Gournay and Maltravers were bored at Corfe, for every pleasure can pall, even that of torturing a king. Besides, Maltravers had left his wife, Eva, at Berkeley Castle with his brother-in-law; and then the people of the neighbourhood of Corfe got to know that Edward was detained there. After an exchange of messages with Mortimer, it was therefore decided to take Edward back to Berkeley.

And when, once again, with the same escort, and now looking a little thinner and a little more bowed, he passed the great portcullis, the drawbridges and the two curtain walls, King Edward II, unhappy as he was, nevertheless felt a great relief, a sense almost of deliverance. His astrologer had lied.

8

'Bonum Est'

QUEEN ISABELLA WAS already in bed, her golden tresses lying across her breast. Roger Mortimer came in without having himself announced, as was his privilege. From his expression the Queen knew what he was going to discuss, or rather re-discuss.

'I've had news from Berkeley,' he said in a voice he hoped sounded calm and detached.

Isabella made no answer.

The window was half-open to the September night. Mortimer went over and flung it wide. For a moment he stood there looking out over the great, crowded town of Lincoln, lying below the castle. There were still a few lights showing here and there. Lincoln was the fourth town in the kingdom after London, Winchester and York. One of the quarters of Hugh Despenser the Younger's body had been sent there ten months ago. The Court, having moved from Yorkshire, had been in residence here for a week.

Isabella looked at Mortimer's high shoulders and curling hair silhouetted in the frame of the window, dark against the night sky. At this particular moment she felt no love for him.

'Your husband seems to be clinging very obstinately to life,' Mortimer went on, turning round. 'And his life is a danger to the peace of the realm. They are still conspiring in the manors of Wales to free him. The Dominicans have had the impudence to preach in his favour even in London, where the riots which took place last July, as you know, may well occur again. Edward is no danger in himself, I grant you, but he is a pretext for sedition by our enemies. I ask you to issue the order, for without it there can be no safety either for you or your sons.'

Isabella sighed in weary exasperation. Why didn't he give the order himself? Why did he not take the decision on his own responsibility? After all, he was all-powerful in the kingdom.

'Sweet Mortimer,' she said, 'I have already told you that you will not get that order from me.'

Roger Mortimer closed the window; he was afraid of losing his temper.

'But why, after all,' he said, 'having suffered so many ordeals and run so many risks, do you now insist on being the enemy of your own safety?'

She shook her head and replied, 'I cannot do it. I would rather run any risk than come to that. Roger, I pray you, we must not stain our hands with that blood.'

Mortimer laughed shortly.

'I do not understand,' he replied, 'why you should so suddenly have this respect for the blood of your enemies. You showed no reluctance in the contemplation of the blood of the Earl of Arundel, the blood of the Despensers, the blood of Baldock, indeed all the blood that has been shed in the town squares. There have even been certain nights when I have thought that shed blood was not altogether displeasing to you. And are not our dear Sire Edward's hands redder than ours could ever be? Would he not willingly have spilt my blood, and yours, had we given him the chance? You cannot be a king, Isabella, nor a queen, if you are afraid of blood; you can only retire to a convent, take the veil of a nun, and resign both love and power.'

For a moment they gazed into each other's eyes. His were the colour of flint and seemed to glow too brightly under his thick brows in the light of the candles; the white scar marked a lip that had too cruel a curve. Isabella was the first to lower her eyes.

'Remember, Mortimer, that he once reprieved you,' she said. 'He must be thinking at this moment that if he hadn't yielded to the prayers of the barons, the bishops, and indeed to mine, and had had you beheaded as he ordered to be done to Thomas of Lancaster . . .'

'That's no argument. Of course I remember; but it is precisely because I do not want to suffer such regrets one day as he must have now. Your compassion for him seems to me both strange and obstinate.'

He was silent for a moment.

'Do you still love him?' he said. 'I can see no other reason for your behaviour.'

She shrugged her shoulders.

'Is that why you want one more proof?' she asked. 'Is this

mad jealousy of yours ever to come to an end? Haven't I sufficiently proved before the whole kingdom of France, and the whole kingdom of England if it comes to that, and even before my son, that there is no other love but the love of you in my heart? What more can I do?'

'Simply what I ask you, nothing more. But I see that you will not make up your mind to it. I realize that the cross you made over your heart, which was to make us allies and give us a single will, was only a pretence to you. I realize that fate has led me to plight my troth to a weak creature!'

Yes, he was jealous, that was the fact. Though he was the all-powerful Regent, though every appointment was in his gift, though he was the young King's guardian, and lived openly as man and wife with the Queen before all the barons, Mortimer was still jealous. 'But is he completely mistaken in being so?' Isabella suddenly wondered. For the danger of jealousy is that it forces its object to consider whether there is any justification for the reproaches. And thus certain fleeting emotions, to which one has paid no attention, suddenly take on a clearer hue. How strange it was! Isabella was sure she hated Edward as much as it was possible for a woman to hate; she thought of him with contempt, disgust and rancour combined. And yet . . . And yet the memory of rings exchanged, of the coronation, of her children being born; memories not so much of him but of herself; the memory merely of having believed she loved him; all this was holding her back now. She could not make up her mind to give the order for the death of the father of her children. 'And they call me the She-wolf of France!' she thought. The saint is never so saintly, nor the cruel man ever so utterly cruel as one supposes. No one can see into another's heart all the time.

And then Edward, even though dethroned, was still a king. Though dispossessed, despoiled and imprisoned, he was still a royal personage. And Isabella was a queen herself, and brought up to be one. Throughout her childhood she had had before her an example of truly royal majesty, incarnate in a man who, by blood and coronation, knew that he stood above all other men, and made others recognize it. To take the life of a subject, even if he were the greatest lord in the kingdom, was never more than a crime. But the act of taking a royal life involved sacrilege and was the negation of that quality of intangibility with which sovereigns were invested.

'And that, Mortimer, you cannot understand, because you are not a king, and you were not born a king's son.'

Too late she realized she had thought out loud.

The Baron of the Marches, the descendant of a companion of William the Conqueror, the Justiciar of Wales, took the blow hardly. He took two paces backwards and bowed.

'I do not believe it was a king, Madame, who gave you back your throne; but it seems to be a waste of time to expect you to agree to that. Being neither a king nor a king's son, my efforts for you have brought me but little merit. Therefore, let your enemies free your royal husband, or rather, go and give him his liberty yourself! Your powerful brother of France will no doubt then protect you, as he did so well when you had to fly to Hainaut, supported in your saddle by me. Mortimer, being no king, and his life having no such protection against the mischances of fortune, will depart, Madame, and find refuge elsewhere before it is too late, outside the kingdom whose queen loves him so little that he feels there is nothing more for him to do there.'

Upon which he went to the door. His anger was controlled; he did not bang the oak door but closed it gently, and the sound of his footsteps slowly faded away.

Isabella knew Mortimer's pride well enough to know he would not come back. She jumped out of the bed, ran in her nightdress through the corridors of the castle, caught Mortimer up, seized him by his coat, clung to his arm.

'Stay, stay, sweet Mortimer, I beseech you!' she cried without caring who heard her. 'I am only a woman, I need your counsel and your support. Stay, stay, please, and act as you think fit.'

She was weeping and clinging to him, nestling against that breast and that heart without which she could not live.

'I only want what you want,' she said again.

Servants, drawn there by the noise, appeared and immediately hid themselves, embarrassed at being witnesses to this lovers' quarrel.

'Do you really want what I want?' he asked, taking the Queen's face in his hands. 'Very well, then! Guards! Go and summon my lord Orleton at once.'

For some months past, and for an absurd reason, there had been a certain coolness between Mortimer and Adam Orleton. It had been due to that bishopric of Worcester to which the prelate had got the Pope to provide him while Mortimer had promised the King's agreement to another candidate. Had Mortimer only known that his friend wanted that bishopric, it would all have been perfectly simple. But

Orleton had acted secretly, and Mortimer, having given his word, did not now want to have to go back on it. He had brought the question up in Parliament, when it was sitting in York, and had had the revenues of the see of Worcester sequestrated. Orleton, who was therefore no longer Bishop of Hereford and was not Bishop of Worcester either, felt this to be ungrateful in the man he had helped escape from the Tower. The affair was still being debated, and Orleton still followed the Court wherever it went.

'Mortimer is bound to end by needing me one day,' he thought, 'and then I shall get the diocese of my choice.'

That day, or rather that night, had now arrived. Orleton realized it as soon as he entered Queen Isabella's room; she had gone back to bed, and Mortimer was striding up and down. The Queen still had traces of tears on her face. If they were so little embarrassed by the prelate's presence, it could only mean that they really needed him.

'Madame the Queen,' said Mortimer, 'considers, and with reason, that because of the conspiracies of which you know, her husband's life imperils the peace of the realm, and she is concerned that God should be so slow to call him to Him.'

Adam Orleton looked at Isabella, Isabella looked at Mortimer, and then she turned her eyes back to the Bishop and nodded in assent. Orleton smiled briefly, not with cruelty, nor even really with irony, but with an expression rather of chaste concern.

'Madame the Queen finds herself faced with the problem which is always confronting those who are in charge of kingdoms,' he replied. 'So as not to destroy a single life, must one risk the death of many others?'

Mortimer turned to Isabella, and said: 'Do you hear?'

He was pleased by the Bishop's support and merely regretted not having thought of this argument himself.

'This is a matter of the safety of the people,' Orleton went on, 'and it is to us bishops that people turn for the elucidation of the Divine Will. Of course the Gospels forbid us to kill. But the law of the Gospels does not apply to kings when they condemn their subjects to death. But I had thought, my lord, that the gaolers you have appointed about the fallen king were going to spare you these problems.'

'The gaolers appear to have exhausted their resources,' replied Mortimer. 'And they will take no further action without written instructions.'

Orleton nodded his head but made no reply.

'And a written order,' Mortimer went on, 'may fall into other hands than those for which it is intended; it can even be used by those who carry it out against those who gave it. You understand me?'

Orleton smiled once more. Did they take him for a fool?

'In other words, my lord,' he said, 'you wish to send the order, yet not send it.'

'I would rather send an order which would be clear to those for whom it is intended, but obscure to those who should know nothing of it. It is on this I wish to consult you, for you are a man of resource. If you will give me your help, that is.'

'And you ask that, my lord, from a poor Bishop who has no throne, nor even a diocese in which to plant his crozier?'

It was Mortimer's turn to smile.

'Now, now, my lord Orleton, let us talk of these things no

more. You have vexed me very much, you know. If you had only told me what you wanted. But since you are so intent on it, I will no longer oppose you. Worcester is yours, I promise it. And you're still my friend, you know that too.'

The Bishop nodded his head. Yes, he knew it. He felt as friendly as ever towards Mortimer; their recent quarrel had changed nothing, and they had only to come face to face to be aware of it. They were linked by too many memories, too many conspiracies as well as a sort of mutual admiration. And this very evening, for instance, when Mortimer, having at last dragged the long-awaited consent from the Queen, found himself in a difficulty, who did he send for? The Bishop with the sloping shoulders, the duck-like walk, and eyes that were short-sighted from too much work on manuscripts at Oxford. They were such great friends indeed that they had forgotten the Queen, who was staring at them with her huge blue eyes and feeling unhappy.

'It was that fine sermon of yours on the text *"Doleo caput meum"*, and everyone remembers it, which made it possible to get rid of the bad King,' said Mortimer. 'And it was you again who obtained his abdication.'

Here was a return of gratitude. Orleton acknowledged the compliments with a bow.

'And now you want me to finish the task,' he said.

There was a writing-table in the room, with pens and paper. Orleton asked for a knife because he could write only with a pen cut by himself. It helped him to think. Mortimer did not interrupt his reflections.

'The order need not be long,' said Orleton after a moment.

He was staring straight to his front with an amused air. He

had clearly forgotton that the death of a man was in question; he was feeling the pride and satisfaction of a writer who had just solved a difficult linguistic problem. With his eyes bent close to the table he wrote a single phrase in a clear handwriting, sanded it, and handed the paper to Mortimer, saying: 'I will even seal the letter with my own seal, if you and Madame the Queen think it better not to apply yours.'

He seemed very pleased with himself.

Mortimer went close to a candle. The letter was in Latin. He read rather slowly: '*Eduardum occidere nolite timere bonum est.*' Then, looking at the Bishop, he said, '*Eduardum occidere*, I understand that all right; *nolite*: do not . . . *timere*: fear . . . *Bonum est*: it is good . . .'

Orleton smiled.

'Which is it: "Do not kill Edward, it is good to fear",' asked Mortimer, 'or: "Do not fear to kill Edward, it is a good thing"? Where is the comma?'

'There isn't one,' replied Orleton. 'The Will of God will be made plain to the understanding of the letter's recipient. But no one can be blamed for the letter itself.'

Mortimer was somewhat perplexed.

'The fact is,' he said, 'I don't know whether Maltravers or Gournay understands Latin.'

'Brother William, whom you asked me to send to them, understands it well enough. And then the messenger can say, but say only, that all action resulting from this order must remain without trace.'

'And are you really prepared to seal it with your own seal?' asked Mortimer.

'I shall do so,' said Orleton.

He really was a good friend. Mortimer accompanied him to the bottom of the stairs, then came back to the Queen's room.

'Sweet Mortimer,' said Isabella, 'don't leave me to sleep alone this night.'

The September night was not cold enough to make her shiver so much.

9

The Red-hot Poker

COMPARED TO THE HUGE fortresses of Kenilworth and Corfe, Berkeley was a relatively small castle. Its stones had a rosy glow and its dimensions made it habitable. It lay immediately next to the cemetery that surrounded the church where the gravestones, in a very few years, became covered with a small green moss, fine as a silk cloth.[44]

Thomas de Berkeley was a decent enough young man, who bore his neighbour no ill-will. Nevertheless, he had no reason to show any particular kindness to ex-King Edward II, who had kept him in prison at Wallingford for four years, together with his father Maurice de Berkeley, who had died during their imprisonment. Moreover, he could not but be devoted to his powerful father-in-law, Roger Mortimer, whose eldest daughter he had married in 1320. He had followed him through the rebellion and had been freed by him the year before. Thomas received the considerable sum of a hundred shillings a day for lodging and guarding the fallen

King. Nor were his wife, Marguerite Mortimer, and his sister Eva, the wife of Maltravers, wicked people.

Edward would not have found his stay there altogether intolerable had he had to do with no one but the Berkeley family. Unfortunately his three tormentors were there too, Maltravers, Gournay and the barber Ogle. These gave Edward no respite; their minds were fertile in cruelty, and there was a sort of competition between them as to who could add the greatest refinements to his tortures.

Maltravers had had the idea of imprisoning Edward in the keep, in a small circular chamber only a few feet in diameter in whose centre was an old dry well, an oubliette. One false step and the prisoner would fall into this deep hole. Edward had to be constantly on his guard. He was now forty-four, though he looked over sixty. And here he had to live, lying on an armful of straw, his body edged close up against the wall. Whenever he fell asleep, he would wake again at once in a sweat, afraid he had moved nearer to the well.

To this torture of fear, Gournay had added another, that of smell. He had the stinking carrion of dead animals gathered from all over the countryside, badgers taken in their earths, foxes, polecats, and rotten dead birds. These were all thrown into the oubliette so that their stench tainted such little air as the prisoner had.

'Here's good venison for the fool!' the three torturers cried each morning when the load of dead animals was brought.

Their own noses were not over-delicate, for they sat, or took turns to sit, in a little room at the top of the keep staircase which commanded the wretched chamber in which the king was growing ever weaker. Nauseating gusts would sometimes reach them; but they were merely a subject for ribald jokes.

'How the old fool stinks!' they cried as they shook the dice-box and drank their pots of beer.

The day Adam Orleton's letter arrived, they had a long discussion. Brother William translated the message, leaving them in no doubt as to its real meaning, but pointing out the clever ambiguity with which it was phrased. The three rascals slapped their thighs for a good quarter of an hour, repeating: *'Bonum est ... bonum est!'* and roared with laughter.

The rather dim-witted courier who had brought the letter had faithfully delivered the oral message: 'without trace'.

And this was the subject of their discussion.

'These Court people, these bishops and lords, really do ask you to do some odd things,' Maltravers said. 'How do they expect you to kill someone without its being apparent that you've done it?'

How were they to set about it? Poison left the body black; besides, you had to get the poison from someone and he might talk. Strangling? The mark of the cord would show on the neck and the face turned blue.

It was Ogle, once barber in the Tower of London, who produced the stroke of genius. Thomas Gournay suggested a few improvements to the plan, and tall Maltravers laughed aloud, showing his huge teeth and all his gums.

'He'll be punished where he has sinned!' he cried.

The idea seemed to him positively brilliant.

'But it will need four of us,' Gournay said. 'Your brother-in-law Thomas will have to give us a hand.'

'Oh, you know what Thomas is like,' Maltravers replied.

'He takes his five pounds a day all right, but he's a sensitive fellow, he might well fail us halfway through the job by going off in a dead faint.'

'I think that big Towurlee would help us willingly enough, if we promised him a good reward,' said Ogle. 'Besides, he's so stupid that even if he does talk no one will believe him.'

They waited till evening. Gournay had a good meal prepared for the prisoner in the Castle kitchens: a rich pasty, small birds roasted on a spit, and an oxtail in gravy. Edward had not had such a supper since the evenings at Kenilworth with his cousin Crouchback. He was astonished, and to begin with a little anxious, but was soon comforted by the unaccustomed food. Instead of merely bringing him a bowl to his straw bed, they set him a stool in the little room next door, which seemed to him a marvel of comfort; and he enjoyed the food, whose taste he had almost forgotten. Nor was he deprived of wine; they gave him a good claret which Thomas de Berkeley got from Aquitaine. The three gaolers winked at each other as they watched him eat.

'He won't even have time to digest it,' Maltravers whispered to Gournay.

The huge Towurlee stood in the doorway which he filled completely.

'You feel better now, don't you, my lord?' said Gournay, when Edward had finished his meal. 'Now we're going to take you to a good room where you'll find a feather-bed.'

The prisoner with his shaven head and long trembling chin looked at his gaolers in surprise.

'Have you received new orders?' he asked.

His voice was humble and afraid.

'Oh, certainly, we've received orders. And we're going to treat you properly, my lord,' replied Maltravers. 'We've even ordered a fire for you where you're going to sleep, because the evenings are turning cooler, aren't they, Gournay? Oh, well, it's seasonable; we're already at the end of September.'

They led the King down the narrow staircase, then across the grassy courtyard of the keep, then up on the other side within the thickness of the wall. His gaolers had told the truth; there was a bedroom, not a palace bedroom of course, but a good room, clean and white-washed, a bed with a thick feather mattress, and a sort of brazier, full of burning embers. It was almost too hot in the room.

The King's mind was in a state of some confusion, and the wine was making him feel a little giddy. Was merely a good meal enough to make him start enjoying life again? But what were these new orders? What had happened that he should suddenly be treated so well? A rebellion in the kingdom perhaps; Mortimer fallen and disgraced. Oh, if that could only happen! Or was it simply that the young King had become concerned at last about his father's fate and given orders that he should be treated more humanely? But even if there was a rebellion and the people had risen in his favour, Edward would never agree to return to the throne; never, he vowed it to God. Because if he became King again, he'd begin committing errors again; he was not fashioned to reign. A quiet monastery was all he wanted, and to be able to walk in a pleasant garden, and be served with the sort of food he liked. And pray, too. And then to let his beard grow again, and his hair, unless he kept the tonsure; though perhaps the razor going over his skull each week would evoke memories that were too appalling. What spiritual neglect and what ingratitude not to thank the Creator for the simple things that are enough to make life agreeable: savoury food, a warm room . . . There was a poker in the brazier . . .

'Lie down, my lord! The bed's a good one, you'll find,' said Gournay.

And indeed the mattress was soft. To have a real bed again, what a joy! But why did the other three remain in the room? Maltravers was sitting on a stool, his hair hanging over his ears, his hands between his knees, and he was staring at the King. Gournay was poking the fire. The barber Ogle had an ox-horn in his hand and a little saw.

'Sleep, Sire Edward, and don't worry about us; we have work to do,' Gournay went on.

'What are you doing, Ogle?' the King asked. 'Are you making a drinking-horn?'

'No, my lord, it's not for drinking. I'm just cutting a horn, that's all.'

Then, turning to Gournay, and marking a place on the horn with his thumbnail, the barber said: 'I think that's the right length, don't you?'

The red-headed man, whose face was like a sow's, looked over his shoulder and replied: 'Yes, I think that'll do. *Bonum est.*'

Then he went on fanning the fire.

The saw grated on the ox-horn. When he had sawn through it, the barber handed the piece he had cut off to Gournay, who took it, looked at it, and inserted the red-hot poker. An acrid stench suddenly filled the room. The poker emerged from the burnt point of the horn. Gournay put it back in the fire. How did they expect the King to sleep with all this going on round him? Had they removed him from the carrion in the oubliette merely to smoke him out with burnt horn? Suddenly Maltravers, who was still sitting there staring at Edward, said: 'Was that Despenser you loved so well endowed?'

The other two burst out laughing. On hearing that name mentioned, Edward felt as if his mind were being torn asunder and he suddenly knew these men were going to kill him within the hour. Were they going to inflict on him the same atrocious death as had been suffered by Hugh the Younger?

'You're not going to do it? You're not going to kill me?' he cried, suddenly sitting up in bed.

'Kill you, Sire Edward?' said Gournay without even turning round. 'What makes you think that? We have our orders. *Bonum est, bonum est . . .*'

'Go on, lie down again,' said Maltravers.

But Edward did not lie down again. His eyes, starting out of his bald, emaciated head, turned like those of a trapped beast from Thomas Gournay's red neck to the long yellow face of Maltravers and to the barber's chubby cheeks. Gournay had taken the poker from the fire and was looking at the red-hot end.

'Towurlee!' he called. 'The table!'

The giant, who was waiting in the next room, came in carrying a heavy table. Maltravers went to the door, closed it and locked it. What was this table for, this heavy plank of oak that was normally placed on trestles? For there were no trestles in the room. And of all the strange things that were going on round the King, this table carried in a giant's arms seemed to him the strangest and most terrifying. How could you kill a man with a table? It was the King's last clear thought.

'Come on!' said Gournay, signing to Ogle.

They came up, one each side of the bed, threw themselves on Edward and turned him over on his stomach.

'Oh, you brutes, you brutes!' he cried. 'You shan't kill me!'

He struggled and fought, and Maltravers came over to lend them a hand, but even the three of them were none too many. The giant Towurlee came forward to help them.

'No, Towurlee, the table!' cried Gournay.

Towurlee remembered what he had been told to do. He picked up the heavy plank and let it fall flat across the King's shoulders. Gournay pulled up the prisoner's robe, and lowered his breeches with a rending of worn cloth. A fundament so exposed was contemptibly grotesque; but the assassins had no heart for laughter now.

The King, who had been half knocked-out by the blow and was suffocating under the table which was forcing him down into the mattress, fought and kicked. He was still surprisingly strong.

'Towurlee, hold his ankles! No, not like that, apart!' Gournay ordered.

The King managed to free his neck from the table and turned his face to one side to get a little air. Maltravers leaned on his head with both hands. Gournay seized the poker and said: 'Ogle, insert the horn!'

King Edward started up with desperate strength as the red-hot iron entered his vitals. The scream he uttered passed through walls and keep, over the gravestones in the cemetery, and awakened the people sleeping in the houses in the town. And those who heard that long, grim and appalling cry knew on the instant that the King had been assassinated.

The next morning the inhabitants of Berkeley came up to the castle to find out what had happened. They were told that the King had died suddenly during the night with a loud cry.

'Come and see him. Yes, you can come in,' said Maltravers and Gournay to the notables and clergy. 'He's being laid out now. Come in. Everyone can come in.'

And the townspeople saw that there was no mark of a blow, no hurt or wound on the body. For it was being washed and care was taken to turn it over and over before their eyes. Only a terrible grimace twisted the corpse's face.

Thomas Gournay and John Maltravers looked at each other; it had been a brilliant idea to introduce the poker through an ox-horn. In a period particularly inventive in methods of assassination, they had discovered a really perfect means of committing murder without trace.

They were a little worried, however, by the fact that Thomas de Berkeley had left the castle before dawn, having business, so he had said, at a neighbouring castle. And then Towurlee, the brainless giant, had taken to his bed and been weeping for some hours.

During the course of the day Gournay left on horseback for Nottingham, where the Queen then was, to announce to her the death of her husband.

Thomas de Berkeley stayed away for a full week and declared that he had not been at home when the death occurred. On his return, he had the unpleasant surprise of discovering that the body was still in the house. No monastery in the neighbourhood would take charge of it. Berkeley had to keep his prisoner a whole month in a coffin, during which period he continued to receive his hundred shillings a day.

The whole kingdom was now aware of the ex-King's death; strange stories, which were not very far from the truth, were going the rounds concerning it, and it was whispered that his assassination would bring no luck either to those who had committed it, or to those, however highly placed they might be, who had given the order for it.

At last, a priest came to take delivery of the body in the name of the Bishop of Gloucester, who had agreed to receive it into his cathedral. The remains of King Edward II were placed on a wagon covered with black cloth. Thomas de Berkeley and his family accompanied it, and the people of the neighbourhood followed in procession. At every mile halt the peasants planted an oak.

After the lapse of six hundred years, some of those oaks are still standing and they cast dark shadows across the road that runs from Berkeley to Gloucester.

Historical Notes

1. In the fourteenth century the Tower of London was still the eastern limit of the City, and was even separated from the City proper by the gardens of monasteries. Tower Bridge did not exist; the Thames was spanned by London Bridge alone, upstream from the Tower.

If the central building, the White Tower, built about 1708 on the orders of William the Conqueror, by his architect, the monk Gandulf, looks to us, after nine hundred years, very much as it originally was – Wren's restoration, in spite of the enlarging of the windows, has altered it but little – the general aspect of the fortifications was considerably different at the period of Edward II.

The present outer fortifications had not then been built, with the exception of St Thomas's Tower and the Middle Tower, which were due respectively to Henry III and Edward I. The outer walls were those which today form the second line of fortifications, shaped like a pentagon with twelve towers built by Richard Cœur de Lion, and constantly altered by his successors.

One can appreciate the astonishing evolution of the medieval style during a single century by comparing the White Tower (end of the eleventh century), which, in spite of its huge mass, preserves in its general shape and proportions the tradition of the ancient Gallo-Roman villas, with the fortifications of Richard Cœur de Lion (end of the twelfth century) by which it is surrounded; these latter works have already the characteristics of the classical stronghold, of the type of Château Gaillard in France, which was in fact also built by Richard I, or the later Angevin buildings in Naples.

The White Tower is practically the only intact example that remains to us of the style of architecture of the year one thousand, and which has been in continuous use throughout the centuries.

2. The title 'Constable', which is a contracted form of the word *connétable*, and which today means a policeman, was the official title of the commander of the Tower. The constable was assisted by a lieutenant. These two appointments still exist, but they have become purely honorary and are given to famous soldiers towards the end of their careers. The effective command of the Tower is nowadays exercised by the Major and Resident Governor.

The 'Major' lives in the Tower, in the King's House, a Tudor building beside the Bell Tower; the first King's lodgings, which dated from the time of Henry I, were demolished by Cromwell. Incidentally, at the period of this story, 1323, the Chapel of St Peter consisted only of the Norman part of the present building.

3. In 1054, against King Henry I of France. Roger Mortimer I was the nephew of Richard I, Sans Peur, third Duke of Normandy and grandfather of the Bastard Conqueror.
4. The 'shilling' was at this period a unit of value, but not one of money as such. Similarly for the 'livres' and the 'marc'. The silver 'penny' was the highest coin in circulation. It was not until the reign of Edward III that gold coins appeared with the 'florin' and the 'noble'. The silver shilling was first minted in the sixteenth century.
5. Very probably in the Beauchamp Tower, though it was not yet known by that name which came into use only after 1397, when Thomas de Beauchamp, Earl of Warwick, was imprisoned in it. It is a curious coincidence that he should have been the grandson of Roger Mortimer. This building had been erected by Edward II and was, therefore, at the time of Roger Mortimer, quite new.

   The apertures for latrines were often a weak point in fortified buildings. It was through an opening of this kind that the soldiers of Philip Augustus, after a siege that seemed hopeless, were enabled one night to enter Château Gaillard, the great French fortress built by Richard Cœur de Lion.
6. The term 'Parliament', which strictly speaking means an assembly, was applied both in France and in England to institutions of common origin, that is to say in the first instance to an extension of the 'curia regis', but which rapidly assumed forms and attributes utterly different to each other.

   The French Parliament, which was at first peripatetic, then became fixed in Paris, while secondary parliaments were ultimately set up in the provinces, was a judicial assembly exercising legal powers on the orders and in the name of the sovereign. To begin with, the members were appointed by the King and for one judicial session only; from the end of the thirteenth century, however, and during the beginning of the fourteenth, that is to say during the reign of Philip the Fair, the masters of Parliament were appointed for life.

The French Parliament had to deal with important conflicts of private interest as well as cases brought by individuals against the Crown, criminal cases of importance to the existence of the State, questions arising out of the interpretation of custom, and, in fact, with everything that came under the heading of general legislation, including the law of accession to the throne, as for instance at the beginning of the reign of Philippe V. But, to repeat, the role and powers of Parliament were entirely juridical and judicial.

The only political power the French Parliament had was due to the fact that no royal act, ordinance, edict, pardon, etc., was valid unless it was registered and confirmed by Parliament, but it only began to use this power of veto towards the end of the fourteenth century and the beginning of the fifteenth, when the monarchy had grown much weaker.

The English Parliament, on the other hand, was both a judicial assembly, since the great state trials were conducted before it, and a political assembly. No one sat in it by right; it was always a sort of enlarged council to which the sovereign summoned whom he wished, that is to say the members of his privy council, the great lords of the kingdom, both temporal and spiritual, and the representatives of counties and cities, generally chosen by the sheriffs.

The political role of the English Parliament was originally

limited to a two-way process of information, by which the king informed the representatives of his people, whom he had selected, of the general policy he intended pursuing, while the representatives informed the sovereign, by means of petitions and speeches, of the wishes of either the classes or the administrative districts to which they belonged.

In theory, the King of England was sole master of his Parliament, which was in fact a sort of privileged audience from which he demanded no more than symbolic and passive adherence to his political policies. But as soon as the Kings of England found themselves in serious difficulty, or showed themselves weak or bad rulers, their Parliament tended to become more exacting, to adopt a frankly deliberative attitude and to impose their will on the sovereign at least to the extent that the sovereign had to take into account the wishes Parliament had expressed.

The precedent of the Magna Carta of 1215, which was imposed on King John by his barons and contained the basis of English liberties, was always present to the minds of Parliaments. That held in 1311 forced Edward II to accept a charter which imposed on the King a committee of great barons elected by Parliament who drew up the Ordinances and really exercised power in the name of the sovereign.

Edward II struggled all his life against this arrangement; refusing to accept it at first, he submitted after his defeat by the Scots in 1314. He succeeded in ridding himself of this tutelage, to his own ultimate disadvantage, only in 1322 when the struggle for influence divided the members of the Committee, and he was able to crush the Lancaster-Mortimer party, who had taken up arms against him, at the Battles of Shrewsbury and Boroughbridge.

Finally, it must be remembered that the English Parliament had no fixed meeting-place, but that Parliament could be summoned by the sovereign, or could demand to be summoned, in any town in the kingdom where the King happened to be.

7. In 1318, five years before, Roger Mortimer of Wigmore, appointed Justiciar and Lieutenant of the King of England in Ireland, had defeated, at the head of an army consisting of the Barons of the Marches, Edward Bruce, King of Ireland and brother of Robert the Bruce, King of Scotland. The taking and executing of Edward Bruce marked the end of the kingdom of Ireland, though the authority of the King of England was far from established for a long time to come.
8. The obscure and complicated affair of the county of Gloucester was born of the fantastic pretensions of Hugh Despenser the Younger to that county. His claim would have had no chance of success had he not been the King's favourite.

Hugh the Younger, not content with having acquired the whole of Glamorgan as his wife's inheritance, demanded from all his brothers-in-law, and in particular from Maurice de Berkeley, the entire possessions of the late Earl, his father-in-law. All the nobility of the south and west of England had become alarmed at this and Thomas of Lancaster had headed the opposition. His determination had been all the greater because his worst enemy, the Earl of Warenne, who had stolen his wife, the fair Alice, was a member of the other party.

The Despensers, who, for a time, had been exiled by a decree of Parliament, promulgated under the pressure of the Lancastrians in arms, had soon been recalled, for Edward found life intolerable without his lover and under the tutelage of his cousin Thomas.

The return of the Despensers to power had been the signal for a renewal of the rebellion, but Thomas of Lancaster, as unfortunate in war as he was in his marriage, had led the coalition extremely badly. Having failed to go to the assistance of the Barons of the Welsh Marches in time, they had been defeated at Shrewsbury, in January 1332, where the two Mortimers had been taken prisoner, while he himself, waiting vainly for Scottish reinforcements in Yorkshire, had been defeated two months later at Boroughbridge and condemned to death immediately afterwards.

9. The commission given the Bishop of Exeter, according to the *Calendar of Close Rolls*, is dated 6 August 1323. Further orders were dispatched concerning Mortimer, notably on August 10 to the sheriffs of Kent, and on the 26th to the Earl of Kent himself. It does not appear that King Edward knew of the fugitive's destination before October 1.

10. Marie of France, the earliest of all French poetesses, lived in the second half of the twelfth century at the Court of Henry II Plantagenet, to which she had been taken, or summoned, by Alienor of Aquitaine, an unfaithful princess, at least to her first husband, the King of France, but certainly extremely beautiful, and who, in England, had created about her a true centre of art and poetry. Alienor was the granddaughter of Duke William IX, himself a poet.

The works of Marie of France were extremely popular, not only during the author's lifetime, but also during the thirteenth and the early part of the fourteenth centuries.

11. The Tolomei Company, together with the Buonsignori, one of the most important of the Sienese banks, had been

both powerful and famous since the beginning of the thirteenth century. It had the papacy as principal client; its founder, Tolomeo Tolomei, had taken part in an embassy to Pope Alexander III. Under Alexander IV the Tolomei were the sole bankers to the Holy See. Urban IV excepted them by name from the general excommunication decreed against Siena between 1260 and 1273. It was at about this time (the end of the reign of Saint Louis and the beginning of the reign of Philippe III) that the Tolomei began to appear at the great fairs in Champagne and that Spinello founded the French branch of the company.

There are still a Tolomei Square and Palace in Siena.

12. Charles IV's decree forbidding the export of French currency must certainly have given rise to trafficking, since another decree, promulgated four months later, forbade the buying of gold and silver at a higher price than that of the currency of the kingdom. A year later, the right of domicile was withdrawn from the Italian merchants, which did not mean that they had to leave France, but simply that they had to purchase once more the authorization to carry on business there.

13. 19 November 1323. Jean de Cherchemont, Lord of Nemours in Poitou, Canon of Notre Dame in Paris, Treasurer of the Cathedral of Laon, had already been Chancellor at the end of the reign of Philippe V. Charles IV had replaced him by Pierre Rodier on his accession. But Charles of Valois, whose favour he had gained, restored him to his position on this date.

The Chancellor, who had the royal seal in his keeping, prepared and drew up acts and appointments; he combined the functions of Minister of Justice, of Foreign Affairs and of

Ecclesiastical Affairs. He sat in the Assembly of Peers and presided by right over all the judicial commissions. On appointment he had to take the following oath:

'You swear to the King our Lord that you will serve and counsel him well and loyally to the honour and advantage of his Kingdom against all and sundry; that you will preserve his inheritance and the public weal of his said Kingdom to the best of your powers, that you will serve no other master or lord but him, that you will hereinafter take no estates, pensions, profits or gifts, nor other presents, from whatever lord or lady, without the permission and licence of our said Lord the King, and that you will not petition for them nor have them petitioned for by others without licence from him to this end; and if you have received from anyone, man or woman in the past, or still have, pensions, estates, or other presents and gifts, you will renounce them all; and, similarly, that you will take from no one whomsoever any corrupt gift, and this you swear on God's Holy Gospel, which you are now holding for the purpose.'

14. The arrangement suggested to the Pope, after a royal council held at Gisors in July 1323, was that the King would receive 300,000 livres out of the 400,000 required for ancillary expenses. But it was also specified – and this was where Valois showed his cunning – that if the King of France, for whatever reason, did not lead the expedition, this role would fall by right to Charles of Valois, who would then benefit personally from the subsidy furnished by the Pope.

15. It is generally forgotten that there were two wars of a hundred years between France and England.

The first, which lasted from 1152 to 1259, was considered

terminated by the Treaty of Paris concluded by Saint Louis, and mentioned here. In fact, between 1259 and 1338, the two countries were twice again at war, and each time over the question of Aquitaine, in 1294 and, as will be seen, again in 1324. The second Hundred Years War, which began in 1328, was not, in reality, so much concerned with the quarrel about Aquitaine as with the succession to the throne of France.

16. This is an example of the inordinately complicated state reached at this period by the feudal system, a system which there is a general tendency to look on as extremely simple, and which was so indeed to begin with. It ended, however, by strangling itself with complications born of its own practice. But this is a vice, or rather a fatality, common to all political systems; and they die of it.

It must be realized that the question of Saint-Sardos, and the affair of Aquitaine in general, were no exceptions, and that the same conditions were true of Artois, Flanders, the Welsh Marches, the kingdoms of Spain, that of Sicily, the German principalities, Hungary and, indeed, of the whole of Europe.

17. These figures have been calculated by historians from fourteenth-century documents, and are based on the statistical returns of the number of parishes and the number of fires per parish at an average of four inhabitants a fire. The figures apply to the period round about 1328.

During the course of the second Hundred Years War, fighting, famines and epidemics reduced the total of the population by more than a third; it was only four centuries later that France recovered the level of population and wealth which had been hers under Philip the Fair and his sons. Even at the beginning of the nineteenth century, the average density of the population in five French departments had not yet reached the figures of 1328 once more. Even in our day, some towns, which were prosperous in the Middle Ages and were ruined by the Hundred Years War, have never recovered their former condition. This is a measure of what the English war cost the nation.

18. The *busines* (derived from the *buccina* of the Romans) were long, straight, or slightly curved trumpets used for calling armies to battle. The short trumpet, which began to come into use in the thirteenth century, did not supplant the *busine* until the fourteenth.

19. A game played with dice and counters which seems to have been the ancestor of tric-trac and backgammon.

20. The use of bombards in the siege of La Réole in 1324 may surprise the reader, for the traditional date for the first appearance of gunpowder artillery is the battle of Crécy in 1346.

    In fact, Crécy was the first time the new artillery was employed in open warfare and in a battle of movement. The weapons used were of relatively small calibre; they did little damage and created no very great impression. Some French historians have exaggerated their effect to explain a defeat which was due much more to the impetuous folly of King Philippe VI and his barons than to the employment of new weapons by the enemy.

    But the light cannon used at Crécy were but a derivative of the ordnance employed at sieges for twenty years past, concurrently with the traditional artillery – one might say even the classical artillery, for it had altered little since Caesar, or indeed since Alexander the Great – which hurled at towns, by a system of levers, balances, counterweights or springs, stone balls or fire-raising materials. The first bombards threw nothing but stone balls similar to those of the ballisters, mangonels and other catapults. It was the method of projection that was new. It seems certain that gunpowder artillery came to birth in Italy, for the metal with which the bombards were hooped was called 'Lombard iron'. The Pisans were using these engines in the years with which we are dealing.

Charles of Valois seems in all likelihood to have been the first French commander to use this new artillery, which was still in its very early days. He had ordered it in the month of April 1324 and had made arrangements with the Seneschal of Languedoc for it to be assembled at Castelsarrasin. His son, Philippe VI, would not therefore have been particularly surprised by the much smaller balls fired at him at Crécy.

21. It must be remembered that the King of France was not at this period suzerain of Avignon. Philip the Fair had, indeed, been careful to surrender his title as co-lord of Avignon to the King of Naples so as not to appear, in the eyes of the world, to be holding the Pope in direct tutelage. But by the garrison established at Villeneuve, and by the mere geographical position of the papal establishment, he held the Holy See and the Church entirely at his mercy.

22. This actually happened in 1330, when the Romans elected the Antipope Nicolas V.

23. The Palace of the Popes, as we know it, is very different from John XXII's castle of which some small portions are still extant in the area known as 'the old Palace'. The huge building which has made Avignon famous is largely the work of the Popes Benedict XXII, Clement VI, Innocent VI

and Urban V. John XXII's building was altered and absorbed almost to the extent of disappearing completely amid the new edifice. Nevertheless, John XXII was the real founder of the Palace of the Popes.

24. Ten years later, Jacques Fournier was to become the next Pope, Benedict XII.

25. John XXII had also a zoo in his palace, which contained among other inmates a lion, two ostriches and a camel.

26. The question certainly required asking, for the princes of the Middle Ages often had six or eight godfathers and godmothers. But, in Canon Law, only those who had actually held the infant at the font were considered as such. The proceedings for the annulment of the marriage between Charles IV and Blanche of Burgundy, which had never been translated before the study we have had made of the documents, are one of the richest mines of information concerning royal religious ceremonies of the period. The congregation was numerous and very mixed; the lower classes crowded in as if to a play and the officiants were almost suffocated by the crowd. The throng and the curiosity were almost as great as at the marriages of film stars today, and reverence was equally absent.

27. Blood-brotherhood by the exchange and mingling of blood, practised since earliest times and in so-called primitive societies, was still in use at the end of the Middle Ages. It existed in Islam; and it was in use among the nobility of Aquitaine, perhaps owing to a tradition inherited from the Moors. Traces of it can be found in certain depositions taken at the trials of the Templars. It appears still to exist, as an act of counter-magic, among certain tribes of gypsies. Blood-brotherhood could seal a pact of friendship or comradeship,

as well as a pact of love, whether spiritual or not. The most famous blood-brotherhoods recorded in the medieval literature of chivalry were those contracted by Count Girart de Roussillon and the daughter of the Emperor of Byzantium (which took place in the presence of their respective spouses), by the Chevalier Gauvain, by the Countess de Die, and by the celebrated Perceval.

28. This dispensation had been granted him by Clement V in 1313, when Charles of Valois was only forty-three.

29. Wautier, or Wauter, or Vautier, are varying forms of Walter. This is a reference to Walter Stapledon, the Lord Treasurer. The originals of this and the subsequent letters are in French, as the English royal correspondence of this period usually was, when it was not in Latin.

30. The six temporal peers at this time were the Dukes of Brittany, Burgundy and Aquitaine (the last being, therefore, the young Prince Edward), the Counts of Flanders and Valois, and the Countess of Artois. It may seem surprising that Jean de Marigny, who at the time of Philip the Fair had been Archbishop of Sens, from which depended the diocese of Paris and which was therefore the most important religious appointment in France, should now appear as Bishop of Beauvais. But it must not be thought that he had reverted to an inferior rank in the hierarchy. On the contrary, the bishopric of Beauvais conferred one of the six spiritual peerages, a dignity which was not attached to the Archbishopric of Sens.

31. The traditional year began on January 1, but the administrative year at Easter. This divergence, one may suspect, had for object, in a period when communications were slow, the allowing of time in which to collate all the accounts of the

royal officials, and incidentally the dispatch of the various decrees in suspense. The administrative year would then begin when the balance-sheet for the previous period had been presented to the King.

32. This manner of carrying a child on a journey was not unusual, though it must have been far from comfortable. The travelling saddles, at the end of the thirteenth and at the beginning of the fourteenth centuries, though they had very high cantles, forming a back for the horseman to lean against, had no pommel and were comparatively flat over the horse's withers.

It was the war saddle which had a high pommel, so that the knight, heavily armoured and liable to have to withstand violent shocks, was, so to speak, wedged between cantle and pommel.

33. This transaction had taken place, in August 1317, between Philippe V and Clémence. The latter possessed in addition, either by gift or legacy from Louis Hutin, the castles of Corbeil, Fontainebleau, Moret, Flagé, Lorrez-le-Bocage, Grez-en-Gâtinais, Nemours, and several estates in Normandy; the houses and manors of Manneville, Hébicourt, Saint-Denis-de-Fermeil, Wardes, Marigny and Dompierre; and the forests of Lyons and of Bray.

Clémence did not, however, go to live in the Temple at once; on the advice of the Pope himself, she had to retire to a convent in Aix-en-Provence and deposit her jewellery as security till she could pay off the many debts contracted during a strange fury of spending that had come over her after she became a widow and her child had supposedly died. The revenues from all her estates had not sufficed to cover her expenditure.

34. Four hundred and sixty-seven years later, Louis XVI was to come out of this very same door in the tower of the Temple on his way to the scaffold. One cannot help feeling that the curse of the Templars took some effect on the Capet family.

35. Chaâlis, in the Forest of Ermenonville, was one of the earliest Gothic buildings in the Île-de-France. On the foundations of the ancient priory, which was a dependency of the monks of Vézelay, King Louis the Fat founded in 1136, a year before his death, a huge monastery of which there remain, owing to its being demolished during the Revolution, only some impressive ruins. Saint Louis often stayed there. Charles IV stayed there briefly in May and again in June 1322, and once again on the present occasion, in June 1326. Philippe VI was there at the beginning of March 1329, and later Charles V. At the Renaissance, when Hyppolyte d'Este, Cardinal of Ferrara, was the titular Abbot, Tasso spent two months there.

The frequency of royal stays in abbeys and monasteries, both in France and England, cannot be accounted for by the piety of the sovereigns concerned but rather by the fact that in the Middle Ages the monks had a sort of monopoly of the hotel industry. There was no monastery of any importance without its 'guest house', which was considerably more comfortable than most of the neighbouring castles. Sovereigns therefore stayed in them on their journeys with their travelling courts, rather as today they reserve for themselves and their suites a whole floor in a hotel in a capital, a seaside resort or a watering-place.

36. By a letter of 19 June 1326: 'And also, my dear son, we charge you that you should not get married before you come back

to us, nor without our assent and command . . . And listen to no counsel contrary to the wishes of your father, which is what the wise King Solomon teaches . . .'

37. Harwich had received its charter as a municipal borough from Edward II in 1318. The port was soon to become the headquarters of trade with Holland and the place from which kings took ship for the Continent during the Hundred Years War. Edward III, fourteen years after landing at Harwich with his mother as we tell here, sailed from its port for the Battle of Ecluse, the first of a long series of defeats inflicted on the French fleet by England. In the sixteenth century Sir Francis Drake and the explorer, Sir Martin Frobisher, met there, after the former had destroyed Philip II's Armada. It was also at Harwich that the famous passengers of the *Mayflower*, commanded by Captain Christopher Jones, embarked for America. Nelson also stayed there.

38. Jean de Hainaut, as a foreigner, did not attend this Council; but it is interesting to note the presence of Henry de Beaumont, the grandson of Jean de Brienne – King of Jerusalem and Emperor of Constantinople – who had been excluded from the English Parliament on the pretext of his foreign origins and had, because of this, rallied to Mortimer's party.

39. The functions of the Marshal of England, which post was held by the Earl of Norfolk, must not be confused with that of a Marshal of the Army.

    The Marshal of England was the equivalent of the Constable of France (we would today say Commander-in-Chief). Edward II's frivolity is evident in the appointment to this office of his half-brother Norfolk, a very young man with but little character or authority.

The Marshals of the Army (the French army had two, the English army only one) corresponded more or less to our present Chiefs of Staff.

40. It is more than probable that Despenser the Elder threw the blame, in particular, for the defeat of Bannockburn, in 1314, on to the barons and attributed it to the reluctance with which they had fought on that occasion. For, indeed, the barons had asked the King to give the army a day's rest. But Edward, in one of those tempers which were habitual with him, ordered them to attack at once; exhausted and discontented, they had offered little resistance to the enemy and were very soon put to flight.

41. The map painted by Richard de Bello, and still preserved in Hereford Cathedral, antedates by several years the provision of Adam Orleton to the see. It was, however, during Orleton's episcopate that the map revealed its miraculous properties.

It is one of the most extraordinary documents extant concerning the medieval conception of the world and a curious graphic synthesis of the knowledge of the times. The map is painted on a parchment of considerable dimensions; the earth is shown as a circle of which Jerusalem is the centre; Asia is placed above and Africa below; the location of the Garden of Eden is marked as well as that of the Ganges. The world seems to be arranged about the Mediterranean basin, with all kinds of illustrations and notes on fauna, ethnology and history, in accordance with information drawn from the Bible, Pliny the naturalist, the Fathers of the Church, the pagan philosophers, the medieval bestiaries and the romances of chivalry.

The map is surrounded by the following circular

inscription: 'The measurement of the round world was begun by Julius Caesar.'

An element of magic formed part at least of the map's inspiration.

The library of Hereford Cathedral is the largest, so far as we know, of the chained libraries still in existence today, since it has 1,440 volumes.

It is both strange and unjust that the name of Adam Orleton should be so little mentioned in historical works on Hereford, considering that this prelate built the most important of the town's monuments, namely the cathedral tower.

42. These Norman castles, which date originally from the eleventh century, and whose architectural type lasted till the beginning of the sixteenth, had either square keeps, in the buildings of the earlier period, or round keeps from the twelfth century onwards. They could stand up to anything, both to weather and assault. Their surrender was more often due to political circumstances than to military enterprise, and they would still be standing today, more or less intact, if Cromwell had not had them all, with the exception of three or four, dismantled and partially destroyed. Kenilworth is twelve miles north of Stratford-upon-Avon.

43. The Chroniclers, and many historians after them, who have seen in the journeys inflicted on Edward II towards the end of his life nothing but gratuitous cruelty, do not seem to have grasped the connection between these journeys and the Scottish war. It was on the very day Robert the Bruce's defiance arrived that the order was given for Edward II to be moved from Kenilworth; and it was at the precise moment the war ended that his residence was changed once again.

44. Berkeley Castle is one of the four Norman fortresses which escaped the general dismantling ordered by Cromwell and is probably the oldest inhabited house in England. The owners are still Berkeleys, descendants of Thomas de Berkeley and Marguerite Mortimer.

A Note for English Readers

Each of my historical novels has brought me a number of letters asking for sources and references.

Since I am well aware how concerned the English reader is about the history of his country, particularly when it is treated by a foreign writer, I would like to attempt in advance some reply to his questions and objections. I assure him that I have taken as much care over the facts of English history as I have over those of French.

In particular, for that part of my book which deals with the pursuit, abdication and death of King Edward II, I have compared the various versions of the events, among others those of the *Dictionary of National Biography*, of James Mackinnon, and of Sir James Ramsay (*The Genesis of Lancaster*), who does not, as do so many historians, confuse Thomas de Berkeley with his father, Maurice.

I have naturally consulted the primary sources and

compared them: the Chronicles of Murimuth, Thomas de la More, the Monk of Malmesbury, and Holinshed. The last is famous for having been used by Marlowe for his play, *Edward II*. But a thesis recently put forward at the Sorbonne (by M. Christian Pons) goes to show that Marlowe drew also on the Chronicles of Thomas de la More and on those of Stow.

I have also used Froissart, though with some reservations, for he used the narratives of Jean le Bel in this part of his work, and is as uncertain as his predecessor over dates and places.

The royal journeys, the dates of sojourns in various places, and the extracts from official documents have been, wherever possible, checked with the *Calendar of Close Rolls*.

And if, after all that, I have still committed errors, which indeed can always occur, either from lack of information or by too audacious an interpretation, I crave your forgiveness. This book claims to be nothing but a novel, yet one that keeps as closely as it can to the truth about the actions of human beings.

NORTH
KINGDOM of ENGLAN
ENGLISH CHANNEL
Cherbourg
Brittany
Le Mans
Anjou
Poitou
BAY of BISCAY
Saintonge
KIN
Bordeaux
Gascony
Bearn